"Don't be fooled by the history and politics. Bill Pezza's *Stealing Tomatoes* may be a tale replete with dramatic world events, but at its heart, it's a love story with characters so engaging you'll be cheering for them from the first time they meet."

Dr. Joseph F. Ruggiero
Author of *A Rose on Ninth Street* and *Raggabooty*

"Bill Pezza is a master at blending engaging fictional characters into high interest historic events. The premise of his latest book is that the United States has been at war since the bombing of the Marine barracks in Lebanon in 1983. In *Stealing Tomatoes*, Bill reminds the reader that those entrusted with enormous responsibilities to ensure our safety may be the kids who grew up down the block."

William J. Frake, CDR USN (Ret)
Former Commanding Officer,
USS Montpelier (SSN 765)

"In his first novel, *Anna's Boys*, Bill Pezza proved to be an able storyteller whose characters remind us that the members of our Armed forces and their families have hopes and dreams similar to any other American's but who must pursue them against a backdrop of enormous courage and sacrifice. I look forward with great anticipation to reading his second novel, *Stealing Tomatoes*."

Colonel William Davis, USA (Ret)
United States Army Special Forces
Awarded the Combat Infantryman's Badge

"As a former student of his and a career Chief Warrant Officer in the Marine Corps who participated in Special Operations, I naturally gravitated to Bill Pezza's first book, *Anna's Boys*. He didn't disappoint. Bill does his homework, puts a human face on history, and provides a unique, bottom-up perspective to world events. His works make for excellent reading experiences."

F. "IKE" INACKER
CWO5 USMC ret

Stealing Tomatoes

Bill Pezza

authorHOUSE®

AuthorHouse™
1663 Liberty Drive, Suite 200
Bloomington, IN 47403
www.authorhouse.com
Phone: 1-800-839-8640

First published by AuthorHouse 3/26/2009

ISBN: 978-1-4389-6714-1 (sc)
ISBN: 978-1-4389-6715-8 (hc)
ISBN: 978-1-4389-6716-5 (e)
Library of Congress Control Number: 2009903063

Printed in the United States of America
Bloomington, Indiana

This book is printed on acid-free paper.

Author's Note & Acknowledgments

Writing a novel is supposed to be fun; at least it usually begins that way for me. However somewhere in the process, maybe in the ninth or tenth month, it becomes a lonely and arduous task. It would have been impossible to complete **Stealing Tomatoes** *were it not for the patient support of my wonderful wife Karen, who served as a first line of protection against inferior plot decisions and shoddy writing. I've considered making a public apology to her for the countless hours I spent working when I could have been assisting with household chores, but that would be dishonest. I do, however, thank her deeply for her support.*

Managing 171,000 words can be cumbersome, and I am indebted to Vince Cordisco and Bert Barbetta for their assistance. Vince's prompt and enthusiastic feedback and subtle suggestions were invaluable. I'm grateful for his help, but even more so for the growing friendship our collaboration fostered. In addition, my long-time friend, Bert Barbetta, demonstrated at each of our sessions the skills and demeanor that earned him the status of Master Teacher in the eyes of the students he taught for so many years.

I am also grateful to three individuals who served with distinction in the armed forces and fielded my endless questions during this process. To my college fraternity brother and friend, Colonel William Davis of the United States Army Special Forces, a true American hero whose service and sacrifice are well documented and who still proudly wears the Green Beret. To hometown hero and Bronze Star recipient U. S. Navy Captain (Ret.)Bill Frake, who commanded a Los Angeles Class submarine, the USS Montpelier and launched missile strikes against Saddam Hussein on the first day of the Iraq War. To my friend and former student Chief Warrant Officer 5 (Ret.) "Ike" Inacker of the United States Marine Corps Special Operations. Ike was deployed on the battleship USS Missouri in the Persian Gulf during operation Desert Storm.

There are others who provided guidance including Andy Bidlingmaier, Anna Mancini, Sue Monte, Dr. Vincent Virgulti, Harold Mitchner, and Connie Zimmer. I appreciate the part they played in the process. I should add that the people acknowledged on this page bear no responsibility for the book's flaws but deserve significant credit for its improvement.

Finally, I want to thank Al Feuerstein and John Ivanchenko for their graphic assistance and cover design.

As was the case with my first novel, **Anna's Boys**, I chose Bristol, Pennsylvania, as the backdrop for this story because it's the town I love. However, aside from the events and personalities from history who are obviously real and clearly identified, the characters in this book are purely fictional and any similarity to real persons, living or dead, is entirely coincidental.

That being said, some have suggested the character of Old Man Lombardi found on these pages bears a resemblance in physical description, demeanor and life experience to my father, Ernesto Pezza. That was not an accident. I miss him and, like most fathers and sons, I wish we would have talked even more- I mean really talked. This work is dedicated to him and immigrants from throughout the world who sought a new life in America.

Bill Pezza
Spring 2009

Introduction

October 23, 1983

Brian Kelly was a gifted child who found interest in things uncommon for a boy his age. He was an accomplished reader by age four, and by the time he was five he had mastered every children's book his parents could gather. By first grade he was reading the daily newspaper. At first all of this was a source of pride for Brian's parents, but their pride changed to concern as Brian became increasingly distressed by the news he read. At times the Kellys would find their son at the kitchen table with the newspaper spread in front of him and tears streaming down his face. Earthquakes, house fires, auto accidents, missing children, all took an emotional toll on the young boy.

Brian's parents stopped delivery of the paper and tried to steer him to more age-appropriate activities like watching television, but it didn't work. He would channel surf until he found a news program and then sit transfixed as the events of the world unfolded.

Now, on his eighth birthday, October 23, 1983, Brian sat in his room watching Peter Jennings and *World News Tonight* on ABC. Jennings had become the network anchor earlier that year, and Brian had quickly settled upon him for his daily dose of world events.

Jennings' tone was somber as he delivered the lead story. Two hundred and twenty-one United States Marines had died in a terrorist attack on the Marine barracks at the international airport in Beirut, Lebanon just after dawn that morning. Twenty-one additional servicemen were killed and eighty others were seriously injured. It was the bloodiest day in Marine Corps history since the battle on Iwo Jima.

The program shifted to the scene of the attack where a network correspondent continued the story. A suicide bomber, driving a truck loaded with explosives estimated to be the equivalent of 12,000 pounds of TNT, crashed through the gate of the Marine complex, ran over the guard shack and detonated its load just as it reached the front door of the four story building.

The camera zoomed in to a mound of smoldering rubble and what was left of the structure behind it.

"Many of the Marines were killed instantly by the blast," the correspondent reported. "Others were crushed under tons of debris." Brian sat riveted to the broadcast as the correspondent provided background.

"The Marines had been redeployed to Beirut by President Reagan in September of 1982 to help keep the peace in the Lebanese capital torn by civil war for almost seven years…"

As the story continued, Brian heard references to terms and places like: Southern Lebanon…PLO…Sunni… Shiite… Syria… Hezbollah… Israel. He grabbed a pad and pencil and recorded the words. Then he went to his book shelf and removed his world atlas. It was one of his favorite books. He had used it recently to memorize the countries of Eastern Asia just for fun. He checked the index for Lebanon and turned to the corresponding page, where he found a map of the Middle East. He located Lebanon and made note of the bordering countries of Syria and Israel. He scanned the next ring of countries: Jordan, Iraq, Saudi Arabia and Iran   He promised himself that he would study each of them, as well as the terms he had written on his notepad.

He turned his attention back to the TV. The correspondent was describing the grizzly, day-long ordeal of rescue teams sifting through the rubble for survivors. As the reporter spoke, the network showed images from earlier in the day. Brian saw Marines carrying bodies on stretchers. Some of the victims looked seriously injured, but most of the stretchers held bodies that had their faces covered. He knew what that meant.

The faces of the surviving Marines showed grief and anger. They certainly looked ready to lash out at someone. He wondered who the enemy was, what their uniforms looked like, who their leader was. But nothing seemed to be happening.

Soon President Reagan was speaking from the White House. Brian liked Reagan. As the President talked about the attack, Brian thought about the men who had died. He imagined them asleep in their bunks and awakened by a thunderous explosion. He imagined the weight of cinder blocks crashing down on their chests. He imagined the smoke and the screams. He tried not to think of those things, but he couldn't help it. That was his problem, his mother had often said. His imagination was much too vivid. He visualized things a child his age should not visualize. He felt the pain of others in a way a child his age shouldn't and became too upset by it. That's why his parents tried to shield him from the news.

Brian knew he should change the channel, but he couldn't. Instead, he thought about the injured. They were thousands of miles away from home with no family nearby. He thought about being half-buried in debris and hoping someone would find him.

Reagan was talking about the families of the victims and Brian's eyes began to fill. He wished there was something he could do to help. He wished someone would get the guys who did this. It was then that he heard his mother's footsteps on the stairs, and he switched off the TV.

1- Johnny's Plan

July 1988

Johnny Marzo was restless, and that was a bad sign. He and his friends were gathered at the log, their usual spot in the woods that bordered the old Delaware Canal. There were five of them: Johnny, Mickey Morelli, Bobby Myers, Tommy Dillon, and Brian Kelly. They called themselves the Pac Men, a play on words adopted from the popular video game. It was late July of 1988, the summer before they were to enter ninth grade. With the exception of Brian "Brain" Kelly, who was a relative newcomer and earned his nickname soon after he arrived in town, the boys had been friends since kindergarten.

"I'm bored," Johnny said. "It's summertime; we're supposed to be doing exciting things. We need some action."

The Pac Men loved excitement as much as anyone else, but Johnny's schemes usually offered far more action than the boys wanted. There was no middle ground with Johnny. Sometimes he'd be happy to just sit around and shoot the breeze, but when he was bored, he tended to stretch things way too far.

The boys eyed Johnny warily and could see that an idea was taking shape. Finally, he smiled broadly and said, "I think it's time that we steal some tomatoes."

2- The Raid on Old Man Lombardi

July 1988

Tomato growing was a big deal in town. Old Italian men would toil for hours in their backyard gardens, tilling the soil, putting in the plants, weeding, and watering. By late July and early August their work would yield plump, juicy tomatoes. Then the men would gather at their favorite meeting places and talk about their prized crops.

The giving of tomatoes was also a big deal in the Italian community. The men would fill small baskets of the baseball-sized beauties and deliver them to relatives and neighbors. Finally, the remainder of the crop, the ones with small imperfections, or those that only grew to the size of a peach, were turned over to their wives to be crushed, canned, and stored for spaghetti sauce.

The two things the old men feared most, especially once the tomatoes were nearly ripe, were squirrels and kids. At times, squirrels would sample the tomatoes, nibble on them just enough to ruin them and then move on. This problem was usually solved by spraying the tomatoes with a solution of hot pepper and water.

The far more serious problem was kids who stole tomatoes for sport. They raided the gardens at night. Some did it only for the thrill and would take only one or two to eat while they walked home, savoring the taste of adventure. Others, of lesser integrity, took more and tossed them at stop signs or cars, in a woeful display of disrespect to those who had nurtured the fruit.

By mid-summer the old men took steps to protect their gardens. Some locked their gates, while others posted warning signs. Still others sat on guard in their back yards in the evening, listening to Phillies games on the radio or smoking their stogies. Their efforts to guard their crops made the sport of stealing tomatoes all the more exciting.

Now, Johnny wanted the guys to go on a tomato raid. The suggestion wasn't nearly as bad as the boys feared. Tomato raids were risky, but they had done them before.

"So how about it, guys?" Johnny said. "How about a nice little raid tomorrow night?"

Mickey was on board right away, as he was with anything Johnny wanted to do.

Tommy's eyes lit up. "Count me in," he said. Tommy was fearless and always enjoyed a good adventure. It was Bobby and Brain they would have to convince.

"I don't know," Bobby said. "We could get caught. I'm already in the doghouse for having to go to summer school. I don't need more trouble." Then Bobby had an idea.

"My aunt has a garden. I bet she'd give us some tomatoes if we asked her."

"Asked her?" Tommy howled. "You want us to ask your aunt for tomatoes?"

"Now that's exciting," Johnny said. "How about it, Mickey? When we go back to school and when the guys ask us what we did this summer that was cool, we can say we asked Bobby's aunt for tomatoes. Sounds like a blast."

Bobby looked hurt, and Johnny felt bad. He put his arm around him and said, "Look, no pressure. It's no problem if you don't want to come. I just hate to see you miss out. When we're telling the girls at school, I'd hate for you to have to say that you got your tomatoes from your aunt. That's all."

Bobby softened. "I wanna do it," he said. "I just can't get caught."

"Never been caught yet," Johnny said.

"And never will be," Tommy added.

"Okay, I'm in," Bobby said reluctantly.

"That's it, Bobby boy," Tommy said. "Stick with us and you'll be fine."

"What about you, Brain?" Bobby asked.

"Forget it." Brain replied quickly. "You know I don't do that stuff. Besides, we're right in the middle of the Democratic National Convention. Michael Dukakis is giving his acceptance speech tomorrow night on TV. I've gotta hear it."

"Are you serious?" Mickey asked.

"I love this stuff," Brain said. "Last night Texas Governor Ann Richards gave the keynote address and said that Vice President Bush was born with a silver foot in his mouth. It was pretty funny."

Brain was getting blank stares from the guys, but he went on. "Next month the republicans are having their convention, and that'll be cool too. They'll nominate Bush, and Reagan will give a sort of good-bye speech. I can't wait to see that."

Mickey shook his head and said sadly, "I give up on you, Brain. You're just a friggin girl."

"Come on, Mickey," Brain said. "You know I love this stuff. Would you go out if the World Series were on TV?"

"This is different, man. Who gives a crap about Michael Dukakis or Vice President Bush? We're trying to help you be a real guy, but you're still just a friggin girl."

"Drop it, Mickey," Johnny said. "Brain doesn't have to go."

Things got quiet for a minute and then Mickey nodded reluctantly. Everyone knew Johnny was Brain's protector.

"So who should we hit tomorrow night?" Mickey asked.

Johnny flashed the famous smile he reserved for his most adventurous schemes.

"I think it's time we hit Old Man Lombardi on Lafayette Street."

The group fell silent. Old Man Lombardi was the most feared tomato grower in town. He was short, but powerfully built, with fingers like sausages and close-cropped gray hair. His skin was weathered and dark from years of toiling in his garden. It was not wise to raid Old Man Lombardi.

Bobby withered immediately. Even fearless Tommy looked apprehensive. Mickey spoke first. "I don't know, Johnny. It's been a while since we've done a raid. Maybe we need an easier target. Maybe we should save Old Man Lombardi until after, when we've had some practice."

"Yeah," Bobby said. "Like next summer."

Johnny eyed Tommy. Tommy looked scared but nodded his approval. He would never leave Johnny out to dry.

"Look," Johnny said. "If we're gonna do this, we might as well make it exciting. I've checked the place out. It's no big deal. I think people just made up stories about this Lombardi guy over the years. He's a myth, just like the hook man."

"Not true," Mickey said. "Joey Ringoli told me that Lombardi chased him down the alley once with a shovel, and when he couldn't catch him, he threw the shovel like a spear. Joey moved out of the way and the spade landed so hard that it made sparks on the pavement. Lombardi wasn't just trying to scare Joey; the crazy bastard was trying to kill him." With that, Bobby looked as if he were going to faint.

Johnny shrugged. "Joey lies. He told everybody he had Joe Montana's autograph, but he never showed it to anybody."

Johnny let that sink in. Then he said, "Tommy and I are hitting Old Man Lombardi's garden tomorrow night. Anybody else coming?"

Mickey grinned. "What the heck, I'm in. I can outrun a shovel."

Bobby still looked doubtful. "Are you sure Joey lies?" Bobby asked.

"Like a rug," Tommy said.

"You think we'll be okay?"

"Guaranteed," Johnny added.

"Okay. I said I was going and I'm going," Bobby said.

"Okay," Johnny said. "Then it's on for tomorrow."

They met in the woods the following night and waited until it got nice and dark. Then they went to the alley that ran between LaFayette Street and Jefferson Avenue, the alley that ran behind Old Man Lombardi's back yard garden.

"Okay," Johnny said. "We're real quiet from here. When we get in the yard, spread out, grab the biggest tomato you can find and get out of there. If Old Man Lombardi shows up, run like hell. It's every man for himself. If we get separated we'll meet at the canal."

Bobby looked scared again.

"Just a precaution," Johnny said. "Everything's cool."

They reached the yard and squatted by the rear chain link gate. The houses on Lafayette Street were twins, with only about ten feet separating each pair. Lombardi's yard was long and narrow, about twenty feet wide and forty feet deep. A shed ran along the rear of the property separating the yard from the alley, except for the opening for the gate. The yard was dark, as was the kitchen located at the rear of the house.

"Maybe they're not home," Bobby whispered. "I hope they're not."

"They're home," Johnny said softly. "Plan on it."

The gate was about four feet high. Johnny reached up from his crouch and confirmed that it was locked.

"Okay," he said. "We're going over. Be quiet and try not to rattle the gate."

Johnny scaled the fence with ease and landed softly on the other side. Tommy went next, followed by Mickey. Mickey was too big to be graceful and made some noise when he landed. Everyone froze for a minute, but the house remained dark and quite.

Bobby was still in the alley, and he looked so scared that Johnny felt sorry for him. It was getting crowded in the walkway between the shed and the side fence, so Tommy and Mickey moved toward the yard. When Bobby grabbed the top of the gate his hands were shaking so badly that the fence rattled. Johnny held it to quiet the noise. Bobby was taking too long, and when Johnny looked in his eyes he saw terror.

"I've got an idea, Bobby," Johnny whispered. "Why don't you keep watch from out there in case someone comes down the alley? I'll get you a tomato."

Bobby's eyes sparkled. "Good idea! I'll stay here and keep watch."

The boys fanned out to search for their prizes. "Look at this baby," Tommy whispered, as he picked a grapefruit sized tomato from the vine."

"Should have brought a salt shaker," Tommy said, as he picked another one and bit into it.

Mickey was closest to the house and was reaching for the largest tomato he'd seen, when suddenly the kitchen door flew open and Old Man Lombardi bounded down the steps like an Olympic athlete.

"Som-a-na-bitch, I kill-uh you!" he roared in his heavy Italian accent.

Bobby let out a scream from the alley, and everyone broke for the gate. Tommy jumped, grabbed the top of the gate with both hands and swung his legs over in one fluid motion. When he landed he saw that Bobby was already halfway down the alley. Johnny was heading for the fence, but looking back he saw Old Man Lombardi catch Mickey. Lombardi grabbed the back of Mickey's belt with one sausage-fingered hand and the back of Mickey's collar with the other. Lombardi was shouting, *"You take my tomatoes? I teach you. You little som-a-na-bitch. I teach-uh you."*

Johnny stopped at the fence as Mickey was screaming, "I'm sorry mister. I'm sorry."

Johnny froze as he looked at Mickey and the old man. Mr. Lombardi ignored Johnny, seemingly content to have caught one of the intruders. Johnny's mind was racing as Lombardi dragged Mickey back toward the house. As big and strong as Mickey was, he seemed helpless in the gardener's grasp.

"You take- uh tomatoes," Lombardi screamed again.

By now, Lombardi and Mickey had reached a rain barrel near the back of the house, and Johnny watched in horror as Old Man Lombardi shoved Mickey's head under water.

"Hey," Johnny yelled. "Leave him alone." But the old man ignored him.

Mickey came up choking and gasping for air. .

"You come my yard! Touch my tomatoes!" Lombardi barked. With that, the old man thrust Mickey's head under the water again.

"My God," Johnny said. "You're gonna drown him."

Johnny was desperate. Lombardi seemed so strong, and Johnny knew that if he got too close the old man might grab them both. Then he saw the garden hose and valve by the shed. He picked up the hose, turned the valve, adjusted the nozzle to a tight piercing flow and aimed. He didn't want to do this to an old man, but the guy was insane with rage. The sharp spray hit Lombardi's ear and Johnny held it there. At first Lombardi ignored it and kept his attention on Mickey's head. Johnny changed his aim to Lombardi's throat and the old man let out a roar and let go of Mickey. Lombardi stood there for a moment, stunned by the audacity of the young fool with the hose. Mickey brushed by him and broke for the gate, gasping and coughing on the way.

"Go," Johnny screamed. "Get out of here!"

Mickey protested for just a second before he thought better of it and bounded for the fence. Johnny stopped spraying. "We're really sorry, mister. It was just a prank. We're sorry."

Lombardi flashed a menacing smile. He was no more than ten feet from Johnny and Johnny was shaking. *"Juust uh prank,"* Lombardi said. He had a crazed look in his eyes. *"Juust uh prank,"* he repeated. *"You gonna pay!"* he said as he moved toward him.

Johnny had no choice. He opened the nozzle again and aimed directly at the old man's eyes. The force of the water blinded Lombardi temporarily and the old man's hands went to his face. Johnny dropped the hose and made for the fence. Mickey was on the other side still choking. Johnny flew over the fence and he and Mickey half raced and half stumbled down the alley. They could hear Lombardi's swearing and screaming fading in the distance.

They slowed down when they were sure they were safe, and Mickey said. "You saved me, man. You didn't leave me."

"That would never happen," Johnny said.

3- Brian Kelly

Brian Kelly had moved to Bristol three years before the great tomato raid, and a week before he entered the sixth grade. He was eager to meet new kids but was anxious about being accepted. Things hadn't gone well at his old school, and he hoped life would be different at St. Theresa's. He wasn't optimistic.

For one thing, he had a baby face. Granted, he was only eleven, but he had the face of a cherub, and it was topped by a head of soft, blond hair. Adults thought he was a cute kid, but Brian didn't want to be cute anymore; he wanted to be a guy. To make things worse, he was easily a head shorter and much thinner than boys his age.

On the first morning of school, his mom made his favorite breakfast. When he finished eating, she handed him his backpack and lunch bag and said, "You're going to love it here Brian; you'll see. And the kids at school are going to love you. Just give things a chance and be yourself." He loved his mom more than anything, so he smiled bravely and went off to school.

As it turned out, breakfast proved to be the best part of Brian's day. He found his way to his classroom and felt awkward as he sat surrounded by strangers excited to see each other after a long summer. Two girls looked Brian's way, whispered something to each other, and giggled. Brian was convinced they were laughing about his size. Others in the class acted as if he were invisible.

He heard a student mumble "Witch Watson" as the teacher entered the room. She was a large, stern-faced woman in her late forties with thinning hair. She certainly didn't match the perky, youthful image Brian had hoped for in a teacher. It wasn't long before he got a taste of her personality.

Miss Watson distributed student record forms and then patrolled the aisles as the students completed them. With his nerves on edge, Brian accidentally transposed the "I" and the "A" when writing his name. When Watson collected the forms and came across Brian's mistake she said, "Where is Brian Kelly?" Brian reluctantly raised his hand and all eyes turned toward him. She gave him a disgusted look and said, "Brian Kelly, you spelled your name B-R-A-I-N, which spells Brain. Surely your parents didn't name you Brain, especially since you barely seem to have one. Now fix this form."

The children exploded with laughter and catcalled "Brain" from around the room. The eruption lasted just a few seconds, but the name stuck.

Later, classmates whispered, "Brain" as they passed him in the hallways, and more loudly during recess, while Brian stood alone by the chain-link fence. Not a single classmate came to his aid or showed him the least bit of kindness that dreadful morning.

At lunch Brian found an empty table in the cafeteria and ate alone. He spilled catsup on his new pants and only made it worse when he tried to dab it out. Later, he misplaced his locker combination. When school was over he waited until most students were gone to avoid their taunts as he walked home. Overall, it was a very bad day, an even worse day than he was used to.

His mom greeted him with a hopeful smile. "Well, how was it?" she asked excitedly.

Brian didn't have the heart to tell her the truth. "It was great, Mom" he replied, forcing his best smile.

"Oh wonderful," she said with a sigh of relief. "I just knew it would be good. Did you make lots of new friends? Do you like your teacher?"

Brian replied in generalizations, trying to avoid too many outright lies. When his mom pressed for more information, Brian said, "I'm pretty tired right now. It was a big day. I think I'll take a nap and then do my homework."

"Of course you're tired, sweetie. You go ahead and we'll talk later," she said, her face beaming.

As Brian walked away his mother called to him, "I'm so happy, Brian. Things are going to be good here."

"I know, mom," Brian replied. "Things will be real good."

Brian went to his room and closed the door. He wanted to cry, but he was too angry. The kids at school were mean, but he learned long ago that kids would be that way. At his old school they called him peanut, shorty, pee wee, and much more. He expected it from kids, but Miss Watson was another story. She was a teacher and should have known better than to humiliate him in front of the class. He had a new nickname because of her. He was now Brain, the new kid. He must have heard it a hundred times already. Sure he ruined his pants, lost his locker combination, screwed up lots of things, but they were all Witch Watson's fault. She was the one who shattered his confidence early, just when he thought he could make a new start. He vowed to get even.

He looked in the mirror with disgust. He was way too short and far too smart for a kid his age. "Small kid, big brain," he said. Whenever he got into a funk about his size, his mom would assure him that people experience growth spurts at different ages, and his was bound to come. Brian was convinced that wasn't true.

She'd also say proudly that God had blessed him with a brilliant mind, which he knew was true. He read constantly and remembered everything he read. In fact, it was almost freakish. But his skills went far beyond memory. He could analyze, interpret, and put ideas together. He knew stuff, lots of stuff. It could have been nice to be that smart, but Brian saw his intellect as a curse because most kids teased him for it.

He sat on the bed for a long time, thinking about Witch Watson, and an idea slowly emerged. He had once read that knowledge is power, and he certainly had it. At his old school he actually tried to hide his intellect, not wanting to give students another reason to single him out. But here in Bristol, he was singled out after just one day. So, if he were going to be different, he might as well go all the way. He was going to unleash everything he had in his intellectual arsenal and kick Witch Watson's academic ass.

He looked at his homework assignments and nodded slowly. He was mobilizing for war and he had to be ready. He opened his textbook and began to read.

Brian arrived at school the next day feeling cheerful. Whenever someone called out "Brain" he smiled and said hello instead of covering his ears as he had the day before. He took his seat and smiled at the girls who had giggled at him. They giggled again and turned away. Brian didn't mind anymore. They were immature, and he hoped they would grow out of it.

Witch Watson entered the room and the class grew quiet as she began her instruction. "This year we are going to study early American History and the role the state of Pennsylvania played in our country's development."

Brian's hand shot up. "Excuse me, Miss Watson."

Witch Watson eyed him disapprovingly. She didn't like to be interrupted. "Yes, Mr. Kelly, what is it?"

All eyes turned to Brian and the class wondered what the new kid was up to.

"You mentioned that we are going to study the state of Pennsylvania," Brian said innocently.

"That's correct. What of it?"

"Well, technically, isn't Pennsylvania a commonwealth?"

Students perked up. It sounded as though the new kid was challenging Witch Watson, and that was good.

"Yes," Watson stammered for a moment. "Technically, Pennsylvania is a commonwealth, but most people just loosely refer to it as a state. Now, as I was saying…"

A student in the next row put his hand up. Brian knew from yesterday's class that his name was Johnny Marzo. He seemed to be one of cooler kids that the others looked up to. Without waiting to be recognized Marzo said, "So what's the difference between a state and a commonwealth?"

Miss Watson eyed him disapprovingly. "Actually, a commonwealth... Well, a state is different from a commonwealth because... they are just different words actually. Ah... Yes. There is really no legal difference. It's just a name."

Johnny pursued it. "So are we the only state that calls itself a commonwealth?"

Watson shot him a hard stare. "First of all, young man, I am not accustomed to having students call out. In the future you will be recognized before speaking. Now, to answer your question, yes, I believe Pennsylvania is the only state to call itself a commonwealth."

Brian immediately put his hand up, but Watson ignored it. "Now, as I was saying... "

Brian waved his arm to be recognized.

"What is it, Kelly?" Watson snapped.

"I'm so sorry to interrupt," Brian said politely, "But there are actually four commonwealths: Pennsylvania, Virginia, Kentucky, and Massachusetts. There is no real significant legal distinction between them and the other states. As you said, they are just names."

Watson looked as though she wanted to strangle Brian for correcting her in front of the class.

"Thank you," Watson said, clearly not meaning it. "Let's move on."

"Well," Brian interjected, "Maybe we should quickly add that Puerto Rico is also a commonwealth, but in its case there is a legal distinction between it and the other fifty states."

"Enough about commonwealths!" Watson thundered. Our lesson is about early colonial settlements, and it's time to begin.

Johnny Marzo looked at Brian and winked his approval. Brian nodded back.

Miss Watson gave a general overview of the early colonial settlements in Jamestown, Plymouth and Massachusetts Bay. As lunch break approached she said, "You will have two assignments tonight for social studies homework, one about Pennsylvania and one about colonial America." She held up a worksheet. "This sheet contains factual questions about Pennsylvania which you will find the answers to by using an encyclopedia." She handed out the assignments. "The second assignment is much more ambitious and will require research from your textbook. It seems that those people who settled in the early New England colonies were much healthier than those who settled in Jamestown, Virginia. Your job is to read your book and determine why one group was healthier than the other."

Brian couldn't resist, and his hand went up.

Watson eyed him suspiciously. Brian thought he saw a slight trace of sweat above her upper lip. "Do you have a question about the assignment?"

"Well," Brian said sheepishly. "Aside from the fact that doctors feel the cooler climate of New England is healthier than the warm, humid climate of the marshy area of Jamestown, I read that the Jamestown settlers built their outhouses too close to the source of their drinking water. So in effect, they were drinking their own, well, you know."

The class laughed and Watson looked as if she would explode. When she spoke, her voice was shaking. "This is exactly why I don't want students calling out. You just ruined the assignment for everyone. The assignment was to *discover* the things you just said."

"I'm sorry, Miss Watson. I thought you wanted us to find things other than the obvious."

Watson stared at him for a long time without speaking. Then she said to the class, "Forget the assignment. Just complete the worksheet on the *Commonwealth* of Pennsylvania."

Lunch time arrived and the class filed out, grateful for the reprieve from a research assignment that the new kid had just won for them.

Brian sat alone again in the cafeteria, next to a table with several students from his class. One of them said something and they all looked his way. Then Johnny Marzo said, "Hey, Brian, you really kicked ol' Witch Watson's butt today."

"Do ya think so?" Brian replied cautiously.

"Are you kidding?" Johnny said smiling. "It was beautiful." The others at the table agreed. Then Marzo said, "Why don't you slide your tray over to our table? There's plenty of room."

"Yeah," Mickey Morelli added. "Come on over."

Brian wasn't sure if the invitation was sincere or if they were setting him up for another taunt, but he decided to take a chance and went over. Everyone was friendly as Johnny introduced them, and Brian even heard one of the girls say he was cute.

The group peppered him with questions about where he came from and where he lived in town. Then, Bobby Myers said, "Hey, Brian. You seem to know a lot of stuff. Are you some kind of genius or what?"

"I don't think so," Brian said. "I just read a lot and remember things."

Bobby said "Do you know the stuff on the Pennsylvania worksheet Watson gave us?"

"I don't know," Brian said. "I just stuck it in my bag. What's on it?"

Bobby had his out and looked it over. "Do you know the Pennsylvania state bird?"

"Sure," Brian replied casually. "It's the Ruffed Grouse."

"Really?" Bobby said.

"Yeah, really."

Bobby asked him to spell it and Brian did.

Bobby looked at the worksheet again. "How about the state flower?"

Brian finished chewing before he said, "That's the Mountain Laurel."

By then everyone was pulling out their homework sheets and taking turns asking questions.

"State tree?"

"The Hemlock."

"State animal."

"The Whitetail deer."

"State dog?"

"The Great Dane."

"Are you sure?" Mickey asked.

"Damn sure," Brian replied with a smile.

Brian's lunch mates were writing feverishly. And then Tommy said, "Hey, are you screwing with us? Are you making this stuff up?"

"Look it up," Brian said casually, wiping some chocolate milk from his chin.

"I believe him," Johnny said. Things got quiet for a minute as everyone pondered Johnny's judgment. They Bobby went on. "State nickname?"

Brian laughed. "It's the Keystone State. Do you want to know why it's called that?"

"No," Bobby said, "That's not on the list and I don't care." Then he added, "Damn, is there even a state fish?"

"Yeah," Brian said. "It's the Brook Trout, but I don't like fish."

Mickey said, "Why do we need a state fish? Who decides this stuff?'

"Who cares?" Bobby said. "Just write it down." Finally, Bobby scanned the homework sheet and said, "That's just about it."

Brian took the last bite of his sandwich and said, "Isn't the state insect on the sheet?"

"Nope," Bobby said. "I don't see it."

"Well,' Brian said playfully, "if it ever comes up, it's the firefly."

"Amazing," Johnny said with a laugh. "You kicked Watson's butt and saved us a couple hours of homework. Welcome to St. Theresa's, Brian."

"Thanks," Brian said smiling. "But can you do me a favor?"

"Name it," Johnny said.

"Please call me Brain in honor of good ol' Agnes Watson." Then he took his last gulp of chocolate milk.

4- EMT

Two weeks after the ill-fated raid on Old Man Lombardi's, Johnny and Mickey were sizzling under the late July sun as they rode their bikes to the 5th Ward pool. Johnny's father, Angelo Marzo, allowed him to go to the pool twice a week with the understanding that Johnny would finish his chores at the family deli first. Mickey would help, and Mr. Marzo would pay the boys five dollars each. The money was just enough to cover their guest fees and buy a hamburger and coke at the snack bar.

The boys rode side by side and Johnny shouted, "I hope that new girl, Carrie Boyle, is at the pool today."

"She will be," Mickey shouted back. "I hear she's there every day."

"Yeah, but today is special. I really need her to be there today."

"What's the big deal about today?" Mickey asked.

Johnny grinned broadly. "She's going to notice me today because I'm going to jackknife off of the diving board to impress her."

Mickey visualized the scene and hollered back, "It's risky, Johnny."

"Why?" Johnny replied. "You know I can do one. All we need to do is get her attention. After that, she's mine if I nail it, guaranteed."

"Maybe," Mickey said. "But what if all eyes are on you, and you blow it? What if you slip or something? You'll be finished before you even start."

Johnny smiled. "There you go again, Mickey, always being careful. You're afraid to live on the edge a little. I'll nail the dive exactly because I know she'll be watching. I'm taking my shot today. That's it."

They pedaled on for a while and then Mickey said, "What if she doesn't see you? What if you make the perfect dive and she isn't even looking?"

"I've got it covered," Johnny said. "Brain Kelly is taking care of it."

"Brain!" Mickey replied. "He knows a lot of stuff, but what does he know about girls?"

"The girls at the pool warm up to Brain. They see him as a little brother. They're friendly because they know he's not trying to pick them up."

"So what's he going to do?"

"He's going to tell Carrie that a great diver is coming to the pool today, and she should make sure to watch him. Then I'm gonna walk in, pretend I don't even see her, stretch a little and then make the dive. And before I do, Brain is going to get her attention."

"I guess it's a plan," Mickey conceded.

"Damn right it is," Johnny said. "This is a big day for old Johnny boy."

They were motoring down Pond Street now when Johnny shot Mickey a mischievous look and turned down Old Man Lombardi's alley. Mickey skidded to a stop at the mouth of the alley and waited. Soon Johnny looked back, shook his head sadly, and doubled back to meet his friend.

When he got close, Mickey said, "Are you crazy? This is Old Man Lombardi's alley. He'll kill us if he sees us!"

"No way," Johnny said laughing. "He's old and he had water in his eyes that night. This is the quickest way to the pool. Let's go."

Mickey wasn't budging. "Let's take Jefferson Avenue instead, just to be safe."

Johnny shook his head again. "See what I mean, Mickey. You've got to take a chance once in a while. Live on the edge a little."

"We took a chance the night of the tomato raid, and I almost died!"

"Hey, you got a little wet; that's all. And speaking of getting wet, I'm melting under this sun. Let's go swimming." With that, Johnny rode off, and Mickey reluctantly followed, just as Johnny knew he would.

Mickey began to pedal frantically as they got closer to Lombardi's yard, intent on zooming by as quickly as possible, and Johnny kept up the pace. Then they heard an awful scream.

"Ernesto morta! Ernesto morta!" It was a female voice. "Ernesto, Ernesto."

Mickey pedaled harder and shot by Lombardi's. But Johnny had a different reaction. He slowed, peered into the yard, and couldn't believe what he saw. Old Man Lombardi was lying on the ground. An elderly woman was kneeling beside him screaming hysterically.

Johnny stopped and sat frozen as the woman sobbed and cradled Lombardi's head in her arms. Then her eyes met Johnny's and she cried out, *"Help-uh, please, help-uh."*

Mickey had stopped at the far end of the alley and looked back just in time to see Johnny jump off his bike, run to Lombardi's gate, and rush in.

The old woman stopped crying and looked at Johnny pleadingly, *"Please. My Ernesto. My husband."* The old man's weathered face was gray and his lips were turning purple. Johnny felt helpless. He wished he had paid more attention during the CPR assembly at school.

He knelt beside the old man, eased his head out of his wife's arms and placed it gently on the grass. He knew he should try to blow air into the man's lungs, but he couldn't bring himself to do it. Not knowing what else to do, he began pushing rapidly on the man's chest. At least it was something, he thought.

Johnny was terrified. He kept pushing steadily as he considered what to do next. Then he saw Mickey standing at the gate, his jaw agape.

"Call an ambulance!" Johnny shouted. Mickey froze and Johnny screamed, "Do it!"

"Okay," Mickey said weakly as he looked around helplessly.

"In there," Johnny said, motioning with his head to Lombardi's house.

Mickey entered the yard, looked at Mrs. Lombardi and said, "Phone?" But she was in no condition to communicate.

"Just find it!" Johnny yelled. "Go Mickey! Call a God-damned ambulance, now!"

Mickey sprinted for the door as Johnny continued to pump Lombardi's chest. Mickey seemed to be gone forever. When he returned he said, "They're on their way. I didn't know the address, so I told them to turn at the alley and I would flag them down."

"Good job," Johnny said as he kept pushing. "How long?"

"Don't know," Mickey said. "I told them to come real fast."

Johnny was tired. His arms hurt, and Mrs. Lombardi's sobbing was driving him crazy. He wished he could tell her to shut up, but her anguish gave him added energy.

"How is he?" Mickey asked weakly.

"How the heck should I know?" Johnny thundered. Tears were streaming down his face, and his sweat was burning his eyes. "I think… I think he's alive." He said. "Where's the stinkin' ambulance?"

"I'll check," Mickey said. He moved to the alley and realized the bikes would be in the way, so he moved them.

He came back and said, "No sign yet."

It had only been minutes, but Johnny's arms felt like lead.

"Go back to the ally," he yelled, "or they might not find us."

Mickey went back and waited. Then he heard a siren in the distance.

"I think I can hear them," he called back. "I think they're coming."

"Do you see them?" Johnny said, frantically. "Where are they?" His arms were cramping, but he kept pushing.

"Not yet," Mickey said.

Seconds passed, but they seemed like hours. As the siren grew louder, Johnny felt another surge of energy. Then the tactical truck turned into the alley and Mickey yelled, "Here they are!" He began waving his arms frantically, crying almost uncontrollably and shouting, "We're right here! Over here!"

Johnny's rhythm was slower now. He just couldn't help it. He tried not to look, but his eyes were drawn to Old Man Lombardi's weathered face. Johnny had kept his enormous guilt to himself after the tomato raid, but he couldn't shake the idea of aiming a hose into an old man's face. Now, Johnny looked at Lombardi's eyes, and the guilt returned three-fold. It wasn't his fault, he told himself. He had no choice. Lombardi might have drowned Mickey. Still the guilt was oppressive, as was his fatigue.

Finally Johnny heard the truck stopping in the alley and Mickey's frenzied directions to the ambulance crew. Soon they were in the yard, two EMT's and Mickey. Johnny kept pushing on Lombardi's chest as one EMT spoke into his radio to the Lower Bucks Hospital emergency room and the other eased Johnny aside. "Great job, kid," he said as the team went to work.

"How long has he been out?" a crew member asked.

"Don't know," Johnny replied weakly. Johnny sat dazed as the team quickly applied oxygen, checked vital signs and transmitted information to the emergency room. The arrival of the crew set Mrs. Lombardi off again. She was still kneeling, and Mickey knelt beside her, put his arm around her shoulder and did his best to calm her. "He'll be okay, lady," he said softly, not knowing if Lombardi were even alive. "He'll be okay now, you'll see."

Johnny looked up and saw a policeman standing next to him. Soon there was another. He hadn't even heard their car arrive. The policeman looked at Johnny. His name tag said Lebo. "You guys called this in?"

"Yes. Mickey did," Johnny said softly.

"Are they your grandparents?"

"No," Mickey said. "We were riding by on our way to the pool. Johnny did CPR."

"Sort of," Johnny said. The tears began to flow again. The policeman took their names and addresses for his report. "You did a real good thing today, boys."

Somebody shouted, "Okay, we're moving. Let's go!" Old Man Lombardi was on the stretcher and they were wheeling him to the ambulance. The police had Mrs. Lombardi now and were leading her to their car. Johnny and Mickey followed everyone to the alley and watched them load the gurney into the vehicle. As the paramedic got in he said to Johnny, "You did a great job, kid. He's stable and I think he has a good chance to make it."

The emergency tactical truck raced off, and Johnny and Mickey watched until it turned at the end of the alley. They stood frozen, without speaking, until the sound of its siren faded in the distance.

5- The Deli

Johnny and Mickey stood quietly, still too stunned to speak.

Finally, Mickey said, "You okay?"

"Don't know," Johnny said softly.

"Me neither," Mickey said. "So what do we do now?"

"I'm going home," Johnny said, rubbing his arms. "I don't feel so good."

"Yeah, I'm not feeling so hot myself, but my parents are still working."

"Come to my place," Johnny said. "My Dad's in the store. We'll get something to drink."

Marzo's deli was a popular gathering place for friends of Johnny's dad, men who went there almost every day to chew the fat and pass the time. They had been friends since high school and had graduated at the height of the Vietnam War. The war had taken a heavy toll on each of them in different ways. There was Nick, a war hero who had served five years in a North Vietnamese POW camp, and Jimmy, who had his own especially horrific experience as a tunnel rat during his tour of duty. Big Frankie was a different story. He had received a medical deferment and had been haunted by guilt ever since because Nick and Jimmy had served and he didn't. But the true winner of the guilt award was Johnny's father. Angelo Marzo fled to Canada with his girlfriend, Donna, when he received his draft notice. They married and lived in exile for ten years until President Jimmy Carter granted amnesty to draft dodgers shortly after young Johnny was born. The four men reunited after the war, but the scars ran deeply for all of them, and the deepest scar of all was the death of their best friend, Johnny Francelli. Johnny was killed in action during his tour of duty. He had been the heart and soul of the gang during their high school days, and they were devastated by his death. But fond memories of him were very much alive in each of them. In fact, young Johnny was named after their slain friend and watching him grow gave each of them a semblance of peace.

Nick and Jimmy were pretty eccentric, and their quirky behavior was well known in town. But they were great guys who loved young Johnny as a son, and Johnny loved them in return. He called each of them uncle, and they ate it up.

The whole gang was there when Johnny and Mickey arrived, and they greeted the boys with the usual fanfare.

"There they are," Jimmy said. It's Mark Spitz and his buddy Johnny Weissmuller, back after a tough day of swimming."

"They don't know who those guys are," Nick said. "They're too young."

"Sure they do," Jimmy shot back. "They teach that stuff in school."

"Like hell, dimwit," Nick said good-naturedly. "They don't teach anything in school anymore. They just ask the kids to share how they feel about things."

Big Frankie just shook his head as his two friends went through another of their mindless arguments. Finally, Nick waved Jimmy off and turned his attention to the boys. "It's boiling outside." He winked at Johnny. "Your cheap old man has the air conditioner on low, but it's better than nothing."

"Hi, son," Johnny's father said from behind the counter. "Back already?"

"Hi, dad," Johnny replied faintly.

"Did you guys meet any hot girls at the pool?" Jimmy asked.

Mickey didn't know what to say and just looked at Johnny. "Nah," Johnny said. "We didn't go."

It was then that Big Frankie realized something didn't seem right. "Hey, Johnny, are you okay?" Johnny looked up and tried to speak, and then tears ran down his cheeks. He tried to hold himself together, but couldn't, and he began crying openly. Seeing this, Mickey broke down as well.

Angelo left the counter to join the boys, and the rest of the guys gathered around. "Sit down, son," Angelo said, leading Johnny to one of the chairs that surrounded an old card table. "Here, Mickey," he added, pulling out another chair, "sit here." Angelo noticed that Johnny's hair and shirt were soaked with perspiration.

"Jimmy," Angelo said, "get the boys some cold sodas from the case."

While Jimmy got the sodas, Nick went to the freezer to get some ice. He made ice packs by wrapping hand towels around the cubes and returned to the boys. "Here ya go," Nick said. Let me put this on your neck for a while and you'll cool down. Big Frankie took one and held it on Mickey's neck while Nick applied the other to Johnny's. Jimmy returned with the Cokes, and both boys drank deeply.

Angelo waited until the boys composed themselves and then asked gently, "So what's wrong? Did anyone bother you guys?"

"Better not have," Jimmy said. "We'll..."

Angelo waved him off. "Come on, son. It's okay now. Talk to us." Angelo looked at Mickey too, hoping to get a response from someone, but Mickey wasn't talking.

"Old Man Lombardi," Johnny stammered between sniffles. "I was afraid he would die. It was awful." With that he lost control again.

The men looked at each other. "Who's this guy Lombardi?" Angelo asked. Nick shrugged. Jimmy shook his head. Then Frankie said, "There's an old guy on Lafayette Street named Lombardi. Don't really know much about him though."

"That's him," Mickey said. "That's where he lives."

"Okay," Angelo said, trying to be as soothing as possible. "So what's this about him dying? What happened?" Johnny tried to compose himself again but still couldn't, and Mickey had already decided that it was Johnny's story to tell.

Just then, Donna Marzo burst through the door from the family residence. The Marzo's home was attached to the deli and a door near the meat counter connected the two. "Johnny!" She said when she saw the boys. "Thank God you're here." She rushed to the group and put her arms around her son. "Oh, my God. You poor baby, are you okay?" Johnny nodded. Then Donna turned to Mickey and ran her hand through his hair. "Mickey, I'm glad you came here. I just spoke to your mother and she's going to leave work early. Stay here until she comes." Then she looked at the group and said, "The police just called and told me everything. And then I called Mickey's mother."

"That's great," Angelo said anxiously. "But what's going on?"

"The boys didn't tell you?" she asked, surprised.

"Not yet," Angelo said.

"They're pretty upset," Jimmy added.

"Of course they are," Donna replied, putting an arm around both of them.

Donna took a deep breath and began. "Johnny saved a man's life today. An old man had a heart attack and Johnny administered CPR until the EMT's came. She kissed the top of her son's head. "Officer Lebo said that you are a hero."

"Mickey helped," Johnny said faintly.

"Nah, I didn't do nothin' much. It was Johnny."

With that Nick said, "Way to go man!" and patted Johnny on the back.

Jimmy added, "You've always been our hero, big guy."

"Great job," Frankie said. "We're proud of you."

Then Johnny's mother said gently, "It must have been awful for you."

"I was afraid he was going to die," Johnny said, sobbing. "Then I thought maybe he did die."

The men remained quiet as they visualized what the scene must have been like. Then Johnny asked his mother, "Did the policeman really say Old Man Lombardi would be okay?"

"Yes," she said reassuringly. "He'll need lots of rest, but the doctors think he should recover nicely."

Then Donna looked at Angelo. "Officer Lebo said that when the EMT's arrived, thanks to Mickey's call," she smiled at Mickey and then continued, "Johnny was administering chest massage, which the team said was very important. The officers took Mrs. Lombardi to the hospital. But they called me from the hospital to see if the boys were still alright."

Angelo nodded. "I'm real proud of you, son. We all are."

"Damn right," Nick added.

"You're a hero, Johnny," his mother said softly.

Johnny closed his eyes. He saw flashes of himself squirting the garden hose directly at Old Man Lombardi's face. He didn't feel much like a hero, not even a bit.

6- Johnny and Brain at the Log

After Mickey's mom picked him up, Johnny went to his room to take a nap. It was a restless, fitful sleep, interrupted by visions of the day. He soon abandoned the idea and opted for a long shower. He stood under the pulsating spray, hoping to wash away his memory of the afternoon. By the time he dressed and went downstairs, his mom was putting dinner on the table.

His parents handled him gingerly throughout the meal, but after some quiet small-talk, Johnny said, "Have you heard any news about Old Man...I mean Mr. Lombardi?"

"I thought you might want to know," his father said. "I closed the store while you were resting, and the guys and I took a ride to the hospital."

Johnny was surprised. His father almost never closed the deli.

"He's in intensive care, which is to be expected. But he's stable and his prognosis is good. The nurses said he's a pretty strong guy."

Johnny recalled the image of Mr. Lombardi holding Mickey's head under water and said, "Yeah, he looked like he might be strong."

Mr. Marzo continued, "The nurses pointed out his wife in the waiting room, so I introduced myself to her. She was still very upset and her English is a little rough, but once she understood who I was she hugged me and said thank you about a thousand times."

Johnny didn't respond, but he had a flash of her kneeling by her husband, begging Johnny to help her. It was quiet a little longer and then Johnny's father said, "The Phillies are on tonight. They're playing the Pirates. Wanna watch a few innings?"

"Thanks, Dad," Johnny replied. "But I think I need to go out for a while, see some of the guys."

Johnny's mother started to protest, but Angelo thought it was probably a good sign. "Sure, son. You go ahead. But don't be late. Maybe we'll catch the later innings together when you get back."

Johnny left the house and went straight for the log, just as he did almost every night. This time he was a little early and was surprised to find Brain sitting on the log waiting for him.

"Hey, Brain," Johnny said, taking a seat next to him. "What are you doing here?"

"Waiting for you. I thought you'd come early."

"Yeah? Why?"

"I heard about what happened today. Eddie Boomer's older brother is a volunteer fireman, and he heard the news at the firehouse. He came around the pool and told everyone. He said you may have saved the guy's life."

Johnny's guilt felt like a dead weight in this throat. He'd heard enough hero references for the day and quickly changed the subject. "I almost forgot about the pool. Was Carrie Boyle there?"

Brain lit up. "She sure was, man."

"How did she look?"

"Are you kidding? She looked great. It was like Helen of Troy was at the pool."

"Helen of Troy? Who's that?"

"You know, Helen of Troy," Brain said, sounding a bit exasperated. "From ancient history. The face that launched a thousand ships."

Johnny was clueless. "Yeah sure," he said dismissively. "What color was Carrie's bathing suit?"

Now Brain was fully animated. "White, set against a beautiful, deep tan. I can still see it. She had on a bikini, kind of skimpy if you ask me. But, man she looked real..."

"Shut up," Johnny said shaking his head. "I've got the picture."

"Hey, you asked."

"Did you tell her about me and the jackknife?"

"Are you kidding? That was my assignment, wasn't it? I had her prepped for an Olympic performance, but you had to go and save some guy's life, a guy who would have gladly killed you a week ago."

Johnny ignored that and asked, "Was she interested in seeing the dive?"

"Now you're making me mad," Brain said playfully. "When Brain Kelly is given an assignment from his lord and mentor, he gets it done. She was damn interested. But, of course, after all of my hard work, you managed to stand her up before you even met her. I've been thinking about the psychological implications of that, and I'd say you've got yourself a problem. This is not the way to begin a relationship."

"Did she wait long?"

"Well, long is a relative term. Know what I mean? When you're a tanned, bikini-clad goddess with golden hair, made lighter by the sun, and you're surrounded by every young male within sniffing distance, you can afford to have an abbreviated wait time. There were a lot of pressures at play..."

Johnny punched him on the arm. "Just tell me how long she waited!"

Brain rubbed his arm feigning pain, but he would not be rushed. "I gave it my best shot. I told her you were performing the masterful dive at 1:00. Then, to kill time, I described the dive. I explained the athleticism required. I told her how you would eventually enter the water while barely disturbing the surface. As more time passed and I became more desperate, I even broached the physics behind the spring in the diving board. I..."

"Don't make me punch you again," Johnny said. "How long did she wait?"

Brain lowered his head, reluctant to deliver the sad news. "She lasted until 1:22," he mumbled softly. "That's when Sammy Neale led her away to the snack-bar. The girl got hungry."

"Sammy Neale!" Johnny thundered.

"Like I said, the girl got hungry and Sammy always has extra cash."

"Sammy Neale's a dweeb."

"He's a dweeb with cash. And today he was the dweeb who got the girl."

Johnny got quiet. Then he said, "Does she know about what happened this afternoon with Mr. Lombardi?"

"Unfortunately, no. The hunger pangs set in before Eddie Boomer spread the news. It's a shame. I mean, if I had that information I would have had something to work with. I could have said, 'Excuse me your highness, but my friend is delayed. It seems he's saving a man's life. I think she would have given that concept a lot of weight, don't you?"

"I'm glad she doesn't know."

"Why? It's a big deal."

"I'm just glad; that's all. I wish nobody knew. Everybody's making a big fuss over it when they shouldn't. I didn't do anything."

Brain turned serious. "Johnny, the heart is a muscle. It expands and contracts. That's how it pumps the blood. During a heart attack it is under great stress. By pushing on Old Man Lombardi's chest for ten hours, or however long it took, you relieved that stress. You helped it do its work. That's a pretty big deal."

Johnny was constantly amazed by Brain's knowledge. He looked at him and asked, "How old are you?"

"Fourteen," Brain said. "Just like you."

Johnny shook his head. "You're a freak, you know that?"

"Thanks," Brain said, smiling.

Johnny sat quietly again. Brain studied him and said, "You've got more on your mind than missing Carrie Boyle at the pool, don't you?" When Johnny didn't answer, Brain added, "You're really not good with this hero thing are you?"

Johnny nodded. "All I can think about is that night when we were stealing Lombardi's tomatoes. He's an old man, Brain. I aimed that hose right at his face, right at his eyes. What's wrong with me?"

Brain gathered his thoughts. "Listen, Johnny. First of all, I'm glad I wasn't there that night because I know I would have wet my pants. But, from what I hear, you had to do it; the guy might have drowned Mickey. Ask Mickey whether he thinks you did the right thing. You know what he'll say."

"It was all my fault to begin with," Johnny countered. "I'm the one who talked everyone into going. Nobody wanted to do it until I convinced them. Why do I always have to do that stuff?"

"You're a kid, Johnny. You like to have fun. That's why everyone likes you so much. You've got chutzpah."

"Chutzpah? What the hell is chutzpah?"

"You know, gall, audacity."

"Huh?"

"Balls, Johnny. You've got balls. That's just the way you are. It's what makes you a leader."

Johnny shook his head. "Some leader I am."

"Listen, Johnny. You changed my life. Before I met you, I was picked on by every kid I ever met. Sometimes it seemed that the only people who accepted me were my parents. Then that day in the cafeteria you told me to slide my tray over and join you and everything changed. The other kids accepted me because you accepted me."

Johnny shook his head again. "No way. They accepted you because they liked you. Don't put it on me."

"You're wrong, Johnny. You did a good thing that day whether you like it or not. Confucius said, 'Forget injuries, never forget kindness.' I'm trying to forget my past injuries, but I will never forget the kindness you showed me."

"Confucius said that, huh? How do I know you're not jerking me around with that Confucius crap? How do I know you're not making it all up?"

"You don't I guess, unless you look it up, which is highly unlikely. Or, you can trust me. Why would I lie about Confucius? But let's get back to the point. I owe you big time. Don't beat yourself up over a prank you tried to pull a few weeks ago. You did a good thing today. Just roll with it."

"I wish I could," Johnny said sadly. "But right now it just doesn't feel right. Nothing feels right."

7- Opening Day

By Labor Day the boys were ready for the change back to school. This school year would be more important than most because the boys were entering ninth grade and were making the jump to public school. They'd be attending Bristol High, and they couldn't wait to make the transition. For Johnny, starting school meant that he'd be in the same building with Carrie Boyle every day, and that was a good thing.

Unfortunately, it also meant that there would be a ton of other guys competing for her attention. Still, Johnny was determined to meet her sometime soon.

The school district encompassed just a little over two square miles and did not offer school busing. So the boys would walk to school each morning, just like generations of Bristol students did before them. They planned to converge on the corner of Jefferson Avenue and Pond Street and walk along Wilson Avenue for the final leg to school.

Johnny and Bobby lived near each other and walked to the corner together. They had a good-natured laugh when they saw Brain already there waiting for them. The little guy still looked like a sixth-grader. Tommy arrived next and the four of them waited for the perennially late Mickey Morelli.

"Think he's still in bed?" Bobby asked.

"I called him," Tommy said. "He's awake, but did you ever see him get moving in the morning? He may not get here until nine o'clock."

Brain checked his watch. He was the only one who wore one. "It's seven-twenty now. I clocked it yesterday and it took twelve minutes to walk to school from here. We have to be there at seven-forty, so we should leave here no later than seven-twenty-eight."

"Wait," Tommy said, laughing. "Are you telling me that you timed the walk yesterday? Are you serious?"

"I've been waiting a long time to start high school," Brain retorted. "I'd hate to be late on my first day."

"I can't believe this guy," Tommy said. "He timed it."

Everyone had a good laugh, and Bobby said, "You're priceless, Kelly."

"Besides," Johnny said. "We're friends. We stick together. We can't just leave without Mickey." Johnny winked at Tommy and Tommy joined in.

"That's right. Like I said, I called Mickey, and he's coming. So we wait here until he shows up. If we're late, we're late together."

Brain looked nervous and checked his watch again. It was approaching seven-twenty-two. He struggled to appear calm, but his stomach was churning. He absolutely did not want to be late for school.

The rest of the boys seemed totally relaxed and pretended not to notice as Brain tried to sneak glances at his watch. It was seven-twenty-six when Brain shouted, "There he is!" Mickey had just turned the corner from Logan Street and was a block away. The closer he got the more disheveled he looked. When he got close enough, Tommy said, "Going all out on the first day, Morelli?"

"What?" Mickey said, sounding half asleep. "What's that mean?"

"You're wearing the same clothes you had on last night," Tommy replied.

Bobby piled on. "Did you look in a mirror? Your hair, man, it's all over the place."

Mickey struck back. "So what's today, the prom or somethin'? How about you guys? You look like your moms dressed you."

Brain looked at his watch and said, "We really should be going now."

"Yeah," Johnny said. "Let's go before Brain has to go home to change his pants"

The day began in homeroom with typical first day stuff. This time, Brain was careful to fill out the forms properly. Following homeroom, the entire school went to the auditorium for the opening day assembly, presided over by the principal, Mr. Doug Baxter.

Mr. Baxter was a legend at the school, and the students loved him. He made it a point to know all of them by name and was blessed with a limitless memory bank on each. He was always in the halls between classes greeting kids. "Hey, Amanda. I see you got the cast removed. How's that wrist feeling?..Joey, big game this weekend. Are we gonna take those Spartans? Mitch, that shirt is killing me! Day-glow orange? That'll keep your classmates awake...Carol, I saw that bowl you're working on in ceramics. It's beautiful!... Welcome back, Art. Feeling better?"

He'd rattle off similar comments from bell to bell, making kids feel that he had a genuine interest in them. He made it seem easy because his interest was sincere, and his enthusiasm was infectious.

To add to the persona, he owned a 1986 Harley-Davidson that he rode to school every Friday. He was also a weight-lifter who lifted with the sports teams in the school weight room. Last year he bench-pressed three-hundred and fifty pounds, a feat that did not go unnoticed by the tougher elements of the school. To round out his image, he insisted on having a small acting part in the school plays and sang badly, but with spirit, at the annual talent show.

Nice guy that he was, Mr. Baxter was no pushover. He was a firm but fair disciplinarian who set high expectations for kids and seemed genuinely hurt when students behaved poorly. Kids often left his office after receiving a suspension feeling sorry that they let him down. He made it a point to greet every student who returned from a suspension with his patented line, "Welcome back. I'm glad you're here. I have a lot of confidence in you, and I know that you've learned from your mistake. If you need help with anything, stop in to see me."

Johnny and the boys had heard all about Mr. Baxter from upperclassmen, but the assembly would be their first chance to see him in action.

Mr. Baxter stepped to the podium and the students got quiet. "Good morning, Bristol High!" He shouted into the microphone. The students laughed and he did it again, "I said, good morning Bristol High!" This time he was greeted by a thunderous, "Good morning, Mr. Baxter!"

"That's more like it." He paused and then said. "Well, here we are, ready to begin the 1988-1989 school year, and I hope you're as excited as I am about what that means. Because it means that we get to see friends and teachers we haven't seen all summer. It means new experiences, new opportunities, and new challenges. I know that sounds trite, but whether it is or not depends upon you.

"There are people in this building who care about you: your friends, your teachers, your counselors, your coaches, and, of course, me." With that some students cheered. Mr. Baxter went on. "And that's not just rhetoric. It's real. We care and we want to help. Your job is to take advantage of our help. Your job is to set goals, to stretch yourselves, to say good-bye to past failures, to cast off past mistakes, to live for the future. You know that old Fleetwood Mac song, *Don't Stop?* Think about those lyrics and don't stop thinking about tomorrow." He paused again. "Yes, yesterday is gone. And that means that if you've had past success, that's great, but remember that you can't live on past success; you need to push forward. You need to find new ways to challenge yourself."

Mr. Baxter was on a roll and his voice grew louder. "And, as I said earlier, if you've had past failures or mistakes, cast them off. If you've got a psychological boogie man hanging on to you and weighing you down, now is the time to look him in the eye and say, 'get off of my back because I'm moving on!'"

The teachers applauded and most students joined in. Johnny looked around at his buddies and then started to clap as well. Mr. Baxter gathered himself and continued, this time in a much softer voice. "I know high school can be a difficult time in your life. Believe me, its not easy being my age either. I'm going to be forty soon. Can you believe that? Forty! The Harley is starting to rattle my bones when I ride it."

He allowed the kids to chuckle before he went on. "Seriously though, I know high school can be tough. So here's my offer. If you're feeling down about something, come to see me. If you're worried about something, come to see me. If you're scared, or if someone is giving you a hard time, come to see me. If you have a personal dream, but you're reluctant to pursue it, come to see me. If you screwed up because you weren't thinking, come to see me. Come to see me, come to see me, come to see me. I'm here for you," he added. "We all are."

Mr. Baxter took a breath and turned somber. "Now, let's get back to that part about screwing up. It's that time in the speech when we talk about being good school citizens. Now some schools have a long list of rules for students to follow. But I just want you to remember one rule, and that is, do the right thing. That's it. You don't need a long explanation of what that means. You know whether or not it is the right thing to deface school property. You know whether or not it is the right thing to be disrespectful to your teachers or to bully someone. You know. I don't think anyone in this room can say, 'Gee, I didn't know I wasn't allowed to throw food in the cafeteria or fight in the halls. We all know what the right thing is; now we just have to choose to do it."

Mr. Baxter smiled again and said, "Okay, we're running out of time and that's enough of that negative stuff. I want to leave you with something positive; something that I think exemplifies what we value at Bristol High. A couple of weeks ago I received a call from Mayor Tosti informing me about two young men, incoming students, who did a remarkable thing this summer. While on their way to the swimming pool, they witnessed an elderly gentleman having a heart attack..."

"No," Johnny said under his breath. "Don't do this." Mickey was sitting next to him and had the same reaction.

Mr. Baxter went on. "One boy administered CPR while the other called the ambulance and consoled the man's grieving wife."

"I can't believe this is happening, " Johnny whispered.

"Me too," Mickey replied.

"The mayor informed me that because of their efforts, the man survived and is well on his way to a full recovery. In light of this, I have decided to establish a new award, the principal's award for outstanding community service. At this time I would like the two boys in question to come to the stage to be the first recipients of the award. Once again, they are new students to our building. Please join with me in welcoming and congratulating Johnny Marzo and Mickey Morelli."

Johnny sat frozen as the audience began to clap. "I'm not going up," Johnny whispered. "We have to, man. He called us," Mickey said.

Brain was sitting on the other side of Johnny and nudged him. "Go, big guy. You have to do this." Johnny and Mickey finally stood and climbed their way over the feet of their classmates. Tommy Dillon goosed Johnny quickly as Johnny passed him in the row. "I'll get you later," Johnny mumbled. Then they made it to the aisle and began what seemed like the longest walk of their lives. When Johnny reached the stage and turned to face the audience, he saw that his teachers and classmates were giving them a standing ovation.

8- After School

Mickey had a guidance appointment after school and Johnny was waiting for him in front of the building when he heard a girl's voice behind him say, "Excuse me." He turned to see that it was Carrie Boyle.

"Hi," she said, flashing a bright smile. "Aren't you the boy they honored at the assembly this morning?"

Johnny was dazed. He wasn't prepared for this, at least not yet. His heart raced and it was only with great effort that he managed to say, "Yeah, that's me."

She put out her hand to shake. "I'm Carrie Boyle," she said, still smiling.

Johnny readily took her hand and stammered, "I'm Johnny Marzo."

She was dressed in light blue shorts and a white blouse. Her hair was pulled back, away from her face, and her summer tan was still with her. It was a hot afternoon, but she looked cool and fresh. Johnny was struck by her clear, blue-green eyes, and her smile that seemed permanently fixed.

"I'm sorry to bother you," she said, "but I noticed you standing here and I just wanted to tell you how much I admire what you did."

Johnny couldn't bring himself to capitalize on Old Man Lombardi, even if to impress a girl. "It was really no big deal," he said flatly.

"Oh, you're too modest," she replied. "It sounded like a very big deal to me." Then she laughed and gently tapped his arm. "Wow! I mean, you saved someone's life, Mr. Johnny Marzo. I'd say that's pretty big!"

A handshake and an arm tap, Johnny thought. That was two touches in less than a minute. He began to feel clammy. He had fantasized about what it would be like when they met, but this was different than he had imagined. She certainly was pretty up close, but there was something he found much more appealing. Seeing her smile, feeling her hand, hearing her kind words, it was clear that there were no pretensions about her. The girl was special. He searched for the right word to describe her. Then he found it. She was nice. Carrie Boyle was very nice.

Still somewhat dazed, Johnny extended his hand and managed to say, "I'm Johnny Marzo."

"I know," she said with a giggle as she gave his hand a second exaggerated shake. "I think we just did this."

"Yeah, right. I guess we did," he said awkwardly. At that moment he would have jumped in front of a train if one were nearby.

"You're funny," she said, still smiling.

"Yeah, I'm a real blast."

"No really," she persisted. "You should have seen yourself on the stage today. You stared at your shoes the whole time Mr. Baxter was talking about you, and you were so bashful while everyone was clapping. It was so cute."

Johnny couldn't believe this was happening. Nothing this good ever happened to him.

"A lot of guys would have enjoyed being a hero, but you didn't," Carrie said. "That's really special."

He managed to mumble "thanks." By now he was totally disgusted with himself. After all, he was the man, formerly the coolest guy at St. Theresa's and destined to become the same at Bristol High. Yet, all he could manage to say was "thanks."

Tragic images raced through his mind. He was on a stage somewhere, the spotlight was on, the audience was present, but he couldn't perform. The opportunity was passing. There would be no *carpe diem* here. He saw himself fumbling on the final drive, double-dribbling with seconds left in a tie game, taking a called third strike in the bottom of the ninth. He was crashing and burning when he should have been soaring. He needed to say something meaningful soon or Carrie would be gone.

Miraculously, he was given another reprieve when Carrie said, "I'm new to town. We just moved here in early July."

"I know," Johnny said.

Carrie looked surprised and Johnny quickly added. "Small town. Everybody knows everybody. I've never seen you before, so I figured you were new." Okay, Johnny thought, a harmless lie.

"I don't feel as though I know many people," Carrie said. "I mean, I met some people at the pool, but… you know," she said, trailing off.

Yeah, Johnny thought. Like that dweeb, Sammy Neale. He was bad enough, but Johnny knew there would be plenty of other guys once word spread that there was a new girl in school. He needed to tie her up early.

Johnny slowly began to recover. His heartbeat was returning to normal and he had stopped sweating. He managed another sentence. "So why are you here so late after school?" Not bad, he thought. It actually sounded normal.

"I was getting my schedule changed in guidance, and there was a long line. There were still some students lined up when I left."

Johnny thought of Mickey and hoped he wouldn't show up any time soon.

"What did you change?" Johnny asked. He was feeling much better now.

"My Mom is from France, so my parents wanted me to take French instead of Spanish."

Johnny surprised himself by saying, "Too bad, for some reason I'm decent in Spanish. I could have helped you."

Carrie looked disappointed. "The change was complicated," she added. "The courses weren't offered at the same time, so they had to change my second period Spanish class to social studies and my seventh period social studies class to French."

Johnny had social studies second period. His heart began to race again as he formed his next question. "Who is your new social studies teacher?" He asked it as casually as he could and waited hopefully for the right answer.

"Mr. Swilli," she replied.

Bingo!

"Mr. Swilli is my second period teacher too," Johnny gushed. "He's seems like a pretty cool guy. It should be a good class."

Carrie jumped when she heard the news, and he liked the way her hair bounced. "That's great," she said. "It will be so much fun."

At that moment, Johnny promised God that he would go to church forever as a gesture of thanks. After all, he'd met the girl he'd been dreaming of and they had already touched twice, three times actually, if you counted the second stupid handshake. And he would see her every day in social studies class.

There was an awkward silence and Carrie filled it again. "Well, I guess I'll be going. I'm so glad we met, Johnny Marzo." Johnny fought the impulse to shake hands again.

"Yeah, me too. I'm glad we met."

"So I guess I'll see you in class tomorrow."

"Yeah, second period, right?"

She giggled again. "Yes, second period."

She flashed one more smile as she turned to leave, and Johnny felt a wave of panic. What if she met another guy between now and class tomorrow? What if someone else already had his eye on her, maybe someone with a car? How could he compete with a car? What if she met someone walking home? Relationships could happen fast. She could be going steady by the time he saw her again. Everything he gained today could be lost by the following morning. He summoned his courage and said, "Where do you live?"

She stopped. "I live on Radcliffe Street, a couple of blocks past the library, toward Mill Street." Then she made it easy again. "Are you going that way?"

I am now, Johnny thought. "Yeah, right by there." It was his second little lie, but Johnny felt it was for a good cause. "I'll walk you if that's okay."

"That would be great," she said beaming. "We had busses at my old school, but I think walking home is neat."

"Like I said, Bristol is a small town."

Johnny glanced back at the school doors, but there was still no sign of Mickey, and that was good. Mickey would have to walk home alone, and Johnny knew he would understand.

As he fell in beside her their shoulders touched ever so slightly. That made three touches, four actually, if you counted the second stupid handshake.

9- Oral History Lesson

It was mid-October and school was in full swing. Johnny and Carrie were a couple, and the world was a good place. Johnny sat three rows from the back of the room, a few rows behind and to the right of Carrie. The seating was perfect because it allowed Johnny to look at her any time he wanted, which was often.

Mr. Swilli's class was Johnny's favorite. Johnny didn't care much for school, but Swilli was a cool guy in his late twenties who obviously liked kids and knew how to relate to them. He was a good teacher who worked hard to make social studies interesting.

Johnny listened as Mr. Swilli opened his lesson for the day. "Most of the American History we study is about wars and generals, elections and presidents, major legislation and landmark court cases. It's called 'top down' history because we study the important people who are at the 'top' of society so to speak, society's leaders. That approach is important, but today we're going to look at another way to study history."

One way is more than enough, Johnny thought, but he was willing to keep an open mind.

Mr. Swilli continued. "I'd like you to imagine that a new movie has been released and you're thinking about seeing it." He paused to allow that to sink in.

"Okay, assuming that we don't want to waste our time or money on a lousy movie, we might want to do something to find out if it is good or not before we go. Agreed?"

Bobby Meyers jumped in. "Hey, Mr. Swilli, I'm gonna go see *Caddyshack II*. It's coming out soon. I saw the first one when it came out and it was pretty good."

"Okay, great," Swilli said. "Let's use Bobby's *Caddyshack II* as an example. How many of you think you might want to see it?" Several hands went up and Swilli nodded.

"Now I have to warn you, some sequel movies can be pretty bad. So I'm back to my original position that we want to find out if it's good before we go. So how might we do that?"

Patti Wayne called out, "We could watch the advertisements for it like Bobby did."

"Exactly," Swilli said. "We all get bombarded by the ads when a new movie is released and they give us an idea of what the movie is about. Is there a problem with relying upon the TV ads?"

"I've seen some pretty bad movies that looked great in the ads," Johnny said.

"Right," Mr. Swilli replied. "The movie companies pay for the ads, so they obviously make their product look good. So the ads have value, but we probably shouldn't rely only on them." He scanned the room and asked, "What else can we do?"

Carrie said, "My family always reads the movie reviews in the newspaper."

"Ah, yes. Movie reviews," Swilli said. "Using professional reviewers is much safer than just watching the paid ads. Film experts like Siskle and Ebert are hired by newspapers or television networks to do reviews. Reading or watching them would certainly help."

Swilli paused again and then asked, "Is there anything else we can do?"

Mickey Morelli said, "Mr. Swilli, I'll be honest. I ain't gonna read no movie review in the newspaper. If I want to know if a movie is good I'll ask one of my friends who has seen it already. That's all."

"Bingo!" Swilli shouted. "How many of you would just ask a friend?" Lots of hands went up. "So let's see, we could read what an expert has to say, but most of you said you'd prefer to find out what the average Joe thinks about the movie instead because we're average Joe's ourselves." Most nodded their agreement.

"Okay, now let's get back to my history example. Suppose we wanted to find out what was happening at a particular time in history. We could read what the expert historians had to say, right? It's kind of like consulting with the expert movie critics. It's what we usually do as students of history. We read the experts. Now that's the 'top down' approach I mentioned earlier. But wouldn't it also be cool to find out things that happened in history from the perspective of the average people who lived it? Wouldn't it be cool to ask common people their feelings and beliefs about what happened just like we ask friends what they think of movies we might want to see?"

The class seemed willing to accept that. Swilli went on. "There's a guy with a funny sounding name, Studs Turkle, who wrote history just that way. He wrote about what it was like to live during the Great Depression, not by interviewing Presidents, economists or other historians. He wrote about the Great Depression by interviewing common citizens who actually lived in the 1930's. He called it 'History from the bottom up.' It's also called oral history because it was done by conducting oral interviews."

Swilli scanned the room and felt as though he still had them. "Okay," he said, "so why am I making such a big deal about using oral history and conducting interviews?"

No hands went up.

Swilli smiled and said with exaggerated enthusiasm, "Because you, my good friends, are about to become oral historians."

Their initial response was neutral at best, so he quickly plunged on. "That's right! You will be conducting interviews with older people from town who have experienced things like the bombing of Pearl Harbor, the Great Depression, man's first walk on the moon, Woodstock..."

Bobby interjected. "Are you saying there are people from Bristol who walked on the moon?"

Swilli stifled a laugh and said gently, "No, Bobby. I guess I didn't make things clear enough. What I mean is that people from town lived during the time that these things were happening. Not that they played a major role in them."

"Oh," Bobby said, smiling at his own mistake. "Now I get it."

Swilli went on. "But talking with them is still important because we want to know what they were thinking and feeling when major events took place."

Now Swilli shifted gears. "Who remembers when the space shuttle *Challenger* exploded two years ago?" Several hands shot up. "Of course you do. You were in seventh grade then."

Patti Wayne's hand went up. "We were watching it on TV in science class, and we saw it happen live. It was awful."

"Right," Swilli said softly. "If you remember, Christa McAuliffe was to be the first teacher in space, and schools across the country were encouraged to watch to get kids more interested in science."

"It was so terrible," Patti added. "One minute we were all excited and then we saw all the thick white smoke and… it was just terrible."

Other students offered brief recollections of the tragedy and Swilli let their comments sink in for a while. Then he said, "At that very moment you were living history. You were experiencing a riveting event that would leave a lasting mark on you."

It was clear that the students got the message. "Years from now anyone can read a history book about the *Challenger* tragedy to learn more about it. They can read about the technical reasons why the tragedy occurred or the political ramifications it had for the space program. But if they really want to know what people were *feeling* at the time. If they want to know how everyday people *reacted*, they can ask you. Heck, someday your children may ask you about it, and you'll be able to tell them because you lived it." Heads nodded and Swilli smiled.

"Now, I want to connect you guys with older people from town who experienced things that you haven't experienced. We're going to make a list of the eras or events we want to investigate and a list of the people from town you can interview. Then you're going to develop questions and then," he added with much more enthusiasm, "You're going to conduct your interviews and report back to class."

By now the students were excited.

Tommy Dillon, asked, "Who are these people?"

"Anyone old enough," Swilli said. "If you're lucky enough to still have grandparents living, you can use them. They have a lot to tell and it's a great way to spend time with them. What I'd like you to do tonight is talk this over with your parents and see if they can come up with someone, a grandparent, a neighbor, a friend of the family, someone who is a little older, who you can interview. I'm going to pass out this sheet now which will explain to your parents what this is all about. And there is one more thing. I already have a list of people in the community willing to do this. So if you can't come up with someone, I'll match you up."

At the end of class Swilli said, "Hang on a minute, Johnny; I need to tell you something." Johnny ran a quick inventory of things he'd done that could land him in trouble. When they were alone, Swilli said, "I have great news."

Johnny relaxed.

"I've been thinking about the man you saved this summer, Mr. Lombardi. As you know, he's an Italian immigrant, and I think the topic of the immigration experience could be an interesting one."

Johnny didn't like where this was going.

"Anyway," Swilli beamed. "I called him, explained our project and asked if he'd be willing to let you interview him."

Johnny was stunned as he heard Mr. Swilli's next words. "He said he was feeling fine and that he'd love to talk with a student, especially you. He said he has wanted to meet you ever since he got out of the hospital and this will be his chance. You are going to interview Ernesto Lombardi!"

10- Meeting Lombardi

Johnny had dreaded this day ever since Mr. Swilli announced his assignment, and now, as he approached Old Man Lombardi's house, he walked like a man going to the gallows. His eyes were cast downward and each step was slow and deliberate.

He was scared out of his mind that Lombardi would recognize him, wring his neck, and then eat him for dinner with some sliced tomatoes. But his fear was secondary to his overbearing guilt. He simply couldn't shake the image of him aiming a stream of high pressured water at an old man's eyes.

Johnny was having a hard time coming to grips with who he was as a person. He reviewed the long list of pranks and adventures he had led over the years, the dangers he had exposed his friends to, the pressures he had put on them to go along with his antics, the disregard he had shown to the victims, and he had become uncomfortable in his own skin. Sure he still fooled around, teased Brain, acted out in school, and talked tough, but inside, he was not pleased at all. And the recent attention he was receiving just made him feel worse.

He thought of his funeral after Lombardi killed him and wondered who would be there. Surely his parents would, and his unofficial uncles from the deli: Nick, Jimmy, and Big Frankie. He'd never seen any of them in a suit and wondered if they owned one. His friends would be there for sure, and he hoped Brain would be asked to write the eulogy; he would know just what to say and what to leave out. Then he thought of Carrie, the light of his world, his reason for living for the past forty-eight days that they had been dating. He wished her happiness, as long as it wasn't with that dweeb, Sammy Neale.

He decided to enter the house by the alley, reasoning that the familiar terrain would be good if he needed to make a quick escape. He tried to convince himself that his fears were irrational. There was no way Lombardi would recognize him. The raid was three months earlier. It had been dark. Lombardi was focused on Mickey until the very end, and from then on, the old man had a steady stream of water in his eyes. Still, Johnny was scared. Damn scared. Heart-pounding, almost wet-your-pants scared.

Johnny reached the rear gate and stopped. He wished he had stopped at the same spot in July and turned around. He remembered letting Bobby off the hook when Bobby was shaking with fright. Johnny wished now that he had canceled the raid and sent everyone home. But that wasn't Johnny's style. He needed to be the fearless one, the hard guy. He had picked Old Man Lombardi's place because he wanted to prove that he wasn't afraid of anything, but he didn't feel so brave now.

He entered the yard and moved along the walkway that bordered the vegetable garden. The yard looked different now. The vegetation was gone. The soil had been tilled in preparation for the winter months. Johnny considered the possibility that Old Man Lombardi had bodies buried in the yard, victims of previous tomato raids who he had caught, mutilated, and used as fertilizer. He knew that was crazy, but still, the thought lingered as he moved forward. He noticed the rain barrel at the rear of the house and remembered the sounds of Mickey choking and gasping for air between each of Lombardi's dunks.

There were two steps leading to the back door. Johnny climbed them, whispered a brief prayer and then looked around. He was hoping a neighbor was watching, someone who would testify later that he saw Johnny enter the house about eleven o'clock and never saw him come out. But the yards were deserted. Johnny exhaled slowly and knocked.

Seconds later the door swung open and Johnny saw Mrs. Lombardi. She smiled broadly and said, *"Saluti! Saluti!"* Then she added, *"Vieni, Vieni,"* motioning for him to come inside.

He stepped through the doorway into the kitchen. There was an old-fashioned pasta maker on the counter and countless pots and utensils hanging from ceiling hooks. Spaghetti sauce was simmering on the stove.

She gave him a hug and said, *"Buon giovanotto!"* Then she called in the direction of the next room, *"Ernesto, vieni. Un buon giovanotto!"*

Old Man Lombardi entered the room and looked even more imposing than Johnny had remembered. He wore a ribbed, sleeveless undershirt, and his stocky build filled the shirt well. His hair was gray and tightly cropped. His skin color was good. In all, he looked far more vibrant than he did the day Johnny found him on the ground.

"Ah, Marzo!" He thundered. *"Grazie. Grazie! Thank you."* He crossed the room and gave Johnny a bear hug. *"You save my life. Grazie."*

Mrs. Lombardi smiled, pinched Johnny's cheek and said, *"Piccolo dottore."*

Lombardi gave a hardy laugh and said, *"She call you 'little doctor.' She no speak good English, but she call you little doctor. What about you? You speak Italiano?"*

"Not really," Johnny replied. "Just English."

"Why? Marzo, no speak Italiano?"

Johnny shrugged, "My grandfather used to teach me a little before he died, but I don't use it anymore."

"Your fadder, he speak Italiano?"

Johnny thought of lying to please the old man but thought better of it. "No. He just speaks English."

Lombardi shook his head and grumbled something in Italian. Mrs. Lombardi gave her husband a chiding look, smiled at Johnny again and said, *"Nice boy. Very nice boy."*

Mr. Lombardi looked at the boy sternly. *"Language is good. Promise me you learn some day."*

Johnny shrugged. He didn't see much harm in appeasing the old man since he'd never see him again. "Sure, okay. I'll learn."

"Good," Lombardi said motioning to the kitchen table. *"Sit. We eat."*

Johnny had no intentions of eating, but when Lombardi repeated the command, Johnny sat and Lombardi took the chair across from him.

Mrs. Lombardi put a plate of cheese, black olives, roasted peppers, and, of course, sliced tomatoes on the table along with squares of homemade tomato pie. *"Mangia, mangia,"* she said. *"Eat."*

The food produced a harmony of smells that reminded Johnny of his father's deli. Johnny held out briefly before reaching for the pizza, and the Lombardis were delighted.

Mr. Lombardi put a piece of cheese in his mouth and followed it with pizza. "Wine!" he said while still chewing, and Mrs. Lombardi returned promptly with a bottle of red wine and a glass. Mr. Lombardi looked at the glass and said, *"Two glass!"*

His wife looked at him disapprovingly. Then she looked at Johnny and said, *"Giovanotto."*

Lombardi laughed again. *"She call you uh little boy."* He turned back to his wife and his smile faded. *"Two glass!"*

Mrs. Lombardi shrugged and placed a glass in front of Johnny. Then Lombardi reached out, pulled his wife toward him and playfully grabbed the cheek of her behind and held it. The move took Johnny by such surprise that he almost spit out his food. Mrs. Lombardi flushed and pushed her husband's hand away.

Lombardi roared with laughter. *"My wife, Angelina. Old now, but you should have seen her before. You know Sophia Loren?"*

Johnny shook his head and Lombardi looked disappointed again.

"You know Gina Lollobrigida?"

Johnny reluctantly shook his head again and Lombardi shrugged.

"Two beautiful women, but my wife, is even more beautiful." He went for her backside again, but she scooted out of reach.

"Sciocco," she said, half kidding and half serious.

Lombardi laughed again and turned to Johnny. *"She call me crazy. You think so?"*

I think you're a crazy bastard and maybe a mass murderer, Johnny thought. But he said, "No. I guess not."

Lombardi slapped his hand on the table so hard that Johnny jumped. *"Well, I am crazy. Crazy about life,"* he said laughing, *"and you save my life! Grazie."* When he finished laughing he poured each of them a generous glass of wine, turned to his wife and said, *"We talk now."*

Mrs. Lombardi nodded, smiled at Johnny, and left.

11- The Interview

Mr. Lombardi sat in silence for a long time, and Johnny considered the possibility that the old man had finally recognized him. Johnny's seat was closer to the door than Lombardi's, and he calculated that if he bolted suddenly he could make it out alive. Then he recalled how quickly Lombardi had bounded down the steps to grab Mickey, so he leaned back in his chair just in case the old geezer tried to lunge across the table.

Finally, Lombardi placed an olive in his mouth, spit the pit out into his hand and took a deep drink of his wine. He stared at Johnny for a long time and then said, *"So, ask da questions!"*

"Okay," Johnny said nervously, "I'll get started." He had brought a notebook with him and a small tape-recorder, and he fumbled now to get things ready.

"You take too long," Lombardi said laughing. *"I be dead by da time you get ready."* Then Lombardi got quiet, shook his head and said softly, *"Sorry, bad joke. Take-uh you time."* It was the first sensitive thing Lombardi had done, and Johnny relaxed a little.

Johnny finally got himself in order and turned on his tape recorder. He had some   questions that he and Mr. Swilli had developed. He checked his notes and began. "When and where were you born?"

"October twelve, nineteen twenty-three. Near Jesolo, Italy."

Johnny noticed that Lombardi's accent wasn't as bad when he was relaxed.

"Tell me about your hometown."

Lombardi softened considerably and explained that he came from a rural area in Northeast Italy, about fifteen miles inland from the resort town of Jesolo, on the Gulf of Venice near the Adriatic Sea.

Jesolo was located in the wine growing region of Veneto. Lombardi's voice lowered as he spoke of his boyhood. His father had died when he was five. His mother had some cousins who had gone to America, and for a time she considered taking young Ernesto to join them. But when she was invited to move in with her brother's family and to work in his modest vineyard, she accepted. Mr. Lombardi spoke fondly of his work in the vineyards as a boy and the closeness of his extended family. They worked side by side to nurture the grapes. Lombardi went on extensively about the art of grape growing and the care his uncle took to teach him the craft.

At first Johnny just wanted a brief answer to his question, but seeing the transformation of the gruff old man's personality fascinated him. He finally sat back and let the tape recorder do the work.

Lombardi spoke warmly of the ripening process; the color changes in the grapes, the role of rain, temperature, and sunlight in determining when to harvest. He described the rush to harvest once it was determined that the time was perfect. He recalled the day his uncle gave him his first harvesting knife. Lombardi brought it with him to America and kept it in a trunk in the attic.

He described the thrill of loading the trucks for the trips to the wineries. He explained how crucial it was to deliver the harvested grapes quickly because each hour in the hot sun diminished the quality of the grape. His recalled the look of determination on his uncle's face as he drove the lead truck at nearly break-neck speed on the dirt roads with young Ernesto in a seat of honor by his side, and the look of satisfaction when the grapes were finally delivered and the price agreed upon.

Johnny was shocked to see Lombardi's eyes fill as he spoke of the great dinners they would share upon their return. He described his uncle's table as the biggest he had ever seen, and how family, hired workers, and neighbors, twenty or thirty people in all, would share in the celebration. Johnny's mouth watered as Lombardi described every course of the meal. Finally, Lombardi talked about the wine served at the dinner. Each harvest, his uncle would hold back enough grapes to make wine for the family's consumption throughout the year, and each year, at the harvest dinner, he would open the first bottles taken from the previous year's harvest.

With that, Lombardi finished the rest of his glass and then noticed that Johnny's wine hadn't been touched. He looked hurt. *"You no like da wine?"* He asked the question as if this would be the greatest sin imaginable. In fact, Johnny didn't like wine. He had only had it once when Bobby stole a bottle from his parents and brought it to the Log. They couldn't drink it right away because no one had realized they would need a corkscrew. They hid the bottle for two days until Tommy Dillon showed up with one. Johnny didn't have much; there were four of them sharing one bottle, but the wine was sweet, and the little he had made him sick. But now, Johnny looked at the full wine glass and then at Mr. Lombardi. He raised his glass and took a sip. It wasn't sweet at all. In fact, it tasted pretty good. He took another sip and returned the glass to the table. He was about to ask his next question when Lombardi continued his monologue.

He spoke of his leisure time in Italy and how he liked to run as a young boy. He would run long distances through the hills to adjoining villages. He told Johnny that he would often run to the next town, almost five miles away, because there was a girl there he wanted to see. He'd never met her, but he had noticed her during one of his runs and often ran there hoping to see her again. He rarely did, but the few times he got lucky made the trips worth it.

"Women," he said smiling, *"dey make men do crazy things."*

Johnny smiled and Lombardi added. *"You gotta da girlfirend?"*

Johnny nodded.

"Den you know."

Johnny smiled and said, "Yeah, I know."

"What's her name?"

"Carrie," Johnny replied shyly.

"Carrie. 'Med-uh-cann name, but dat's okay."

Lombardi looked over his shoulder and then lowered his voice. *"My wife? She's da boss of da family. Maybe no look dat way, but she's da boss. And dat's okay too."*

Lombardi poured himself more wine. Then he motioned to Johnny's glass and said, *"Drink."*

Johnny sipped and reached for another piece of pizza.

"Good. Eat!"

Johnny was still chewing when Mr. Lombardi started talking again. His eyes glistened when he described trips with his family to the Jesolo beach. He loved the sea and would swim until his uncle ordered him to stop. It was during his trips to the sea that he dreamed of long voyages to experience the rest of the world one day. He went on about this for a while and then stopped, as if he had nothing more to say.

Johnny checked his notes and said, "Why did you leave your native country?"

Lombardi's mood changed and Johnny saw a flash of anger in the old man's eyes. *"Benito Mussolini, dat somm-a-na-bitch. He's-uh why I leave Italy."* His accent grew worse as he became agitated. He explained that Italy had fallen on difficult times after World War I and Mussolini took advantage of the circumstances to come to power. He said that Mussolini was a fascist. Johnny had heard the term before, but wasn't sure what it meant. Lombardi explained that Mussolini gradually gained more and more power until he finally became a dictator. At first, many Italians didn't mind. He had restored order and the economy was improving, but many others still saw him as bad for the country.

Often, while at the dinner table, Ernesto's uncle would complain about the erosion of freedom and his fears about what the future held. In time his fears were realized. Mussolini militarized the country and dreamed of using warfare to re-establish a Roman empire in the Mediterranean rim. He invaded Ethiopia in an unprovoked war in 1935 when young Ernesto was twelve. Mussolini then sided with fascists in the 1936 Spanish Civil War, and entered Italy into an alliance with Hitler's Nazi Germany that same year. By then, all forms of free speech and press in Italy had been crushed.

Johnny was glad he had the tape recorder and hoped Mr. Swilli would help him sort things out. Lombardi wasn't even coming up for air. He explained that as Mussolini's growing war aims became more apparent, Ernesto's mother feared for her son who was approaching the age for the military draft. Then Mussolini's local henchmen charged Ernesto's uncle with being an enemy of the state. The family had seen this tactic before. First accusations were made, and then steps would be taken to strip families of their assets. Some had even lost their land. That was enough for Ernesto's mother. She knew it was time to get her son out of Italy while she still could. She wrote to her relatives in America who agreed to sponsor her entry into the country, promising immigration officials that she would have a place to live and a job prospect. Her brother gave her what money he could, and she used it to bribe an Italian passport official and to pay for passage to the United States. Then, she packed what she could, said painful good-byes to her family and set sail for America as Ernesto was nearing his sixteenth birthday.

A tear ran down Old Man Lombardi's face as he described his separation from his beloved uncle, his extended family and the land and vineyards that had been his life. Finally he fell silent.

Johnny was overcome by the old man's story. He reached for his wine and drained the glass. Still waiting for Mr. Lombardi to recover, he grasped the bottle and poured himself more. By then Lombardi composed himself enough to say, *"So dat's why I come to America."*

Johnny nodded. Then Lombardi added wistfully, *"Sometimes, when I work in da garden, I think of da days in da vineyards. It's not da same, but…"*

At that moment Johnny hated himself. Not knowing what else to do, he reached for his glass to drink again, but before he could, Old

Man Lombardi raised his glass as well and said carefully, *"To my new friend."* And they drained their glasses together.

12- Carrie's House

Johnny peered through the back window of Carrie's house and saw her sitting at her kitchen table. He tapped lightly on the glass and motioned for her to come to the back door.

"Hi, Johnny," she said as she stepped to the patio. "You're early. I didn't expect to see you until tonight. How was the inter..." She stopped in mid sentence and said, "Hey, what's wrong? You don't look so good. And what's that smell?" She sniffed and said, "Have you been drinking?" She stepped outside and closed the door behind her.

Johnny put his forefinger to his lips and said, "Lower your voice a little." Then he looked over her shoulder into the house again. "Are your parents home?"

"Dad's in the den watching a football game, and mom's at the store. What's going on?"

Johnny rubbed his eyes. "I think I'm drunk."

Carrie was incredulous. "Drunk!" She whispered. "Are you serious? How can you be drunk? It's three o'clock in the afternoon. Do you have a drinking problem or something? And what about the interview?"

"It's a long story," Johnny said. "Mr. Lombardi made me drink wine while I was there." Johnny was aware that he was slurring his words.

"He made you drink wine!"

"Well, he didn't actually make me, but he kept offering, and I was trying to be polite. One thing led to another and I guess I had more than I realized." He swayed slightly and braced himself against the wall. "I knew I was a little buzzed when I was there, but it really hit me on the way home." Johnny felt even more unsteady and said, "Can I sit down?"

Carrie hesitated. "Ah, sure, but my parents will flip if they see you like this."

"Mine too," Johnny said. "That's why I came here. I couldn't go home yet."

"Obviously not. Would it help if you ate something?"

"No! No food." Johnny said. "I had plenty to eat, and I'm afraid I might lose it."

Carrie cringed. "Should I try to make coffee?"

"No coffee. I just need to sit a little while. Can I use your phone? I'll call my parents and tell them I stopped here and you invited me to dinner."

"I guess so, but if my father sees you…"

"I'll be quick; I promise."

Johnny called home. He told his parents the interview went well and that he'd tell them all about it later. He got off the phone quickly, and he and Carrie went back outside and sat.

Johnny buried his head in his hands. "You wouldn't believe the interview. It was nothing like I expected. I could have listened to him for hours if it wasn't for the damn wine."

Carrie stroked his arm. "Tell me about it."

"He told me to come back next week because he has more to tell. I think I might go."

"Really? That's great."

"Yeah, he's nothing like I thought he was. He's a little rough around the edges. I mean he's crazy and all, but in a good way, a funny way. He laughed, he cried, he ate like a cow, he drank like… Well, I guess I drank too. But I never heard someone with such a strong laugh. And you should have seen him. He grabbed his wife's butt and…"

"What! He grabbed his wife's butt? And he made you drink wine! What the heck happened today?"

Johnny laughed. "It's not like it sounds."

"I think you'd better start from the beginning."

Johnny did. He told her about Mr. Lombardi's childhood in Italy, his love of the vineyards and the beach, the problems with Mussolini and his sadness over leaving his family and what he had hoped would be his life's work.

Carrie was touched. "Quite a story," she said. "Mr. Swilli will do cartwheels when he hears it. Maybe you can invite Mr. Lombardi to come to school. Mr. Baxter will love it too. Was the newspaper there? Maybe…"

Johnny put up his hand. "Wait, Carrie. Please don't. No newspapers, no more hero talk. There's something I have to tell you. You're probably going to hate me when I'm finished, but this whole thing has been eating me up inside, and I have to get it out. I haven't been honest with you, my parents, Mr. Baxter, Mr. Swilli or anybody. It's not that it was intentional. But..." Carrie thought she saw tears.

"Come on, Johnny," she said, putting her arm around him. "It can't be that bad. Are you saying that you didn't help Mr. Lombardi?"

"No, I helped him, just like everybody says. But I have to tell you what I did before that. You need to know that I'm not the person you think I am."

Johnny told her everything about the night of the tomato raid and the guilt he felt ever since. "I feel worse every time someone makes a big deal out of me helping Old Man Lombardi. And today, after meeting him..." He sobbed. "It just isn't right."

Carrie waited for him to compose himself. Then she said softly, "You're wrong, Johnny Marzo. You are the boy I think you are. You just proved it. I wish you wouldn't do the things you do with your childish friends. I guess it's just part of being a guy, although it's probably time to grow out of it. But seeing you so bothered by all of this tells me a lot about you." She leaned in and kissed him.

When they parted she smiled and said, "You smell awful. Find yourself another girl if you're going to be drinking on Saturday afternoons."

Johnny laughed. "I know one thing. I'll never drink wine again."

"Are you feeling any better?"

"Things aren't spinning as much, but my head still hurts."

"I'm not talking about physically, dummy. You're getting what you deserve. I mean are you feeling better inside?"

"Yeah, a little better. The kiss helped. Maybe a few more..."

She laughed and kissed him again. "That's it for you until you find a breath mint. What did you eat?"

"Pizza, cheese, olives, peppers, lots of stuff."

"And wine."

"Yeah," Johnny said, rubbing his temples, "and wine."

"Like I said, if you're gonna eat that stuff, then find a mint or we will be shaking hands from now on."

"Count on it," Johnny said.

Carrie turned serious. "Now I have to tell you something, and I'm afraid you're not going to like it very much."

Johnny looked concerned. "Are you seeing someone else?"

"No, silly. Nothing like that."

"Okay, it's no big deal then. What is it?"

"Well, I'm telling you as a friend, and you don't have to take my advice if you don't want to."

"Okay, fine. What is it?"

"From what you're telling me, I don't think you did something so awful. I mean, it sounds really bad, but under the circumstances, what else could you have done? I'll bet Mickey really appreciated it."

"He did. And I know all that. But we shouldn't have been there in the first place, and that was my fault. I can't shake this guilty feeling and it's been three months!"

"I know. And that's why, Mr. Tough Guy, if you really want to feel better, if you really want to put this all behind you and get rid of the guilt, then you are going to have to suck it up and tell Old Man Lombardi that it was you that night with the garden hose."

13- Dr. Brain

Johnny was reeling from Carrie's advice. There was no way he could see himself owning up to Mr. Lombardi. He envisioned the old man flying into a rage again, but this time with Johnny as the victim. On the other hand, he thought Carrie had a point. Maybe telling Lombardi the truth would finally end the guilt.

Johnny decided to run his conflict past the guys at the log. He asked Mickey, Tommy, Bobby and Brain to meet him by the canal Sunday night. They were waiting for him when he arrived, discussing a bottle of slow gin that Tommy had smuggled out of his house. Tommy had paper cups for all the guys. Mickey looked at the label and frowned. "Where did you get this junk?"

"My dad won it in a basket of cheer three years ago. He hates the stuff; says it's too sweet. It's been in the back of the liquor cabinet ever since. He'll never miss it."

"But what if he does?" Bobby asked.

"Here we go again with nervous Nellie," Tommy said. "Trust me, he won't miss it."

He began pouring and Brain said, "Just give me half. With my size and weight my ability to absorb alcohol is half than…"

"Please shut up, Brain," Tommy said. "We don't want to hear it tonight. Just drink what you want."

Brain feigned being hurt. "I was just explaining the relationship between body weight and …"

"Stop it!" Mickey said. "We don't want to learn any more of your worthless crap tonight."

Tommy reached for Johnny's cup, but Johnny passed.

Tommy gave him a quizzical look and said, "So what's up with you? Are you okay?"

"I'm fine," Johnny said. "I just don't know why we have to drink on a Sunday night."

"Because we have it," Tommy said. "If we had it on Tuesday, we'd drink it then."

"Fine," Johnny said. "Do what you want."

Brain planned to dump his when no one was looking, so he steered the conversation away from the booze. "Okay, Johnny, so why did you call us here tonight?"

Johnny took a breath and began. He told them about his guilt, his interview with Lombardi and Carrie's suggestion. When he was finished he said, "So, I'm asking your advice. Should I tell him?"

"I don't know, man," Tommy said. "I'm only going from that night, but that guy is one crazy son-of-a-bitch."

Bobby spoke up next. "I'm not just saying this, Johnny, but I really think he might kill you."

"I'm telling ya," Johnny said, "he was a different guy when I met him on Sunday."

Mickey shook his head. When he spoke, they could still sense his fear. "Listen, Johnny, I still have nightmares about that night. I'm telling ya, the guy was trying to kill me. I mean, he was in a rage. His hands were like a vice. I think he came that close to just holding my head under water until it was too late. I can't believe you'd risk telling him."

Everyone fell silent. There wasn't any dissension. Finally, Johnny said, "What about you, Brain? You haven't said anything."

"Well," Brain said. "If you remember, I wasn't there that night."

"We remember all right," Tommy said. "You were conveniently absent. Good ol' no balls Brain."

"I told you," Brian protested. "I was watching the convention speeches, Michael Dukakis…"

"Yeah," Mickey interrupted. "Maybe the speeches were an excuse. Maybe you had a ballet lesson. I think that's it."

Johnny jumped in. "Will you guys knock it off! I'm looking for some help here." Then he looked at Brain. "I'd like to hear what you have to say."

"Just do it, Brain. You know we're kidding," Tommy said.

"Well," Brain said. "I guess it was a day or two after he saved Old Man Lombardi that Johnny confided to me about how guilty he felt." Brain enjoyed letting the guys know that he had had a private conversation with Johnny. "I hated seeing Johnny suffering like that so, of course, I became interested in the topic of guilt."

"Of course," Tommy said. "We wouldn't expect anything else."

Johnny gave Tommy a dirty look and told Brain to go on.

"Let me start with the good news. At least we know you're not a psychopath."

"That's great," Johnny said. "What does that mean?"

"Well, a psychopath is someone who exhibits a complete lack of remorse or empathy for his actions. In other words, it is a person who is unable to feel guilty. You seem to have an abundance of guilt. You have a conscience. So, even though you exhibited behavior that night that would usually be considered highly aggressive and anti-social, your remorse, your guilt, is really a very normal and healthy reaction."

Tommy shook his head. "Jesus!" he said. "With your brains, can't you just show us how to rob a bank or something without getting caught?"

Brain shook his head. "Talk about lacking a conscience."

"Just ignore him," Johnny said. "He's being a real smack tonight."

"Sorry," Tommy said smiling. "Must be the slow gin."

Johnny got back to the topic. "So, do I tell Old Man Lombardi or not?"

"Well, let's get back to the guilt. That's the only reason why you would even consider it, right?"

"Yeah, I guess so."

"Psychologists say there are different ways people deal with guilt. One is accepting punishment. If Old Man Lombardi beats you until you're nearly dead, you'll probably consider yourself even and the guilt will go away."

"Right," Mickey said. "And if Old Man Lombardi kills him it will definitely go away."

Brain ignored him and went on. "The next way people attempt to alleviate guilt is by seeking forgiveness. So, I guess if you tell Lombardi and he takes your hand and sings 'Let There Be Peace on Earth,' then I guess you'll feel better."

"Yeah," Mickey said. "That's probably what will happen. I think after one or two more dunks that night, Lombardi probably would have forgiven me and invited me in for brownies."

"Can I hear this please?' Johnny pleaded.

Brain went on. "The next avenue is the one you have taken and which doesn't seem to be working. And that is to bury yourself in private remorse until the guilt eventually goes away. I have no idea how long that would take."

Brain sensed the guys were getting restless, so he pushed on quickly. "There is one more avenue, and it's the one I think you should use. Psychologists say that some people deal with their guilt by using cognition. That is, reaching the realization that the extent of your guilt is illogical, that it doesn't match the wrongdoing. I think everyone here knows that what you did was necessary under the circumstances."

"I'll drink to that," Mickey said. "I'm telling you, Johnny, you saved my life."

Tommy jumped in. "So is that it for the psychology lesson?"

"That's it," Brain said. "Those are Johnny's options."

The group fell silent again until Johnny said, "Okay, Brain, so answer the question. Do I tell Old Man Lombardi or not?"

Brain paused for a long time. "It's your decision," he said flatly. "But if you ask me, I think the guy is crazy, bi-polar maybe, and has anger issues. He might kill you in a fit of rage before he even realizes what he's done. I'd avoid him like the plague."

14- Saturday

On Monday morning Johnny decided that the guys were right. He wouldn't risk telling Lombardi. He'd just deal with his guilt some other way. In fact, he decided that he wouldn't even do the second interview because he didn't want to push his luck about being recognized. Besides, he'd already gotten more than enough material for Mr. Swilli's report. So, he would just let Saturday morning pass and not show up.

He was at peace with his decision until Thursday when new urges to return to Lombardi's began to surface. At first he suppressed them, but that night, in his dreams, he saw images of the old man laughing, affectionately grabbing his wife's behind, wistfully recalling his boyhood, and tearfully retelling the story of his exodus from Italy. They had a powerful effect. Like sailors of Greek mythology lured by beautiful maidens to almost certain disaster on the dangerous rocks near shore, Johnny was being drawn, once again, to Old Man Lombardi's.

He slept well Friday night, perhaps because he knew what his decision would be. On Saturday, he rose early and did his routine of pushups, sit-ups, and chin-ups that his Uncle Nick had devised. "Ya gotta be strong in this world, Johnny- boy," Nick had said. "Mind, body and spirit, isn't that how it goes? Stick with it and it'll pay off later."

"I will, Uncle Nick," Johnny had promised. And he did. It was difficult at first, but over time he became so pleased with his progress that he felt uncomfortable if he missed a workout. He especially liked the chin-up bar that Nick had bolted to the wall with the approval of Johnny's mother.

"Chin-ups are good for you, Johnny," Nick said with his trademark twinkle in his eyes. "They're uplifting in more ways than one. The more you elevate yourself the more elevated you feel. Get it?"

"Yeah, Uncle Nick, I get it," Johnny had said.

Now, as Johnny completed his last set of chin-ups, he felt better than he did in a long time, and the feeling was more than physical. His mind was clear and less troubled. He sang in the shower, and for some reason, Michael Jackson's *Man in the Mirror* was on his mind.

"I'm starting with the man in the mirror, ...asking him to change his ways..."

He dressed quickly and went down to the deli. His mom worked on Saturday mornings but he knew he'd find his dad and at least some of the regular guys there.

"Hey, there he is," Jimmy said when he spotted him first. "We thought you'd sleep 'till noon."

"Nah, not today," Uncle Jimmy, Johnny said smiling.

"Better not," Nick added. "It's a beautiful fall day out there. Get outside and enjoy it."

"He will," Johnny's father added from behind the counter, "as soon as he stocks some shelves." Then he turned to Johnny. "Bacon and eggs?"

"Thanks, Pop," Johnny said.

Just then Big Frankie walked in.

"There he is," Jimmy said. "Speaking of hungry, Big Frankie was born hungry and hasn't stopped eating since." Frankie grunted at his friends and said hello to Johnny.

"So what's on tap today, kid," Frankie said as he poured his coffee.

"Not much," Johnny said. "I've got some stuff to do."

Nick said, "Hey Jimmy, how do you spell stuff?"

Jimmy thought for a minute. "I'm pretty sure it's S-T-U-F-F, why?"

Nick grinned. "I think Johnny spells it C-A-R-R-I-E. How about it, Johnny-boy, am I right?"

Johnny smiled. "I guess I'll fit her into my schedule sometime today."

Johnny loved fooling around with his father's friends. He loved their joking and story telling. He knew they had been friends since they were his age, younger even, and he'd heard all about their football days, their trips to the shore and the doo wop group they once had. But he wished he knew more about other things. Growing up in the nineteen-sixties like they did, the Vietnam War was obviously a big deal in their lives. Johnny knew some things. He knew Nick was a war hero, Jimmy had a terrible experience, and Big Frankie and Johnny's dad, Angelo, hadn't served. Johnny also knew that he had been born in Canada, which he thought was pretty cool. But he wished he knew more about their experiences and promised himself he'd try to find out.

After breakfast he stacked some shelves, swept the floor, emptied the trash cans, said good-bye to the guys, and headed out. Things were crystal clear to him now. He was going to Old Man Lombardi's and he wouldn't need his notepad, pencil or tape-recorder for this visit.

It was a crisp, sunny day, just as Nick had promised, and there was a bounce in Johnny's step. He walked the first few blocks and then broke into a jog. As he ran, he visualized Old Man Lombardi in Italy, running to the next town just to steal a glimpse of a girl. He chuckled as he recalled the old man's words, *"Women make men do crazy dings."* They certainly did, Johnny thought. He hoped he wasn't doing something crazy now. He didn't think so.

15- Coming To America

Johnny entered through the back gate again and chuckled at his earlier thoughts of bodies buried in the garden. It was amazing what fear could do to a person's imagination. He knocked on the door and was greeted by Lombardi himself. *"Hey, giovanotto, you come back. Vieni, vieni."* He moved aside and Johnny was greeted by an aroma that made his mouth water. What he smelled wasn't pizza, but it was clearly something very good.

"Sit," Lombardi said. *"Eat da lunch."* Johnny checked the clock on the wall. It was just after eleven and he had barely digested his bacon and eggs. Soon, Lombardi was at the stove loading a generous piece of Italian sausage on a long roll and smothering it with peppers and onions. He placed it in front of Johnny and fixed another for himself. Eyeing the food, Johnny reminded himself that he had sworn off wine forever. But when Lombardi reached for the bottle and said, *"Vino?"* Johnny shrugged and said, "Just a little."

Lombardi let out one of his hardy laughs. *"Juust uh little. Who drinks juust uh little?"* He poured them each a full glass and sat down. Johnny was tempted to say, "Hey, Ernesto, I'm only fourteen and you got my ass drunk last week." Instead, Johnny took a bite of the sandwich and rolled his eyes in delight.

"Good?" Lombardi asked.

"The best," Johnny said, wiping some grease from his chin.

"Damn right," Lombardi said proudly. *"My wife make-uh for you."*

Johnny looked around, wondering where she was and Lombardi read his mind. *"She's resting. No feel good today."*

"Oh," Johnny said. "I hope she feels better soon."

The old man nodded his appreciation. *"Mangia,"* Lombardi said, and they both attacked their sandwiches. After a few bites, Lombardi said, *"So, we talk."*

"Yes," Johnny said quickly. Remembering the old man's impatience last time, he plunged right in. "I was wondering what your trip to America was like."

Lombardi began by describing his changing emotions during the two week journey across the Atlantic. He explained how his intense sadness over leaving Italy dissipated after a few days and was replaced by the growing excitement of going to America. Unfortunately, that feeling soon gave way to a crippling fear of what the future might hold.

Next he spoke of the conditions on the ship: the cramped quarters in steerage, the foul smell of passengers who could not bathe for days, the small portions of bland and often cold food they were served, and the terrible sickness he felt as they encountered rough seas. He spoke of his mother having to guard their modest possessions against thieves. He described the swindlers who roamed the decks touting their new world connections and offering assistance on shore for a small advance fee. He recalled fondly the people who entertained their fellow passengers by singing, playing simple instruments, doing card tricks and telling stories of the wonders of America. They made the trip bearable.

When he was finished, Johnny asked the question that he had been saving all morning. It was one that he and Mr. Swilli had developed, and Johnny couldn't wait to hear the answer. He glanced at his wine glass that was still untouched and said, "What was it like when you first saw the Statue of Liberty?"

Lombardi looked puzzled, so Johnny tried again. "You know, what did it feel like when you sailed into New York harbor and saw the Statue of Liberty for the first time?"

Lombardi shook his head and leaned forward. He spoke slowly, choosing his words carefully. His accent was more pronounced. *"I'm-uh sick as uh dog on ship. We have almost no money. We don't know if my cousin will be at da dock to meet us. I'm so scared I almost pee-uh my pants.*" Then he paused for emphasis and added, *"What da hell do I care about uh God-damn-uh statue?"*

Johnny was floored. Mr. Swilli had said that the question was so good that it would probably be a defining moment of the interview. Johnny thought so too. He had imagined Lombardi's feelings of pride or honor at his first sight of Lady Liberty. Instead, Lombardi had called one of the most recognizable symbols of America a God-damned statue.

Johnny sat in silence. He looked at the wine again and took a small sip to stall for time. He didn't know what to say next. Lombardi sensed his discomfort and laughed before turning serious again. *"Hey, kid. I love dis country. I love da statue. I love da flag, especially da flag. But dat day, I want food. I want-uh bed, I want-uh doctor. Dat's what I'm thinking when I come to New York. Not da God-damn statue."*

Now it was Lombardi's turn to drink.

They sat quietly again and Johnny's mind wondered. He thought about the sleep-over summer basketball camp his parents had sent him to for a week at a college in Philadelphia when he was in sixth grade. The food was terrible, the beds were uncomfortable, and there was no air-conditioning in the dorms. His muscles ached from constant running, his team was getting its ass kicked on the court day after day, and he was homesick. One of the selling points of the camp was a scheduled visit by Philadelphia '76er great, Julius Erving, the legendary Dr. J. But by the time Dr. J. arrived on the fourth day, Johnny was so miserable that he couldn't have cared less and would have gladly traded the visit for an early ticket home. Johnny looked at Old Man Lombardi and nodded. Okay Ernesto, he said to himself. I guess I get it. He took another small sip of wine and continued the interview.

"What were your early years in America like?"

Lombardi talked about his arrival at the dock and his relief that his cousins were there to greet them. They lived in Bristol and had driven to New York to meet the boat. He and his mother lived with their relatives for two years before they were able to rent an apartment with money Mrs. Lombardi earned as a seamstress and Ernesto earned as a quarry laborer in nearby Tullytown.

Johnny had his list of questions memorized and asked another. "Did you ever go to school in America?"

Lombardi frowned. "One *year. I go to school, but I no speak good English like now.*" Lombardi thought that was pretty funny and had to gather himself before continuing. *"Da first day, da kids make fun, so I smile. Second day dey make fun again, and I keep quiet. Dat night I'll tell mama."* He smiled at the memory of his mother's response. *"She said, 'Ernesto, no take-uh no shit'. Den she said, 'Who's da biggest one? I tell her, and she nod her head. I understand. Da next time dey make da fun I punch da biggest one in da face and he falls down. Nobody make fun any more."*

Johnny laughed. "No kidding? You hit the guy!"

Lombardi smiled proudly. *"In Italy, I lift boxes of grapes all da time. Twenty-eight pounds. I'm strong."*

"Did you get in trouble with the principal?"

"No trouble," Lombardi said. *"He like it so much dat he let me stay home for a week."* With that Lombardi roared.

Johnny was howling too. "Are you serious? You got suspended!"

"No suspend. Vacation!" Lombardi bellowed.

Johnny was laughing so hard that he got caught up in the moment and reached for his wine glass, but then thought better of it and leaned back. "So after one year of school you went to work?"

"At da quarry in Tullytown. I shovel stones all day long. Feel da muscle." Lombardi was wearing another sleeveless undershirt and he flexed for Johnny. Johnny thought the request was symbolic and just smiled. But Lombardi kept his arm flexed and thundered, *"Feel da muscle!"*

Johnny leaned forward and grabbed Lombardi's bicep. It felt like an anvil, and he nodded with admiration.

"And you? You soft?"

Johnny surprised himself by flexing right away. Lombardi grabbed his arm and whistled. *"Not too bad!"*

With his masculine credentials clearly established, Johnny treated himself to a sip of wine and then moved on. "So what happened next?"

Lombardi told Johnny that he and his mother kept informed about events in Europe in the late 1930's. As Americans watched the storm clouds of war develop in Europe, President Roosevelt had asked them to remain neutral. But the days of neutrality had passed for most Americans as Nazi aggression grew. To be sure, many still hoped to avoid war at all costs, and some even sided with Hitler, but the vast majority of Americans were sympathetic to their traditional allies in Britain and France.

Lombardi recalled the pact Mussolini had signed with Germany and Japan, just before Lombardi and his mother left Italy. The dictators had called it the Rome-Berlin-Tokyo Pact and it had made Lombardi sick. Once in America, he watched with growing concern as Hitler invaded Poland and then France. He was horrified when Italy joined Hitler in the war against France in 1940 and was soon fighting against Britain in North Africa.

Johnny was amazed by Lombardi's clarity and decided there was much more to this man than growing tomatoes and drinking wine.

"I'm American," Lombardi said. *"But I still love my native country."* Then he said he could have wrung Mussolini's neck for what he was doing to Italy's place in the world. Johnny believed him.

Lombardi said that when he was eighteen, he received a letter from his uncle saying that Mussolini was drafting men his age and that a notice, no doubt generated from old registration records, had arrived at the house ordering Ernesto to report for military duty.

"I wrote back to my cousin, 'Please tell Mussolini if he wants me, he'll have to come to America.'"

Lombardi finished his wine and poured himself more. He looked at Johnny's still mostly filled glass but said nothing. Johnny could sense a growing anger when Lombardi spoke again. *"Mussolini!"* He turned his head away and mimicked a man spitting. *"I'm embarrassed. I'm angry. And den..."* Lombardi stopped and shook his head. He struggled to compose himself before he explained his feelings on the day he heard the radio broadcast that the Japanese had attacked Pearl Harbor. With Italy part of the Rome-Berlin-Tokyo alliance, it was as if the Italians had mounted the attack themselves. Two months later, with his mother's blessing, Lombardi enlisted in the United States Army.

Johnny was surprised. "Really? You joined the army? You were an immigrant."

Lombardi nodded. *"Immigrants fight too."* Then he told Johnny to wait a minute and he left the room. He returned with a photo and what looked like an old yearbook. He slid the photo across the table. It was a black and white of a young man in a military uniform. Johnny studied the face and looked at Lombardi. "Is this you?"

Lombardi nodded proudly. Then he pointed to the insignia on the soldier's arm. *"See da patch."* Johnny did, but couldn't make out what it said.

"Dat's da Screaming Eagle, Da one-hundred and first airborne division."

Johnny didn't know much about the Screaming Eagles, but Lombardi made it sound like a pretty big deal. Lombardi thrust out his chest and said, *"Screaming Eagles were paratroops."*

"Paratroopers!" Johnny said, almost leaving his seat. "You jumped out of airplanes?"

Lombardi showed him the yearbook. It was titled:

The 101ˢᵗ Airborne Division
The Screaming Eagles
Activated August 16, 1942
"A Rendezvous with Destiny"

Johnny was disappointed that he didn't know more about the war, but he tried to imagine a young Lombardi, new to America, who spoke only broken English, enlisting to defend his adopted country. Over the next half-hour Johnny was mesmerized as Lombardi went through the book and recounted his experiences in the war. He traced the travels of the division as they trained at Camp Claiborne, Louisiana and Fort Bragg, North Carolina before they left for Europe. Johnny was struck by the irony of Lombardi and the rest of the troops embarking from New York in 1943 for the trip to England where they trained for another year in preparation for the D-Day invasion of Normandy. There was just something interesting about recent immigrants making the trip back to Europe to fight for their new country.

Johnny noted Lombardi's disappointment when Johnny admitted that he didn't know much about D-Day. He wanted to explain that his class would study it later in the semester, but the explanation, although true, felt hollow and he decided not to use it.

Lombardi described his long months of waiting in England for the invasion of Normandy, the long hours of training, the frequent trips to the pubs with the guys in his company, and the British girls they met.

All of this raised a question for Johnny. "How were you accepted by the other soldiers?"

"They make da fun at first, but I prove myself. I run, shoot, climb. And, when da time come, I'm da first to jump from da plane for practice. I earn respect and we become friends, good friends, friends who would save each other's lives, like you did for me."

Johnny felt a sharp pang of guilt but shook it off. He was eager to get to the action. "So what did you do during the invasion?"

Lombardi explained that the 101st was assigned to parachute behind German lines hours before sunrise on the morning of the invasion to cut enemy communication lines and secure bridges for the troops that would follow.

"No kidding!" Johnny said. "You jumped behind enemy lines! Was it exciting?"

Lombardi sat back and shook his head. He waited before speaking, and when he spoke he sounded sad. *"I'm sorry. I forget dat you so young and don't understand."*

Johnny felt uncomfortable. He'd obviously said something to upset the old man. Again, he didn't know what to say. He thought about the wine again but resisted.

Finally, Lombardi decided to try again. He leaned forward and spoke softly. *"I'm twenty years old. Some of da men are younger. It's two o'clock in da morning. We fly behind enemy lines. If da Germans see us jump, dey shoot us before we hit da ground. I worry if my chute will open, but who knows? I look at my friends in da plane, some cry, some pray. Da captain says it's time and I move to da door. All I see is da big black hole outside.. The captain says 'go.' I bless myself and jump. I was never so scared in my life. Nothing exciting. Men die in uh war, Johnny."*

Johnny felt foolish. This wasn't a movie or teenage prank. He searched for something to say but came up empty. He had never thought about what old men were like in their youth, what they had done with their lives. Mr. Lombardi had risked his for his country, a country he had only recently adopted, and Johnny had tried to steal his tomatoes.

Suddenly, Lombardi looked tired and Johnny hoped he felt okay. Lombardi said, *"We stop for today, okay?"*

Lombardi started to get up, when Johnny heard himself say, "Wait! There's something I want to tell you."

Lombardi relaxed, but said nothing.

Before Johnny could change his mind, he said, "Back in July, when boys tried to steal your tomatoes, I was one of them. I was their leader. And when you were dunking my friend, Mickey, in the rain barrel, I was the one who squirted you in the face with the hose. I'm so sorry. The whole thing was my idea, and it was wrong."

Lombardi remained expressionless. Johnny summoned more courage and looked him in the eyes. "I just wanted you to know it was me."

Lombardi remained stone-faced for as long as he could, but finally, he broke into a grin, which grew to a laugh that grew stronger until he was almost out of control.

Johnny was stunned. He wasn't sure what Lombardi's reaction would be, but he never anticipated this. "What's so funny?" Johnny said.

"I'm sorry," Lombardi said, composing himself. *"But I already know. I know last week."*

"How?" Johnny said numbly.

"Da voice." Then Lombardi said in a mimicking tone, *"We real sorry mista. It was jusst uh prank. We sorry."* In spite of Lombardi's accent, Johnny recognized the words as those he had said to the old man on the night of the raid.

Johnny lowered his head and said nothing. Lombardi could see that he was shaking. He said tenderly, *"Listen kid. You save me two times, and I appreciate."*

Johnny looked up. "Two times?"

"Once in da yard with my heart and once with da hose when I try to kill da kid."

"Really? Do you think you would have drowned Mickey?"

Lombardi shrugged. *"Maybe not, but who knows? Bad temper."*

"I feel stupid." Johnny said. "Why didn't you say something last week?"

"Because I wanna find out what kind of man you are. Now I know. You good man. Uh very good man, and you got guts. I like dat."

"But what I did wasn't right," Johnny protested.

Lombardi shook his head. *"Who knows what's right? In da army, we do whatever is necessary to save da friend. And dat's what you did."*

Johnny's eyes filled and Lombardi stood and came around the table. He put his hand on Johnny's shoulder and said, *"I like you kid. I respect you. You honest. You make me mad as hell last July, but now, I like you."*

Johnny wanted to say he liked him too. He wanted to say he admired what he did in his life. He wanted to say a lot of things, but they all felt stupid. So instead he said "thank you."

It was time to leave, and Lombardi opened the door for him. As Johnny was ready to step outside, Lombardi said, *"You come back any time, and we talk."*

"I will Mr. Lombardi, I promise." Johnny reached out his hand to shake and Lombardi took it. The old man's grip felt like a vice.

16- Bush and Dukakis

Brain had followed the 1988 election campaign closely, and by late October he had decided to support George Bush over Michael Dukakis. He even started wearing a Bush campaign button. When the guys at the deli heard about it they asked Johnny to bring him around. As Nick explained, he wanted to "talk some sense into the kid."

Johnny knew the discussion would be fun. Nick loved Brain and enjoyed squaring off with him. Although Nick was eccentric, he was also the smartest adult Johnny knew, but Johnny was confident that Brain would hold his own. The meeting was arranged for a Saturday morning. Everyone was there when the boys arrived and the fun started right away.

"Here they are," Nick said, speaking into a salt shaker as though it were a microphone. "It's a fine fall day. The smell of burning leaves is in the air, college football will be played this afternoon, and in just eleven short days, on November 8, 1988, this great nation will select its leader for the next four years. Will it make the right choice?"

"It will if it selects George Bush," Brain said confidently.

"Bang," Jimmy said. "He got you early, Nick, even before he said hello. This guy plays for keeps."

Jimmy gave Brain a high five and Nick said, "I thought you were for Dukakis?"

"I am," Jimmy said. "But he still got you."

Nick said, "Just to show I've got class, let's get these boys some Cokes before I carve them up. They're on me."

"Hold on, Nick," Angelo called from behind the counter. "Every time these kids come in you say the Cokes are on you, but you never pay."

"Geeze, Angelo. You'd think you could spare a Coke for your kid and his friend."

"I'm happy to, and I do every time," Angelo said smiling. "So either pay up or stop saying they're on you."

"Damn," Nick mumbled, "Won't even give his kid a Coke. It's a disgrace."

"Okay, let's get started," Frankie said. "I'll buy the sodas today."

Nick turned to Brain. "Okay, Mr. Kelly, let's..."

Jimmy interrupted and announced, "Calling Brain Mr. Kelly was my idea. We're gonna use his last name, get him out of his comfort zone, knock him off his game a little. We practiced last night and decided to do it."

"You practiced?" Frankie said. "You practiced debating politics against a kid?"

"Never underestimate your opponent," Jimmy said.

"Ya know something, Jimmy," Nick said. "It was really brilliant of you to let our strategy out of the bag. Great move, you dimwit."

"That's it," Jimmy said. "I've taken enough of your abuse. I'm voting for Bush."

"You just said you were for Dukakis," Nick said.

"I was," Jimmy said smugly. "But this debate changed my mind. I'm for Bush."

"But the debate hasn't started yet," Nick protested.

"My mind is made up, Nick. Don't try to change it."

Nick rolled his eyes and said, "Know what, Jimmy? People like you shouldn't be allowed to vote."

"Yeah, well I am allowed," Jimmy said. "And I hope Bush wins by one vote. It will be your fault if he does."

Nick waved him off and turned to Brain. "Okay, my Republican friend, tell us why you're for Bush and then I'll explain why I'm for Dukakis."

"Who says I'm going first?" Brain said with exaggerated firmness. "It's a disadvantage. We'll flip for who goes first."

"Bang!" Jimmy said. "The kid got you again! I guess you thought he'd be a pushover. Then he turned to Frankie and Angelo. "We planned this last night too. I'm ashamed that I was a part of it, but we planned to let him go first. The strategy backfired."

"Is that true?" Frankie asked Nick. "Did you really plan that?"

Nick stared at the floor. "We were just passing time. Jimmy's just…"

"You guys are pathetic," Frankie said, smiling. "Both of you."

"I didn't want to do it," Jimmy said.

"Pathetic," Frankie repeated.

Brain took charge. "Get a coin, Johnny."

Johnny pulled out a quarter.

"Call it, Uncle Nick," Johnny said and quickly flipped the quarter into the air.

"Tails," Nick said.

Johnny caught the coin and flipped it on to the back of his hand. It was heads.

"Bang, bang, bang," Jimmy said as he did a little dance. "The kid is pitching a shutout. He's kicking your butt all around the deli. Someone should stop this before it gets too ugly. Is there a mercy rule in debate?"

"I wasn't ready," Nick shouted. "Johnny flipped the coin too fast. I wanted to call 'heads.'"

Johnny shook his head. "Sorry, Uncle Nick, looks like you're going first."

Nick winked at Johnny. He was having fun. "I guess I am. Is there a time limit?"

Johnny suggested five minutes and both sides nodded their approval.

"Okay," Nick said. "Here goes, so let's get serious. I'm for Michael Dukakis because I'm a Democrat, and he supports Democratic values. I'm a democrat for lots of reasons. I'm a democrat because history shows that the Democratic Party is the party of the people. It's the party of the little guy. It's the party of guys like Jimmy who worked in a steel mill his whole life and Frankie who's a carpenter. It's the party of labor unions.

It's the party of civil rights. It's the party of those who can't always make it on their own without a little help to get over the obstacles.

"I'm a democrat because it's the party of Franklin D. Roosevelt, who gave the country hope during the depression and strength during the Second World War. I'm a democrat because it's the party of John and Bobby Kennedy who lent their voices to people who had few willing to speak for them: African- Americans, migrant workers, the young and the poor.

"I'm a Democrat because I hate the fact that if we give a needy family some food stamps, or an extra few weeks of unemployment compensation to a worker who lost his job, or a student loan to a kid trying to further his education, or a free health exam to a sick child, the Republicans say we are ruining the country.

"The Republicans say everyone should make it on his or her own. But they have no problem allowing the fat cats to claim three martini lunches in expensive restaurants as tax deductions. Same thing with their country club memberships, and fancy company cars.

"I'm a Democrat because I believe that the workers who worked sixteen-hour shifts in the coal mines and steel mills of Pennsylvania did as much to build this country as John D. Rockefeller and Thomas Edison. I'm a democrat because the little guys came up big when there was a skyscraper or railroad to be built or a war to be fought. I'm a Democrat because the Democratic Party has stood by those people.

"This time the candidate is Michael Dukakis. Next time it will be someone else. But as long as the Democratic nominee remains true to the party's principles, then I'll be there for him whoever he may be. No country club guy named George Herbert Walker Bush is going to give a damn about me. I've never trusted anyone with too many middle names anyway. "

Jimmy clapped when Nick finished and Angelo and Frankie joined in.

Then Jimmy turned to Brain and said, "Sorry kid. I wanted you to win just to bust 'em on Nick, but Nick just said what's in my heart. Guys like me, Angelo and Big Frankie, the Republican Party doesn't care about us. So we're voting for Dukakis.

"That's fine, Jimmy," Brain said politely. "But do I get a chance to talk."

"Sure, kid," Jimmy said. "Go right ahead."

"Well," Brain began. "I'm glad you guys are democrats. I am too. I've been one for four or five years, ever since I was nine."

"This kid is priceless," Nick said. "Since you were nine?"

"No, really, Nick. I'm not kidding. The more I read the more I identified with the values of the democrats."

"Hey, don't get me wrong, kid. I know you're not kidding. That's what makes you priceless. You know things."

"I read."

"Hear that, Johnny," Angelo said. "The kid reads."

"I know, Dad. I'm working on it."

"Anyway," Brain continued. "I'm a democrat, but I believe we still need to take a look at the man and not just the party. I'm sorry to say that when I look at Bush and Dukakis it's not even close."

"Okay, we need to hear some reasons," Nick said.

"I've got three. The first is experience. Dukakis has never been involved in the federal government. Being a governor is nice, but George Bush has been Vice President of the United States for eight years! I think he wins the experience factor."

"Okay," Frankie said, "We'll give you that one. So what else have you got?"

"I've got a question for Nick," Brain said.

"Fire away. As long as it isn't math; I hate math," He winked again at Johnny.

"Nick, give me your honest opinion. What is the single most important thing government can do for us?"

Nick thought for a moment. "Well, there are a few things, but I think the most important is to keep its citizens safe."

Brain smiled. "As Jimmy would say, Bang! I think it's government's most important job too. I'm sure you guys know that George Bush used to be Director of the CIA. I'd say that plus his eight years as VP makes him better prepared to protect us. And I didn't even get into his time as ambassador to China. All of that trumps Dukakis as Governor of Massachusetts, which, as Johnny can tell you, is a Commonwealth."

"That's right! Johnny said. And Virginia and Kentucky too."

The men look perplexed and Brain said, "Sorry, that's a private joke."

Brain continued. "So let's see. Bush is more experienced in general and has better national security credentials. Now I have a question for Jimmy."

"I'm not taking questions today. Call my office and we'll set something up."

"It's just a simple question," Brain said.

"Nah, I'm not playing. Ask Frankie or Angelo."

"I want to ask you," Brain persisted.

"Answer the damn question," Angelo snapped. "He's just a kid. What can he ask?"

"Okay, fine," Jimmy said. "I'll answer a question."

"Okay, keeping with the idea that government should keep us safe, here's my question. Now it's a little rough, but stay with me."

"Okay," Jimmy said. "I'm with you."

"Okay, you're not married, right."

"No," Jimmy said shyly. "I haven't found the right girl yet."

"I told him," Nick said. "There are plenty of girls who work at the carnival that comes to town each year, but he doesn't listen."

Jimmy gave Nick's arm a shove.

"So where is this going?" Jimmy said.

Brain looked around the room before speaking. "Jimmy, I want you pretend that you are married. Are you seeing it?"

"Yeah," Jimmy smiled. "I'm seeing it."

"Is it nice?"

"Yeah," Jimmy said. "It's nice. She's pretty, she has a good job, and she loves to watch sports. She cooks good. She let's me shoot darts on Wednesday nights and she always tells me I'm her man."

"Wow, Jimmy," Nick said. "I'm happy for you."

"Thanks, Nick," Jimmy said. "You were the best man in our wedding."

"I remember," Nick said. "It was beautiful."

Angelo pounded his fist on the counter. "Will you guys shut up and let the kid ask his question?"

"Calm town," Nick said. "We were just enjoying a beautiful moment. Go ahead, Brain. Ask Jimmy the question."

"Okay, now here's the tough part, and I apologize for asking, but I have to. You have a beautiful, wonderful wife. What would you do if someone raped and murdered her?"

The room got quiet and Jimmy's face began to twitch. He didn't speak for a long time and then he said, "I'd find the son-of-a-bitch. And I wouldn't stop until I did."

"And I'd help him," Nick said.

"And then you'd turn him over to the cops, right?" Brain asked.

Jimmy shook his head. "Just so some candy-ass judge can let him go? Hell no," Jimmy said, his voice rising. "I'd rip his eyes out. I'd tear his heart right out of his chest. I'm not kidding."

"No, I don't think you are," Brain said softly.

"Then I'd tie him to the back of my truck and drag him through town until all the skin came off his body, and then, maybe, I'd drop him off on the police station steps."

"It sounds like you don't have much faith in the government to protect us against criminals?"

"Too many bad guys go free," Jimmy said.

Brain looked at the rest of the men. "How about you guys?"

"Pretty much the same," Angelo said.

"Me too," Frankie added. "But Jimmy only gave you the short version of what we'd do if we caught the guy."

Angelo said, "So what's this have to do with Bush and Dukakis?"

"A lot," Brain said. "Did any of you watch the Bush-Dukakis debate the other night.?"

"No," Nick said. "But I'm betting you did."

"I sure did," Brain said firmly. "The TV commentator, Bernard Shaw, asked Dukakis the same question. He even used Dukakis' wife, Kitty, as his example. They were talking about capital punishment and Shaw said, 'Governor, if Kitty Dukakis were raped and murdered would you favor an irrevocable death penalty for the killer?'"

"That was a cheap-shot question to ask," Frankie said.

"I think so too," Brain said. "But he asked it anyway." He paused for effect, and Jimmy took the bait.

"And what did Dukakis say?"

Brain shook his head. "He never flinched, never changed his voice or expression. He gave some cold fish answer about his opposition to capital punishment and that was it. I was on the fence until that moment. But that answer turned me off. I just thought to myself, this guy's not a leader; he's a robot. So, if I were old enough to vote, I'd vote for Bush. You've got to protect people from the bad guys."

17- A Christmas Surprise

Brain was in his room reading about satellites when his mother called up to him, "Brian, Uncle Ray is on the phone." Brain's family didn't like his nickname at all and still called him Brian.

Brian tossed his book on his bed and raced downstairs. Uncle Ray was Brian's favorite person in the world. He was his mother's unmarried brother, and, with no children of his own, he treated Brian like his son.

For as long as Brian could remember, Uncle Ray had given him a crisp, one-hundred dollar bill on every birthday and another one every Christmas. But those weren't Uncle Ray's best gifts. He sold communication technologies to America's allies and corporations around the world, and he made it a point to bring Brian an interesting gift from each country he visited.

Brian enjoyed the gifts, but what he cherished even more was the time he got to spend with Uncle Ray during his visits. He came for most major holidays, and he and Brian would talk for hours about the places he visited and the people he met. It was fascinating stuff, but each time they spoke Brian would try to steer the conversation to telecommunications and the associated satellites Uncle Ray worked with. Brian knew that his uncle's company's best customers were the United States government and our NATO allies in Europe, both of whom found military uses for his equipment. Although Uncle Ray remained guarded about his work, Brian enjoyed pumping him for information.

Brian got to the kitchen just as his mom was ending her conversation. It was December 21 and his uncle was flying into JFK from Europe that night. Brian and his parents were going to New York to meet him at his hotel the following morning. They would spend the day together in New York and then drive Uncle Ray to their Bristol home for the holidays.

Brian's mom finished and handed Brian the phone.

"Hi, Uncle Ray!" Brian said, excitedly.

"Hey, Pal. How's it going?"

"I'm good. How about you?"

"I'm great, Brian. It's good to hear your voice."

"So where are you?"

"Well, I'm in Frankfurt, Germany right now. In a few minutes I'm hopping on a flight to London, making a switch there and flying out of Heathrow early this evening for New York. With the time difference, I should land with plenty of time to get some rest before I see you guys tomorrow."

"That's great, Uncle Ray. I'm excited."

"Wanna hear what I've planned for you guys tomorrow?" Ray had insisted that he treat Brian's family to a day on the town.

"Sure. Let's hear it."

"Your mom said you'll be leaving Bristol after the morning traffic on the Jersey Turnpike and get to New York about eleven. You'll park at the hotel, and we'll walk a few blocks to St. Patrick's Cathedral for a Christmas visit. You can't spend a day in mid-town Manhattan and not visit St. Patrick's, especially at Christmas."

"Neat," Brian said. "Bobby Kennedy's funeral mass was held there. I saw a program on PBS about it."

"You really know your stuff, Brian."

"I try, Uncle Ray."

"After St. Patrick's we'll grab a hot dog from a street vendor and a bag of those roasted peanuts you like."

"Great," Brian said. "I want the dog with chili and cheese."

"Got it, chili and cheese. But we'll have to hustle because we have tickets for the early afternoon Christmas show at Radio City. It's a little hokey, but it's for your mom. Besides, if you like girls with long legs, you'll love the Rockettes."

"Uncle Ray, I'm 5'0" in ninth grade. I need girls with short legs. But I'm sure mom will like the show."

"You're gonna grow, Brian. Count on it. Anyway, the show lets out about five and it should be dark by then. We'll be heading for

Rockefeller Center to see the Christmas tree and watch the ice skaters. Who knows? If it's not too crowded, maybe we can rent some skates."

"Like Holden Caufield in *Catcher in the Rye*."

"I'm sure our trip will be better than Holden's ever was."

"That's true. He was a pretty messed up character."

"Anyway, we'll wrap up the day by driving to Lower Manhattan for dinner at the Top of the World restaurant at the World Trade Center. It's the most magnificent night view on the entire east coast. You'll love it."

"That's a fantastic plan, Uncle Ray," Brian gushed.

"Then we'll drag our tired bodies home for some much needed rest before Christmas."

"I'm pumped, Uncle Ray. I hope I can sleep tonight."

"You better, Brian. I need you fresh tomorrow."

"I'll read a book until I fall asleep. It's what I do every night."

"Sounds good, pal. Look, Brian, I have to run to catch my flight. I'll see you tomorrow."

"Bye, Uncle Ray. See you in the Big Apple."

Brian slept fitfully and awakened early to shower and dress. It was approaching seven o'clock, so he turned on CNN to get caught up on the news. That was when his life changed.

The news anchor said, "We begin this hour with our top story, and a grim one it is. Pan AM flight 103 from Heathrow, bound for New York's JFK airport, exploded in mid-air just shortly after seven p.m. last night, London time, killing all 287 passengers on board. Much of the debris from the explosion landed on the town of Lockerbie, Scotland, killing at least eleven residents."

Brian sat paralyzed as the anchor continued, "The cause of the explosion is unclear at the time, but officials reported that communication from the cockpit was normal just seconds before the plane disintegrated on the radar screen. Unnamed British officials suspect a bomb may have been placed or carried on board and are exploring the possibility that this tragic event was the work of terrorists."

Brian willed it not to be as images of the cockpit and what remained of the fuselage appeared on the screen. The reporter in Lockerbie called it a grizzly scene and said that debris and body parts were spread over a corridor of several miles.

Brian's mom entered the room and was saying something about having breakfast.

Without looking at her, Brian said, "Mom, what was Uncle Ray's flight number?"

18- The Vigil

There was no Christmas at Brian's house or visit to New York. Instead, the Kellys kept a sad vigil by their phone, waiting desperately for news about Uncle Ray. They used every resource they could muster to obtain reliable information, but the process was agonizingly slow. It didn't help that Christmas was on a Sunday, and by the afternoon of Thursday, December 22, the day they first saw the news report, workers in government offices were either in their holiday shut-down mode or deeply immersed in office parties.

By Thursday afternoon, the airline had posted a family hotline number with the networks. It took the Kellys several phone calls to finally convince officials that they were indeed Ray Murphy's closest next-of- kin, only to learn that no definitive information was available anyway. On Friday, they were finally able to speak with a staffer from their congressman's district office. He kindly put aside his hope for an early holiday break to open some doors across the Atlantic. In spite of those efforts, it wasn't until Christmas Eve that the airline confirmed that Raymond Murphy was indeed booked for Pan Am flight 103 and that he had been issued a boarding pass. The airline also confirmed that there were, as of that moment, no known survivors. They further explained that exceptionally high winds at the time of the explosion spread debris and body parts over an eighty mile corridor, and it could take weeks to make positive identification of the victims.

One network did a short piece about how the once popular Motown singing group, the Four Tops, had been scheduled for the flight but had gotten stuck in London traffic and missed it. That story was enough to convince Brian's mom to hold out desperate hope that her brother had, for some reason, not boarded the plane. So while Brian's father tried gently to ease his wife to accept the inevitable, Brian dealt with the reality that he had known from the moment he first heard the news report- Uncle Ray was dead. Brian was sure of it, just as sure as he was that his uncle had been murdered by a terrorist driven by an unknown cause and sponsored by an unknown group.

Faced with this certainty, Brian withdrew. He barely communicated with his parents and didn't return calls from his friends. He refused to return to school after Christmas break and spent most of his time in his room. After a week Brian's guidance counselor referred his parents to the school psychologist to arrange a grief counseling session. Brian participated, and the counselor concluded, incorrectly, that Brian was in denial and that some sort of closure would be helpful to allow him to move on. It was then that the Kellys planned a quiet memorial Mass.

The service was held at St. Theresa's on January 17 and was attended by a modest group of friends, neighbors and co-workers. Brian's friends came, and Brian was touched to see Johnny, Bobby, Mickey and Tommy in jackets and ties. Frankie, Nick, and Jimmy, Johnny's unofficial uncles from the deli, also came, as did Mr. And Mrs. Marzo. Brian always thought it was a little odd that Johnny referred to his father's friends as uncle, but having just lost the only real uncle he had, he saw things in a different light.

The parish priest didn't know Raymond Murphy, so he spoke in general terms of the sudden and premature loss of a loved one. It was a nice effort, but void of any real feeling. At one point Brian was tempted to stand and tell everyone what a kind and wonderful man Uncle Ray was. He wanted to say that Uncle Ray was his favorite person in the world, but he sat quietly instead, holding his grieving mother's hand and vowing privately to live a life worthy of his uncle's admiration. He thought about his uncle's line of work, and another vow, still somewhat fuzzy, began to take shape.

19- The Think Tank

Brain didn't return to classes the Monday after the ceremony, so Johnny called Mrs. Kelly after school to ask if he and the guys could pay a visit.

"Oh, Johnny, I'm so glad you called," she said. "I'm very concerned about Brian. He stayed home Friday because he wanted to watch Bush's inauguration. You know he loved Ronald Reagan, and didn't want to miss his last day in office. Knowing how much he thrives on the news, I thought it was okay. But he's spent his time alone. We don't want to force him to go to school, but I'm afraid we'll have to. Would you talk with him?"

"We'll try, Mrs. Kelly," Johnny said.

"Thank you. You'll find him in the garage. He's fixed it up with a TV and computer and it's become his little refuge. He spends much of his time tinkering in there."

"We'll be right over," Johnny replied.

The Kellys' garage had always been used for storage, and the boys found Brain there working on his new layout. He had moved the lawn mower and other tools to one side and covered them with a tarp. The rest of the area was occupied by a desk he had moved in that held a computer. There was also a bookcase that was half full and a small television. There was an old swivel chair on coasters and two walls held large cork bulletin boards covered with postings.

"Hi, guys," he said cheerfully when the boys walked in. "It's good to see you."

"Hey, Brain," Johnny said. "Hope you don't mind that we dropped in."

"Heck no. Mom said you were on your way over." His expression changed and he said quietly, "I want to thank you guys for coming to Uncle Ray's service last week. It meant a lot to me."

Tommy spoke first, "Are you kidding, man. We wouldn't miss it. Uncle Ray was a great guy."

"We'll never forget that Phillies game he took us to last 4th of July," Mickey said. "Best seats we ever had."

"He bought us all the hot dogs we wanted and then took us down to the outfield after the game for the fireworks. He was a great guy, Brain," Bobby added.

"Thanks," Brain said softly.

"You must miss him a lot," Johnny said.

"A whole lot," Brain replied. "More than I can say."

It got quiet and Bobby said, "We were worried when you didn't come back to school."

Brain perked up. "I'm going back tomorrow. But as you can see, I had work to do first. How do you like the place?"

"Pretty neat," Tommy said. The others agreed.

"So this is where you'll do your homework and stuff?" Johnny asked.

"Nah, I'll still do that in my room. This is where I'll do a special project I'm working on. I need a place where I can focus."

"Really?" Johnny said. "What kind of project?"

Brain lowered his head and his voice softened. "My Uncle Ray was murdered, along with a couple hundred other Americans. Someone planted a bomb on the plane."

Brain paused to let that sink in. Then he said, "I'm going to get the bastards that did it."

The boys looked at each other, each not sure what to say. Finally, Johnny said reassuringly, "Sure, Brain. Sure you will."

Brain didn't like the sound of Johnny's response, and his face hardened. "Don't blow me off, Johnny."

Johnny didn't respond. The other boys shifted their weight and looked away. No one knew what to do.

"Look at me!" Brain said, his voice rising. "All of you. I'm only going to say this once more and then you guys can stay or leave. I'm going to get the bastards that did this to my Uncle Ray. Do you understand?" Brain's lips were quivering and his face was red. No one had ever seen him like this before.

"Listen, Brain," Johnny said softly. "You know how we feel about you, and we understand. We know you're pissed and want to do something. Heck, we'd like to help you. But you're a kid. You're fourteen going on fifteen. How would you do it? Where would you start?"

"I've got resources," Brain said confidently.

"What kind of resources?" Tommy asked.

"The best kind," Brain said. "Money. I'm rich."

"Well, you kept that a pretty good secret," Mickey said.

"No secret," Brain said. "I just found out. Uncle Ray's lawyer called a couple of days ago. Uncle Ray had a good job that paid well. He was unmarried, and my mom was his only living relative. He left all of his assets, which were substantial, to her."

"Wow," Tommy said. "I never thought about that."

"But that's not the end of it," Brain added. "Uncle Ray took out a million dollar life insurance policy when I was born and named me as his sole beneficiary. It's just like Uncle Ray to do something like that." Brain's eyes began to fill, and a tear ran down his cheek.

The boys were too stunned to speak.

"There's more," Brain said. "Uncle Ray's policy had a double indemnity clause."

"What's that?" Bobby asked.

"It means that the amount of the policy doubles if the insured person dies an accidental death," Brain said.

Mickey whistled. "Two million dollars!"

"That's right. Uncle Ray set everything up in a trust that my parents will administer. I'll get a generous allowance until I'm twenty-one and then the money is mine to do with as I please."

"Unbelievable," Johnny said. "So what will you do?"

Brain put his head down. "I'm not sure. Uncle Ray loved to have fun, and I know he'd like me to enjoy it. But I'm not gonna throw it away or waste it on frivolous stuff. One thing I'm gonna do is buy equipment to help catch and punish the people who killed my uncle."

No one replied.

"Listen, guys," Brain said. "I know this sounds crazy, but I've given it a lot of thought and my head is on straight about this. I know my age and my limitations. I'm a kid, and this may take years to do. But I will do it. And I may not get the actual person who planted the bomb. Heck, he may have even been on the plane, although I doubt it. My goal is to get the people or country behind the attack, and someday I will."

Johnny put his hand on Brain's shoulder and said, "You've always done everything else you said you'd do. So I'm starting to believe you."

"You're definitely smart enough," Bobby said.

"It's not going to be easy," Brain said. "I know that."

"So where will you start?" Tommy asked.

"Right here in my workroom," Brain said proudly." From now on this garage will be called the Kelly Think Tank. As you can see, I've already started to gather my tools. Of course my parents don't know my plans, and I won't ever tell them. But once they saw what a funk I was in they were more than willing to buy me this computer and TV and the best Internet access available, anything to get me out of my shell. At this point they don't care much about money."

"Internet?" Bobby said.

"Yeah." Brain replied. "Hardly anybody has it. It's something that lets you find information quickly if you know how to look. It's cutting edge. My Uncle Ray told me all about it. I've got some new books too," Brain said, pointing to the bookcase. "They're mostly high-tech topics related to Uncle Ray's field. I'm going to learn all I can about it."

"I'm surprised you don't know it already," Johnny said.

"Give me time," Brain said. "I'm working on it."

"So after you're set up, then what?" Johnny asked.

"Well, for starters, I might sue the airline. I'm not sure yet, but I think I have a year to decide. I'm looking into it."

"You've got two million bucks. Why bother to sue?" Mickey asked.

"It wouldn't be for the money, and I'm pretty sure I wouldn't win. I'd be doing it to get information. We'd say they were negligent in not preventing this. We could subpoena airline records, find out what they know. That kind of stuff."

"Okay," Bobby said. "You lost me already."

Bobby was usually lost, so Brain continued. "I'll wait until I see what kind of job Great Britain and the United States do in investigating and releasing information."

"Sounds like you're in charge of things, man," Mickey said.

Brain gave him a hard stare. "Remember 'no balls' Brain Kelly?" There was resentment in his voice.

"We were only kidding, Brain." Mickey said sheepishly, "You know that."

"Well, I just grew a pair," Brain said.

Mickey nodded.

"And one more thing," Brain said. "Let's drop the Brain thing. I grew up a few weeks ago. Please call me Brian."

"You got it," Mickey said. "It's Brian from now on."

Johnny broke the tension. "So what do you do while you're waiting to sue?"

"I've got lots to do. I have two prime suspects that I have to research."

"Cool," Bobby said. "Who are they?"

Brian exhaled slowly before answering. "Look, guys. No offense, but this isn't stealing tomatoes or knocking over people's trash cans for fun. We're not stealing Halloween candy from little kids. This is real business, and it's complicated. I don't want to bore you with it if you don't really want to know."

The garage got quiet. Johnny thought about his meetings with old man Lombardi and the things Lombardi said about responsibility and manhood. He scanned the faces of his friends and then said, "Maybe it's time we all grew up a little. I think we all want in."

The others nodded and Brian smiled. .

"I'd really like to have you guys around now and then so I could bounce ideas off of you."

"Okay," Johnny said. "We're in. So who are these suspects?"

20- The Suspect

Brian drew the boys' attention to the cork boards mounted on the far side of the garage. The first board displayed several maps, photographs and photocopied news clippings.

"You guys sure you want to hear this?"

"We're sure," Johnny said.

"Okay," Brian said. "Here goes." He drew their attention to a map of North Africa and the Mediterranean Sea. Pointing to the map he said, "This is Libya, and this body of water that juts into Northern Libya is called the Gulf of Sidra." Then he pointed to a photograph of a man with a dark, ruddy completion. He was wearing an embroidered, flowing gold tunic and matching kufi skull cap. "And this crazy bastard is Colonel Moammar Gaddafi, the ruler of Libya."

"Sounds like you don't like the guy," Johnny said.

"Who gets him dressed in the morning?" Bobby asked. "Looks like he's ready for Halloween."

Brian ignored them and went on. "In the early 1980s Gaddafi declared that the Gulf of Sidra belonged to Libya and ordered all foreign ships out of it, including our naval vessels on maneuver. But he was wrong. International law says that most of the gulf is in international waters, and my man President Reagan ordered the ships to stay."

Bobby was already lost and Mickey said, "Who cares? Why didn't we just leave?"

"It was a matter of principle," Brian said. "Reagan already suspected Libya of sponsoring terrorism around the world, and he wasn't going to give in on this point."

"Okay, so what happened?" Johnny asked.

"The simple bastard ordered his planes to attack our ships or at least act like they were attacking."

"So what did we do?" Tommy asked.

"Simple," Brian said. "We shot 'em down." Brian shook his head in disgust. "It was reckless of Gaddafi to order the attack in the first place. His pilots didn't have a chance."

"I guess he learned his lesson," Johnny said.

"Wrong," Brian said. "The idiot ordered another confrontation, but using boats this time."

"What happened then?" Tommy asked.

"We sunk them," Brian said flatly.

"Cool," Tommy said.

Johnny recalled Old Man Lombardi's lesson about the costs of war and shot Tommy a disapproving look. "No more games, remember?"

Tommy nodded and turned back to Brian. "Did that end it?"

"We're dealing with a nut here," Brian said. "Gaddafi waited a little while to retaliate, and then ordered his agents to detonate a bomb in a West Berlin nightclub where American servicemen hung out. One American died and fifty others were injured."

"Jesus," Johnny said. "The guy really is a nut."

Brian nodded. "Once our intelligence forces assured Reagan that Libya was behind the nightclub bombing, he ordered an air attack against military targets in Tripoli, Libya's capital, and Benghazi."

"Damn," Mickey said. "These guys don't mess around."

"For the most part the attack was swift and devastating," Brian said. "But, unfortunately, one of our missiles went haywire and hit a civilian target. The Libyans claimed that Gaddafi's stepson was killed in the explosion."

Mickey whistled. "Are you serious?"

"It's all here in the news articles," Brian said.

"That had to piss him off," Bobby said.

"That was in April of 1986," Brian said. "And we waited to see what he might do next. But by all accounts, Gaddafi went quiet." Brian paused and wiped a tear from his cheek. "That is until he blew up my uncle's plane over Scotland."

"Sweet Jesus," Johnny said. "You think Gaddafi did it?"

"Yeah, I do." Brian said, "Or paid some other government or nut-job organization to do it."

"Has our government said that Libya did it?" Mickey asked.

"Not yet," Brian said. "But we'll see." Then Brian lifted a picture frame from the table. "After things calmed down, I wrote a letter to President Reagan. I told him my Uncle Ray died at Lockerbie, told him I thought Libya did it, and said I hoped he would get them."

"Damn, Brian," Johnny said. "You wrote to the President?"

Brian nodded. "I didn't expect to receive an answer because he only had a couple of weeks left in office. But I received this a few days ago. It's hand written on Reagan's personal stationary. The return address was Rancho del Cielo, his place in California."

"He wrote back!" Tommy said.

Brian handed them the framed note and they gathered closely to read it.

> *Dear Brian,*
>
> *I apologize this reply has been delayed. As you can imagine, I have received thousands of letters since leaving office, and my staff has worked diligently to review them and draw the most poignant to our attention.*
>
> *It was with profound sadness that Nancy and I read your recent letter, and we want to convey our sincere condolences over your tremendous loss. Your moving account of the closeness you shared with your uncle brought both of us to tears. I hope you can take some comfort from*

*knowing that his influence will remain with you and the
unbreakable bond you shared will continue in spirit.*

*At this point we simply do not know the cause of the
Pan Am Flight 103 explosion or who, if anyone, may have
been responsible. But I am confident that the government
of the United States will not rest until it determines the
cause of this tragic event and seek justice if it is deemed
appropriate.*

God Bless you and the United States of America.
With deepest sympathy,
Ronald Reagan

"Wow, Brian," Johnny said. "This is really something."

"It doesn't say much," Brian said. "But it was nice of him to write. Maybe it will be a reminder to him that this is personal for the families who lost someone."

The room got quiet and then Johnny said. "You were talking like you had more than one suspect. Is there someone else?"

"Yeah, there is," Brian said. He steered them to the second cork board. It too was cluttered with photos and news clippings. One photo was of a passenger airliner with the word IRANAIR painted on the fuselage. Another showed a United States Naval vessel.

The boys looked puzzled, so Brian began. "Do you guys remember the U.S.S. Vincennes incident?" He was met with blank stares.

"Damn, don't you guys ever watch the news?" There was continued silence and Brian just shook his head. "Six months ago, in July of 1988, the U.S.S. Vincennes, a guided missile cruiser, was on patrol in the Straight of Hormuz in the Persian Gulf. Tensions were high in the area because of the Iran-Iraq war. A radar technician aboard ship thought he detected an Iranian F-14 Tomcat fighter heading toward the ship. It was flying directly at them and increasing speed. The Captain and crew didn't have much time to react, and they fired on the aircraft and made a successful hit. Unfortunately, it wasn't an enemy fighter at all; it was an Iranian passenger aircraft with 290 innocent people on board, including sixty-six children. Most of the passengers were Iranian and everyone died."

"Damn," Johnny said.

"Pretty big mistake," Bobby added.

"We apologized profusely to the Iranian government and offered to make reparations to the families, but they are convinced that we did it on purpose."

"So you think they might have wanted revenge?" Tommy said.

"Wouldn't you?" Bobby asked.

"The Iranians are crazy," Brian said. "Or at least the government is."

"Seems like the whole world is crazy," Bobby added.

"Remember, these are the guys that attacked our embassy and held Americans hostage for hundreds of days back when Jimmy Carter was President."

"How can we remember?" Tommy said. "We were in kindergarten when Carter left office."

"That's why we read, Tommy." Brian chided. "Anyway, trust me, they're nuts, and they think we took out the plane to get even for the past."

"Do ya think we did?" Bobby asked.

"No," Brian said. "It wouldn't make sense. There are plenty of other ways to get them. But it helps their government's 'Hate America' campaign."

"So you think they may have hit your uncle's plane?" Johnny asked.

"Maybe," Brian said. "I'm not ruling them out."

The room got quiet again and Johnny spoke first. "Listen, Brian. This is heavy stuff, and I don't blame you for wanting to get the killers. But I don't want to see this eat you up. You've got a life to lead. We need to see some of the old Brian laughing it up."

Brian smiled. "I'm with you. Tomorrow, I'll be back at school and I'll be my old, smiling self. But I promise you, and Uncle Ray, I won't forget this and I won't stop working to get even. Don't underestimate me."

Johnny smiled, "That's one thing we never do."

21- Carrie's Birthday

A jovial, wise-cracking Brian returned to school as promised and things got back to normal. Johnny was relieved to see his change in mood from the previous day in the garage. He and Brian shared the same lunch period and they sat together in the cafeteria.

"It's good to have you back, Brian. My grades have been dropping without you."

"Good to be back," Brian said. "I guess it was irresponsible of me to leave you alone like that, with nothing but your teachers and books to guide your education."

"I'll say," Johnny said. "But we'll catch up."

Carrie walked by on her way to join her girlfriends. She stopped at the table and said cheerfully, "Hi, Brian, it's good to see you again."

Brian sat taller in his chair. "Good to see you too, Carrie."

"I'm sure you're already caught up with your school work," she kidded.

"Piece of cake."

"Well, I'll let you guys get back to whatever it is you do. Nice seeing you, Brian."

"Nice seeing you," Brian said, beaming.

Then she turned to Johnny. "See you after school?"

"I'll meet you out front," Johnny said.

"Great," she said, smiling. "Bye."

Brian followed her with his eyes until she crossed the room and sat with her friends. Then he said wistfully, "That is one of God's greatest creations, maybe the greatest. Of course the sun is important too. I suppose the universe needs the sun more than it needs Carrie. You know, heat, light, the whole solar system. But she's a close second. I still can't figure out why she settled on you instead of me. I could make her so happy. Have I told you that I get heart palpitations each time I see her?"

"I guess it's okay, as long as she doesn't get them when she sees you."

"That's the problem, Johnny boy. I think she does. I think she's crazy about me. I think she only dates you to get close to me. It's just a theory, but there's mounting evidence to support it."

Johnny just smiled. He was happy to have the old Brian back.

Brian pressed on. "Did you notice that she looked at me a lot more than she looked at you just now?"

Johnny took a large bite of his sandwich.

"I'm telling ya, Johnny. I think she's on the verge of revealing her true feelings for me, and I have to prepare myself for the day when I have to choose between your friendship and her love. I'm sorry to say that friendship can only go so far."

Johnny swallowed and smiled. "I need to ask you something when you're finished with this crap."

"Sure, Johnny. Go ahead, change the subject. It's a defense mechanism. You can't face reality so you…"

"Please shut up for a minute. The bell is going to ring, and I need some advice first."

"Okay. I'm yours. Fire away."

"Carrie's birthday is coming up, and I don't know what to get her."

Brian thought for a minute.

"I want it to be something special," Johnny continued. "I'm thinking about going to Mignoni's and getting her a nice bracelet or something like that. Or maybe a necklace."

Brian nodded. "That might be nice."

"You don't sound very enthused," Johnny said.

"Hey, jewelry is always nice," Brian said. "It's just that I think I understand girls better than you do."

"Okay, wise ass. The act's getting old. What are you thinking?"

"I'm thinking that you really want to impress her, right?"

"Yeah, I do."

"Then instead of giving her a thing, a material object, give her yourself."

"She's not like that, Brian. I…"

"That's not what I mean, bonehead. I mean give her your time, your undivided attention. Do something with her on her birthday that says there is no one you want to be with that night more than her. Take her someplace special. Chicks love that stuff."

Johnny thought about that and said, "She loves Cesares's pizza. I could take her to Cesare's."

Brian shook his head. "You're hopeless, man. You really are. You know I love Cesare's as much as you do. But you take her there once a week already, and that's great. But I've been with you guys at Cesare's and I've seen your act. Once you get your hands on a slice with extra cheese and pepperoni you seem to crave the pizza more than the girl. I mean, you've got strings of melted mozzarella dripping down your chin, your eyes roll to the back of your head with pleasure, and you make noises that sound sexual. All the while Carrie, the classy lady that she is, waits patiently to engage in nice conversation. And when you finally swallow you say something poetic like, 'Good, huh?'"

"That's an exaggeration," Johnny said laughing.

"Yeah, you're right. Sometimes you just say, 'Good.'"

"Okay, fine. So where should I take her?"

"You've got to take her to the King George."

The King George was the most expensive restaurant in town and boasted of being the oldest inn in continuous operation in the United States. It was a classy place, not a place teenagers go for dinner.

"No way!" Johnny said. "That's not me, and besides, I don't have that kind of money. Give me another idea. How about the diner? Maybe Charlie Karp's Pub. You get a ton of food at Karp's. Plus they have all you can eat nights. We could…"

"Shut up, Johnny, and let me paint this picture for you. First, don't worry about the money. I'm rich remember? I'll spot you fifty bucks and if you ever amount to anything in life you can pay me back. I know it's a bad investment on my part, but what the heck, we're friends."

"I can't do that…"

"Shut up, Johnny, the bell's going to ring."

Johnny did.

"Carrie's a classy girl. She'll like this."

Johnny nodded his agreement.

"Okay, so you put on a jacket and tie and…"

Johnny started to protest again and Brian placed his hand over Johnny's mouth.

"You put on a jacket and tie," he said firmly, "and you pick her up at her house. See, here's the thing, Carrie's parents don't like you."

"Sure they do. They're nice to me."

"Trust me, Johnny. They don't like you. They may be polite and tolerate you out of respect for Carrie, but they definitely don't like you."

"I think they..."

Brian interrupted again. "Are you in the National Honor Society?"

"No."

"Are your parents upper crust wealthy?"

"No."

"Are you destined to be a doctor or a lawyer?"

"Maybe," Johnny said sheepishly.

"I think the correct answer to that one should have been 'no.'"

Johnny shrugged his acceptance.

"Carrie is everything a parent could want in a daughter. She's nice, she's kind, she's perky, she's intelligent, and she has angelic beauty. And you! Look at you! You're minor league at best while she's a star in the majors, a shining star. And you have the audacity to date their daughter, to hold her hand, to kiss her lips? How dare you? That's what they're thinking, Johnny, as they force their smiles each time you stop over."

"Gee," Johnny said softly, "I thought..."

"Don't worry about it. Because when she tells them that you're taking her to the King George, it will raise some eyebrows. And when you walk in that house with your jacket and tie and you help her with her coat- and you damn well better help her with her coat- they'll start to view you differently." Brian paused and said, "Are you seeing it, Johnny?"

Johnny nodded. "Yeah, maybe I am."

"Oh, and I forgot. When you show up, you give her mom a small bouquet of cut flowers."

"No!" Johnny said.

"You have to. It's important," Brian insisted.

"It's phony, and I won't do it. I mean it."

"Fine," Brian said. "No flowers for mom. That was one of my throw-away points anyway, a negotiating ploy to manipulate you. But I guess I shouldn't tell you that."

Johnny shook his head. "You're amazing, Brian. You really are." Then he said, "Okay, so I'll take Carrie to dinner at the King George. Thanks for the advice."

"Slow down, pal, we've got plenty more to discuss."

Johnny sighed. "Like what?"

"You need to call for reservations and ask for a table near the piano. I was there once with my parents, and they have a piano player who plays soft, classy music."

"I've never made reservations before."

"It's easy. I'll even show you how to use the phone book. It's about time you learn."

Johnny smacked him on the arm.

Brian rubbed it and kept talking. "Okay, when you get to the table you don't sit until the waiter helps Carrie with her chair. If he doesn't, then you do it."

Johnny rolled his eyes.

"Listen, Johnny. You're painting a picture here. You're showing Carrie what life will be like with you, how caring and sensitive you can be when you're not being a smacked ass."

Johnny nodded. "Okay."

"Now, when you get the menu you look it over for a minute and find the most expensive thing. Let's say it's lobster tail. Then you say, 'I hear the lobster is really good here.' It's your subtle way of saying she can order whatever she wants without worrying about the price. Now normally, you'd be sweating bullets hoping she uses restraint anyway. Except this time you don't care because I'm paying."

"You shouldn't do that," Johnny protested again.

"It's okay. I'll get vicarious satisfaction knowing you're having a good time."

Johnny looked perplexed. "What's vicarious mean?"

"Never mind that; we're running out of time."

Johnny shrugged again.

"Okay, so you placed your order and everything is cool. Now you've got that awkward time before the food arrives. What kind of music does she like?"

"Lots of stuff, she likes Bon Jovi, U2..."

"That's nice," Brian said. "But I mean classy stuff. Didn't you say her parents take her to Broadway shows?"

"Yeah, they went a couple of months ago. I forget what they saw, though, something about being miserable. But she said she loved it."

"Les Miserables?" Brian asked with his best French accent.

"Lay what? Nah, I don't think so. I don't remember."

Brian shook his head. "I'm sure it was Les Miserables. Okay, so here's what you do. Put a couple of dollar bills in your shirt pocket when you get dressed that night. Then, while you're waiting for dinner, excuse yourself, walk up to the piano player, throw the two bucks in his tip jar and ask him to play something from Les Miz."

"Huh?"

"Let me hear you say it, 'Play something from Les Miz.'"

Reluctantly, Johnny mumbled, "Play something from Lay Miz."

"That was beautiful. Then you stroll back to the table and say, 'I asked him to play something for you.'" Of course, she will have seen it all go down because you'll have a table near the piano. Just then, he'll play a nice selection and you'll be a friggin' hero." Brian smiled, but Johnny's expression remained blank.

"Are you feeling this?" Brian asked.

"Yeah, I guess so."

"Okay, we're almost finished. When the song is over you reach across the table and put your hand on hers. Don't grab it. Just put it on hers lightly and say, 'I just want you to know.' Then stop like you're too shy to say what you're thinking. Then pause a second and say, 'I'm just glad you're here.' That's it. That's all you say. Then smile and gently take your hand away."

Johnny looked him in the eyes and said, "Have you ever been out with a girl?"

"Not yet," Brian said, "But I'm optimistic."

"And you want me to do all of this crap?"

"I insist," Brian said. "Just trust me. You will own her when you're finished and she will bubble to her parents about what a gentleman you are."

"Maybe," Johnny said. "I'll think about it."

"Two more quick things."

"Hurry up. I won't remember all this stuff."

"Don't worry. I'll write it down and we'll practice."

"No way," Johnny said.

Brian ignored him and spoke firmly. "Two things. First, do not eat any of her food. Do not tell her you'll finish her mashed potatoes if she doesn't want them. Don't do anything like that."

"Fine," Johnny said. "What's the other thing?"

"Okay, this is important. Don't maul her when you get her alone. Don't act like some thug who thinks he's entitled to some nookey because he spent a little money on a girl. Walk her straight home. Don't try to steer her to the park by the river to be alone. I know that's what you're thinking."

Johnny smiled.

"Walk her to her door. Tell her you had a great time and give her one four-second kiss."

Johnny laughed. "Four seconds?"

"Four seconds. Anything shorter and she'll think something is wrong. Anything longer and she'll think you're trying to cash in. Just give her one four second kiss. And you're on your own for that; we're not going to practice it."

Brian put is hand on Johnny's shoulder. "Trust me, man. Follow the script and it will be the best birthday she ever had."

Things went well. When Johnny picked up Carrie, her mom commented on how handsome he looked. Of course, Carrie looked stunning. He detected a little tension between Carrie and her parents, but both her mother and father were nice to him, so he shrugged it off.

It was a cold but comfortable January night, and the three block walk down Radcliffe Street felt good. Carrie seemed a little tense but managed to keep the conversation going. They passed the Bristol

Riverside Theater just as people were going in for a show, and she said, "We should go to a play sometime. That would be nice."

"Sure," Johnny said. "We can do that." But he began to worry about what he was getting himself into, nice dinners, plays. He wondered what would come next.

They arrived at the restaurant and Carrie giggled when the hostess called Johnny, Mr. Marzo. They were seated at a corner table in the glass enclosed room that overlooked Lions Park and the Delaware River. It was two tables away from the piano. Carrie didn't care for lobster and chose crab cakes instead. Johnny ordered the king's cut prime rib.

Johnny followed the script. He excused himself as Brian suggested, strolled to the piano, flashed the money and said, "Play something from Lay Miz," just as he had practiced.

Carrie smiled, and when she heard the notes of "On my Own," she put her hands to her mouth and said, "Oh my God, this is my favorite." She stretched across the table and gave him a peck on the cheek. Johnny thought she actually looked a little sad, but he'd have to run that thought by Brian later to understand.

Johnny didn't do the hand thing when the music ended. It just didn't feel right. So they talked about school until their food arrived.

Carrie ate like a bird, and Johnny forced himself not to devour his beef. It was nice. When they finished, Johnny gathered his courage, reached across the table, took her hand and said something like, "I just want you to know how glad I am that we're together."

Carrie looked at him, managed to say, "Me too," and then started to cry.

Johnny was stuck and didn't know what to do.

She wiped her tears and said, "I love you, Johnny." Then, before he had a chance to respond, she leaned over the table again and gave him a long, tender kiss.

Johnny felt like he was in a movie. He decided right then that he would take her to nice restaurants, plays, and the friggin' ballet if that was what she wanted. He was in love.

When they parted, she started to cry again, but harder this time. Through her tears she said, "I have something terrible to tell you."

Johnny felt himself deflate. She had just told him she loved him, what could be wrong?

She gathered her courage and said, "My parents and I are moving. They just told me today."

Johnny heard the words, but they didn't make sense.

"Moving?

"Yes," she said sobbing. "My father's been transferred."

Johnny heard himself mumble, "But you just came here this summer."

"I know," she said. "My father is some big-time chemist for an international company and gets moved around a lot for special projects. We usually last a couple of years in one place. I hoped he'd be at Rohm and Haas for a few years, until I could graduate. It's never been this short before."

Johnny was speechless.

"I just want to die, Johnny. I really do."

Finally, Johnny said, "Where are you moving to?"

It was almost as if she couldn't bring herself to say it.

"Look, Carrie. I'm not going to let you just go away. We'll visit each other. I'll take the train until I get my license; then I'll drive every weekend. Where are you going?"

She covered her face with her hands.

Johnny asked again. "Carrie, where are you going?"

She composed herself and said, "My father works for a French company."

"Okay," Johnny said cautiously.

"We're moving to France!"

Johnny felt as if he would pass out. "France?"

Just then the waiter approached and began to clear the table. They watched him in silence.

When the plates were gone, the waiter said cheerfully, "Can I interest you in some dessert? We have an excellent crème bruele tonight."

22- The Limo

Johnny and Carrie sat on her front steps, waiting for the limousine that would take her family to the airport. Ever since their dinner at the King George, the departure date loomed as the day their world would end.

The limo arrived and Carrie's parents came out of the house. Carrie wrapped her arms around Johnny and sobbed uncontrollably. She kissed him long and passionately, not caring that her parents, the driver, or anyone else would see. Johnny felt her tears on his cheeks, and soon they mixed with his own.

When they parted, her mom said gently, "We really must go, honey." But Carrie wouldn't release her embrace. "I love you, Johnny. I really do. And we'll be together. Promise me we'll be together again."

"We will," Johnny said, his voice cracking. "I promise we will."

Carrie's mom touched her shoulder and said, "Please come, dear. This only makes it harder."

"No!" Carrie screamed, pulling away from her. "I'm not going! I'm staying here. How can you do this to me?"

Her father stepped toward her and Carrie moved behind Johnny, using him as a shield. "You can't make me go!" she shouted. She was hysterical now.

Her father was choking back tears of his own. "Carrie, please. This isn't helping any of us. Please come."

Carrie shook her head violently.

Mr. Boyle looked at Johnny and said softly, "Son, you're going to have to be strong and help me with this."

Johnny felt as though he would throw up, but he nodded slowly and turned to Carrie. "He's right, Carrie. There's nothing we can do. You have to go now."

"No, Johnny," she said sobbing. "I want to stay here."

Johnny looked back at Mr. Boyle whose eyes pleaded with him. Then Johnny turned back to Carrie. "It's time," he said softly. He took her hand and moved her slowly to the car.

When they reached the open door, she turned and kissed him again. Then she said, "We'll be together right, Johnny? You won't forget me?"

"We'll be together," he sniffled, "I promise." He wanted to die.

She smiled bravely and slid into the back seat.

"Good luck, young man," Mr. Boyle said. "And thank you."

Johnny nodded.

Then, Mrs. Boyle kissed him on the cheek and said warmly, "Good luck, Johnny. Write to us."

"I will," Johnny said, without moving his gaze from Carrie. He closed her door and watched as the limo pulled away. Then he sat on the curb and cried.

23- Mr. Baxter

Almost two months had passed since Carrie left, and Johnny still wasn't coping with her absence. They wrote to each other daily, and the hour it took to read her letter and write his response was the only bearable time in his day. He went to the log less frequently, did virtually no school work, and generally brooded in his room.

It was early June and he couldn't wait for the year to end. He was walking by the principal's office on his way to class when he saw Mr. Baxter. Baxter smiled and said, "Hey, Johnny. How's it going?"

"Okay, Mr. Baxter," Johnny mumbled and kept walking.

"Hold up, Johnny. It's good that you passed by. I was just about to send for you. Come in to my office."

Johnny's mind raced. What could he have done to prompt a discussion with the principal? He stalled for time. "I have a class now."

"I know," Mr. Baxter said lightly. "I'm sure Mr. Swilli will understand." He opened the door and said, "Come on in."

"It's a pretty important class," Johnny said, weakly.

The principal's smiled faded and he said, "Come inside." Mr. Baxter was a great guy, but you didn't want to cross him.

"Sure," Johnny said. "If you think it's okay."

Baxter followed him in and closed the door. "Have a seat."

Johnny sat and scanned the office. He had never been there before. The wall behind the principal's desk was lined with photos. There was one of Mr. Baxter posing on his Harley, with a bunch of other bikers in the background. The caption read, "Bucks County Riding Club-Hog Heaven." There were several pictures of Baxter on class trips with students, and a few from his former football coaching days. Johnny noticed a nicely framed certificate touting Baxter's induction into the Bucknell University Football Hall of Fame, and another document certifying his graduation with Summa Cum Laude honors. Mr. Baxter was an interesting guy.

Baxter offered Johnny some M & M's and Johnny decided this couldn't be too bad if Baxter was offering candy. He politely declined.

"So how are things going?" Baxter said.

"Good," Johnny lied. "Real good."

Baxter sat back and studied his visitor. Then he said, "Johnny, do you have any uncles?"

"No," Johnny said, thinking the question was strange. "Not really."

"Not really? I'm not sure what that means. You either have uncles or you don't. Do your parents have any brothers?"

"No. No brothers. No sisters either."

Baxter nodded and looked at the wall.

Johnny summoned some courage and said, "Mind if I ask what this is about?"

"Sure," Baxter said. "I had a strange visit yesterday from two men who said they were your uncles." He picked up a tablet from his desk and read from it. "They said their names were Nick Hardings and Jimmy Wright. They said they went to school here and played football back in the sixties, long before I was hired. They also said that your other uncle, Frankie, would have come too, but he had to work."

Johnny shot forward. "Are you serious? Uncle Nick and Uncle Jimmy came here? Why?"

"I thought you didn't have any uncles?"

"I don't," Johnny said. "At least not real ones. Those guys are my father's best friends. I've always called them uncle. Why were they here?"

"The whole thing seemed a bit strange," Baxter said.

"You have to understand, Mr. Baxter. They're a little different. My dad says they are Vietnam vets and had a rough time in the war, a real rough time. But they're great guys."

Baxter nodded. "Well, they certainly care about you. And don't get me wrong; they were actually pretty funny. They were strange and concerned, but funny."

"What's going on, Mr. Baxter. Why were they here?"

"They said no one knew they were coming, not you or your parents, but they were here because they were worried about you. They said you've suffered a trauma and you haven't been yourself for a long time."

Johnny didn't want to have this conversation. "Trauma?"

Baxter leaned forward. "Look, Johnny, this is awkward. But everyone in school knows how close you were with Carrie Boyle and how upset you were when she transferred. Your Uncle Jimmy called it," Baxter checked his notes again, "Post-Romantic Stress Syndrome. He's an interesting guy, that Uncle Jimmy."

Johnny snickered at Jimmy's comment. It sounded like him. Still, he wanted this conversation with Baxter to end. "It's no big deal," Johnny said. "Besides, it's personal."

"Yeah, you're right. It is personal. When someone tells me I have a student with a problem, it becomes personal for me."

"It's got nothing to do with school. You don't have to worry about it. I'll handle it."

Baxter ignored that and said, "When your uncles left I called the guidance office for your records. Ms. Quattrocchi said it was a coincidence that I called because your mom had just called to express her concern, too. You've got a lot of people worried about you."

"Geez," Johnny said. "Why doesn't everyone just back off?"

Baxter ignored him again. "I have your records here, Johnny."

"Great," Johnny said. "This is going to be fun," he added sarcastically.

"You weren't exactly a stellar student at St. Theresa's, but you did a fair job your first semester here. You earned a B in social studies, an A- in foreign language and B's and C's in your other courses. But this semester, which happens to coincide with Carrie's leaving, your grades have fallen significantly. You earned a D in Biology and you flunked Algebra."

Johnny stared at the ceiling.

The only classes you did well in besides Phys. Ed. were social studies and foreign language. You earned an A in each."

"Mr. Swilli is cool, and I've always had an easy time with language."

"Good." Baxter said. "We should build on that." He turned his attention back to Johnny's transcript, and Johnny rolled his eyes.

"Do you know what strikes me most about your records?"

"No," Johnny said. "But I can't wait to hear."

Baxter shot him a cold stare. He was not accustomed to any backtalk from students. "As I was saying, I'm always interested in comparing a student's achievement and ability levels, and guess what?"

"I give up," Johnny said.

"You're not achieving anywhere near your potential. Your IQ is high, and you do well on standardized tests. But when it comes to completing assignments, well, let's say you fall a bit short."

Johnny had had enough. "Look, Mr. Baxter. I appreciate your concern, but if I haven't broken any rules I'd like to get back to class. He started to stand and Mr. Baxter roared, "Sit down, Marzo!" Johnny was stunned and slid back into his chair.

Baxter stood. His face was red and veins were popping in his neck. Johnny decided he may have wised-off just a bit too much.

Baxter walked to the window and looked out at the courtyard, obviously trying to compose himself. When he turned he was calmer. He pulled a chair up next to Johnny and sat down. Then, in a soothing voice he said, "I'm going to cross the line here, Johnny, and say some personal things. I'm doing it because I like you and I see a lot of myself in you."

Johnny listened.

"Carrie Boyle is an incredible girl. She is bright, friendly, energetic and attractive. I mean, everyone on the staff loved her. And I used to watch you guys together. I watch everyone. You know that. And I thought you were great together. I thought she was a classy kid and a good influence on you.

"You know, after I honored you at the assembly in the beginning of the year I heard some interesting stories about your disciplinary record from St. Theresa's. So I expected the worst from you as the year went on. But you were okay."

"Look, Mr. Baxter. I apologize for being disrespectful before. But really, what's the point here? I'm not bothering anyone."

"Fair question," Baxter said. "You said you were okay earlier, but you and I know that you're not okay, and I'm concerned. This is my school, Johnny. I entered education because I love kids and I want to help them. I also did it because I was a lot like you when I was your age." He leaned in and spoke in a conspiratorial tone, "Just between us, I needed my ass kicked a little when I was a kid, and fortunately a teacher cared enough to do it for me. Not literally, although he would have if necessary. But he took me under his care and challenged me. He stopped me from really screwing up my life.

"You're one of my students, Johnny, and I will not stand by and watch you mess up your future. You can't walk around here in a daze anymore. You need to pick yourself up. You have a problem, and we want to help."

Johnny shook his head. His lips were quivering, but he managed to say, "You don't understand…." He couldn't finish.

"I think I do, Johnny. Like I said, your uncle called it post-romantic stress syndrome. The term would almost be funny if it weren't true. You've had your heart broken, and it hurts. Two months later and it still hurts."

Johnny put his head down to hide his emotion.

"I'm thirty-seven years old, kid. I have a pretty good memory of being a teenager. I know what it's like to feel that sense of loss, to feel empty inside. I know what it's like to wake up at five in the morning and not be able to get back to sleep, just thinking about a special girl. I know what it's like to miss someone five minutes after you just left her. So I can imagine what this is like for you."

Johnny's eyes filled up. "Sometimes I get out of bed before the sun comes up and walk by her old house. I look up at the window that used to be hers. I don't even know why."

Baxter put his hand on Johnny's shoulder. "Women make us do crazy things, Johnny." Johnny thought of Old Man Lombardi saying the same thing.

"Yeah, I guess they do."

"Sometimes it's good to just talk about things," Baxter said.

Johnny shrugged. "Nobody to talk to."

"You've got a ton of friends; I can see that."

"I'm too embarrassed to talk with them. I'm not supposed to let one girl wack me out. That would be a sign of weakness. I can talk to Brian a little, but you know Brian. He's way too logical."

Baxter smiled. "Brian's quite a guy." Then he added, "How about family?"

Johnny shook his head. "Way too awkward to talk with Jimmy, Nick, and those guys. I mean, I love them, you know, they're great. But I couldn't do it."

"Your parents?"

"Same thing," Johnny said. "I love them both. They're good to me, too good. But I couldn't talk with them about this, especially my Pop. He's kind to me and all, but sometimes fathers and sons just can't talk. Like we hardly ever just fool around or tell jokes or anything. We're fine together, but we're not relaxed. Mom told me once that Dad sees the world as a hard place, without much to joke about. Fun is something you have if everything else is okay."

Things got quiet and Mr. Baxter left it that way for a long time. Then he said,

"I spoke to your Dad today."

Johnny shot forward. "You talked to my Dad! Why?"

"When your Mom called guidance she asked that I call her back. I dialed and he answered."

"And?" Johnny seemed highly anxious.

"And we spoke, " Baxter said calmly, "for a long time. He said he's worried sick about you."

"Really?"

"It was interesting," Baxter said. "He said a lot of the same things you just said about your relationship. He said he loved you to death, but didn't always know how to show it. He said he has a hard time talking with you about personal stuff. He said the two of you never got into the fishing or hunting thing. You didn't go to ball games much because he was always bogged down with the store."

Johnny's eyes filled again. "We're okay together," he said softly. "We know how we feel about each other. We're good. He's a great dad."

Baxter smiled. "I think you're right. Your Dad feels the same way about you. But, he's worried sick and is at a loss to do anything. So he asked me for some help. I shared some ideas with him and he liked them."

Johnny looked apprehensive. "What ideas?"

"Now I don't want you thinking we're ganging up on you, because we're not. Just think of us as being on the same team of people who want to help you. As your Uncle Nick put it so lovingly, "Straighten his ass out.""

Johnny smiled, but still looked apprehensive.

"So here's the plan. There are two plans actually, one for me and one for you. My plan is to stay on top of things with you, to check on how you're doing, to offer you support and advice. There's no room in my plan for letting you off the hook."

Johnny didn't respond.

"I have a plan for you too, and it's in effect until you show me a better one. Psychologists say I can't do this. They say people have to come up with their own plans for self help. Well, that's garbage because, so far, your lack of a plan over the past few months has you unhappy and failing.

"So here's what you're going to do. First, you're going to do the best you can to salvage something of this school year by studying for your finals. And I don't mean pretending to study. I mean locking yourself in your room for hours and really working at it. I'm going to check those grades.

"Then, this summer, you're going to run and lift weights. The weight room is open in the evenings and I expect to see you there. Your Uncle Nick went on and on about how you do pull-ups on a bar in your room. He got into this long thing about pull-ups being uplifting. I had to cut him off. But his point was well taken. You're a big, strong kid. You should work at it more. Mr. Kemp says you're a good athlete in gym class. That's good because you're going out for football this August."

Johnny looked startled and began to protest, but Baxter said, "Hey, your uncles suggested it. They said they were stars, and your dad was too. Everybody's on board."

Johnny broke a smile. "They tell me the same football stories over and over."

"So, get off your ass and play. Then you can tell them your stories."

Johnny didn't protest, and Baxter went on. In late September we elect class officers. You are going to run for something. I don't care which office, and I don't care if you win, but you are going to put your name on a ballot and run for something in student government."

Johnny didn't like this idea at all and said so. Baxter listened briefly and then cut him off. "You're a leader, Johnny. I watch you. Kids gravitate to you. Brian Kelly is the brightest kid in the school and he follows you like a puppy dog. You declare what is cool and your classmates fall in behind it. It's about time you put your skills to appropriate use. So start making your campaign signs. You're running."

Johnny didn't respond.

"Now here's the final piece. Starting next year you are going to learn how to spell H-O-N-O-R R-O-L-L, and you're gong to make it. This gap between ability and performance is going to close."

Baxter could tell Johnny was buying some of this, but still felt the need to resist.

"You can't change a person just like that," Johnny said.

"We're not trying to," Baxter said soothingly. "I see a bright, athletic kid, with natural leadership ability with way too much time on his hands. I'm just making a coaching change. We're taking you off the sidelines of life and putting you in the game. That is, unless you're too afraid to compete in the real world."

Johnny stiffened. "I can compete, all right."

"I think you can," Baxter said. "I'm sure of it."

Then Johnny grew melancholy again. "It won't bring Carrie back."

"Maybe not," Baxter said. "But her family said when she transferred that this might be a temporary assignment, and that they might be back some day."

"Yeah," Johnny said without much conviction.

"Ask yourself this, Johnny. Supposes she does come back. Which Johnny would you like her to find? The person you've been for the past two months, drowning in self-pity, or the person we believe you can be. Which one is more likeable? It's your call, Johnny."

24- Mr. President!

"The criminal always returns to the scene of the crime," Brian said as he and Johnny entered old man Lombardi's yard.

"That's right," Johnny said. "I'm here at least once every two weeks."

"Free food?" Brian said.

"The food's great, but so is my Dad's at the deli. I come because I love to talk with this guy."

"So tell me again, why am I here?"

"Because the old man wants to meet you. I told him you're a genius and he said only Italians are geniuses- Michelangelo, Leonardo da Vinci, Galileo, Enrico Fermi."

Brian laughed. "There are plenty of Irish intellects."

"Hey, I'm just telling ya what the guy said. By the way, who was Enrico Fermi?"

"An Italian physicist. He helped develop the first nuclear reactor that eventually made the atomic bomb possible. I guess you could say he helped the allies win World War II. He also worked on the quantum theory and particle physics, lots of stuff. He even has a synthetic element named after him. It's called Fermium. It has an atomic number of..."

"Stop!" Johnny shouted. "I get it."

"I thought the new Johnny wanted to learn stuff."

"I do," Johnny said. "But Jesus..."

When they reached the back door, Johnny said, "Listen, Brian. The guy is a little different, a little gruff sometimes. Just roll with things."

"Fine, as long as you can guarantee my safety."

"Trust me. He's harmless."

"I wonder if Mickey would agree with that," Brian said.

"That was different. Lombardi was defending his turf. He's big on that. Besides, it was a long time ago. He's mellowed."

"Let's find out," Brian said as he reached around Johnny and knocked on the door.

Lombardi opened the door immediately and shouted, *"Mista President! Vieni."*

Lombardi had taken to calling Johnny Mr. President ever since he read about Johnny's election as head of Bristol High's student government in the *Bucks County Courier Times.*

Johnny entered and Brian followed.

"Mr. Lombardi, this is my friend, Brian. He's the one I told you about."

Without any greeting Lombardi said, *"Okay, Mis-ta smart ass Irishman. What's- da time in Roma?"*

"You want to know what time it is in Rome?"

"Dat's what I said."

Brian checked the wall clock and added six hours. "It's ten after five in the afternoon."

Lombardi shrugged and fired another question. *"How far to Venice?"*

Brian smiled. "From Bristol or Philadelphia?"

"See," Lombardi said to Johnny. *"Wise guy."* Turning back to Brian he said, *"From Philadelphia. Airport to airport."*

"About 4200 miles." Brian replied quickly.

"Mile!" Lombardi roared. *"No mile. We talk Europe. Kilometer!"*

Brian did a quick calculation. "About 6800 kilometers."

"Damn," Lombardi said to Johnny. *"Som-a-na-bitch is smart!"*

"I told ya, Mr. Lombardi," Johnny deadpanned.

Lombardi turned back to Brian. *"What's you last name?"*

"Kelly," Brian said proudly. "I'm Irish."

Lombardi winked at Johnny. *"Can't be. Your mama, she must be Italiano."*

"Sorry," Brian said. "Her maiden name was Murphy."

"Murphy! Not possible," Lombardi said grinning.*"Maybe somebody make da mistake at da hospital, send home Italiano baby with Irish family."*

With that, Lombardi roared with laughter and grabbed Brian in a bear hug. *"I'm juuust bust-uh you ass."*

Brian laughed as he struggled to breathe in the old man's grasp. Lombardi released him and said to Johnny, *"I like dis guy. Smart som-a-na-bitch. I like him."*

"Genius," Johnny said.

"*Genius,*" Lombardi repeated. Then the smile on his face changed to a scowl. "*He steal my tomatoes too?*"

"No!" Brian said quickly. "I wasn't there. Right, Johnny?"

"That's true. He wasn't," Johnny said.

Lombardi looked Brian in the eyes. "*Why? You afraid?*"

"Terrified," Brian replied.

Lombardi roared. "*No guts!*"

"I've got guts," Brian protested. "But I've got brains too. And brains are better than guts."

Lombardi nodded. "*Brains good. But you need brains and da guts. Dat's why you two make-uh good team.*"

"Johnny has brains too," Brian said. "But he's just now starting to use them."

"*Sure,*" Lombardi said. "*He's da president! My friend win big election. You help?*"

"Brian was my campaign manager," Johnny said.

"*Good! We celebrate. I get da wine.*"

"No!" Johnny said, louder than he intended. "It's not even lunch time yet. No wine for us."

Lombardi looked hurt. He looked at Brian. "*Little bit?*"

"Sorry, can't do it."

Lombardi shrugged again. "*I drink myself. Sit. I get some food.*"

Lombardi produced a loaf of Italian bread still in the Macozzi's bakery bag, olive oil, aged provolone and soprassata, an Italian salami delicacy.

Brian sampled the soprassata. "This is great. What's in it?"

Lombardi grinned. "*No ask. Just eat.*"

The boys obeyed and Lombardi joined them. After a while Johnny said, "So how is Mrs. Lombardi?"

"*She's good,*" Lombardi said, not looking like he meant it. "*She get's tired. Take da nap.*"

"Please give her my best," Johnny said.

Lombardi nodded and changed the subject. "*Two big shots. Mr. President and his smart-ass advisor. Good!*"

The boys laughed. "That's us I guess," Brian said, reaching for more provolone.

Lombardi put his hand on Brian's shoulder in the same vice grip that Johnny was used to. *"You know I kid you about da Irish. I love da Irish. My friends in the army, many Irish. Catholic like me."*

Lombardi released his grip but continued. *"We pray together on the plane before we jump. We shit our pants; we hold hands and we pray. Den we jump in da dark."*

Lombardi paused as though he were reliving the moment. *"Good men. We were close. Italiano, Irish, no difference. We both come to dis country, and people make it very hard. But, in time, everything okay. Dis uh great country for immigrants. But it take time. You work hard, you take some shit, you save da money and wait. Den, everything okay. Same today with da Cubans, Puerto Ricans, Mexicans, Asians. Nobody like dem now. But soon..."*

"I guess assimilation is difficult," Brian said.

Lombardi laughed and sat forward. *"What's dat word?*

"Assimilation," Brian said sheepishly.

Lombardi smiled and repeated it carefully. Then he said, *"It means A-mer-ic-a. kicks you ass for a while and den everything okay. ASS-simulation."* Lombardi roared again and pounded the table with his fist.

Brian understood.

Lombardi treated himself to a slice of soprassata and a swig of his wine. When he swallowed, Brian said, "Johnny tells me you're a war hero."

"No hero," Lombardi said firmly. *"Just da soldier."*

"Johnny said you were a paratrooper on D-Day, dropped behind enemy lines during the first wave of the invasion. I'd say that qualifies you as a hero. You served your country well."

"No hero," Lombardi said softly. *Da heroes are buried in France."*

"Still," Johnny said. "You did your part."

Lombardi nodded and looked at Brian. *"You know D-Day?"*

"Sure do," Brian said and recited the facts as if he could still see the page in the textbook. "It was one of the noblest and most important days in western civilization. It was the largest amphibious landing in modern military history. Over 150,000 men, including thousands of paratroopers, took part in the initial assault on Hitler's Atlantic Wall. Thousands of aircraft and vessels crossed the English Channel to Normandy with troops and supplies. By the end of the month almost 850,000 troops had landed. It was the beginning of the end for Hitler."

Lombardi nodded. He spoke slowly and Brian noted his accent was less pronounced when he took his time. *"People at home... dey part of it too. President Roosevelt ask da people to pray during da invasion. Churches open all night, full of people. Everybody knows many will die. Wives and mothers hope da loved ones live. My beautiful girlfriend, Angelina, she tell me she's in da church all night. But everybody knows we have to beat dat som-a-na-bitch, Hitler, so dey sacrifice."*

Then Lombardi had an idea. *"Wait. I be right back."*

Lombardi left the room and returned quickly holding the famous photo of General Eisenhower surrounded by a group of paratroopers the day before D-Day. The photo was in all the textbooks, and Brian had seen it several times. It showed Eisenhower speaking to members of the 101st Airborne Division. The men were in full battle gear, their faces painted black. They were ready to depart for the early stages of the mission and Ike was wishing them luck.

Lombardi pointed to Eisenhower and tried to pronounce his name. *"Dis is da General Eisa, General Eisen. Dis is Ike! Great man. I was there!"*

"You're in the picture?" Johnny said as he and Brian leaned in to get a better look.

"No," Lombardi said. *"I was there, but not in picture. Bad luck."* He pointed to a spot just beyond the photo's edge. *"I was standing here. Like I said, not in da picture. But I hear Ike's words. I see his face."*

"But he had his back to you," Brian said.

"That's right," Lombardi said. *"But when he finish he turned my way and I see his face."*

The boys nodded their understanding. "It must have been something," Brian said, imagining being visited by the celebrated general and eventual president just hours before America's greatest operation.

Lombardi ignored the comment and said, *"Know what I see? Know that I see on da General's face?"*

The boys remained silent.

"Tears," Lombardi said softly as his eyes seemed to fill. *"When he turned toward me, General Ike had da tears in his eyes because he knew*

what da men had to do. He knew many would die." Lombardi took a breath. *"When I see da tears; Dat's when I know Ike was uh great man."*

Johnny remembered Mr. Swilli talking about the emotions soldiers must have when they go into battle. They had just read Stephen Crane's *The Red Badge of Courage,* a story of a young Civil War recruit who must come to grips with his cowardly act of fleeing in battle while his fellow soldiers stayed to fight. The young man eventually overcomes his fears, performs valiantly, and wins the respect of his fellow soldiers. It was a good story. Swilli provided another perspective by asking the class to think about what it must be like for a general to order men into battle, knowing that many will die. It had been a good discussion, but Lombardi's story made it very real.

The story affected Brian as well because he had read that Ike had written a note prior to the invasion stating that if the plan failed, it would not be the fault of the brave men who landed on the beaches; the responsibility would be his alone. Brian imagined himself as Eisenhower. If the invasion failed, it would be viewed as the biggest military screw-up in the history of the United States, and Ike would indeed shoulder the blame. Not to mention that Hitler could have very well gone on to win the war or at least negotiate a peace that would have left him in power.

Lombardi composed himself and said softly, *"Der's good and bad in da world. You protect da good and you fight da bad."*

The boys nodded.

Lombardi drank some wine and exhaled deeply. When he spoke his accent was more pronounced. *"You country is like da tomato garden. You plant da seeds, you water, you watch grow. Everything nice. But somebody try to take da tomatoes, you stop dem. You protect. You fight like uh som-a-na-bitch. A-mer-i-ca da same. Some som-a-na-bitch try to hurt da country, you fight."*

Lombardi paused and the boys thought about what the old man had just said. Then, Lombardi said, *"So what about you? Some day you serve da country?"*

"I guess so," Johnny said. "I hadn't really given it much thought."

Brian didn't respond, but he had given it a lot of thought, and he had a pretty good idea of what he planned to do.

25- A Distinguished Graduate

It wasn't unusual for Johnny to be summoned to Mr. Baxter's office. He and Mr. Baxter had met weekly since Johnny's election as President of the Student Council. What was unusual was that they had just met the previous day, and now Mr. Baxter wanted to see him again.

The principal greeted him with a smile. "Hi Johnny, have a seat." Johnny did.

"Peanut or plain?"

"Peanut," Johnny said.

Baxter opened his desk drawer and tossed Johnny a small bag of M & M's chocolate covered peanuts and opened a bag for himself.

"I just spoke with Ms. Quattrocchi about your college applications, and she said they're all in."

"That's right," Johnny said. "I've applied to three schools. West Chester is my 'safe school' because Ms. Q. feels that I should get in easily with my SAT scores and class rank. Penn State is the school I hope to get into. The standards are higher, but Ms. Q. thinks I have a pretty good shot."

"I think so too," Baxter said, examining Johnny's transcript.

"My dream school is Georgetown. I know I don't have much of a chance, but I love Washington and my friend, Brian, said I should shoot big."

"Can't hurt," Baxter said. "It will be tough, but it certainly is possible."

Johnny sat forward. "Mr. Baxter, I want to thank you for all you've done for me. I don't think we'd be having this conversation if you hadn't taken an interest in me back in freshman year. Same thing for Ms. Q. She's been great."

Baxter smiled, tossed an M & M in the air and caught it with his mouth. They both laughed. "Johnny, there is no greater satisfaction than seeing a kid pick himself up and do a complete turn around. The effort you've put forth was all the thanks we needed. We're both proud of you. The entire faculty is proud of you."

"Well, I'll never forget what you did," Johnny said.

Baxter's expression changed. "There is one minor thing on my mind."

Johnny looked concerned, but Baxter added quickly, "Don't worry. Nothing is wrong. But I want to make sure you understand the financial issues involved here. Fortunately, you selected two state schools, which will keep the costs down. But even though Penn State is a state school, it can still end up costing $15,000 a year once everything is counted. There are student loans out there, but they're limited. I'm just afraid that your family might be in that income bracket where they earn too much for you to qualify for full financial aid but not enough to pay the whole amount. This is especially true about Georgetown which is even more expensive. I want you to know we'll do everything we can from our end to help, but I don't want you to be disappointed if things don't work out with the more expensive schools."

Johnny nodded. "Thanks, Mr. Baxter. Ms. Q. already went over this with me. We have all the financial aid forms filled out, and we'll try for the max. But just between us, I've got it covered."

"You do?" Baxter was obviously surprised.

My parents are going to pay what they can, and I'm going to apply for aid. But I already have a commitment from someone to make up the difference if there is any."

"Really?" Baxter looked pleased, but he was obviously curious and wanted to hear more.

"Yup," Johnny said confidently. "Let's just say it's a friend of the family."

Baxter nodded. It was clear that was all the information Johnny planned to offer. "Hey, that's great," Baxter replied. "Well, as I said, we'll do our part at this end, and things should be fine."

What Johnny wouldn't reveal was that Brian had encouraged him to apply to any school that interested him. Brian's encouragement came with a confidential promise that he would use his hefty allowance from Uncle Ray's estate to pay the balance of any expenses Johnny couldn't cover. Johnny had refused the offer, but Brian was adamant, saying that he owed Johnny more than he could ever repay for his friendship and that he needed to do something in return.

Johnny thought back to the exchange. "This isn't just for you," Brian had said. "It's for me too. Besides, I've spoken with my parents about stuff like this. They said I've always been responsible, and I can do whatever I want with the money as long as I don't exceed twenty-five percent of the principal until I'm twenty-one. I want to do this, and I can definitely afford it."

Johnny had agreed reluctantly, but only with the stipulation that he would repay Brian once he began his career, whatever that might be.

Mr. Baxter brought Johnny back to the moment. "Well, that's one topic covered, but it isn't the main reason why I called you here today."

"Okay," Johnny said. "So what is?"

Baxter smiled again. "We're having a special school-wide assembly next week and a former student, a distinguished 1980 graduate, will be addressing our students. I would like you to introduce him."

Johnny's response wasn't very enthusiastic. "Why me?"

"Because you're Student Council President," Baxter said. "You're the obvious choice."

Johnny pondered that for a moment and said, "We've had plenty of speakers in the past, and you always introduce them, not the Student Council President."

Baxter laughed. "Okay, you got me. The truth is that I never thought of it before. In fact, the real reason is because of what I said earlier. You've been a great example to the other students. Since our little talk your freshman year, you've done everything I've asked of you. Your grades have soared. You've been a student leader, and you're on the football team."

"I'm no star," Johnny interrupted.

"You've been a starting linebacker on a winning team three years in a row and you've made a ton of tackles. I'm sure your parents and those guys you call your uncles who are in the stands for every game would disagree with you."

Johnny laughed. "They're crazy; aren't they?"

Baxter laughed with him. "Let's just say they're very colorful."

"And intense."

"Oh, very intense," Baxter agreed. "But they're former Bristol players, so I get where they're coming from. I just control my emotions a little better than they do. But they're good guys and the fans love them."

"Yeah, me too," Johnny said.

"So, anyway, because of all of your accomplishments, I'd like you to introduce our speaker."

"Thanks, Mr. Baxter, but I don't know. It just seems like it would be better if you did it."

Baxter tossed another M & M into the air and shifted his head slightly to catch it. He chewed the peanut and smiled, "This is not optional, Johnny. You're doing it. It will be a good experience for you, and I have all the confidence in the world that you'll be fine. An educator's job is to stretch students now and then. Consider yourself stretched."

Then he slid a folder across his desk. "Here is some information on our guest's background. Look it over and write a one minute introduction. Come back in a few days and show me what you've written."

He tossed another M & M and caught it with ease.

Johnny sat on the auditorium stage with Mr. Baxter and the guest speaker as the students filed into the assembly. He thought back to the first time he was on the stage almost four years earlier. It was the first day of school during his freshman year, the day Mr. Baxter recognized him and Mickey for saving Mr. Lombardi's life. It was also the day he spoke to Carrie for the first time. He remembered how weak-kneed he felt. He could still picture her standing in front of him, the most perfect girl he had ever seen. He smiled at his awkwardness and the ease with which she had carried the conversation. She had kidded him that day about how shy he looked on stage, and he wished she was in the audience today to see his second act.

His memory turned to a far less pleasant image, the day the limousine took her and her parents to the airport for their trip to France. In spite of their impassioned promises to somehow sustain their relationship, they had not seen each other again.

Carrie's dad was a high- powered chemist whose services were sought by companies around the world. As a private contractor, he would work on special projects, complete them and then move on to work for the next highest bidder. Their stay in France had lasted just two years. It was followed by a year-long stint in Copenhagen. From there they moved to Florence, where they currently lived.

The heart-felt letters they exchanged after their separation, letters in which they vowed to remain faithful to each other and find a way to reunite, soon fell victim to the circumstances that separated them.

Carrie had been required to assimilate with new surroundings so frequently that it was virtually impossible to squeeze in a return visit to the United States, even for a short time. Sadly, Johnny knew that it was more than just logistics keeping her away. In spite of the clear affection she still held for Johnny, Carrie had become a cosmopolitan woman of Europe, enthralled by the art, architecture and languages of the continent. She became fully immersed in the cultural nuances of each new location and was rapidly becoming multi-lingual. They still exchanged letters regularly, although not as frequently, and eventually came to an understanding that they would see other people. Johnny's only hope was that her frequent relocations would reduce the chances of her building a lasting relationship with someone.

Brian had insisted that Johnny fly to Europe for a visit and offered to pay the airfare and expenses, but Johnny refused, partly because he couldn't bring himself to take the money and partly because he feared that a visit after so long might result in disaster.

From the photos they exchanged, he knew that the girl he remembered had become a strikingly beautiful woman. But her smile and the tone of her letters revealed that she was still as easygoing and genial as ever, still the sweet, unassuming girl he had met in front of Bristol High School. Still, he feared what a meeting might bring.

"Okay," Brian had said when Johnny refused his offer. "Let's hope her old man gets transferred every two months until you finally get the guts to go see her. But in the meantime, you better make sure she knows that the Johnny she fell for has emerged as a new guy. Still the same old Johnny in many ways, but now he can read and write, is a leader of men, and is a kick-ass football player.

"This is a classy girl we're talking about here, Johnny boy. She may have been into that puppy love crap when she fell for you. Maybe she even had a little bit of the bad-boy attraction in her, but that stuff fades in the circles she's traveling in now.

"In fact, I'll bet that this very minute she's being smoozed by some one-hundred and twenty pound European gigolo, sipping coffee in some outdoor café and discussing the work of some famous artists. You need to build your credentials, man. You need to keep yourself in the running by letting her know that Johnny Marzo has become a scholar, statesman and athlete."

Now, Johnny was becoming preoccupied by thoughts of what he would be doing with the rest of his life and whether or not he would ever have her back.

26- Lieutenant William J. Frake

The students entered the auditorium and began to settle down, Johnny noticed the Pac Men sitting together. When their eyes met his, they did everything they could to make him laugh. Mickey pulled his cheeks apart and stuck out his tongue. Bobby scratched under his arms like a monkey, and Tommy grasped his neck pretending to choke. Brian saluted in a gesture he had adopted after Johnny's election.

Johnny just smiled and shook his head. He reminded himself to savor his senior year because he knew his friendships would never be the same once he and his friends graduated.

Brian was already accepted to the Massachusetts Institute of Technology. In addition to receiving a full scholarship, he was awarded a monthly stipend to assist in laboratory work. It was one of many similar offers Brian had received from distinguished engineering and technology schools across the country. Brian settled upon MIT because, in his words, "The Boston area has the largest collection of colleges and the greatest concentration of female students in the United States. It's a gold mine for girls. I'll probably flunk out because of my social life." The fact was that Brian had finally experienced the growth spurt his mother had always promised would come, and, with it, his confidence grew as well.

Tommy dreamed of becoming a Physical Education teacher and had already applied to Slippery Rock University in Western Pennsylvania. When Johnny asked why he had chosen Phys. Ed. he said, "I've been observing teachers for four years. Seems to me they do the least work. Just roll out the ball and wait for the period to end. I'm into it."

Bobby wisely recognized that college was not for him and decided to follow his passion for working on cars by enrolling in the Pennco Tech automotive repair program for the fall.

Mickey had been fascinated by the heroic rescue efforts during the Baby Jessica drama that unfolded before the nation four years earlier. Baby Jessica McClure, an eighteen-month-old child from Midland, Texas, had fallen into an eight inch diameter abandoned well-shaft and became trapped. The news coverage was extensive as rescue crews worked fifty-eight hours to free the little girl. Mickey never forgot the joy he felt when the drama unfolded and a rescue worker emerged from a parallel shaft, dug by a rescue team, with the child alive and well. Nor did he forget the admiration he felt for those who worked tirelessly to free her. That event, reinforced by the experience of seeing, first hand, the skill of the emergency services team that worked on Mr. Lombardi during his heart attack, convinced Mickey that he would pursue a career as an Emergency Medical Technician.

Next, Johnny caught the glance of Jenny Ryan, his current girlfriend. Jenny was a cross country runner, with a slender body and long dark hair, which she wore pulled back from her face. Jenny was a perky, happy, fun-loving girl who never declined an invitation from Johnny for a Sunday night movie, a mid-week basketball game or weekend party.

She was smitten by Johnny and he liked her a lot as well. She was no Carrie, he'd confess privately, but Carrie was in Europe doing who knows what and Jenny was here. Johnny decided there were far worse ways to spend his senior year than to spend it with Jenny. Jenny smiled when their eyes met and gave him a thumbs-up. Johnny winked back.

When Johnny turned his attention from the Pac Men to Jenny, Brian turned his to the guest speaker seated on stage with Johnny and Mr. Baxter. He appeared to be in his late twenties. He wore the sharply creased uniform of a United States naval officer. This guy was the real deal, Brian thought, and he was interested in what the officer had to say. Lately, he was interested in the military in general.

Operation Desert Storm, or the war in Iraq as it was commonly called, had come to an end in February of 1991 during their junior year, and Brian had been fully absorbed by the conflict from the time

Saddam Hussein's troops had invaded oil-rich Kuwait and posed a very real threat to Saudi Arabia, until Saddam was defeated and a cease-fire declared.

He became a big fan of General Colin Powell, Chairman of the Joint Chiefs of Staff, and General Norman, "Stormin' Norman," Schwarzkopf. Powell was the guy at home running things from the Pentagon, and Schwarzkopf was deployed to manage things in the field.

Brian watched as President Bush put together an alliance of thirty-four nations to repel Saddam's aggression, and Schwarzkopf patiently assembled his multi-national force. When the deadline imposed by the United Nations for Saddam's withdrawal from Kuwait passed without compliance, Brian marveled as CNN broadcasted the air war live from Baghdad. After several days of softening the enemy from the air, allied ground forces advanced through Iraq's defenses with lightning-quick precision.

Of everything he watched, Brian was most impressed by the new weapons technology deployed by the United States. Dessert Storm was being called the first computer war for good reason. Allied forces made extensive use of weapons like Tomahawk BGM 109 Cruise Missiles, F117A Stealth fighters equipped with laser guided bombs, and Airborne Warning and Control Systems (AWACS). The AWACS were a flying command center. They were able to detect enemy airborne threats and direct F14's or F 15's to eliminate the threat. Equally fascinating to Brian was the use of Global Positioning Satellites, or GPS Technology, used by ground forces to guide their advance through unfamiliar territory. The list went on and on and included night vision goggles and combat platoons linked by small laptop computers. Brian felt sure that if his Uncle Ray were still alive he would have been on the cutting edge of such technology. Brian had become increasingly interested in making technology his career, just as his uncle had. Hardly a day passed when Brian didn't think of his Uncle Ray and the other Flight 103 passengers who perished over Lockerbie, or the Marines killed in their barracks in Beirut, or the twenty-eight reservists from Pennsylvania who died when one of Saddam's Scud missiles hit their barracks in Dhahran, Saudi Arabia. Just under three hundred Americans lost their lives on Operations Desert Shield and Desert Storm, roughly one-half from battle related deaths and the other half from combat support accidents.

These were widely considered to be relatively small numbers given the scope of the conflict, but not to Brian or the families who lost their loved ones.

To Brian, the attacks in Lockerbie, Beirut, Dhahran and elsewhere, were all the same, although their origins appeared to be varied. We were at war with an amorphous, but dangerous enemy, and we would have to be vigilant in our defense.

Brian's thoughts were interrupted when Mr. Baxter took the podium and made some general announcements. Then Baxter said, "And now, it is my pleasure to turn the program over to your President, Johnny Marzo, who will introduce our guest speaker."

The auditorium erupted with whistles, cheers and chants of "Marzo, Marzo." Mickey and the rest of the Pac Men rose from their seats and saluted until their homeroom teacher gave them the evil eye and they sat down.

Johnny laughed at his classmates' response and motioned for everyone to quiet down. "Now that's the kind of enthusiasm we need from you when we play Lower Moreland this Friday night. I expect to see all of you at the game." The room burst into cheers again, and Johnny let it go on for a few seconds.

When the room was quiet again, Johnny said, "Let's move on to more serious things" and he began the remarks he'd worked on with Mr. Baxter.

"Today's guest speaker graduated from Bristol High School in 1980, where he distinguished himself in academics and extra curricular activities. During his senior year he was nominated to and ultimately accepted an appointment to the United States Naval Academy at Annapolis, Maryland. He graduated with merit from the academy in 1984 with a degree in Aerospace Engineering. Following graduation, he underwent two years of intensive training in nuclear power and submarine warfare. In April 1986, he was assigned to the attack submarine, USS Seahorse, where he and the crew were deployed, among other places, to the Artic Circle.

"For the past two years he was assigned as a nuclear engineer at the headquarters of the Navy's Nuclear Propulsion Program in Washington, DC. This was a handpicked position where he worked directly with the technical teams that design and maintain the hundreds of nuclear reactors in our submarines and ships. Next month he will attend the Submarine Officer Advanced Course in Groton, CT. When he graduates he will be assigned as the Engineer Officer in the attack submarine, USS Oklahoma City."

Johnny paused and scanned the audience. "I know a lot of this is over my head as I'm sure it is for you too, but it should be inspiring to all of us to know that this gentleman, who walked the same halls that we walk, who had many of the same teachers that we have, and whose parents still live right down the street in our town, has gone on to so much success. It is inspiring to know that our government has entrusted him with such responsibility on nuclear submarines that cost hundreds of millions of dollars.

It is my honor to introduce to you one of the most distinguished graduates Bristol High School has ever had. Please join me in welcoming Lieutenant William J. Frake, United States Navy.

The students applauded as Lieutenant Frake stepped to the podium and shook Johnny's hand. "Thank you, President Marzo," Frake joked. "I wasn't sure whether to salute or shake your hand. From the reaction of your constituents in the audience, I'd say there are plenty of politicians in Washington who would love to have your approval rating."

There was laughter in the audience. "It is certainly a pleasure to be back at Bristol High today. Some people say that when people return to their alma maters everything looks smaller, but when you spend as much time on a submarine as I have, I assure you, everything else looks big.

"I was able to have breakfast with the faculty this morning and thoroughly enjoyed seeing many of my former teachers. If I say nothing else today, I want you to know that the things I learned from them formed a solid foundation for my future studies, and I owe them a great deal of gratitude. I know this will sound trite, but I hope you will soak up as much as you can from them during your time here.

"When Mr. Baxter invited me to speak, I readily accepted because I welcomed the idea of speaking to students, especially Bristol students, and because it would give me the opportunity to visit my parents. Fortunately I was available to come because, as Johnny said, I'm currently stationed in Washington DC. The navy's normal procedure is to rotate its officers on two year cycles. Usually, you spend three years at sea and two years on land for advanced training or work in areas supporting our operational submarines. My stint at Washington DC will end next month, and I will attend six months of intensive training in Groton, CT and will report to the USS Oklahoma City where I will serve as Engineer Officer. I can't tell you where we'll be going. The navy keeps that a secret. But sometimes we can tell you where we've been after our mission is completed."

Lieutenant Frake went on to tell the students about his experiences at the Artic Circle while serving on the USS Seahorse. He recounted the experience of breaking through ice to surface and what it was like playing touch football on the frozen landscape, dressed in shorts and a t-shirt. He spoke of life at the military academy, and in general terms of the research and development work taking place in Washington and other military facilities.

He closed by offering the students encouragement about their own careers. "When I sat where you are sitting now, I knew I wanted a career in military service, but I had no idea what path it would take. I know many of you may feel confused about your own futures. My advice to you is to open as many doors as you can for yourself, and that means giving yourself the skills and education necessary to pursue your future. I don't know what the navy has in store for me, but I know my dream is to command my own submarine some day, and I've been fortunate enough to have pursued the training and experiences that could one day make that possible. I hope you will pursue your dreams as well. And if you're not sure what they are, I hope some of you will consider a career in military service. There is a great deal of satisfaction involved in willingly assuming responsibility for the safety and well-being of your fellow countrymen.

"Thank you for having me as your guest. I wish you the best of luck as you pursue your dreams."

27- Canada

Johnny entered the family deli and found Nick writing a letter at his favorite table. Nick was a volunteer at the Veterans Outreach Center in Philadelphia, and he wrote to Washington each day on behalf of the servicemen he encountered there.

As soon as Nick saw Johnny, he stopped writing and hummed a few bars of "Hail to the Chief." "Know something, Johnny? Ever since you've been president the weather has improved. Keep up the good work."

Johnny smiled. "Thanks, Uncle Nick; glad you noticed."

"Jimmy and your dad are out delivering lunches. They'll be back in a half-hour. I'm minding the store."

Johnny knew they would be gone and had timed his visit for that reason. "Do you have a few minutes, Uncle Nick?"

"You know I always have time for you, kid. Have a seat, and grab a Coke first. It's on me."

Johnny laughed. "Thanks, but I'm fine."

Johnny sat and Nick closed his writing tablet. "So what's on your mind, young man?"

Johnny got right to the point. "I'd like to talk about Vietnam."

Nick's smile faded. He started to speak, but Johnny interrupted. "I know you don't like to talk about your time as a POW, and I respect that, but I need to know some things about the whole Vietnam deal and how I fit in."

Nick was a hometown hero who'd been a Green Beret and a recipient of the Distinguished Service Cross. He had been captured while freeing downed pilots from a North Vietnamese village and was held as a prisoner of war for five years. During that time he was beaten, tortured, and denied medical treatment. He didn't like talking about his experiences and rarely did, preferring instead to work on behalf of other veterans.

"What I really want to talk about is Canada." Johnny added.

Now Nick looked even more uncomfortable. Johnny's father had fled to Canada in 1968 with his girlfriend, Donna, just after he received his draft notice. He and Donna lived there for eight years. During their stay they married and had Johnny. They returned to the United States in 1977 when President Carter granted amnesty to draft dodgers. At the time it seemed that Angelo had taken the cowardly way out and had gotten off easily.

Nick stammered, "I don't know, Johnny. That's a tough topic. Maybe someone else would be better."

"I need to hear things from you, Nick," Johnny persisted.

"Why me?"

"I'm not sure. I guess it's because you're the war hero. I need to know what was going on with my parents. Heck, I was born in Canada and know almost nothing about… about anything."

Nick looked torn. He'd do anything for Johnny, but this was too personal. "You should talk to your dad. It's not right coming from me."

"I will someday. I promise. But first I need some background."

Nick exhaled deeply. "Okay, just some background."

"Thanks, Uncle Nick. It's important. Sometimes I feel like I'm adopted or something."

"Don't worry; you're not adopted. So here's some general stuff."

Johnny nodded and Nick began. "It was a very complicated time. Everyone had different views about the war, strong views."

"What were yours?"

"I supported the war and signed up to fight it. Things didn't work out so well for me, but I think signing up was the right thing to do. And I still think we could have won."

"What about Jimmy?'

Nick shook his head at the thought. "Jimmy was against the war, but he went when he was drafted. To this day he regrets going. He was made to do things that few men could do, and he wasn't mentally equipped to handle them. He came home a much different person, seriously damaged, we all did, but he's still bitter."

"Toward my dad for not going?"

"No, toward the people who sent us there."

"What about Big Frankie?

"Frankie's story is different. I was already away at the time Frankie got drafted, but…"

Johnny interrupted. "Frankie got drafted? I thought he didn't go to Vietnam, like my dad."

"He didn't. As I said, I was already gone when he got drafted, but from what I hear, he was prepared to go, scared as hell about going, but prepared."

"So what happened?"

"He flunked his physical because of his diabetes. He never had to go."

"So he got off easy then," Johnny added, searching for a parallel with his father's experience.

"There's no way Big Frankie got off easy," Nick said emphatically. "Johnny Francelli was Frankie's best friend. You know all about Johnny," Nick added. "Hell, you're named after him."

Nick paused and it looked as though his eyes were filling up. "I wish you could have known him. He was an incredible guy. You'd love him. Everybody did."

Johnny nodded. The guys talked about Johnny Francelli all the time, not about his dying in the war, but about the fun they had growing up together. But young Johnny wanted to hear more about how the man he was named after fit into the Vietnam picture.

Nick continued, "As I said, Johnny and Frankie were best friends, so when Frankie got drafted Johnny surprised everyone by enlisting in a program that supposedly would allow them to go through training together. But the unfortunate surprise was on Johnny because Frankie flunked his physical later and Johnny still had to go. So the short story is that Johnny went to Vietnam and died. He died a hero, I should add. He's the hero, not me."

"Wow. That's pretty sad," Johnny said softly. "Johnny Francelli joined for Frankie."

"Frankie still believes that it's his fault his best friend died. He visits Johnny's mother all the time and takes care of her. He treats her like his own."

Johnny didn't say anything and Nick added, "Still think Frankie got off easy?"

"No, "Johnny mumbled. "I guess not."

Nick took a breath and said, "Then there's Billy."

Johnny looked surprised. "Who's Billy?"

"He was one of the original gang. We all played ball together. The guy could really motor with the football, but that's another story. Anyway, Billy was the smart one. He went to college after high school, so he got a student draft deferment. The war was still going on when he graduated. He pulled a bad draft lottery number and was likely to go sooner or later, so he enlisted. He went to officer's school, became a Lieutenant, went to Nam, got wounded and was sent home."

"How come I haven't met him?"

"He went to law school in North Jersey, met a girl, got married and started a life up there. None of us heard from him until he invited us to that reunion at his shore home in September."

"So that's where all you guys and my mom and dad went last month?"

"Yup. Your dad didn't want to go. He was afraid Billy would hold Canada against him. But we all made him go."

"Did Billy hold it against him?"

"Hell no, Billy had his own explaining to do, like where the hell he'd been for twenty years and why he forgot about his friends for so long." Nick paused. "Always remember to hang on to your friends, Johnny."

"So how did the reunion go? My dad doesn't say much. "

"It was great. I mean everything about it was terrific. Plus, I fell in love with Billy's wife."

Johnny laughed.

"Don't laugh. I mean it."

"You fell in love with someone in one weekend?"

"In five minutes. There's just something about her."

Johnny thought back to his first meeting with Carrie. "I guess I see how that could happen. But she's married, Uncle Nick. You can't…"

"Of course I can't," Nick interrupted. "But love's love, and she got to me. Don't tell Jimmy."

Now Johnny knew Nick was fooling around a little, so he played along. "Why not Jimmy?"

"Because he loves her too. It's so obvious. He combed his hair for her."

Johnny nodded and smiled.

"I guess we shouldn't tell Billy either. He might take offense. In fact, we better not tell Trish either. Trish is her name by the way. I think it would just spoil things. It's better if I love her from afar as the saying goes. That way I won't be disappointed."

"Sounds like a plan," Johnny said.

Nick winked at him. "It'll be our secret."

Johnny wanted to steer Nick back to the topic. "So anyway, it sounds like seeing Billy at the reunion was a good thing."

"It was great," Nick said. "It was painful in some ways, but great."

Johnny had been clicking off the list of his dad's friends in his mind. Ralph was the last one he knew about. "Tell me about Ralph."

Nick chuckled. "Yeah, then there's Ralph."

Ralph was a local undertaker who came to the deli a couple of times a week for a coffee and chat with the guys. It was obvious he was a friend from the old days, but he always took a lot of ribbing and never seemed to be totally accepted.

"You want the truth about Ralph?"

"Yeah," Johnny said, "the truth."

"Ralph never paid a price in the war. Except for the loss of Johnny, which the whole town suffered, Ralph floated through the whole Vietnam thing like a butterfly. First he got a college deferment and when that ran out he pulled a good draft lottery number. He had a free ride. Deep down I think everyone holds some resentment against him. He's got a wife, kids, makes plenty of money, drives a BMW."

Nick shook his head. "Even with guys who opposed the war like Jimmy, there is a bond you build with guys when you pay a price, and Ralph never paid a price."

"What about my dad? He never paid a price; he went to Canada."

Nick looked at Johnny and waited a long time before responding. "Let's talk about the price your father paid. Of course, I knew your dad before he went. He was never the same after he came back. He paid a big price, Johnny, a different kind of price but a heavy one."

Johnny didn't see it. "How?"

"Let's start with your grandparents. They supported his decision to go, but they suffered a lot because of it. Eventually, your grandfather got too weak to travel to Canada every few months, so they spent the last few years of your father's exile without seeing their only child, or their grandson once you were born. That tore your father up.

"Your grandparents were also shunned by people in town, people who thought your dad was a coward, people who resented the fact their sons were in danger while your dad was safe.

"Then there was the family deli. Business dropped off sharply. Lots of people shopped elsewhere. Your grandfather struggled to keep the store open while his health was failing. Big Frankie used to come to the store to help him stock the shelves. Your dad knew all of this and it tore him up even more."

Johnny started to speak, but Nick had more to say and pushed on.

"Then there was your mom and you. Your mom went with him to Canada because she loved him. But think about it. She left behind everyone she knew. It didn't matter much with her parents because they had a terrible relationship. But she left her town and all of her friends behind. Then when you were born she really freaked out. She wanted her son to live in America."

"Maybe Dad should have come home to help my grandfather," Johnny said innocently.

"Wouldn't have done much good," Nick replied. "They were prosecuting draft dodgers. He would have gone to jail."

Johnny shook his head. "This was pretty messed up."

"Like I said, Johnny, it was a complicated time. Your parents spent nine years in exile to avoid the draft. Nine years."

Now it was Johnny's turn to pause. He'd never fully considered the impact fleeing to Canada had on his family. He had three more questions and knew he'd have trouble asking them.

"Nick, do you think my dad was a coward?"

Nick answered immediately. "No way! Absolutely not."

Nick leaned forward. "Listen, your dad was a bad ass on the football field. He used to flatten people. He used to seek out contact even when it wasn't necessary. One of the reasons why we won our big Thanksgiving game was because he decked Morrisville's place kicker so hard that they had to help the kid off the field.

"He was the same way off the field. In fact, sometimes he was a pain in the ass to have around because he was always picking fights. We'd go to a dance at the Number 3 firehouse and he'd pick a fight with guys from Croydon or Trenton. Their friends would jump in and before you'd know it, we'd all be fighting. "Heck," Nick winked, "I was there to pick up girls, not fight."

Johnny smiled.

"Your dad wouldn't back down from anybody, even at times when he should have." Nick paused again. "Now don't get me wrong. There are different kinds of courage, and it's still a whole heck of a lot safer to get your ass kicked at a dance than to carry an M-16 in Nam. But I think your dad would have been a good soldier, maybe too good. I just don't think courage was the issue."

"So what was it then? Why did he go to Canada?"

"He had very strong convictions against the war. He was always tuned in to world events, and he thought the war was wrong long before he was drafted. He used to go to anti-war rallies. He used to lecture us about foreign policy while we drank beer by the canal. He'd tell us about leaders who opposed the war. We weren't paying much attention, at least I wasn't. To me, if our leaders said Nam was a necessary war, then that was good enough for me. Maybe I should have listened more. Keep in mind, Johnny, the country was split right down the middle, and it got nasty on both sides."

Johnny considered that before moving to his next question. "Uncle Nick, did you resent my dad?"

Nick was taken back. Then he gave a shrug as if to say he'd just air everything out. "Keep in mind that I was shut off from the world for five years. We didn't even know that Neil Armstrong had walked on the moon. We didn't know King and Bobby Kennedy were assassinated, or that Nixon had been elected. We didn't know anything. They finally freed us after the war in 1973, which was four years before Carter granted amnesty to your dad and the rest of the Canada bunch to come home.

"I was shocked when I learned how the anti-war movement had intensified while I was gone. And to be truthful, when I learned that Johnny had died and your father had fled to Canada, I hated your father, hated him. I swore that if I ever saw him again I would punch him in the face. No hello, no warning, just the best punch I could throw with this bad arm of mine, right to his face."

This was a much stronger reaction than Johnny expected. "So what changed?"

"Lots of things, I guess. This may sound lame, but it's the best I can do. It was a screwed up time, and when I look back, I'm just not sure who was right. Don't get me wrong, I still think we could have and should have won the war, just because we committed ourselves to do it, and we should honor our commitments. But then again when I visited The Wall, the Vietnam War Memorial in Washington..."

Nick stopped speaking and drifted off briefly. It was as though his eyes were focused elsewhere. When he came back he asked softly, "Ever been to The Wall, Johnny?"

Johnny shook his head.

"Every American should go. I've only been there once and will never go again. It was too painful. I didn't want to go at all, but Jimmy made me go with him." Nick sighed and said, "When I saw all those names on the wall I couldn't help but wonder whether it was all worth it. I get the same feeling when I work with the disabled vets. I mean, look at Vietnam today. It's doing well. I'm sure that in ten years or so, maybe by the year 2000, we'll have normal relations with them. Americans might even travel there, it's a beautiful country. So in the end, I just thought screw it; Angelo's my friend and the past is the past."

Johnny absorbed that for a minute and then said, "Can I ask one more question?"

"Sure," Nick said. But he sounded as though he'd already had enough.

"This one isn't personal," Johnny added.

"Good," Nick said. "I like to keep things loose if I can."

"Why was there so much protest against the Vietnam War and almost none for Desert Storm?"

Nick smiled. "Good question. In my opinion the biggest reason was the military draft. We had a draft during Nam and we didn't have one for Dessert Storm. The American people are much more tolerant of wars if the people fighting them are someone else's kids, kids who volunteered. We had a draft during the Civil War and there were anti-war riots then too.

"Another reason is that Desert Storm was considered to be a 'good war' with a clear purpose. Saddam's invasion of Kuwait and the dangers it posed for Saudi Arabia seriously threatened our oil supply, and Americans love their oil.

"Here's another reason. Vietnam lasted ten years. Ten years, Johnny! It took almost 60,000 American lives and left countless Americans seriously injured. Desert Storm was over in weeks and claimed relatively few lives. America didn't have much time to get mad."

Nick paused and said, "Get me a Coke, will ya please. All this talkin'..."

"Sure," Johnny said.

Johnny returned from the soda case and handed Nick the Coke. Nick unscrewed the cap, took a long swig and said. "Your old man lets me have three a day. This is my second. You'd think he'd give me more for all the work I do."

Johnny smiled and Nick resumed his story. "We could get into some academic arguments too, like Vietnam being a civil war that we should have stayed out of, but I think the other two reasons are more important."

Johnny nodded. The distinctions seemed clear.

Nick leaned forward. "Now here's another twist for you, Johnny boy. Regardless of why we fought Desert Storm, the fact is that many people felt America and its military needed a good war." Nick added.

"Needed a war? I'm not sure I get that," Johnny said.

"Prior to Vietnam, wearing an American uniform was a source of pride. After Nam, rightly or wrongly, the American military took a big dip in popularity. Sure it was still held in high esteem with many, but to most, the war was long, costly, bloody and divisive. And, of course, we lost. It hurt our national pride and sent us into a funk. It tainted our trust in government too. After all, it was our leaders who got us involved in the mess in the first place. So we took a pretty good hit and needed to restore our pride. We had lost our swagger and were trying to get it back for a long time. Reagan tried with his 1983 Grenada invasion."

"I never heard of it," Johnny said.

"It's no wonder. Grenada is a small island country in the Caribbean. President Reagan was itching to fight somebody and got his chance when American students there were caught in the middle of an internal political struggle. We sent troops and it was all over in a few days. We even fought some Cubans there, and it was good to see us win something, but it was a joke really. Then came George Bush and the invasion of Panama in 1989."

"I kind of remember that one," Johnny said. "It was the middle of my sophomore year, but I didn't pay much attention."

"Panama's leader was Manuel Noriega, who was a bad guy. He used to be on the CIA's payroll at the same time he worked against us, especially in our efforts to limit drug trafficking. Finally, Panama had an election, and he lost, but as head of the military, he nullified the election and refused to give up power. At that point Bush ordered an invasion. We used about 50,000 troops and the whole thing was over in two weeks. Again, it was good to do something right, but, you know, it wasn't as if we had saved the world or anything. Know what I mean?"

"Yeah," Johnny said. "I do. By the time I got interested, the whole thing was over. Besides, it was confusing. First this guy Noriega was our friend and then he was a bad guy."

"Anyway," Nick continued, "America needed a 'good war,' a kick-ass win over somebody that mattered. We got it in Iraq with Desert Storm. Everybody is feeling good again. Everybody loves the military. Armies are a lot like sports teams. A little bit of winning can make the blues go away."

"Yeah," Johnny said. "It seems that way."

"I wish our guys had the kind of reception when they came from Nam that guys got after Desert Storm," Nick said. "We even have heroes again- General Powell, General Schwarzkopf.

"I'm sure the country appreciates what you guys did, Nick."

Nick didn't bother to respond. He looked at the clock instead and noted that Angelo and Jimmy would be back soon.

"I'm curious, Johnny. Why this sudden interest in the military?"

""I've just been thinking about things lately. I've been thinking maybe I'd like to join up. Maybe become a Green Beret like you."

Nick was shocked. "You're going to college, Johnny. Your parents are thrilled."

"Yeah, I know. Actually, I think I want to do both. Can I do that?"

Nick got quiet. He didn't like hearing Johnny's plans before his parents did.

"Will you tell me how to become a Green Beret?"

28- Moving On

April 1992

In spite of the different paths their lives had taken, the Pac Men continued to meet at the canal every other week. Tommy was still their rum runner and proudly produced a twelve- pack of Miller Lite he lifted from a neighborhood party hosted by his parents. "The key," Tommy said, "is to stash the stuff while the party is still going on. That way, it's never missed."

Tommy passed out the beers and even Brian took one and offered a toast, "To the Pac Men!" They clinked their bottles and drank.

"So, two months until graduation," Brian said. "Bobby, are you ready for your big move to Pennco Tech?" Bobby was enrolled in an automotive program at the local technical school for the fall.

"I'm ready," Bobby said. "I can't wait to get out of high school." Then he added with less enthusiasm, "I hope I graduate."

"Don't sweat it," Brian said. "You know I'll help you with your senior paper. What's the topic again?"

"Something about T.S. Elliot," Bobby said. "I don't even know who the guy is." Then he added, "It is a guy, right?"

"Yeah," Brian said. "It's a guy. "Like I said, don't sweat it. We'll have you under the hood of a car in no time."

"Hey," Tommy needled, "Do they have frat parties at Pennco Tech?"

"Screw you, Tommy," Bobby said. "I'm doing what I want to do. What's wrong with that?"

"Nothin'," Tommy snickered. "I'm just bustin' a little. You'll be a great mechanic some day."

"I'm gonna get hooked up with a NASCAR team, maybe Dale Earnhardt's or Jeff Gordon's," Bobby said.

"Cool," Mickey said. "Maybe you'll pick up one of those Daisy-Mae chicks that hang out at the track. You know, like the girl in the cutoff jeans from the Dukes of Hazard."

"Forget Daisy-*may*," Bobby said. "I want a Daisy-*will!*" Everyone had a good chuckle.

When things quieted down Brian said, "So what about you, Mickey? How's the EMT training going?"

"Pretty good," Mickey said. He had been spending most of his spare time at the Goodwill Hose Company No. 3, a firehouse on the other side of town.

"I completed my CPR and First Aid courses, and now I'm studying for the state EMT certification test. I already go on most of the emergency medical runs. I like it and the guys at the firehouse treat me good. The trainers from the county are pretty cool too."

"Gee," Tommy said, "do they let you blow the siren on the truck?"

"Know what, Tommy? You're a real jerk sometimes," Mickey said. "Maybe a good ass-kicking would help."

Tommy wasn't fazed. It was obvious he'd been drinking long before they opened the twelve-pack. "Just kiddin' man."

"Yeah well don't, at least not with me and not about that. If you ever saw the look in people's eyes when we answer an emergency call, how desperate and scared they are, maybe you'd understand. Maybe you need to see what happens when we roll into the Emergency Room at Lower Bucks Hospital with a life threatening situation. Right, Johnny?"

"Right," Johnny said quietly, flashing back to Old Man Lombardi and his wife. "You're doin' a good thing, Mickey, a real good thing."

"Whatever," Tommy shrugged.

"What about you, Tommy?" Johnny retorted. "What's with the Slippery Rock thing?"

"I'm goin' to Slippery Rock University in September," he said proudly.

"Why Slippery Rock?" Brian asked. "It's in the middle of nowhere."

"Somebody said *Playboy* rated it the number one party school in the East or something like that," Tommy said proudly. "And last year Guns N' Roses played there. I can't wait."

"What are you going to study?" Brian asked.

"Nothin' if I can help it," Tommy quipped.

"What about your major?" Johnny asked.

"Don't have one," Tommy said. "Don't want one. They have a thing called undeclared. That's me. Did I mention that the male to female ratio on campus is almost two to one in my favor?"

"Sounds like you're all set then," Brian said, with a hint of sarcasm.

Tommy missed it. "I'm ready."

"So I guess we all know what we're doing," Bobby said. "I'm goin' to Pennco, Mickey's gonna be an EMT, Brian's goin' to MIT to be some kind of scientist or something, and Johnny's off to Penn State." He shook his head sadly. "The Pac Men are breaking up."

"I'm gonna miss you guys," Mickey said.

"Don't worry," Johnny said smiling, "Tommy will be home soon, after he flunks out."

"Hey," Tommy protested. "I have a plan. I'm gonna get a part time job."

"How's a part time job gonna keep you in school?" Johnny asked.

"I'm gonna use the money to pay someone to do my school work," Tommy said confidently, "preferably a hot girl."

"One semester," Johnny said. "Then you'll be back in good ol' Bristol."

"We'll see," Tommy said. Then he had a thought. "Hey, did I show you this?" He reached for his wallet and pulled out a fake I.D. "My cousin got it for me in Trenton. Twenty bucks. It'll get me in any bar I want."

"Looks real," Bobby said.

"That's the point my friend," Tommy said smugly.

Johnny looked at the card and shook his head. "Forget about lasting a semester; they're gonna toss your ass out of school in a month."

"Come on, Johnny. What's with this Boy Scout routine? It's like you're a cop or something."

"Just worried about you, Tommy."

"Johnny Marzo, defender of the weak. It's like you're in the National Guard or something" Tommy mocked.

"You're close, Tommy," Brian said.

Johnny shot Brian a look that said keep quiet, and Tommy noticed it. .

"What's that supposed to mean?" Tommy said.

"Never mind," Brian said. "It's no big deal."

"Bullshit," Tommy said.

"Yeah," Mickey added. "What's going on?"

"Just tell them," Brian said to Johnny. "I don't know why it's such a big secret."

Johnny shrugged. "I guess you're right. I'm joining the ROTC when I get to Penn State."

"What's that?" Bobby asked.

"It stands for Reserve Officer Training Corps. I'll train with the army a few hours a week while I'm at school, plus some summer training at Fort Knox, Kentucky."

"Sounds like a blast," Tommy said.

"Tommy, I swear, you're gonna end up in the canal tonight if you don't shut up," Johnny said.

When Tommy didn't reply, Johnny continued. "I can also take Airborne or Mountain Warfare courses and train with military units around the world. If I stick with it, I'll be commissioned a second lieutenant when I graduate."

The Pac Men were quiet. Finally, Bobby said, "You're gonna join the army? Why?"

Johnny thought for a minute and said, "I guess so I can protect guys like Tommy while he's partying at Slippery Rock."

29- Mrs. Lombardi

Things got quiet when Johnny walked into the deli. Frankie turned and poured a cup of coffee. Jimmy went back to the stock room, and Nick kept his head buried in another letter writing task. Only Angelo, who was making hoagies behind the counter, looked up.

"Hello son," he said quietly. It certainly wasn't the type of reception Johnny was accustomed to from the guys.

"Hey, Pop. What's going on?"

When no one else spoke, Angelo wiped his hands on his apron and came around the counter. "I'm afraid we have some bad news, Johnny."

Angelo took a newspaper from the counter and handed it to him. It was folded to the obituary page. Johnny hesitated and then took the paper.

"Top right column," Angelo said, placing his hand on the boy's shoulder.

Johnny's apprehension grew as he scanned the paper until he saw the name, ANGELINA LOMBARDI. "No!" he shouted, "that can't be. Not Mrs. Lombardi."

"We saw it this morning," Nick said. "Apparently she died yesterday."

"The viewing is tomorrow," Frankie said. "It's at Ralph's funeral home, and the service is Friday morning."

Johnny took a chair next to Nick. "Poor Mr. Lombardi, she was all he had."

"Sorry, kid," Frankie said. "It's really a shame."

"This will crush him," Johnny said. "They were so close."

Jimmy came in and joined the group. "Sorry, Johnny. We already chipped in for flowers from Bristol Florist. We sent them to the funeral home."

Tears welled in Johnny eyes. He scanned the obituary again. He couldn't imagine what Mr. Lombardi was going through. Then he jumped up, handed the paper to his father and said, "I gotta go."

He bolted from the store and sprinted the four blocks to Lombardi's alley. He stopped at Lombardi's gate and stood there debating what he should do next. Maybe he shouldn't visit now, he thought. Maybe Mr. Lombardi preferred to be alone. Maybe he had a house full of relatives. Johnny shrugged and then raced to the door and knocked hard. He was preparing to knock again when the door opened. When Lombardi saw him he began to cry softly. It was more of a moan than a cry. He looked broken, a far less imposing figure than the man Johnny had come to know.

"Amico mio, my friend," Lombardi said. *"Vieni, Vieni."*

Johnny stepped inside, and Lombardi locked him in a bear hug. With that, Johnny broke down and cried openly. "I'm so sorry," he said.

"Thank you," Lombardi said, regaining his composure. *"Thank you for come. Please, sit."*

The house seemed empty. Lombardi needed a shave and smelled as if he had been drinking. Johnny took his customary chair and Lombardi offered him wine. Johnny surprised himself by saying yes right away. Lombardi poured two generous glasses and put the bottle on the table between them.

Johnny was searching for something to say, but Lombardi beat him to it. *"I'm a dead man. When Angelina die, I die."*

"Don't say that," Johnny protested.

Lombardi shook his head. *"Angelina was everything to me; now she's gone. Nothing left."*

Johnny stared into his glass.

"Fifty-two years. We love each other fifty-two years."

"That's amazing," was all Johnny could manage in reply.

They sat in silence for a long time. Lombardi was slumped forward with his elbows resting on the table and his fingers massaging his temples, while Johnny searched desperately for something comforting to offer the old man.

Lombardi raised his head and smiled. *"Good wife, beautiful woman, good partner."* Then he winked. *"You know what I mean, good partner?"*

Johnny wasn't sure.

"In da bed," Lombardi smiled when he said it. *"Make love."*

Johnny felt embarrassed but forced a smile. He was relieved to see the old man's expression change.

"But no children. Very sad we can't have. Angelina heart break. She love children."

"That is very sad," Johnny said.

"Dat's why she like for you to come over so much."

"I liked coming over too, and I loved her cooking," Johnny said. "She was so good to me."

Lombardi looked at him and forced another smile. *"You uh good friend, Mr. President. Very good friend."*

Lombardi took a long pull of his wine and said, *"I tell you uh story?"*

"Sure," Johnny said, grateful that Lombardi was doing the talking. "I'd love a story." Johnny reached for his wine and leaned back in his chair.

"One day. I'm at da grocery store in Tullytown, two years after I come to America. I shop. I'm ready to leave when a girl comes in who is so beautiful I almost shit my pants. I smile, but she no smile back. Because she's there, I keep shopping. She shop, and I shop. The owner, Mrs. Mercandanti, watch me. Finally, the girl finish. When she leaves, I smile, but she still no smile back. Den Mrs. Mercandanti make it uh big joke. She ask me if I like da girl. "I said, 'I love da girl.' Mrs. Mercandanti say, 'Dat's Angelina Tangretti. She here every day at four o'clock.'

"So I go to da grocery store at four o'clock every day for da next five days. Every day, I shop and she shop. I smile, but she no smile back."

"Finally, on da fifth day I said, 'cuse-a me, but I'm broke. I can't shop every day. When you gonna smile?"

Johnny laughed and sipped his wine. "No kidding? You said that?"

"Sure, what else?"

"So then what happened?"

"So den, she laugh da most beautiful laugh I ever heard. I carry her bag home and we fall in love." Lombardi smiled at the memory and added, *"Dat was da best day of my life."* Then he fell silent and buried his head in his hands.

Johnny found himself saying, "You were lucky to have such a wonderful wife for so long."

Lombardi looked up at him. *"I know. But women make men crazy. I miss her so much. I miss everything. Da house is empty, but I see her everywhere."*

Johnny's eyes filled again. Seeing such an imposing figure reduced to such grief was much too painful. He emptied his glass and poured more wine.

Then Lombardi said, *"What about you, Mr. President? How's you girl?"*

"She's fine," Johnny said. "Jenny and I see each other almost every night."

Lombardi shook his head. *"Mr. President, please no bullshit. You know who I mean."*

Johnny looked perplexed.

"Da girl in Europe," Lombardi thundered.

"You mean Carrie?"

"Ah, dat's da one, Carrie."

"I'm dating Jenny," Johnny said without much enthusiasm.

Lombardi rolled his eyes. *"Now you piss me off. You date Jenny, you like Jenny, but you love da girl in Europe."*

Johnny averted his eyes and mumbled, "I haven't seen her in three years."

"So, what the hell you waiting for? Go see."

"I can't do that," Johnny said.

"Why?" Lombardi demanded. He sounded agitated. *"Life is short. Go see the girl."*

"I can't because I don't know how she'd react. We still write letters once in a while, but she probably has another boyfriend."

Lombardi cursed in Italian and pounded the table so hard that the wine glasses shook. Johnny was startled and sat back.

"Sorry," Lombardi said. *"Please' cuse me, too excited. "* Then he leaned forward and spoke softly. *"Mr. President, how many girls do you think you will love in uh lifetime?"*

Johnny shrugged. He was afraid to give a wrong answer.

Lombardi answered for him. *"One, Mr. President,"* he said, pointing his index finger to the ceiling. *"You love, really love, only one time."*

Then Lombardi filled Johnny's glass and said, *"Drink. We talk."*

Johnny drank deeply and Lombardi said, *"I'm disappointed. You sound like baby when you say 'maybe she has uh boyfriend.' You da boyfriend!,"* he roared. *"You have to see her and tell her."*

Johnny didn't respond at first. Then he said, "Maybe I'll tell her in a letter. Maybe I'll ask her how she really fells."

"Bullshit da letter! Face to face!" Lombardi forced himself to lower his voice again and added gently, *"If you don't go, you regret da rest of your life."*

This was hitting too close to home for Johnny and he searched for a way out. "How would I get there?"

Lombardi cursed under his breath. *"How da hell do I know? If you love da girl, swim, take da plane! Just go."*

"I can't. It's too expensive. I don't have the money," Johnny lied, remembering Brian's offer to pay for a trip.

Lombardi shook his head and finished his glass. Then he poured another. *"Stay here,"* he ordered. He left the table and returned quickly with a shoe box. He placed the box on the table and opened it. It was filled with cash.

"What are you doing?" Johnny asked.

Lombardi's eyes filled again. *"Angelina and I save to make da trip to da old country. We save two-thousand eight hundred and seventy-two dollars."* He slid the box across the table. *"Go see da girl."*

Johnny was floored. "I can't use your money!"

"Why?"

"It's not right. You and Mrs. Lombardi saved that. I can't use it. Thank you for your kindness, but please use it for yourself."

Lombardi shook his head. *"For myself? For what? New television? Tomato plants? Da money no good to me now. It make me sad. You go see da girl, dat make me happy. It make Angelina happy too. She's uh..."* He searched for the right word. *"How you say? She's uh romantic. She like dis."*

Johnny's emotions were swirling. He hated seeing his friend this way. And he hated facing his feelings about Carrie. He knew Lombardi was right. Brian had told him the same thing. But he just couldn't summon the courage to go to Europe.

Lombardi interrupted his thoughts. He reached across the table and put his usual vice grip on Johnny's shoulder. *"Mr. President, Johnny, my good friend, please make da old man happy. Please go see da girl."*

Johnny looked into Lombardi's eyes. He remembered the first time he visited the Lombardi kitchen. He remembered the old man grabbing his wife's butt and her laughing as she slapped his hand away and called him crazy. He thought about the life they must have shared together, and he wanted the same thing with Carrie.

He rubbed his eyes to clear his tears and said, "Okay, Mr. Lombardi. I'll go see the girl. Thank you."

Lombardi beamed.

30- The Odyssey

Johnny left Lombardi's and went straight to Brian's garage where he found him installing his most recent purchase of advanced computer and Internet equipment. The Internet was only just beginning to enjoy widespread use, and in a form and speed much inferior to the capabilities of Brian's system.

For the past two months, Brian had taken a break from his research on terrorist activity and was focusing on the primary elections for both parties. President Bush, who had enjoyed an eighty-nine percent approval rating following Desert Storm, had seen his popularity dip considerably by the spring of 1992 when the country entered a recession. In addition, Bush had been challenged in the Republican primaries by conservative, Pat Buchanan. Conservatives were angry with Bush for violating his "read my lips, no new taxes" pledge by negotiating a tax increase with the Democrats. There was no question that the incumbent Bush would receive the nomination, but Buchanan's challenge, coupled with the country's economic downturn, had weakened Bush considerably. On the democratic side, Arkansas Governor, Bill Clinton, was the front runner and probable nominee, but he was still locked in a battle with Governor Jerry Brown of California. Brian found both races fascinating.

"Hey, Johnny," Brian said. "You're just in time to see my new stuff."

"Hi, Brian," Johnny replied weakly.

Johnny seemed subdued and Brian noticed he was carrying the shoebox Lombardi had given him. "What's going on, man? And what's in the box?"

Johnny sat and told Brian about Mrs. Lombardi's death, his visit to the house, their long talk, and Lombardi's insistence that he use his money to visit Carrie.

"Wow!" Brian said. "That's terrible about Mrs. Lombardi."

"The poor guy is crushed," Johnny said. "I don't know how he's going to handle it."

Brian looked at the box again. "He gave you two grand?"

"Two-thousand, eight-hundred and seventy-two dollars," Johnny said softly.

"I can't believe you took it. I mean, you know, I told you I'd give you the money to go see her."

"I know, Brian. But this was different. It's tough to explain, but it wasn't like he wanted me to take it; he *needed* me to take it. I tried to say no, but in the end I just couldn't." Johnny paused and wiped his eyes. "They were saving it for a trip to Italy. Now…"

"It's okay, man," Brian said. "Sounds like you did the right thing."

"Yeah, but what do I do now?"

"What do you mean?"

"I mean I can't just go to Europe."

"Why not?" Brian asked. "Sure you can."

"I won't know where I'm going. I got an A in Spanish, but I don't know how much that will help me. I don't even know how to buy a plane ticket. And what about my parents? They're not just gonna let me go. I can't do it."

Brian thought for a while as Johnny stared at the floor. Finally, Brian said, "I've got it; I'll go with you."

Johnny looked up.

"Sure, that's it," Brian said. "I've been wanting to travel. I speak a little of this and a little of that. I can handle the travel arrangements. Heck, this can be my graduation gift to myself, to both of us." Then he smiled. "You're parents won't mind as much if they know you're going with a responsible and resourceful person like me."

Johnny started to protest, but Brian cut him off. "Shut up, Johnny. We can sell this. I'm excited. I've always wanted to see Italy. Where'd you say Carrie was, Florence? Naples?"

Johnny shook his head. "She moved again. Now she's in Germany."

"Germany!" Brian shouted. "When did that happen?"

"I hadn't heard from her for more than six weeks. I finally got a letter this weekend that said by the time her letter arrived she'd be living in Berlin. She was pretty down about it."

"Germany. Damn! I don't know much German. My Spanish is real good, which I thought would help us in Italy. The languages are similar in many ways. And my French is passable. I know a few words to get us by. You'd be surprised how much my ninth grade Latin course has helped. Latin is the root of …"

"Stop it, Brian. I'm not in the mood. I'm still not sure we should go. I feel so bad about Mr. Lombardi's money."

Johnny sat cradling the shoe box and Brian began pacing the floor. A few minutes passed before Brian broke the silence. "I've got it! You need to go to Germany, but you feel bad about taking Lombardi's money. You won't let me pay for you instead because you feel bad *not* taking his money. I've got a plan.'

"No plan," Johnny said. "We can't go."

Brian ignored him. "Remember when we visited Mr. Lombardi and he told us all about the D-Day invasion of Normandy? Remember how he was a part of it?"

"Of course I remember. He was a paratrooper. So what?"

"So," Brian said proudly. "You and I are going to fly to England. We're gonna cross the English Channel just like he did. We're gonna visit the beaches of Normandy where our troops landed. We're gonna follow the same route that the Americans and Mr. Lombardi's paratroopers followed as they liberated France and closed in on Germany. We're gonna use his money to make the same trip he made almost..." Brian paused to calculate, "almost forty-eight years ago."

Johnny looked interested, so Brian continued. "Look, he wants you to go anyway. He shoved the money at you, but you feel bad taking it. You think it's selfish to use his money to see your girl. Wait until you see his eyes when you tell him what we're gonna do on the way to see Carrie. He'll be reliving one of the most important events in western civilization, and one of the most important events of his life vicariously through you. We'll send him a post card every day. He'll track our route."

Johnny was softening to the idea but still resisted. "I don't know..."

Brian pressed on. "This won't be a vacation, Johnny. This is a mission, sort of a pilgrimage to pay honor to Lombardi and the men he served with at America's finest hour."

Johnny just sat there, shaking his head. "Know what, Brian. That's a great idea. It really is. I mean, I know Mr. Lombardi would love it. But..."

"But what, Johnny? I'll handle everything. We graduate in a month and we'll leave. I'll know enough German by then to get by. This will be great."

"Yeah," Johnny mumbled. "Until we get to Berlin."

"What's that supposed to mean?"

"It means what if Carrie doesn't want to see me? What if she has a boyfriend somewhere? What if I make an ass of myself? I can't do it."

Brian looked disgusted. He sighed deeply and said, "How old are you, Johnny?"

"Eighteen, just like you."

"How old was Mr. Lombardi when he jumped out of a friggin' airplane at two o'clock in the morning on June 6, 1944, into complete darkness behind enemy lines? How old was he when he did that *before* our troops had even hit the beaches?"

"Nineteen," Johnny said sheepishly.

Brian let the answer hang for a few seconds and then said, "To use a time-honored phrase, you, my friend, are gonna grow some balls. We're going to Europe."

31- "Hail to Thee Ol' Alma Mater…"

Final exams were pretty much a joke for the Pac Men except for Bobby whose grades were so marginal that there was a real danger of him not graduating unless he did well. As promised, Brian not only "helped" him with his senior paper, he also tutored him for each exam. In spite of that, Brian still found the time to plan the trip to Europe, order passports, and study German, which was coming easily to him.

Brian had also handled the sales pitch with Johnny's parents. Wisely, he did it when Nick, Jimmy and Big Frankie were in the deli, and they became quick allies, just as he knew they would. Nick and Jimmy loved the fact that the boys would be honoring World War II veterans, and Big Frankie just liked the idea of Johnny having fun. The Marzo's were understandably reluctant at first, but Brian convinced them that the trip was well planed. He knew it was a good sign when Donna cried as she heard the story of Mr. Lombardi's wish. Brian sealed the deal by mentioning the great cathedrals, like Notre Dame, that they would visit in France. Finally, the Marzo's relented.

At one point Brian considered paying for all the Pac Men to join them, but changed his mind. Tommy had become increasingly irresponsible and Brian was concerned about problems he might cause. Bobby was simply too nervous to undertake such an adventure, and Mickey was deeply engrossed in his training. So in the end it would be just Brian and Johnny.

One problem that troubled Johnny was how to deal with Jenny Ryan. She was a lot of fun, and he liked her a lot. She and other girlfriends before her had helped him survive his separation from Carrie. He'd always tried to be honest with the girls he dated, at least somewhat. He never let on about his feelings for Carrie, largely because he wasn't sure what they were. But at the same time, he let everyone he dated know that he was just along for a casual ride. In Jenny's case, she realized that they would be going to different colleges, Jenny to the University of Delaware and Johnny to Penn State, so she swore that she was cool with keeping things loose in their senior year. But that became harder and harder as the end of the year approached. They went to the Prom together, were inseparable on the senior class trip, and, as their final high school days approached, and all the emotions that came with them, they became more attached than they had intended.

"This is just great," Brian said. "It's hard enough that you'll soon be traveling across another continent in search of the girl you love, just like in some Hollywood movie, but now you're latching on to the proverbial girl next store at the same time. I guess it's cool, now that I think about it, as long as you don't tell either one about the other. I guess what they don't know won't hurt them."

"It's not like that," Johnny protested. "I'm not trying to hurt Jenny. I've tried to keep things causal, but I guess we've grown a little attached."

"Hey, Johnny boy, I understand. Psychologists call it separation anxiety. You're leaving high school and you want to hold on to something. Besides, Jenny's cool. She's cute, she's nice, she's smart, and she's on the track team. I love female runners with those slender, athletic bodies. They're all so healthy and fresh looking. In fact," Brian added after a pause, "know who she reminds me of?"

Johnny shot him a look. "No," Brian said. "Don't even say it."

"Sorry, buddy, but it's true. Jenny is Carrie with dark hair."

"That's crap," Johnny said.

"Sorry, but my mind is made up. I'll spare you all the deep psychological implications, but Jenny is definitely Carrie, only she's on this side of the ocean."

"You're wrong, Brian. So drop it."

Brian did, but it was clear that he had struck a nerve. He decided to change the subject. "So how's your speech coming along?"

Both Johnny and Brian would be speaking at Bristol's graduation exercises, Johnny as Student Council President and Brian as Valedictorian.

"Pretty good," Johnny said. "It's supposed to be short, like a minute or so, and Mr. Baxter has been helping me with it. How about yours?"

"I'm all finished," Brian said with a mischievous grin.

"What's that mean? Did Mr. Baxter approve it already?"

"Mr. Baxter and I had some differences of opinion about what I should say."

"So did he make you change much?"

"At first he did, and we really banged heads. Then I thought, life's too short, and I'm not going to win this argument, so I surrendered. I wrote exactly what I thought he wanted."

Johnny gave him a funny look. "Really? That doesn't sound like you."

"Well," Brian said. "Just between us, I wrote two speeches, the one Mr. Baxter approved and the one I'm actually going to give that night."

Johnny bolted forward. "Are you serious? You're gonna swap speeches?"

"Dead serious," Brian said. "It's my right; I earned it, and I'm gonna give the speech I want to give."

32- Commencement 1992

The graduation ceremony was held on the football field, which was sandwiched between the rear of the school and a high speed elevated rail line fifty yards behind it. Year after year the outdoor venue pretty much guaranteed two things: the night would be extremely muggy with a threat of thunder showers looming throughout the event, and an exceptionally long, loud train would rumble by in the middle of someone's speech. The weather proved to be true to form. As for the train, Brian hoped his speech would be spared.

The graduates were seated on a temporary stage facing the bleachers. Parents and family members were offered limited on-field seating while the overflow crowd was relegated to the bleachers.

The ceremony was standard fare. The seniors sang the National Anthem and Mr. James McCool, the Superintendent of Schools, and Mr. Baxter each delivered short but appropriate addresses. Clearly they had decided not to steal the stage on what promised to be a long night reserved for students.

Then it was time for Johnny to give his welcoming address. His main task was to announce the class gift to the school. He did a nice job thanking the teachers and administration for their work and dedication over the past four years, said a few words about how sad it was to be leaving Bristol High and how exciting it would be to face new challenges, wished his classmates good luck, and announced that the senior class would be donating over twelve hundred dollars for two new vandal-proof benches for the school courtyard. Although the speech was largely vanilla, Brian felt Johnny's diction was good, his tone and inflection appropriate, and his volume clear and strong.

Johnny's announcement was followed by an endless list of awards given by every service club and fraternal society in town, not to mention a slew of memorial scholarships given in behalf of prominent citizens or former beloved teachers. Johnny received a few leadership citations, and Brian won a truckload of achievement-based awards. In a poignant moment, Mickey was given a service award in recognition of his countless hours spent as a junior volunteer with the fire department. Even Bobby rose to thunderous applause as he was called to receive a one-hundred dollar bond as the student with the highest academic average who would be attending the local technical school. Ms. Quattrocchi, the guidance counselor reading the names of the winners, tactfully did not mention that Bobby was the only member of the senior class attending the institution.

All that remained before the awarding of the diplomas were the Salutatorian and Valedictorian speeches. Marybeth Watson, the student with the second highest academic average in the class, went first. Brian knew that Marybeth hated him, and he wasn't sure he could blame her. She was head and shoulders above any of the top classmates, except, of course, for Brian. Brian actually felt sorry for her because he knew that she took her studies very seriously, worked extremely hard, and tied herself in emotional knots over her grades. But no matter how hard she worked, no matter how much she kissed up to the faculty, she always found herself in second place to Brian. What made it even more difficult to tolerate was her knowledge that Brian didn't work nearly as hard. In fact, at times it seemed that he didn't work at all. He was simply blessed with exceptional ability that came along only rarely, and Marybeth had the misfortune to be in his class. She had developed a nervous habit of twirling her hair with her index finger which she was doing now as she walked to the podium.

Brian hoped that she would deliver a kick-ass speech, one that would knock everyone's socks off and give her the recognition she so richly deserved. But she didn't. Instead, she victimized the audience with one of those soppy, highly forgettable speeches filled with mundane references to Elmo, their sixth grade goldfish, and Butchie Meyers, the eight grader who left his egg salad sandwich in his desk for the entire Christmas vacation. The highlight of the speech came when Marybeth repainted the unforgettable image of Sally Humbright blowing lunch in the Biology lab the day the class dissected a worm. After a litany of similar stories so heart warming that half the audience was on the verge of duplicating poor Sally's upchucking, Marybeth mercifully brought the speech to a close with tearful admonitions to her classmates to never forget the good times and always remember the great Bristol High class of 1992. The audience responded with light applause, after which Tommy ripped a fart that could be heard at the top of the bleachers.

Marybeth's mush and Tommy's fart were hardly the tone Brian wanted to precede his speech, and he was grateful for the transition provided by the 7:20 Amtrak express from New York to Philadelphia that came roaring by just at the right time, preventing Mr. Baxter from introducing him for a full minute. Baxter waited until the noise subsided and the crowd settled down and then he introduced Brian.

Brian was hugely popular with his classmates and was greeted with loud and sustained applause. Throughout his high school years they had marveled at his intellect, enjoyed his humor and appreciated the help he had so freely given to any student who asked. Brian also took satisfaction for the change in the way girls viewed him. His growth spurt during the summer prior to eleventh grade had transformed him from a cute Teddy Bear type to a handsome young man. Ironically, this long-awaited change produced a new problem. Once he realized that girls were now attracted to him in the same way all girls were attracted to boys, he became shackled with an almost crushing awkwardness that was difficult to overcome. There were no books he could read to help him with this problem. For this he had to rely on his well-trained mentor, Johnny Marzo. But Brian was making progress. As he walked to the podium, his eyes met Jenny Ryan's and he gave her a wink, just in case she became available in the future.

Brian tried not to look at Mr. Baxter. He liked the guy a lot, everyone did, and he felt a twinge of guilt because he wasn't going to give the speech he and Mr. Baxter had worked on. It wasn't that the other speech was bad. Baxter had suggested a theme about the time-honored traditions of Bristol High, and how the class of 1992 would be passing the baton to the next class as the graduates moved on to new challenges, blah, blah, blah. It was typical stuff, but there were things Brian wanted to say instead, and he was going to say them.

As he prepared to speak, he was surprised to find himself thinking back to the unfortunate event in Sally Humbright's life. What Marybeth had failed to mention was that some of Sally's former lunch had landed on Bobby's shoe, and he had bolted to the rest room just in time to deposit his own macaroni and cheese with a bit more decorum. Brian stifled a laugh. Maybe Marybeth's speech wasn't so bad after all.

Finally, he was ready, and he started with the words, "Good evening." That was Mr. Baxter's first tip that something was awry. Baxter had suggested the traditional salutation, "Mr. McCool, Mr. Baxter, members of the school board, faculty, parents, friends, honored guests and fellow graduates." Brian always saw such openings as yawners and it was the first thing he scratched out. Any idiots who didn't realize he was talking to them didn't need to hear the speech anyway.

"This is a wonderful night for all of us, and I'm honored to share the stage with my fellow graduates. I promise I'll be brief because I have a feeling that some of you are eager to begin your family celebrations."

There was a soft murmur of agreement in the crowd.

"I've learned a lot during my twelve years of education. I should add that I didn't go to kindergarten because I was too small for my feet to touch the floor when seated in a desk. But that's an old problem that has thankfully passed me by."

His classmates clapped warmly at that remark.

"Anyway, I'd like to share just two experiences with you tonight, two defining moments in my life that shaped who I am and how I view the world. I'm doing so because I feel these experiences have relevance for all of us.

"The first took place on September 4, 1986. That was the first day I met my best friend, Johnny Marzo. Prior to that day, the world was not a pleasant place for me because, aside from my parents and extended family, I was accepted by virtually no one. I was bullied in school and ridiculed about my size relentlessly. Johnny changed all of that when I moved to Bristol. He guided my acceptance into a circle of friends and taught me that there were good people out there. From that day on I saw the world differently. School became a welcoming place rather than something to dread. I'll never forget how that single act of kindness changed my life. I thank Johnny deeply as well as everyone else who extended their hands in friendship."

There was warm applause from his classmates.

"I hope that each of you present tonight, and I'm speaking to the teachers as well, will be extra vigilant in protecting those who are cast aside, who don't fit in, who have no one in their corner. There are people out there who are easy to overlook, easy to miss. Because of our busy schedules, we plough through life at times never noticing they are there, never knowing that we've inflicted pain by our indifference. I also believe that the more comfortable we are with our own friendships, the less likely we are to be sensitive to those who are isolated. So I urge you to have eyes, notice those who go unnoticed, include those who are not included and take the time to care. My classmates will tell you that I am always willing to help others with their school work. That's because the single act of kindness that opened so many doors for me when I was younger taught me the value of opening doors for others. I hope each of you will do the same. Begin a cycle of kindness that will spread to others."

The audience gave its approval, and Brian noticed Mr. Baxter clapping enthusiastically. Brian hoped that his principal would still be supportive after hearing what was coming next.

"The second defining moment was not as pleasant, and I struggled with the decision over whether or not to share it tonight. But share it I must because it has gnawed at me for four years, and I may never have an audience such as this again. It occurred on December 21, 1988."

Brian paused to gather himself. "It was on that day that I learned with certainty that there is also a dark world out there, where evil lurks beneath the surface and where dangerous fanatics plot the destruction of innocent people. It was on that day that my Uncle Ray, a kind, gentle, brilliant man, an American patriot, was murdered in an explosion along with 252 other passengers and crew aboard Pam Am Flight 103 over Lockerbie, Scotland.

"It was a senseless act of destruction, part of a seemingly unending cycle of violence and retribution. The list of victims is startling: Marines on a peace-keeping mission in Lebanon slaughtered in their sleep, passengers murdered on a hijacked Italian cruise ship, Olympic athletes kidnapped and murdered in Munich for all the world to see, state department officials taken hostage in Iran and brutalized for over a year. The list is endless, and I will spare you more details tonight."

The audience seemed captivated but uncomfortable. Many felt it certainly wasn't the time or place to discuss such matters. Their facial expressions sent mixed messages. Brian expected this and didn't care.

"I share this with you this evening because I'd like all of us to take a moment to reflect upon the fact that as we enjoy this momentous occasion and prepare for well-deserved celebrations, we are being protected by countless people in our armed forces, the FBI, the CIA, the DIA, and other relevant agencies. We need to be thankful for that, but we also need to remember three things:

"First, we are at war. We may have won Desert Storm last year in classic fashion, but we are clearly at war and have been for many years. Unfortunately, the enemy is not as visible as Saddam's army was.

"Second, we need to support the efforts of those charged with protecting us and demand that our government do more as well.

"Third, and I address this mainly to my classmates: as you pursue your education and consider your careers, give some thought to serving your country in some capacity.

"I've given this last point a great deal of thought and I've decided to use the gifts God has given me to acquire the knowledge and skills necessary to defend others. I've chosen the Massachusetts Institute of Technology because I believe I will receive the kind of education that will enable me to function in the high tech world of satellite surveillance, data analysis, laser guided weaponry and whatever else is on the horizon. . I'm not sure in what capacity I will use these skills, but I promise you that I will."

He closed by adding, "I wish each of you God's blessing for a happy, prosperous and safe future. Thank you."

The audience sat in silence for several seconds, not quite sure what to do. Brian's mother, sitting in the front row, had tears streaming down her face. Teachers, parents and classmates were stunned. A reporter from the Bucks County Courier-Times, expecting to write another typically fluffy graduation piece, began writing frantically. Finally, Mr. Baxter stood and clapped. Others joined him, and soon, the entire audience was on its feet."

Brian stepped away from the microphone and slowly made his way back to his seat. It was time to call the roll of graduates.

33- LaFayette, we are here. Again!

The trip to the airport for their early evening flight was a circus. Brian rented a van and driver so that his parents, Johnny's parents, Nick, Jimmy, Big Frankie, and the Pac Men could all go along for the sendoff. At the airport, the mothers begged their sons to be careful and to write. Tommy quietly reminded his friends that there was no drinking age in France, and Bobby wondered whether French girls really didn't shave under their arms. Jimmy, Big Frankie, and Nick each slipped Johnny a twenty in case he ran short. Angelo pulled Johnny aside and reminded him to write to his mother often, while Mrs. Kelly and Brian shared a tearful word about Uncle Ray's generosity.

After they boarded, Johnny was surprised to learn that Brian had booked them in first class. But when Johnny complained about the cost, his friend cut him off.

"I've got bad news, Johnny, but I wanted to wait until we were airborne to tell you"

"What now?"

"You're not paying for anything on this trip."

"No way," Johnny protested.

"Sorry, but that's the way it is. I've had this money for a couple of years now and another chunk just kicked in when I turned eighteen. So far I haven't bought anything for myself except high tech equipment. Like I said, this is my graduation present to us. So just relax and enjoy it."

"I can't relax. It's not right. Besides, I promised Mr. Lombardi I'd use his money. . I can't use yours."

"I've thought about that. First of all, he's so excited that we're going to visit Normandy that he won't care. You saw how touched he was when we told him."

"I know he was."

"And what about that map he showed us of his trek across France into Germany? We're gonna hit some of the same towns he hit and send him a card from each spot."

"He'll love it," Johnny agreed. "But I still can't keep the money."

"That's right. So here's what I'm thinking. Why don't we do something nice with it when we get home, something appropriate that would honor Mrs. Lombardi's memory?"

Brian could tell Johnny liked the idea.

"Like what?" Johnny said.

"Well, you said Mr. Lombardi belongs to St. Theresa's Parish, right?"

"He told me he goes to 7:30 Mass every morning. That's why we never see him. It's too early. "

"You mean 7:30 every Sunday."

"No," Johnny said emphatically. "I mean 7:30 every *day*."

"Perfect. He likes church. St. Theresa's is having a drive to replace the stained glass windows. Each one costs about three thousand dollars. Donors can have a plaque placed below the window in someone's memory. How's that sound?"

Johnny smiled. He could picture Mr. Lombardi's reaction.

"That's a great idea. I think we should do it."

"I'm glad you like it. Now relax a little."

They dined on prime rib and champagne, read their travel guides until the wine caught up with them, and then fell asleep.

They landed at Heathrow and Johnny was floored when he saw a limo driver standing at the gate holding a sign that read, "Kelly."

"Are you serious?" Johnny said.

"Hey, we're only in London for one night. Why waste time looking for transportation and getting lost?"

The driver took them on a two-hour windshield tour of the city while the boys snacked in the back seat. They passed Buckingham Palace, Parliament and Big Ben, the London Bridge, the Tower of London, and St. Paul's Cathedral. They had lunch at a pub at Piccadilly Circus and then drove to Trafalgar Square. Brian had been bombarding Johnny with history all day, and after Trafalgar, Johnny had heard enough. He demanded to go to the hotel.

That night they sent their first post cards. Brian had printed multiple sets of labels for everyone back home. They wrote notes to their parents, Mr. Lombardi, the Pac Men, Nick, Jimmy, and Big Frankie. They even sent one to Mr. Baxter and Mr. Swilli. Brian brought labels for Jenny too, as he said with a wink, just in case they needed them.

They had a light dinner and went to bed. It had been a long day, and the next day would be just as busy. They rose early and traveled by taxi and train to Portsmouth where Brian had made reservations to sail to Le Harve in Northern France. They had three hours to kill before boarding, so they visited the historic dockyard.

"This is the place where the invasion all started, Johnny. Operation Overlord was planned near here at Southwick House. Try to imagine the number of ships and men in this area, the equipment, and the thousands of drums of fuel. It was the largest amphibious landing in history. And somewhere around here, just a little past midnight on June 6, forty-eight years ago, Mr. Lombardi strapped on his parachute and boarded his flight to France."

They visited the D-Day Museum near Southsea Castle, where they saw the magnificent Overlord Embroidery that took five years to make and was almost the size of a football field. It was created to commemorate the 40th Anniversary of D-Day in 1984.

They mailed some postcards from the museum and headed to the ship for their trip across the English Channel.

It was a long trip in choppy water, and both boys got sick. When they disembarked Brian said, "LaFayette, we are here. Again!"

Johnny looked puzzled. "What's that all about?"

"Remember when Swilli taught us that the Marquis de LaFayette helped us win the Revolutionary War?"

"Yeah, actually I do."

"When we sent our troops to France in World War I, our general, Blackjack Pershing, said, 'LaFayette, we are here.' Returning the favor, get it?"

Johnny nodded. "I get it."

"There's another connection you should be thinking about," Brian said. "What street does Mr. Lombardi live on?"

Johnny brightened. "LaFayette Street."

"Bingo!" Brian said. "We've got that whole string of streets in Bristol named after presidents, and right in the middle of them is LaFayette Street."

"Nice gesture," Johnny said.

"So, we helped France in World War I, named a street after the Marquis, and helped France again in World War II. I'd say we've paid our debt."

"Yeah, I guess we did."

Brian knew the law prohibited someone his age from renting a car, so he bought one instead. He paid cash for a used Peugeot from a dealer in Le Harve. After some quick paperwork, they were on their way.

"Are you nuts?" Johnny said. "You just bought a car!"

"Yeah, for the equivalent of two-thousand American dollars. We'll use it now and sell it when we leave. It might be cheaper than renting, and we can't rent anyway. You just get used to the maps and let me worry about the car."

They headed southwest from Le Harve, crossed the Normandy Bridge over the Seine River and continued west along the beautiful Normandy coast. It was cool being in France. They passed the beaches codenamed Sword, Juno and Gold, where the British and Canadian forces landed during the invasion, and they drove on to Omaha Beach where Americans landed at Point du Hoc. The site was incredible. The long beach was bordered by high cliffs that American Rangers had to scale while German defenders fired down at them from their entrenched positions. Two hundred and twenty-five Rangers attacked the cliffs on June 6, but only ninety had clawed and fought their way to the top. Had the Americans not taken the cliff, the massive German artillery behind them would have threatened the success of the invasion and inflicted countless more allied causalities.

The boys toured the German bunkers and saw the system of tunnels that connected them. The place was eerily peaceful now, but they tried to imagine what it must have been like for the Americans to approach the beach in small landing craft rocked by choppy seas. They imagined the soldiers' fear, knowing that German machine gunners would open fire as soon as the landing ramps dropped. They imagined hitting the beach and seeing nothing but the imposing cliffs before them, cliffs they had to scale under impossible odds. The postings stated that over 2,000 Americans died that day in the fierce fighting on Omaha Beach. That was more than ten times the total American combat deaths in the Persian Gulf War that ended the year before.

Next they went to the American Cemetery at Colleville Saint Laurent, located on a high point overlooking Omaha Beach. The boys were staggered by what they saw. Thousands of white crosses, interspersed with white Stars of David, flowed in perfect rows over one-hundred and seventy two acres. The postings stated that over nine-thousand Americans were buried there. Most had died at Normandy and in the fighting that took place in the weeks to come. The graves faced westward, toward the homes across the Atlantic to which these men would never return. Johnny tried to imagine what it must have been like when news hit the United States that the invasion was a success, the beachhead was established, and the long, difficult final push to rid Europe of the Nazi menace had begun. He thought about the relief the country must have felt and the prayers of thanksgiving offered. Then he thought about the grief of the thousands of families in the ensuing days as they received word that their loved ones had died.

The boys visited the 22-foot high bronze statue titled "The Spirit of American Youth Rising from the Waves," which stands in the open arc of the cemetery's memorial. It was a soaring image, depicting the strength and vitality of the young men who fought there. Johnny thought again of Mr. Lombardi who had been the same age as he and Brian when he jumped out of the plane.

The boys left the cemetery and walked back to the car in silence.

They drove west, away from the coast, in the direction of Saint Mere-Eglise, the first town liberated by allied paratroopers during the invasion. The 82nd and 101st Airborne, including Mr. Lombardi's unit, dropped there behind enemy lines just before 2:00 A.M. on June 6th in hopes of surprising the Germans and cutting off a potential troop reinforcement route.

Unfortunately, a building had caught fire that evening and the flames illuminated the sky. With much of the town out fighting the fire, the element of surprise was lost and the Germans were able to fire at the helpless paratroopers as they made their slow descent. The Americans suffered heavy causalities, but they took the town and cut off the access route.

The boys found a small inn near the center of town run by a couple who looked to be in their mid- seventies. They used their passable

French to inquire about a room. The woman smiled and replied in broken English, "American?"

"Yes," Brian said.

Her husband's English was much better, and he welcomed them. "Many Americans visit Sainte Mere-Eglise, so we've learned the language. Two weeks ago the town was full for the 48th anniversary of the invasion. This is a better time to visit."

He pointed them to a shaded veranda where some small tables were arranged. "You must be hungry. Please go sit. I'll take your bags to our best room and my wife will get you something to eat."

The boys went outside, grateful for the chance to relax. The veranda overlooked a large garden with tomato plants, bean stalks, and grape vines clinging to a faded trellis.

Soon the woman arrived with a wedge of cheese, grapes, sliced tomatoes, and bread that smelled as though it had just been baked. She returned a minute later with a bottle of dark red wine and three glasses and then disappeared.

The man joined them and introduced himself as Jean-Henri, and the boys invited him to sit. "I hope you are comfortable," he said.

"Very," Brian replied.

Jean-Henri smiled. "The cheese is a product of this part of the country. Perhaps you would like a different type?"

"Oh no," Johnny said. "This is great."

"It's very good," Brian added. "And the bread is delicious."

"My wife bakes every day. We always have fresh bread for our guests." Then he looked at the wine bottle. "The wine is my gift to you. May I share a glass?"

"Certainly," Brian said. "Did you make it?"

Jean-Henri smiled. "Of course, everyone makes wine."

He filled their glasses and they drank. "After you rest, you must visit the square. There is a museum there and a church you must see. I was twenty-four when the Americans came, part of the French underground, the resistance. They liberated the town from the bastard Germans, and we joined them to drive the Germans out of France. Sainte Mere-Eglise will never forget."

"A friend of ours was in the 101st Airborne," Johnny said.

"Ah, the Screaming Eagles!" Jean-Henri bellowed.

"You know of them?" Johnny asked.

"We will never forget them. Most of the troops that landed here were from the 82nd, but the 101st was here also."

They chatted a while longer until the wine added to the boys' fatigue and they went to their room to nap. Later that evening Jean-Henri took them to the Airborne Museum. It was closed, but Jean-Henri found the caretaker who was more than happy to let them in. When Brian tried to tip him, the caretaker refused.

The museum contained an actual DC-3 aircraft used on D-Day, a glider, a full replica of a paratrooper's uniform, and several other artifacts. They left the museum and walked to the church, where they were surprised to see a parachute hanging from the steeple. Jean-Henri told them the story of John Steel, a paratrooper, whose chute became stuck on the steeple during his decent, leaving him helpless. He pretended he was dead while a battle raged all around him. He lived to tell the story, and the parishioners kept the memory alive.

But it was inside the church that the boys saw the most interesting thing of all. Jean-Henri pointed out two stained glass windows. One depicted the Blessed Mother surrounded by paratroopers. It was a most unusual sight, but one that conveyed the appreciation of the people of Sainte Mere-Eglise. The other was of Sainte Michael, who Jean-Henri explained was the patron saint of paratroopers.

That night the boys wrote more cards to their friends and families. Johnny wanted to write a long letter to Mr. Lombardi. His emotions were swirling, and there was so much he wanted to say. But in the end he wrote:

> *Dear Mr. Lombardi,*
> *We visited Omaha Beach and Sainte Mere-Eglise today. I'm speechless. We'll talk when I get home.*
> *Johnny*

As the boys prepared to leave town the next morning, Jean-Henri's wife gave them a small basket of cheese, bread and fruit for the trip. A handful of residents gathered to see them off. As they headed east to follow Mr. Lombardi's route, Brian could still see them waving in his rearview mirror. Brian turned to Johnny and said, "Know something,

Johnny? American conceptions about the French people just aren't true, at least not these French people." Then he added, "Get the map out. We're heading for Germany."

Germany, Johnny thought, and Carrie.

34- *Oh My Sweet Fraulein Down in Berlin Town ...*

They entered the third country in their European tour and Johnny reflected on the trip thus far. He had marveled at the sights in London and was deeply moved by his experiences at Normandy. But now, as they crossed the German countryside, he became uneasy.

He ignored his surroundings and focused entirely on seeing Carrie and rekindling their relationship. It was an undertaking he feared would fail, and he approached it with considerable trepidation. Brian's attempts to cheer him by repeatedly singing Ricky Nelson's *Traveling Man* didn't help. Each time Brian sang: "Oh my sweet Fraulein down in Berlin town makes my heart start to yearn..." Johnny punched him on the arm.

During their first night in Frankfurt, Brian had laid out the plan. "We're gonna send Carrie a letter telling her that you're touring Europe and will arrive in Berlin by late Friday night. You're gonna ask her to meet you in a public place at noon the next day."

"Why not her house?" Johnny asked.

"Listen, Johnny. You and Carrie have been apart for three years, and we don't know what she's been up to. She may see you and say, 'Let's get married tomorrow.' Or she may be in love with another guy. You have to anticipate that. The thing is, whatever she's dealing with will be complicated enough without including her parents. I don't think her mom and dad miss you. In fact, they'll see you as someone who will complicate her life, and they'll definitely lobby against you. So keep them out of it for now."

"Okay," Johnny said. "Makes sense."

"There's one more thing. You have to face the possibility that she won't show up, and you'll know what that means."

Johnny nodded. "I'm really nervous, Brian. I'm glad you're gonna be there."

Brian put his hand on Johnny's shoulder. "Wrong, Johnny-boy. I'm not gonna be there. "

"What are you talking about? You have to come!"

"I'd stick out like a sore thumb. You guys need to be alone; you have a lot of catching up to do."

Johnny shook his head. "This is all a big mistake. I should have told her I was coming."

"I don't think so. You've got too much riding on this. If you told her you were coming, she might have politely wiggled out of it. Whatever decisions you guys make have to be made face to face."

"I bet she has a boyfriend," Johnny added.

"Who's the most perfect, wonderful girl you know?"

"Carrie."

"So do you think you're the only one who's discovered that? Of course she has a boyfriend. Your best hope is that she's had so many competing for her that she hasn't settled on one. You're here to remind her, in person, that her choice should be you."

"I'm sure she's already made her choice," Johnny said dejectedly.

Brian paused, searching for something to add. Then he said, "Hey, Johnny. Do you have a girlfriend?"

Johnny didn't answer.

"Come on, man. Answer the question. Has Jenny been your girl?"

"Yeah, sure. I guess she has."

"Great girl, right?"

"She's terrific," Johnny said.

"And if you had to choose between her and Carrie right now, what would you do?"

"That's a dumb question. I'm in Germany aren't I?"

"Exactly. And that's the thought you need to bring into your meeting with Carrie. She's gonna have a guy or two in her life; bet on it. But, hopefully, she'll drop them when she sees you're back in the game."

"I'm nervous," Johnny mumbled.

"Damn right you are. But you've been through this stuff before. Football games, tomato raids, you've always liked to be on the edge, remember?"

"Yeah, but this is tougher."

Brian selected the Neptune Fountain at Alexanderplatz as the meeting place. It was an enormous plaza adjacent to one of Berlin's largest transportation hubs. The fountain was a popular rendezvous spot for couples.

Johnny arrived at ten minutes to twelve. He had hoped that Carrie would be there first, but when he circled the fountain she was not to be found. Johnny waited, doing all he could to appear calm. He watched as others arrived, couples happy to see each other. They exchanged hugs and walked off together to enjoy their day.

Noon passed and there was still no sign of Carrie. He reached in his pocket and pulled out a stack of coins. He had one for each of his parents, the guys at the deli, Old Man Lombardi and the Pac Men. His Uncle Nick had given them to him with the suggestion that he toss them into a fountain for good luck. "There are fountains all over Europe," Nick had said. "Find a good one and toss these in. You'll be leaving pieces of Bristol behind."

Sadly, Johnny knew now that he would be leaving a piece of himself as well. He had traveled over four thousand miles to see Carrie again, to make his move to re-enter her life, knowing all along that it would probably end badly. He had at least expected a face to face meeting, but it wasn't to be.

He checked his watch. It was twelve seventeen. Slowly, he began flipping the coins into the water, naming them for the people he cared about as he released them. He'd be going back to them soon, back to where he belonged. When he got to his last coin, his own, he heard a familiar voice behind him say, "It's a beautiful fountain, isn't it?"

Johnny's heart leaped. Carrie had approached him from behind the first time they had spoken in high school, and her voice was unmistakable now. His hand shook as he tossed the last coin. Without turning he said, "Yeah, it is."

"The statue at the top represents Poseidon, the Greek God of the Sea." she said. "The four women surrounding him represent the four great German rivers: Elbe, Oden, Rhine and Vistula."

"Four women, huh." Johnny said. "One is all you need if it's the right one."

He turned to face her and was speechless. The girl he had known had become a woman, even more beautiful than he imagined and far more so than the photos she had sent over the years. Her hair was still blond, although a shade darker, and her clothing gave her a distinctly European look. She smiled as naturally as ever, stuck out her hand and said, "Hi, I'm Carrie Boyle."

Johnny took her hand lightly and said, "I'm Johnny Marzo."

"You certainly are," she said. She pulled him toward her, and they shared a long, tender kiss. Johnny remembered the last time their lips had met. It was the day she left for France. He remembered how their tears had blended as their cheeks touched. Carrie made him promise that day that they would be together again. They were now, but this time sharing tears of joy.

When they parted, Carrie said, "It's so good to see you. I'm sorry I was late. I was so afraid you'd leave that I ran the last two blocks."

"I'm here," Johnny said. "And I can't believe I waited so long to come."

Carrie smiled. "Do you have any plans today, Johnny Marzo?"

"No. I think I'm free."

"Great," she said, draping her arm around his. "Then let me show you my new city."

They crossed the plaza and strolled along Unter den Linden, a broad boulevard separated by a wide, tree lined pedestrian thoroughfare. It was a beautiful summer day, and flowers and foliage were in full bloom.

"That," Carrie said, pointing to a large, elevated statue, is Fredrick the Great. As you can tell by his name, he was one of the revered rulers of Germany. He lived in the seventeen hundreds and died one year before the United States Constitution was written."

"You know a lot for someone who hasn't been here that long."

"You learn to adapt quickly when you move as often as I do. Absorbing a city's culture helps keep me sane."

"It must be hard to move so much," Johnny said.

"Awful would be a good word." For the first time Carrie's smile faded, but she recovered quickly.

"Look around you, Johnny Marzo," she said, extending her arms wide. "You are standing in the middle of Humboldt University, one of the finest schools in all of Berlin, all of Germany actually. And I am enrolled to study here in the fall."

"No kidding?" Johnny said. "You're going to a German college?"

"Europe is much more diverse than the United States. People speak multiple languages. I'm not fluent in any, but I'm passable in French and Italian, and I'm working on German. There are many English speaking professors here, and several courses are taught in English. I'll be fine."

"Wow," Johnny said.

As you can see, Unter den Linden runs right through the campus. I like an urban setting, so I'm sure I'll like it here."

They continued along the walkway past the Russian, Hungarian and British embassies, and Johnny was beginning to like the city.

"Straight ahead is the Brandenburg Gate, the most recognizable landmark in all of Germany. The Berlin wall ran right in front of where we are now until it was demolished three years ago."

"Cool," Johnny said.

"Just beyond the Brandenburg Gate is the Tiergarten. It's kind of like the Central Park of Berlin. That's where we'll relax and have lunch."

They stopped at a small shop and purchased cheese, apples and a bottle of wine. They found a shady spot in the park and Carrie produced a thin blanket from her shoulder bag and spread it on the grass.

"The trees that lined the street were Linden trees," Carrie said. "Hence the name, 'Under the Linden.'"

"They're beautiful," Johnny said. "And so are you."

Carrie smiled and squeezed his arm. "Thank you, my strong, handsome football hero from across the Atlantic. You've aged well yourself."

"Thanks," Johnny said. "I don't know about the football hero part though."

"Let's see," Carrie said. "Twelve unassisted tackles in the Lower Moreland game. Two fumble recoveries at Jenkintown. Team leader in sacks. First team All- League honors. Should I go on?"

Johnny laughed. "Where'd you get that stuff?"

"Remember how hysterical I was the day we moved to France?"

"I'll never forget it," Johnny said.

"Well, one of the things my parents did to placate me was subscribe to the *Bucks County Courier Times*. We've kept the subscription ever since. I get the paper a few days late, but I'm pretty well informed. It's a good thing, since you were too modest to tell me in your letters."

"Wow. The Courier-Times in Germany. It's a small world," Johnny said.

"I wish it were," Carrie replied. "I've missed you."

He kissed her again, and the years of their separation melted away.

They snacked and talked for hours about the past three years. Johnny was fascinated by the changes Carrie faced each time her family moved, and Carrie enjoyed hearing about Johnny's transformation from prankster and academic deadbeat to student leader and scholar.

Each carefully avoided references to other relationships, nor did they mention their future together. They were having a wonderful time, and neither wanted to break the mood. There was one awkward moment when Carrie inquired about Brian.

"He's great," Johnny had said. "You know him. He wanted us to be alone today, so he planned a full day of museum tours. But I told him the three of us will definitely get together tomorrow."

Johnny sensed a change in Carrie's demeanor when he mentioned tomorrow, but it passed quickly, and he shrugged it off.

It was a warm but comfortable day. They finished the wine and drifted off to sleep in each other's arms. Johnny awakened to Carrie's gentle stroking of his arm.

"Tired, Johnny Marzo?"

"Comfortable," Johnny said. "I want to stay right here forever. But we'll need more wine."

"I'm hungry," Carrie said. "Germany isn't known for its food, but there's a nice place not far from here with outdoor tables. Want to try it?"

"Sure," Johnny replied. "Show me the way."

They left the park and headed north in the direction of the Reichstag to a small restaurant and found a table outside.

"That's the Reichstag," Carrie said. "It's the former German parliament building. Hitler's Nazis supposedly burned it in 1933 and blamed the deed on the communists to help him gain power. It's being refurbished now."

"I don't care," Johnny said lightly. "Brian's already given me all the history I need for one trip. I just want to enjoy being with you for as long as I can."

Carrie looked concerned again, but said brightly, "Hey, we're in Germany. Let's order some beer and bratwurst."

"You're the tour guide," Johnny said.

They placed their order, and Johnny reached across the table to take her hand. He couldn't put off talking about the future any longer.

"I have an idea. Why don't you tell Humboldt University you've made other plans and enroll at Penn State. It would be great."

"It would," Carrie replied. "But I can't. My parents would never approve of my going to school so far away."

She saw Johnny's disappointment and changed the subject. "You haven't told me much about what you're going to do there. What will you major in?"

"I'm not sure," Johnny said. "I'm officially undeclared right now."

To brighten things she said, "I could visit you, Johnny. I could fly in for long weekends. My parents can afford it, and they at least owe me that."

Johnny smiled. "That would be a good start. But we'd have to plan it. Some of my weekends are already booked. I've joined the ROTC. When I graduate, I'll be an officer in the United States Army."

Carrie stiffened and eased her hand away. "Why would you want to do that?"

Johnny was surprised by the question. "I'm not sure. I want to serve my country, I guess."

"Most people in Europe don't approve of the American military," she said. "I mean, they appreciate what the Americans did in World War II, and the help they gave afterwards. They love America, but they feel the United States is too willing to use its might around the world and poke its nose where it shouldn't."

Johnny was surprised by her tone. "We just liberated Kuwait from Saddam's invasion last year."

"Right," Carrie replied, "and Europe helped. But it wasn't for any noble cause. We did it for the oil."

Their beers arrived and both welcomed the break in the conversation.

"Cheers," Carrie said, as she raised her glass to his.

They drank and Johnny said, "That's a lot better than the stuff we drink at the canal."

Carrie smiled. "Bad boy Marzo. Speaking of the canal, how are the Pac Men?"

Johnny gave her a quick rundown of how the guys were doing and ended with Brian. "Speaking of Brian, what should the three of us do tomorrow?"

Carrie lowered her head and didn't respond.

Johnny noticed. "Carrie? What's wrong?"

When she looked up her smile was gone. "Johnny, I have a problem."

Johnny remained silent and waited for her to continue.

"I'm having a visitor tomorrow. If I had more advanced notice that you were coming, I would have changed my plans and told him not to come. But…"

"Him?" Johnny interrupted.

"His name is Emilio. And he's on a train right now coming from Italy. I'm really sorry, but I don't know what to do."

Johnny felt his chest tighten. "From Italy? You guys must be tight."

"Come on Johnny, don't do this. You and I haven't seen each other for three years. Surely you've dated people in that time."

"This sounds like more than dating. The guy's coming from Italy for God's sake. Things must be pretty serious." Johnny hated sounding jealous, but he couldn't help it.

"They're not, at least not the way you think. We have a relationship, but it's not a commitment. I'm with you today aren't I?"

Their food arrived and Johnny said, "I guess I should stop taking you to dinner. Bad things happen when I do."

"This has been a beautiful day, Johnny, one I've dreamed about for a long time."

Johnny turned bitter. "I thought it was too. But all the while you knew you had this guy coming. You're kissing me knowing you'll be kissing him tomorrow."

"Now you're not being fair," she protested. "You drop in out of the blue after three years and somehow it's my fault because I have a life. I wasn't thinking about him today, I was happy to be with you. I just don't know what to do about this mess. I feel so bad."

Johnny's tone softened. "Don't worry. I'll make it easy for you. Brian and I will head out tomorrow, maybe tonight."

"No!" Carrie shouted loud enough for the other diners to hear. "No," she repeated more quietly and reached for his hand. "I don't want you to do that."

"Look, Carrie, I'm sorry I messed things up. I should have called you earlier. But I hope my being here tells you how much you mean to me. As soon as I heard your voice today, it made the whole trip worthwhile. I love you, Carrie. I know that now. I knew you'd have other guys in your life, but I didn't think you'd be this involved. I need to get home."

He put some money on the table and stood to leave. Carrie was crying now.

"Listen, Johnny. I like Emilio. I don't deny that. But you can't turn my life upside down in one day and expect me to know how to handle it. After just a short time with you today, it seemed like we were never separated. I don't want to lose that again."

"I'll write to you, Carrie. Give my best to Emilio." He turned to leave.

"Stop!" Carrie shouted again. "You are not going to walk away. I won't let you."

"Sorry, Carrie, but I have to go."

Carrie wiped her eyes. "Look at me, Johnny Marzo."

He did.

"Tomorrow at noon I'll be at the fountain, and Emilio will be with me. If you care about me, you and Brian better be there too."

"Are you serious? What will the four of us do, go bowling together?"

"No. But this is my way of saying that I want to work this out."

Johnny stepped away and said, "I don't think so, Carrie. Bye."

As he walked away Carrie called after him, "Twelve o'clock, Johnny. I'll be there."

35- Packing Bags

"You're pissed at me aren't you?" Brian asked.

Johnny shrugged and unzipped his suitcase.

"I know you are. You think we should have warned Carrie that you were coming."

Johnny opened a drawer and started packing.

"You think if I didn't talk you into it none of this would have happened, right?"

"I'm not mad," Johnny said. "Now please shut up and start packing. The sooner we leave this city the better."

"Would you just listen to me for a minute?"

"I already did, remember. Now I just want to go home."

Brian sat on the bed and watched Johnny fill one suitcase and start on another. When Johnny asked him again to pack, Brian said, "I'm not leaving."

Johnny stopped and looked at his friend. When he spoke, he was controlled but clearly angry. "Listen, Brian. I owe you a lot, and I really appreciate what you've done for me. I really do. But I've had it with this trip and I'm going home. I don't need your car or your plane ticket. I've got my own money, and I'm flying out of Berlin on the next flight I can book. If you want to come, that's fine. If not, I'll see you when I see you. Got it?"

Brian didn't respond.

Johnny went to the bathroom, returned with his shaving kit and found Brian still sitting on the bed. "Damn it, Brian. I'm not kidding. Get a move on."

"I told you," Brian replied calmly, "I'm not going, and you're not either."

"Watch me," Johnny said.

Brian waited a short time and said quietly, "I hid your passport."

Johnny looked in his travel bag and confirmed his passport was missing. "Now you are pissing me off, Brian. Give me the passport!"

"Five minutes," Brian said. Just give me five minutes and if you still want to leave I'll go with you."

"I've had enough Kelly logic for one trip."

"Just five minutes, Johnny. Then we'll do whatever you want."

Johnny sighed and sat on the bed across from him. He looked at his watch. "Okay, five minutes."

"First of all, you had a great day today."

"Yeah, I did," Johnny said. "And a rotten, stinkin, miserable night."

Brian ignored the comment. "You learned today that your feelings for Carrie are as strong as ever."

"Which just makes it worse knowing about this Emilio guy."

"You think it would have been better to tell her you were coming, but it wouldn't. If you told her, she would have either made up an excuse for you not to come or she would have told him not to come. Either way, you wouldn't have known about the guy. And now you do."

"Right, now I do, and I'm going home."

"Let's talk about tomorrow because I think it might be a good opportunity."

"Are you serious?"

"Listen, she's willing to show you off in front of him. That's gotta tick him off, right?"

"And she's gonna show him off in front of me. And that ticks me off. Let's leave."

"If you leave, he wins. If you stay, things get messy. There'll be some friction between them. Look at it his way. He took a train all the way from Italy to spend a day with his girlfriend and her old boyfriend is here. It's beautiful."

"It stinks. Let's go."

"What do you have to lose, Johnny?"

"My time. My pride. My sanity."

"I know you're mad at me and not listening to what I'm saying, so let me ask you this. If you asked your dad, or Nick, or Old Man Lombardi whether you should go home or stay and fight for the girl you love, what would they say?"

Johnny got quiet.

"We traveled four thousand miles. I don't think you're gonna have too many chances. It's crunch time. Stay Johnny. I don't know what will happen, but I know you'll regret it for a long time if you don't take a shot."

36- Poseidon Adventure

As they approached the fountain, Johnny said, "Okay, you talked me into this, but I still don't have any idea what we're doing."

"To tell you the truth, I don't either," Brian said.

"I don't think I've heard you say that before."

"Sorry," Brian replied, "I'm stumped. But I just think we should meet them."

"I'm hurting inside, Brian, real bad. But the more I think about it, the more I need to do something. I can't let things end this way. So we'll give it a shot. Besides, I feel a little tingle of excitement about this. It's the way I used to feel before I became responsible. The new me is kind of boring. I miss the thrill of ... I don't know, conflict, adventure, I guess."

"Okay," Brian said. "Then go with your gut. Just let things rip and see what happens."

As they got closer to the fountain, Brian saw her first. "Well this is interesting, Carrie is here, but she's alone"

"The guy must be here somewhere."

"Maybe," Brian said, "but she looks alone to me."

Carrie looked up and ran to meet them. Without speaking, she threw her arms around Johnny's neck and kissed him. "You came," she said. "I was so afraid I wouldn't see you again."

She turned to Brian and gave him a hug and a kiss on the cheek. "It's so good to see you, Brian." She eyed him up and down. "You look great. What happened to the little guy I knew?"

"Nature finally kicked in, I guess. You look pretty good yourself."

"Don't lie, Brian. I look awful."

Carrie was right. Her eyes were red and puffy from crying, and she looked as though she hadn't slept.

She took each of them by the hand and led them to the rim of the fountain. "Let's sit," she said. "It's hot and the mist feels good."

"Aren't we missing someone?" Johnny said.

"Yes," Carrie said. "Emilio wouldn't come."

"To Germany?" Brian asked hopefully.

"No, he arrived at nine this morning. I met him at the station, but when I explained the situation over breakfast, he got angry and refused to come here."

Brian stifled a smile. Johnny caught his eye and knew what he was thinking. "So," Johnny said, "what exactly is the situation that you explained?'

"The situation is that this is a complicated mess," Carrie said.

Johnny exhaled deeply. "Let me make it easier. Do you want me out of your life?"

"No!" Carrie said, grasping his arm. "Absolutely not. Yesterday was…yesterday was wonderful."

"For most of the day," Johnny replied. "It's not like you're just dating someone. This guy came all the way from Italy to see you. That tells me it's much more than a casual relationship."

Carrie stood to face both of them. She gathered her thoughts and said, "Please try to understand. This moving around is awful. I don't care how much money my father makes. It's ruining my life. It's easier for my parents because they have each other. But when I move to a new city, I have to start fresh every time. Just when I was making friends in France and feeling comfortable, we moved to Copenhagen, where I knew no one. Before I could get my feet on the ground there, we were off to Italy. You have no idea what that is like. I needed someone I could hold on to. I don't know if it was because I really cared about him or because he offered stability. I mean, I won't lie. I do care for him. I like him. We've had fun. But he's not you." Her eyes began to fill again, and both boys felt sorry for her.

"So did you meet this guy in school or what?" Johnny asked.

"No," Carrie said sheepishly. "He's older."

Johnny knew he shouldn't ask, but he had to. "How much older?"

She looked embarrassed. "He's twenty-four."

Johnny exploded. "Twenty-four! Jesus. You just graduated from high school. How can a twenty-four year old guy date a high school student?"

"It's different here, Johnny. That doesn't mean as much. Besides, I'm almost nineteen, and I'd like to think I'm mature for my age."

"So where did you find this guy?"

"At a meeting. Right after we moved to Italy, I saw a poster for an environmental group that was forming. Kind of like a Greenpeace affiliate. I'd been active with an environmental group in France, and I wanted to fit in, so I decided to go. Emilio was one of the organizers, and he welcomed me. As we started to work together, we became friends, got involved in other causes, and eventually started dating."

Johnny sat quietly, just shaking his head.

"See, that's what I want you to understand. I think I was just infatuated by his commitment to causes I value. At least it started that way. Can you see that makes a difference?"

"That's a nice story about how it started," Johnny said. "It's where it went from there that has me wanting to pack and go home."

"Back off, Johnny," Brian said, gently. "The girl is upset, and she's trying to be honest."

Johnny got quiet.

"So what does this Emilio do?" Brian asked.

Carrie knew this answer wouldn't go over well either. "He's an artist. He paints modern art."

"Modern art," Johnny sneered. "Doesn't that mean he can't paint?"

"Come on, Johnny," Carrie pleaded. "I'm trying here. He's sold a few paintings."

"Sorry," Johnny said. "So he just paints all day?"

"Well, he's an artist and an activist."

"An activist?" Johnny said. "What the hell is an activist?"

Carrie was growing tired of Johnny's tone and replied more assertively. "He organizes people. He champions causes like the environment, the world-wide AIDS epidemic, malaria in Africa, land mines maiming children, World Bank loans to third world countries, war refugees. These are causes I believe in too."

Johnny considered a wise crack but thought better of it.

Carrie went on. "Before I left Italy, I attended a rally with Emilio to protest American nuclear weapons on Italian soil. There were hundreds of us there."

Now Brian jumped in. "Those nukes are there to protect Italy. They're part of the NATO defense system."

"Protect Italy from whom?" Carrie said. "The Cold War is over. Does anyone really think the Russians are going to launch nuclear weapons at Italy? Why would they do that?"

"You have to be prepared," Brian said. "It's a dangerous world."

A heavily accented voice said, "Sometimes protections from friends are more dangerous than threats from enemies."

"Emilio!" Carrie said, putting her hands to her mouth.

Johnny disliked him immediately. He was slender, of average height, with dark, shoulder-length hair. He wore a male purse on his shoulder. Johnny decided he fit his image of what an artist-activist would look like, whatever that meant.

"I came for you," he said to Carrie. He put his arm around her shoulder and kissed her forehead. Johnny felt his muscles tighten. That's one, he thought.

"I think you've had enough time to talk," Emilio said smugly. "It's time to go."

Carrie moved to a more neutral position. "I thought maybe all of us could talk."

Emilio frowned. "For what purpose?"

"I'm not sure," Carrie stammered. "I don't know what to do. I'm a little confused right now. I thought seeing the two of you together might help."

"Like a competition?" Emilio said. "This is silly and has lasted long enough," he said smugly. "You had some uninvited visitors. You paid your respects, and now we should go."

Brian tried to ease the tension. "Look, none of us likes seeing Carrie so upset. We should talk. We're all adults here."

Emilio snickered. "Are we?" He turned to Carrie again. "It's not your job to entertain these boys on their little adventure." He had emphasized the word "boys."

That's two, Johnny thought.

The conflict was too much for Carrie, and she started to cry.

"Typical American arrogance," Emilio said, as he looked Johnny straight in the eye. "You come here and intrude on Carrie's life. You throw your weight around just like your government does and expect everyone to conform to your wishes."

"You seem to have a problem with America," Brian said.

"I have a big problem with its war machine, its meddlesome foreign policy, and Americans in general."

"Carrie's an American girl," Brian said.

"Carrie is a woman," Emilio corrected him. "She's a woman with many more experiences and a much broader view of the world than others from your country."

"You need to read your history, pal," Brian said. "You might learn that Italy wasn't too happy under Mussolini and Hitler. I think you have a lot to thank us for."

"Ancient history," Emilio said. "Today, you drink the world's oil, pollute its environment, and exploit its third world workers. It's no wonder that the world hates you."

Carrie interjected. "Hate's a pretty strong word, Emilio."

"It's the appropriate one," Emilio snapped.

Johnny was losing his patience. He had never heard anyone snap at Carrie like that.

"You wonder why people bomb your embassies and attack your citizens," Emilio said. "Just look at your record in the world."

Carrie thought of Brian's uncle and said, "Emilio, I've never heard you talk that way before." She was almost hysterical now.

"It's the truth, Carrie."

Johnny shot a look at Brian who was visibly upset. "Innocent people die in those attacks," Brian said softly.

Emilio was ranting now. "Can anyone be innocent when they embrace such disastrous policies?"

"Women and children die in those attacks," Brian mumbled. "Good people die."

Emilio started to respond, but Johnny stepped toward him and cut him off. "Okay," Johnny said. "We've heard enough. You're upsetting my friend and my girl. It's time you got quiet."

"Your girl?" Emilio laughed. "That's hardly the case."

Johnny looked at Brian. "That's three," he said. It sounded as though he was asking for permission.

"Would everyone please stop!" Carrie screamed. "Please!"

"Watch, Carrie. I think your American friend is going to hit me." He turned back to Johnny. "Go ahead, show her that everything I've said about American aggression is true." Emilio was goading Johnny now.

"I'm not going to hit you," Johnny said. "I just need you to shut up."

Emilio looked at Brian again. "There are no innocent victims."

"Be quiet, Emilio!" Carrie pleaded. Her tears were streaming now. "Please don't hit him, Johnny."

"I won't," Johnny said. "I promise."

Johnny stepped toward Emilio spun him around, and, with one fluid motion, grabbed him by his shirt collar and belt, lifted him off the ground and tossed him into the fountain."

"Oh, my God!" Carrie screamed.

As Emilio flapped in the water trying to get up, Brian said, "I think I'd just stay there for a while if I were you."

Johnny walked to Carrie, wrapped his arms around her and said, "I'm really, really sorry. I guess I messed things up. I love you, and I hope you love me. Time will tell. But for now, I think it's time to go home. He kissed her tenderly on the forehead and whispered, "I love you" one more time as he and Brian stepped away.

37- We are, Penn State!

September 1992

Johnny and the Pac Men sat in the student section of Beaver Stadium watching the Penn State football game. This week it was Eastern Michigan's turn to be one of State's early season victims, and they were playing the part well. The Nittnay Lions had a 45 to 7 lead in the third quarter.

Mickey scanned the ninety-eight thousand people in the stands. He had never seen so many people in one place before. "This place is incredible."

"Unreal," Bobby shouted above the crowd's roar.

"It beats the heck out of Slippery Rock," Tommy added. "We had two thousand people at our game last week."

Mickey patted Johnny on the shoulder. "Thanks for the tickets. This is great."

"Don't thank me," Johnny said. "Brian paid for them."

"Thanks, Brian," Mickey said. "But you should save your money."

Brian laughed. "I bought stocks in Cisco when I turned eighteen. It's been a good year."

Mickey drew a blank. "Cisco?"

"It's a data networking company."

Mickey shook his head. "Forget I asked."

Penn State's second team continued to pour it on, and the boys lost interest. With eight minutes left in the game, they decided to head for the exit.

They walked down College Avenue, a street lined with shops and restaurants that ran along the edge of campus.

"Better hide your face," Bobby said to Tommy. "The cops might recognize you."

"No sweat," Tommy replied. "The evidence is gone."

That morning the boys had walked College Ave to kill time before the game. State College, Pennsylvania is one of the great college towns in America with a carnival atmosphere on game day. That morning was no exception. The sidewalks were packed with fans wearing blue and white, street vendors hawking Penn State shirts and hats, and pep bands playing on each corner. People joked and wore big smiles, confident that State would chalk up another victory. Kids carried balloons, and perky co-eds had lion paws painted on their faces. The place certainly lived up to its Happy Valley nickname.

Tommy had stolen a life-sized cardboard cutout of Joe Paterno from a sidewalk display in front of the campus book store. He picked up the cutout, placed it under his arm and casually blended in with the crowd as he continued down the street. The cutout was a popular sales item in town, and a few fans stopped him to ask where they could buy one. Tommy calmly pointed in the wrong direction and continued to walk.

Paterno's likeness was now safely stored in Johnny's dorm room, and Tommy wasn't worried.

Brian thought again about the scene from the morning: the smiling vendors, the happy children, and the carefree attitude of the students. He remembered wanting to enjoy it all, but he couldn't. The more festive the occasion the more haunted he was by the belief that evil lurked in the world, that there were those who held an irrational hatred for the United States and wanted to inflict serious harm on innocent civilians. Where others saw joy and celebration, Brian saw danger and vulnerability. He tried to fight off those feelings but couldn't. Instead, he imagined his Uncle Ray and the other passengers boarding their pre-Christmas flight 103. He imagined their anticipation of flying home for the holidays, blissfully unaware of their pending doom.

It wasn't fear for his personal safety that Brian felt at these times; that wasn't it at all. It was anger. Brian wanted to protect the innocent and unsuspecting from harm. He wasn't sure how to do that, at least not yet, but he was working on it.

Johnny snapped Brian back to the present. "Let's get something to eat. There's a lot of dead time between the end of the game and the parties later tonight."

Everyone agreed. They stopped at a diner frequented by students and used the time to catch up on what each had been doing. Mickey was fully immersed in the fire department and courses at Bucks County Community College. Bobby loved his experience at Pennco Tech. He was finally out of an academic environment and happy as a lark to be working under the hood. He was as good at it as anyone in his class. Tommy, on the other hand, seemed well on his way to flunking out of Slippery Rock. "Someone forgot to tell the professors that Slippery Rock is a party school," he said sadly. "The work is a bear."

Tommy, Mickey and Bobby had shared a flask of vodka before the game, and now the three were getting tired. "I told you guys it was too early to drink," Brian said. He and Johnny had declined, Brian because he really didn't drink much and Johnny because he'd get booted out of ROTC if he got caught.

After they ate, the drinkers headed back to Johnny's room to rest before what they hoped would be a big night on campus, and Brian and Johnny stayed at the diner to talk.

"So what's up with MIT?" Johnny asked. "What are you studying?"

"I guess you'd say information technology for now. I'm a wire head."

"So how is it?"

"I love it. You know how easily things come to me. But for the first time in my life I feel like I'm learning something in school rather than just reading on my own. I've got some brilliant profs, guys who are tops in their fields. They're consultants for the government and major corporations."

"Impressive," Johnny said.

"I applied for an internship with a professor named Dr. Blake. He's in the technology department, but he's also a part time advisor for the Pentagon on satellite technology and communications. It's an internship freshmen don't usually get, but I applied anyway. I even had to go through a security clearance. It's a big deal."

"So do you think you have a chance?"

Brian smiled and said, "I hope so. I have an interview scheduled."

"Fantastic," Johnny said.

"I'll probably end up just getting the guy coffee or something. We'll see. But I think it's a good way to get my foot in the door."

"Are you kidding?" Johnny said. "You'll be running the place in no time."

"We'll see," Brian said. "I'm excited."

The waitress came and dropped off the check. When she left Brian said, "So what about you? How are things here?"

"Pretty good," Johnny said. "I like my classes, but some of the lecture halls are huge. A guy can get lost."

"Welcome to life at a major university."

"Yeah, I guess so. But things are good so far."

"What about ROTC? What's that like?"

"Not bad. I like it. We do physical training three times a week, which I'd be doing anyway, so that's good. It's not easy, but it's nothing compared to summer football practice, at least not yet. Then I have a class once a week on the organization and function of the army, and a thing they call Leadership Lab once a week for two hours. I'll do a field training exercise later in the semester."

"Sounds like you're busy."

"It's manageable," Johnny said. "Plus the army gives me $300.00 a month."

Brian smiled. "I can't believe I'll be calling you Lieutenant in a few years."

"It's a long way off," Johnny said. "I hope I make it."

"You'll make it," Brian said confidently.

They got quiet for a minute, and Brian asked Johnny if he'd heard from Carrie.

Johnny shook his head slowly. "Not a word. I guess I blew it."

"You mean I blew it, don't you? I shouldn't have talked you into going to Germany."

"It wasn't your fault. I decided for myself. I guess it's over between Carrie and me, and there's nothing else I can do about it. I left the ball in her court and nothing happened. It's killing me, but I guess I'll have to get over it." Johnny didn't sound convincing.

Brian laughed and Johnny looked annoyed. "I don't see what's so funny. Things are pretty screwed up."

Brian smiled and shook his head. "Johnny boy, in matters of romance, never doubt the wisdom of the great Brian Kelly."

"Right," Johnny said sarcastically. "You're brilliant."

Brian reached into his pocket, pulled out a small envelope and slid it across the table. It had foreign postage and was addressed to Johnny Marzo in care of Brian Kelly.

"It came a few days ago," Brian said. "I thought it'd be just as quick to hand deliver it."

Johnny saw Carrie's name and address in the upper left hand corner. His hand shook when he picked it up.

"She didn't know your address, so she sent it to me at school," Brian said.

"How did she know yours?"

"I sent a postcard with my new address to all of my friends when I moved to Boston. It's how people keep in touch. You should try it."

Johnny opened the letter and sat back to read it.

> *Dear Johnny,*
>
> *I hope you're doing well and enjoying college. I've wanted to write this letter for weeks but couldn't get up the nerve. I guess I was hoping I'd hear from you first.*
>
> *I want you to know that I ended my relationship with Emilio the same day you left, partly because I was shocked to see a side of him I hadn't seen before, and partly because seeing you again made me realize how much you mean*

to me. I was a wreck for a long time about everything that happened during your visit, good and bad, but I'm thinking pretty clearly now.

After you left, I had a long talk with my parents. Maybe confrontation is a better word. I spilled my guts about how miserable and confused I am. I mean I love Europe and consider my cultural experiences here to be priceless. But I have no roots, no lasting friendships, and no sense of security. I feel empty inside. They were defensive at first about all of our moves and reminded me of the wonderful opportunities they provided for me and the comfortable lifestyle my father's salary made possible. I countered that I appreciated all of that, but it didn't make up for the sadness I felt. It was hard saying those things because my parents are great people. They felt really guilty about things, but I had to let them know.

Anyway, we talked for hours, the first real talk we'd had in years. We cried and hugged and really aired things out. In the end, they said all they wanted was for me to be happy.

I told them that I wanted to make a trip to America to visit you. I thought they'd give me a hundred reasons why I shouldn't or couldn't, but amazingly, they said yes! I was shocked. In fact, the more we talked the more the idea grew on them.

So, Johnny Marzo, I'm writing to let you know that I have some time off from school next month for Oktoberfest and I'm coming to visit you for a weekend at Penn State. I know I'm not invited, but I learned from you that invitations aren't necessary. So, like it or not, I'm coming. At least I'm giving you three week's notice, so you have plenty of time to hide any new girlfriends you might have.

There are other things my parents and I talked about that you'll be interested in, but that will have to wait until I see you.

Love,
Carrie

Johnny was floored. He folded the letter and returned it to its envelope. He was quiet for a minute and then said, "She's coming."

Brian smiled.

"I can't believe it," Johnny mumbled. "I don't know what to do."

"You have a funny way of greeting good news. What's the problem?"

"The problem is that she's thousands of miles away. Even if we have a great weekend, she'll be back in Europe when it's over, so what's the use. I don't want to be hurt again."

"Makes sense," Brian said. "But you don't have any choice. The girl you love said she's coming and she's interested. There's no way you could live with yourself if you didn't see this through. So just roll with it and see what happens."

38- Dinner at the Tavern

Johnny's heart beat faster as the passengers filed off the Greyhound bus. Carrie had called several hours earlier to let him know she had landed safely in Philadelphia and was scheduled to arrive at State College by five o'clock. The wait had seemed endless, and now it was over, or would be when he finally saw her face. He counted twenty-two passengers before she appeared. If Johnny needed a reminder of why she was the girl who had dominated his thoughts since the first time he met her, he got it. It was dusk now, but even in the diminished light she looked as good as ever. Casual beauty, Johnny thought. Her blond hair was long and parted in the middle, and she wore a loose fitting sweatshirt, jeans and boots.

She seemed tired, but her face lit up when she saw him moving toward her though the crowd. She threw her arms around his neck, and they kissed briefly.

"You made it!" He said cheerfully.

Carrie smiled. "I thought I'd die. The flight took forever, but the bus ride was worse- five hours from the airport to here."

"I'm so glad you're here," Johnny said. "You look great."

"Be quiet, Johnny Marzo. I look terrible and you know it. I'm a mess."

"I'll decide how you look to me," Johnny said, "and you look great."

"Well, you do too, Mr. Penn State college boy."

They moved closer to where the driver was unloading the luggage.

"You'll be happy to know I only have one bag. Europeans travel lightly."

Johnny saw images of Emilio when Carrie referenced Europe, but he shook them off. He was determined that nothing would prevent them from having a beautiful weekend.

He retrieved the suitcase and tipped the driver. "It's just a short walk to your hotel," Johnny said. "Is that okay?"

"That's great. I need to stretch my legs."

Johnny extended the handle on the roller suitcase, took Carrie's hand, and moved her away from the depot.

"I was going to ask some girls I know if they could find you an open room in the dorm for the weekend, but you know Brian. As soon as he knew you were coming, he insisted on putting you up in style. He was here for a football game, and he booked your room before he left.

"So what's the hotel like?"

"It's called the Nittnay Lion Inn, and it's by far the nicest place in State College."

They crossed Atherton toward the campus and Johnny said, "There it is."

The Inn was a white, three story structure with black shutters. A high columned colonial portico dominated the front and opened to a circular drive rimmed with landscaping.

"Oh, it's charming," Carrie said. "Brian shouldn't do things like this."

"Tell me about it," Johnny said. "He claims he hasn't spent a dime of his uncle's money. He bought some Internet stocks that have done very well, and he barely touches the dividends. I don't know much about that stuff, but you can bet that Brian's an expert."

They reached the portico and were greeted by a student bell hop wearing khaki slacks and a navy blazer. He took Carrie's bag and led her to the front desk. Johnny held back while she checked in and then walked with her in the direction of the elevators.

"Nice place," Carrie said. She took an apple from a complimentary fruit display and bit into it."

"That's Brian," Johnny said.

The elevator arrived and they stepped in. The doors closed and they were alone. Johnny wanted to kiss her, but she had a mouth full of apple, so he decided to wait. The elevator doors opened and they headed down a richly carpeted hallway. There were several alcoves along the way, each tastefully appointed with antique tables topped with flower arrangements.

"Cool," Carrie said.

When they reached her room, Johnny opened the door and followed her in. The door closed behind them. He placed her suitcase on the bed and turned to face her. Carrie tossed her apple core in the trash can and walked toward him. She placed her arms on his shoulders and said playfully, "Do I smell like apple?"

Johnny smiled. "You smell like…" He paused for a moment and said, "You smell just like I remember you." Then he smiled and added, "Plus maybe a little whiff of apple." They kissed long and tenderly, and Johnny was happier than he'd been in a long time.

When they parted, Carrie said, "I'm so glad I came."

"Me too." Johnny glanced at the bed and Carrie noticed. She took half a step back and said, "I'm starved. The food on the plane was terrible. Is there a place to eat in the hotel?"

Johnny sighed and then smiled. "There is, but our friend Brian made us dinner reservations off campus."

Carrie laughed. "You're kidding, right?"

"It's called the Tavern Restaurant, and it's the most popular place in town. I'm told President Eisenhower ate there back in the day and that the Governor eats there when he visits."

"I don't have clothes…"

"Doesn't matter," Johnny interrupted. "We'll get in."

"Great. Like I said, I'm starved."

"Okay, then, let's go."

"Wait," Carrie said. "I'm really sorry, but I can't go anywhere until I take a shower. After the plane and bus ride, I've got to get out of these clothes. I promise I'll just be a minute."

"Sure," Johnny said. "No problem." He thought of Carrie taking a shower in the next room and got squirmy. "Eh...where..."

"I saw a small shop downstairs. Why don't you get me some gum and relax in the lobby, and I'll be down right away."

He wanted to say, "I'm a little grungy too. Why don't we shower together?" But instead he said. "Take your time. I'll find something to do." He moved to the door and stopped and looked back. "You know. I'm a little afraid to go to dinner with you."

Carrie laughed. "Why in the world..."

"The last two times we've eaten together you've given me bad news. First it was France and then the guy from Italy."

Carrie understood. "Johnny Marzo, I didn't travel all this way to give you bad news."

"No," Johnny said sheepishly, "I guess not. I'll see you downstairs."

He went to the lobby and found the shop. It was stocked with every item a Penn State nut could want- shirts, jackets, baby clothes, playing cards, mugs, key chains; all adorned with some form of Penn State inscription. He bought a small Teddy Bear dressed in a Penn State sweater and holding a small college pennant. He went to the front desk, wrote Carrie a short note and asked that the note and stuffed animal be placed in her room after they left.

He found a copy of *The Daily Collegian*, selected one of the plush, burgundy leather chairs that lined the lobby, and read about State's away game scheduled for the following day.

Carrie arrived soon after looking radiant and rejuvenated. Her hair was still damp and pulled back in a pony tail. She had changed into a pair of dark slacks and a white pullover that accented her figure.

She smiled when she saw him. "I hope that wasn't too long."

He thought of saying something trite like, "It was worth the wait," but said instead, "It was quicker than I thought."

They exited the hotel and turned in the opposite direction they had come from earlier. It was dark now, and the hotel glowed brilliantly against the night sky. The air was cool, but pleasant, and Johnny took her hand in his and they walked.

"The restaurant isn't far," he said, "and the walk will give you a chance to see some of the campus."

They turned and headed away from the building. They hadn't talked about anything serious yet and the image of Emilio splashing around in the Poseidon Fountain entered Johnny's mind. He smiled inwardly and thought maybe it was better if they kept things light for now.

They came upon a large statue of a mountain lion perched on a rock. "That's the Nittany Lion shrine," Johnny said. "It's tradition to have your picture taken there on graduation day. You'll see Mt. Nittany tomorrow in the daylight. It's pretty cool."

A small group had gathered around the statue and a visiting family was posing for a photo.

"On the weekends of home football games, pledges from different fraternities guard the lion from vandals all night long. Supposedly, somebody from Syracuse painted the ears orange one year, and twice the ears have been broken off. You can't have people coming onto your turf and doing stuff like that."

"That's right," Carrie said playfully. "You would have never done anything like that in your past."

"Never," Johnny smiled.

It got cooler and Johnny put his arm on Carrie's shoulder and drew her closer to him. She put her arm around his waist. As they walked she said, "So how many girls did you have to hide away this weekend."

"None," Johnny said.

She pinched his side. "I'll bet."

"Really, I date now and then, but I always seem to have someone else on my mind."

She leaned her head on his shoulder and said, "It's nice here, Johnny. Do you like it?"

"I love it. I mean, I miss Bristol and my parents and the guys at the deli and the Pac Men. I miss knowing everyone in town. But I like it here. Besides, it was time to move on."

Carrie didn't respond, and Johnny said, "So what about you?"

"That's a good question. I don't have roots like you do. I don't have a place I can call home, so I don't even know what that feels like. I know I miss the United States. I miss football and American television, and all kinds of things. But as far as people go, you have more lasting relationships in that one deli than I have in the whole world.   I'm jealous."

"Do you think your parents will ever come home?"

"My mom's from France. As far as she's concerned, she is home. Europe has become a very integrated place. People move about more freely and speak multiple languages. She's comfortable in just about any country in Western Europe."

"What about your dad?"

Carrie shook her head. "Do you know that stereotype about scientists? Well it's true. He's totally absorbed with his work. He could be happy on Jupiter as long as he had a lab to work in."

They walked down Burrowes Road and Carrie changed the subject. "What's that building across the street?"

That's Rec Hall, the gymnasium. It's where I do a lot of my ROTC training."

Carrie stopped and said, "Why did you do that?" She sounded disappointed.

"Do what?"

"Join ROTC."

"I'm not sure," Johnny said. "I was attracted by the army I guess."

"It seems like it was an impulsive decision. Aren't you committed to the military when you graduate?"

"Yes. I am."

Carrie didn't look happy.

"There are worse decisions I could have made," Johnny said. "And there wasn't anyone around to help me make this one."

She got the message. "That's not my fault," she said softly.

"I know," Johnny said. "Anyway, the army offers opportunities."

"The army fights wars," Carrie protested. "And America seems to like them."

"Now that doesn't seem fair. We try to do the right thing."

"Well, a whole lot of people in the world think we need to try harder."

"We stopped Saddam."

"True," Carrie said. "And that was a good thing. But we put troops in Saudi Arabia."

"So?"

"So, America looks at everything through its eyes. It needs a broader lens. Having Western troops in the land of Mecca drives the Muslims crazy. They think we're infidels desecrating their holiest places."

Johnny shrugged. America led a coalition to stop Saddam Hussein in the Persian Gulf, and he didn't see what the problem was. But he wasn't going to let this conversation ruin their time together.

"Hey," he said playfully. "I thought you were hungry."

Carrie smiled. "I am. Let's get going."

They approached a row of magnificent mansions and Johnny said. "Those are some of the oldest fraternity houses at the university."

"Wow," Carrie said. "Students live there?"

"They get a little beat up inside from the parties, but they're pretty nice places."

"They're beautiful. The whole place is beautiful."

She put her arm around his waist again and he pulled her closer to him as they walked.

They crossed College Avenue and the campus tranquility was replaced by the bustle of the main drag. The street was jammed with Friday night shoppers and students searching for adventure. Outdoor cafes were packed, and street performers strummed guitars or performed magic tricks. A man, who Johnny claimed was a professor, held a sign that read, Honk to Legalize Marijuana, and many cars did. A student group was holding a mini Clinton-Gore rally and Carrie stopped to listen. One of the organizers eyed Carrie up and down. Johnny shot him a menacing stare and the organizer looked away.

"This is wild," Carrie said laughing. "I love it."

Johnny eyed Carrie up and down and decided he really couldn't blame the guy with the Clinton button. She really was exceptional.

They arrived at the Tavern Restaurant and Carrie said, "This is nice. So Eisenhower ate here?"

"Yeah," Johnny replied straight faced. "I think it was the night before the Normandy Invasion. On second thought I think he brought that British babe he was dating in England while poor Mamie sat home praying for his safety."

"That's not nice."

"Sure it is. It's always nice to pray."

"You know what I mean, Silly. Besides, I don't think those stories are true about Ike and his female driver. I think they were just friends."

"Tell that to Mamie"

They entered the restaurant and Johnny gave his name. You would have thought Prince Charles had just arrived. "Mr. Marzo," the head waiter said. "We've been expecting you. Follow me."

Johnny winked at Carrie and said, "I get that wherever I go. I wish people would just treat me like a normal person."

Carrie laughed. "Just follow the waiter, hotshot."

He placed them at a table next to the large window overlooking College Avenue. "I trust this is adequate?" the head waiter asked.

Johnny wanted to say, "Cut the bullshit; this is Penn State, not uptown Manhattan, but he said, "Thanks, this is fine."

"Very nice," Carrie added. "Thank you."

He gave each a menu and said, "Mr. Kelly sends his compliments and asked me to suggest the Surf and Turf, which is excellent. He regrets that he cannot provide you with a bottle of wine, but alas, your age prohibits this. Of course your dinner and gratuity are already taken care of. Please enjoy your evening. Your waiter will be with you shortly.

"Thanks," Johnny said. "Did you ever work at Sardi's in Manhattan?"

Johnny felt a kick under the table.

"No sir. I have not."

Johnny nodded and said, "Must be someone who looks like you."

Carrie gave him a scolding stare.

"Please thank Mr. Kelly if you bump into him."

"I will, sir. Your waiter will be with you shortly."

He left and Carrie said smiling, "That wasn't necessary. He was only trying to make things nice"

"Things are nice already," he said reaching for her hand. "Besides, I can't stand phonies. Alas. Who the heck says alas?"

"Let's send Brian a thank you card tomorrow," Carrie said.

"First thing. We'll look for a picture of the Nittany Lion with orange ears."

Carrie shook her head. They watched the people stream by the window and Johnny said, "I feel like I'm in an aquarium."

"I love watching people."

"I bet that's what the fish say."

Carrie smiled. "I've really missed you. I guess I didn't realize how much."

Johnny wanted to say, "That's because you've been with those European bastards," but he said, "Me too."

The waiter came and Carrie ordered stuffed flounder. Johnny chose the surf and turf. "Brian said his stocks are up, remember?"

The food came, and it was delicious. Johnny dipped a chunk of lobster in melted butter and extended the fork to Carrie. She ate it, and butter dripped down her chin. They laughed, ate, and exchanged stories, and Johnny managed to avoid thinking about the future.

They passed on dessert and sat quietly as the waiter cleared the table. When he was gone, Johnny said, "I hate to ask this, but in your letter you said you had a surprise."

"I know," Carrie said. "But I'm afraid to tell you. Everything is so nice, and I don't want to mess things up."

All of Johnny's fears came rushing back. He exhaled slowly and said, "This is crazy. I'm never going to dinner with you again."

"No," Carrie said. "It's not bad news. At least I hope it's not. I just want us to be this way every night."

Johnny had no idea what she meant. He said, "Look, just get it out. What's the big surprise?"

"I'm afraid."

"There's nothing to be afraid of. The waiter already took my knife and fork, and I love you too much to kill you with my bare hands."

Carrie smiled and cleared her throat. " I told you in the letter that my parents and I had a long talk right after you left, and I told them how miserable I am and how much my life has been messed up from moving all the time."

Johnny nodded.

"They felt terrible and asked what would make me happy."

Johnny was afraid to look at her as she spoke. He was playing with his plastic straw, tying it in knots.

Carrie continued, "I told them I hated Humboldt University and that I wanted to go to college in the United States."

Johnny looked up. This certainly was a surprise.

Carrie pressed on. "I told them I wanted to go to Penn State."

Johnny dropped his straw and leaned forward. "What did they say?"

"They said that was fine."

Now Johnny felt the room spinning.

Carrie was reluctant to get out the final piece, uncertain of what Johnny's reaction would be. She forced her best smile and said, "I'm transferring to Penn State in January."

39- Professor Blake

Brian felt a rush of adrenalin as he entered the building that housed Professor David Blake's office. Dr. Blake was one of the most respected faculty members at Massachusetts Institute of Technology, the kind of professor whose name lent prestige to the institution.

Blake rarely taught. Aside from a weekly lecture for doctoral candidates, his real work was in research and development. The university received enormous contracts from the government and several corporations to use his skills and the university's facilities to provide answers to the most vexing technological problems of the day.

His work was widespread. He'd been a key player in the development of the most recent generation of telecommunication satellites that had revolutionized cell phones. He pioneered military adaptations of ground to air communications, especially with the development of AWACS systems, and he was developing prototypes of drones, remote controlled spy planes equipped with visual and audio monitoring equipment that were adaptable for weapons use.

As if that weren't enough, during the last five years he'd immersed himself in the field of data collection, records retrieval and analysis. At first, the major banks had contracted with him to develop systems to manage the records of the exploding credit card industry. They needed fast, accurate service to keep track of their millions of customers whose transactions numbered in the billions each day. However, it didn't take long for Blake to see the potential for law enforcement and intelligence gathering applications of what he was doing. With the proper modifications of these tools, the FBI and the CIA could revolutionize the tracking of people they had in their sights.

Blake was often frustrated by the government's slow movement in this area. It was 1993, and the technological potential was there, but in many ways, the decision makers were operating with a 1970's mentality.

It had been a month since Brian applied for an internship with the professor. It was a bold move for a freshman. He'd been told by Blake's secretary not to waste his time because a freshman had never even made it to the interview stage. But Brian had read about Blake in technical journals and couldn't resist trying.

Brian reached Dr. Blake's door, knocked and entered. The secretary looked up without smiling and said curtly, Dr. Blake will be with you shortly. She obviously remembered his earlier visit and didn't like being wrong.

Brian wanted to tell her to kiss his ass, but instead he said, "Thank you," and took a seat. It turned out old sourpuss was right. It wasn't long before her phone rang. She spoke briefly, hung up and told Brian he could go in.

Blake's office looked like a Hollywood set, complete with floor to ceiling mahogany book shelves, a huge desk, and plush leather chairs. Blake was old, seventy at least, thinner than Brian had imagined, with gray hair and a thin beard. Brian was grateful there was no pipe in sight. Brian hated guys who smoked pipes, especially academics. They always seemed so full of themselves.

"Sit down, young man," Blake said. He seemed much more personable than his secretary. "I reviewed your academic records and background check and liked what I saw. That's why you're here."

"Thank you, sir." Brian thought back to the background check and suppressed a smile. Because of the sensitive nature of Dr. Blake's work, everyone who worked in his office, even old sourpuss outside, was submitted to a background check. Brian thought it was a blast when his parents told him that an FBI agent had actually interviewed their neighbors, as well as Mr. Baxter and Ms. Quattrocchi at the high school, and Bristol's Chief of Police.

"I'm pressed for time," Blake said. "So let's get started."

They had an extensive academic discussion, and Blake grilled Brian on physics and calculus. The professor fired questions that Brian answered without hesitation. After a while it became a game, with Blake increasing the level of difficulty and Brian keeping pace effortlessly.

Finally, Blake smiled, sat back in his chair and said, "You know some physics, and your calculus isn't too shabby either."

"I try," Brian said.

"The work here is difficult, and I demand a great deal in time and effort."

"I wouldn't expect anything less, sir," Brian said.

Professor Blake wasn't convinced. "That's now, when you're eager for the position. I'm more interested in how you'll sustain your effort weeks from now when I'm working you to the bone."

"That's not who I am," Brian said confidently. "When I'm in, I'm all in."

Blake nodded. "I'd like to know what motivates you, what makes you tick." Blake scanned the office for a moment and added, "You're a pretty bright guy. You could apply your skills to medicine or law, any number of fields. Why this one?"

Brian began to speak but Blake cut him off. "I'd like you to think about a defining moment in your life, something that drove you to pursue a career in a field such as this. Take your time and think before you answer."

Brian responded right away. "With all due respect, sir, there's nothing to think about."

Brian launched into the story of his Uncle Ray. He explained their close relationship and his uncle's work with satellite communications for the Pentagon and in the private sector. He ended with an emotional retelling of his uncle's death aboard Pan Am Flight 103 over Lockerbie, Scotland.

Dr. Blake was stunned. He'd been horrified by the wanton slaughter of the terror attack and was deeply moved by Brian's story. Blake was equally surprised by the depth of Brian's knowledge of the three-year investigation that led to indictments against two Libyan nationals. Brian rattled off forensic details, the complicated trail that linked the killers with the event, and the complicity and cover up by Libyan President Moammar Gadaffi.

"The cowards who murdered my uncle and 270 other innocent people are free, and the Libyan government is harboring them. I'm sure you can imagine the impact this has had on my family. My mother hasn't been the same since her brother was taken."

Professor Blake nodded. "This must have been devastating for you."

"It was," Brian said painfully, "and still is."

Blake wanted to lighten the moment. He left his chair and went to the corner of his office, where he invited Brian to join him. He opened a small refrigerator, took out two cokes and passed one to Brian. "So you want to honor your uncle's memory by following the same interests he had."

"It's more than that," Brian said evenly.

Dr. Blake had a corner office with broad windows on two sides that offered a sweeping view of the snow-covered campus. Brian took a sip of his soda and looked outside. The sidewalks were cleared, and students, bundled against the cold, moved between classes. Some were laughing, and some were holding hands. A few stooped to make snowballs which they playfully threw at friends. Most, however, moved quietly to their next class.

"It's peaceful down there," Brian said.

Dr. Blake followed his gaze but decided not to respond.

"They're innocent people just going about their lives," Brian said softly. When he turned back to Dr. Blake his expression was somber. "I'm convinced that right now there are diabolical people in the world plotting to kill them." Then he quickly added, "Maybe not them in particular, but others just as innocent. I want to use technology to find and destroy the fanatical bastards who would do that."

Blake raised his eyebrows but still didn't speak.

"I'm not a nut," Brian continued. "Nor am I reckless. But I am highly focused."

Dr. Blake nodded but still didn't respond. He took a sip of his soda and waited for Brian to say more, which he did. "In economics they talk about the law of comparative advantage. An entity, be it a country or a corporation, should focus upon those things that it does best." Brian paused. "Thanks to people like you, what America does best is technology."

"And what is the significance of that?" Dr. Blake prompted.

"Our enemies have changed. I'm convinced of that, even if our elected officials are a little slow on the uptake. If we're going to keep up with adversaries who figuratively hide under rocks, and engage in a perverse martyrdom to spread their destruction, then we have to use every tool at our disposal."

Blake walked to his desk, picked up the phone and told sourpuss to cancel his next appointment. Then he came back and said, "Go on."

"We need soldiers of course, boots on the ground as they say. We always will. We need spies, infiltrators, informants, what they call human assets in all the spy novels. But we also need the best technology to monitor who they are, where they are and what they're up to."

Brian paused and added, "I may have just screwed up my interview, but that's how I see things."

Dr. Blake smiled, and then laughed. "Either you've read my book or you've read my mind. Which is it?"

"I read your book in high school," Brian said.

"High school?" Dr. Blake was somewhat taken aback. I'd like to think my work is a little more sophisticated than that."

"I read a lot after Uncle Ray died."

Dr. Blake's demeanor changed. It was as though the interview was over and they were colleagues. The seventy year old genius had found a nineteen year old associate, someone who shared his zeal.

Blake gave Brian a conspiratorial look and confided to his new friend. "We have the most sophisticated military in the world, but we've just scratched the surface of what we can do with foreign and domestic intelligence gathering. One small lead from an informant can open a wide network of surveillance for us. We monitor one person's calls and it leads us to his associates. We monitor theirs and we uncover plots. That's just good old fashioned police work. But we can do it so much better than we are. Hell, it's 1993, but we're still dragging our feet. We can merge the data, share it between agencies. We can monitor suspect's calls, monitor their frequency of contact, and monitor contacts from foreign locations. We can do it in real time speed and provide the FBI, CIA, DIA, and every other agency invaluable information. We can, but we don't, largely because of outdated equipment, but also because of interagency rivalries. The God-dammed FBI and CIA don't trust each other. It's astonishing."

Blake was growing more animated. "We can find one small lead, and we hack into the bad guy's computer without his knowledge and uncover a wealth of new information. We can build voice identification banks and use them like fingerprints, and do the same with DNA banks, and share everything between agencies. But we don't do it nearly enough."

Blake concluded by saying, "We think we're doing a lot in these areas, but we're only scratching the surface."

"So what's the holdup?" Brian said impatiently.

"Two things actually. One, of course is money. Congress likes to flaunt where it spends our taxes because it likes to take credit for projects like new bridges or veterans hospitals. But spending money on intelligence gathering is not something easily shared with the public. Congressmen need to be convinced that additional spending is vital. So far, no one is frightened enough to believe it. Plus they're operating from an outmoded mindset that thinks a strong traditional military alone can get the job done. We're funding billion dollar tank programs while our new enemy, one they don't understand yet, is using crude explosive devices. They just don't get the enemy yet."

Brian asked, "What's the other holdup?"

"Civil liberties," Blake said. "People are wary of a government with too much power, and they should be. I understand that. Congressmen do too. Try to broach the topic of domestic spying with them, and they flip out about personal liberties."

Blake paused. "My mother was Jewish, and she lost her siblings and parents in the Nazi camps. So no one need lecture me about the evils of an oppressive police state. But people need to understand that our constitutional rights to privacy have to be adapted to the technological realities of the twenty-first century and to twenty-first century dangers. Someday they will, but we're wasting valuable time.

Blake continued. "Hell, we all cheered when the Soviet Union collapsed, but their nuclear security collapsed with them. There are nukes missing! Nukes, for Christ sakes, that could have fallen into the wrong hands. Some fanatic could take out Washington or New York, and he wouldn't need a missile. He could stick the damned device in a suitcase and kill a couple hundred thousand Mets fans in one shot.

Blake was sweating as he took a long pull from his Coke. Then he said, "We have to show this country how to protect itself."

Brian thought about his Uncle Ray and wondered whether a better intelligence network would have saved him. He didn't know, but it didn't matter now. The job now was to protect others in the future.

Brian looked at the professor and said, "Dr. Blake, I'd really like to work for you. I'd do a good job."

Blake smiled. "I hired you twenty minutes ago. But I warn you; the work here will be rigorous, and you'll still have a full load of classes. You'll have to stay on top of things or you'll be dismissed."

Brian smiled. "That will not be an issue."

40- "I William Jefferson Clinton Do Solemnly Swear…"

January 20, 1993

Johnny and Carrie sat in Union Station in Washington, D.C. awaiting the arrival of Brian, Mickey and Bobby on the Amtrak from Philadelphia. A week earlier Brian called everyone to share his idea of meeting in the nation's capital for the Presidential Inauguration. They hadn't been together since late September and Brian thought they could witness history and have some fun.

Johnny and Carrie arrived first from State College and the rest were due any minute. Brian had traveled from Boston to Philadelphia where he met up with Mickey and Bobby for the final leg to Washington. Tommy sent his regrets. He had somehow avoided flunking out of Slippery Rock but was on academic probation and couldn't miss any classes.

"This is exciting," Carrie gushed. "Would you believe I've been to most of the major cities in Europe, but I've never seen Washington?"

"See America first," Johnny said. "That's the way to do it."

She leaned closer and kissed Johnny on the check. "And see it with someone special."

Johnny put his arm around her and gave her shoulder a squeeze.

"Do we know what we're doing today?" Carrie asked.

"Not a clue, but I'm sure Brian has a plan."

The train arrived and the couple stood to greet their friends. Mickey appeared first and flashed a big smile. Bobby and Brian followed. They met on the platform and exchanged hugs and high fives. Mickey and Bobby hadn't seen Carrie in almost four years and they made a huge fuss. It was an open secret that they both had a crush on her in high school, just about everyone did, and they didn't take long to pick up where they had left off.

"You look terrific," Mickey said.

"Better than terrific," Bobby added.

Johnny winked at her and she smiled. "You guys look good too. It's great to see you after so long. We have a lot of catching up to do."

Brian was next. Carrie hadn't seen him since the incident in Berlin. She felt awkward about the whole scene and didn't know what to say. But Brian broke the ice by saying, "Okay, everybody, our first stop is a beautiful fountain just a couple of blocks away."

Carrie laughed. "That's very funny, wise guy." She gave him a hug and a peck on the cheek. "No fountains. It's too cold for that!"

"Don't worry," Brian said. "I've got a plan and it doesn't include fountains. Besides, Johnny looks mellow today."

"Everyday," Johnny said, putting his arm around Carrie.

Mickey said, "Before we do anything, I just want to thank Brian for the train tickets, but, like I said before, you shouldn't be spending your money like that." The others voiced their agreement.

Brian shook his head. "It would be stupid of me to squander my money, right?"

"Right," Bobby said.

"Does anyone here think I'm stupid?"

"No," Mickey said, "But..."

"Then just let me handle my money. But if it makes you feel better, let me explain something. Does anyone know how much interest $2,000,000 modestly invested can earn?"

The boys looked at each other and shrugged.

Carrie offered a guess. "Maybe five or six percent?"

"Hold on to her, Johnny," Brian said. "She's beautiful and smart. I'm getting six percent."

That still didn't mean much to the guys, so Brian said, "Six percent of $2,000,000 is $120,000 a year. That's $10,000 a month before taxes and about $6000 or $7000 clear. I allow myself $2000 a month spending money, cover my college expenses, and put the rest in the stock market."

The Pac Men were stunned. Mickey said, "You've come a long way from hanging out at the canal."

"I didn't do anything," Brian said sadly. My Uncle Ray did. "So anyway, will you guys please shut up and let me do things?"

"Got it," Johnny said.

"And one more thing," Brian said. "I told you this before. You guys were always great to me. You," he pointed to Johnny, "always said we had to be where the action was."

Johnny nodded.

"Well, look around," Brian said. "Look at all these people. Today, we're where the action is, and it makes me feel good to put us there. Fair enough?"

"Fair enough," Mickey said. "And thanks."

"So what's the plan?" Johnny said.

"Well, we don't have tickets. I did't get them."

"Cheapskate," Bobby kidded. Everyone laughed.

"I tried. But the word is that they are expecting huge crowds and the Clinton people gave out way too many VIP tickets. I'm told we might be better without them. Let's go see."

They left the station and walked South on Louisiana Avenue. It was a brisk but sunny day, beautiful for mid January. The crowds were enormous and the mood festive. Vendors hawked balloons, hats, buttons, flags and anything else that struck their entrepreneurial spirit. Bobby announced he was starving, so they stopped for hot dogs and coffee. The vendor wore a Clinton-Gore baseball cap and a button that read, "Happy Days Are Here Again."

They finished their dogs and continued down Louisiana until police barriers around the capitol forced them to head west on D Street. Carrie walked ahead with Mickey and Bobby on either side. She playfully hooked her arms through theirs and they laughed and joked as they followed the crowds. Johnny and Brian were behind them, and Brian said, "So how's it going with the two of you?"

"Great," Johnny said. "It's like a dream. Six months ago we're half a world away from here and I'm throwing her boyfriend in a fountain, thinking I was throwing away our future at the same time. Now she's here and it's like we never parted."

"That's fantastic," Brian said. "Storybook stuff."

"It's really good," Johnny replied. "But I wouldn't say it's perfect."

Brian gave him a quizzical look and Johnny explained.

"She's got these political ideas; I guess they're a milder version of that crap Emilio was spilling to us. She's got this European view that America is a bully. She says we always act in our selfish interests. She talks a lot about oppressed people around the world. I mean, she loves America, but she likes to say that she loves it so much that she wants to fix it. And she's not real happy about my military commitment."

Brian shook his head. "I hope you're not going to let that stuff affect your relationship."

"Hell no," Johnny said. "I kind of admire that she wants to help people at home too. She's joined every do-good group on campus- the poor, the homeless, all kinds of causes. It's just that when she gets into the foreign affairs stuff, I feel like it's still Emilio talking and that ticks me off."

"Just be cool about it," Brian said.

"Don't worry; I plan to."

Brian got quiet and then said, "Do you love her?"

Johnny looked at her skipping along with his friends, like the bubbly kid he knew in ninth grade. "Yeah," he said, "I love her."

"Are you sure?"

"Yeah, I'm sure." Johnny stopped walking and looked at Brian. "What's up with these questions?"

Brian smiled. "Well, Jenny and I have been exchanging letters."

Johnny laughed. "No kidding? That's great."

"Just friendly stuff," Brian said. "But I've been thinking that if you wouldn't mind, I'd like to try to turn it up a notch with her."

Johnny laughed and smacked Brian on the back. "That's great. You two would be good together."

"You're sure you wouldn't mind?"

"Listen," Johnny said. "I like Jenny a lot. She's a terrific girl, and we had some great times together. But she wasn't Carrie. She knew that and I knew that. We parted friends, but that's it. Go for it, man!"

"Thanks," Brian said. "I plan to."

They caught up with Carrie and the guys and Brian said, "We're turning left on 3rd Street."

"The guy's a freak," Bobby said. "He knows everything."

Brian smiled. They walked south on 3rd until they reached Constitution Avenue.

"Okay," Brian said. "Now we'll work our way back toward the Capitol and get as close as we can. The crowds were denser as they got closer to the National Mall, and they elbowed their way to a spot near John Marshall Park, where they had a distant, but clear view of the Capitol steps and the speaker's platform.

"This is as close as we're gonna get," Brian said.

"Can't see too good from here," Bobby said.

"You don't have to see," Brian said. "You just have to feel it." He pointed to a loudspeaker on a street poll. "And you'll be able to hear it."

"Cool," Bobby said.

It was twenty minutes to twelve, and the Marine band began warming up the crowd. Carrie snuggled closer to Johnny and he looked down at her. Her cheeks were flushed from the cold, and her eyes sparkled. He put his arm around her and made a vow never to let go.

"Thanks for bringing me, Johnny," she said. "I've never been here before, but today I feel more like I'm home than I ever have. It's nice to be in America again."

"Not as nice as it is to have you here," Johnny said softly.

Someone introduced a poet named Maya Angelou and explained that President-elect Clinton had asked her to compose a poem to commemorate the occasion. The poem was called "On the Pulse of Morning," and Angelou stepped to the podium to deliver it.

Bobby moaned, "Not poetry."

Brian gave him a stare and said, "Quiet, I want to hear this."

Other people in the crowd were talking and the gang struggled to hear. The verse that came through most clearly was:

History, despite its wrenching pain,
Cannot be unlived, and if faced
With courage, need not be lived again.

The crowd clapped politely at the end. It was growing restless in anticipation of the oath of office. Finally Chief Justice William Rehnquist and Bill Clinton approached the podium. The Chief Justice instructed the President-elect to place his hand on the bible and repeat after him. "I, William Jefferson Clinton…"

Brian surveyed the crowd. Police had estimated that over a quarter million people would assemble that day to celebrate the peaceful transfer of authority in the most powerful nation in the world. He looked at the people around him- small children on their fathers' shoulders; young girls with their faces painted red, white and blue; veterans, proudly wearing their service hats and grandmothers braving the January chill. Something stirred inside him. He felt a part of something important. He caught Johnny's eye and could tell that Johnny was feeling it too. They nodded to each other and returned their attention to the podium.

Clinton finished the oath with the words, "…So help me God." The Chief Justice and others on the podium shook his hand and the Marine Band played "Hail to the Chief," to the 42nd President of the United States.

Clinton began his address and Carrie said, "This is incredible. I like this guy. I think President Clinton really cares about the people I care about."

Johnny smiled and said, "It seems that way."

Near the end of his remarks, Clinton said,

Each generation of Americans must define what it means to be an American. On behalf of our nation, I salute my predecessor, President Bush, for his half century of service to America. And I thank the millions of men and women whose steadfastness and sacrifice triumphed over depression, Fascism and Communism.

Today, a generation raised in the shadows of the Cold War assumes new responsibilities in a world warmed by the sunshine of freedom but threatened still by ancient hatreds and plagues.

Brian wondered where those ancient hatreds and plagues would show themselves next.

41- The Blind Sheikh

Omar Abdel Rahman, the radical Muslim cleric better known as the "Blind Sheikh," sat seething in his Brooklyn apartment as news of the World Trade Center bombing took shape. The media was reporting that a massive explosion, believed to be the work of terrorists, had blasted a one-hundred foot hole through six floors of the subterranean structure of Tower 1. Smoke and noxious fumes climbed through maintenance shafts, elevators and stairways and reached as high as the 90th floor. At last count, six people had died and over a thousand had been injured, including hundreds who suffered smoke inhalation as they evacuated the building. Phone and television service was lost throughout Lower Manhattan. Tens of thousands had been evacuated from the area.

An aide to the Sheikh said, "Praise be Allah, the bomb detonated, and the Americans are in panic."

The Blind Sheikh sneered. "You overstate our success. The towers still stand. The infidels have been only slightly wounded. Something went wrong."

Indeed, the terror bombing fell far short of its goal. The 1400 pound mixture of urea-nitrate, laced with sodium cyanide, and coupled with hydrogen tanks added to boost the explosion, created the massive blast intended, but the device, built by the fanatical Ramzi Yousef, Mahmud Abouhalima and Nidal Ayyad, was expected to inflict far greater damage. The plan was to position the truck bomb near the corner support structure of the building, where the bombers believed the blast would cause Tower 1 to collapse into Tower 2. The attackers were convinced that both towers would fall.

"Either the calculations were wrong or the driver did not position the truck at the desired location," the Sheikh said.

"Still the damage is great," his aide said. "The repairs will cost hundreds of millions, and we have instilled fear into the hearts of the Americans. Lower Manhattan is at a standstill."

Sheikh Omar shook his head. An estimated 120,000 people worked in the area of the World Trade Center. Countless people would have died if the explosion went as planned, and the property damage would have been in the billons. The financial capital of Satan's America would have been brought to its knees.

The Blind Sheikh was growing impatient for success. He'd been a powerful voice for radical Islam for decades. He had advocated the assassination of Egypt's President Anwar Sadat for his friendship with the United States and his tolerance of Israel, and offered prayerful praise when Sadat was killed. Later, he turned his wrath against Sadat's successor, Hosni Mubarak, who continued Sadat's policies.

But Sheikh Omar was also an early advocate of Jihad, or holy war, against the United States and preached that terrorism is a justifiable means to defend Islam. As far as he was concerned, Islam was under attack from the United States, and a Holy War was justified as self-defense. Since the Islamic nations lacked the military strength to fight the Americans in a traditional sense, it was justifiable to use well-trained individuals, working in embedded cells within the United States, to engage in what the West called terrorism.

Given the history of his teachings and his advocacy of violence, it was remarkable that immigration officials allowed the Sheikh to enter the United States, but they did, and he had preached his anti-American venom ever since.

While Ramzi Yousef was the mastermind behind the World Trade Center operation, it was the Blind Sheikh who provided the scriptural justification for the action.

"What follows will be better," Sheikh Omar said to his guest. Plans were in the works for bombings of the United Nations, the New York office of the FBI, and the Lincoln and Holland Tunnels.

"We will cripple the city, destroy its economy, and strike terror in the hearts of the infidels. It is Allah's will."

42- Emergency Management

One month after the World Trade Center bombing, over 150 fire, EMT, and other emergency personnel met in the banquet hall of Bristol's American Hose, Hook and Ladder Company, Station 53, for a seminar sponsored by the Bucks County Office of Emergency Management. The office was hosting meetings county-wide to review strategies for dealing with local disasters. The seminar was open to all emergency services personnel, and representatives came from throughout Lower Bucks County.

As a newly trained member of Goodwill Hose Company Number 3 located across town, Mickey appreciated the significance of gathering men from different organizations in the same room. He knew that fire companies, especially those in Bristol, had a love-hate relationship. They shared a common bond between people who risk their lives to protect others, and their interactions during emergencies were professional. But beyond that, the companies were in constant competition to purchase the best equipment, record the quickest response times, and court elected officials for funding.

The companies resembled fraternities steeped in traditions that spanned generations. Many firemen had fathers and grandfathers who had served in the same organization. Mickey thought back to the stories he'd heard about his own company's origins. Railroad tracks virtually divided Bristol in half, and once, a century earlier, a slow moving freight train prevented fire apparatus from responding to a house fire in which four people died, including three children. The residents were mortified by the disaster and vowed such a tragedy would never happen again. Neighbors began soliciting donations to build a station on their side of the tracks. Eventually, land was acquired, and volunteers poured the foundation for a new firehouse. The story was repeated each time the company had to roll up it sleeves to deal with financial difficulty, which was often.

Mickey soon learned that life in the fire and rescue services included long periods of boredom interrupted by periods of intense activity. Volunteers spent their free time at the station. Training exercises and equipment maintenance took up some of their time, but most was spent shooting pool, watching TV, and swapping stories. All that changed whenever the alarm sounded.

Mickey remembered his first live run. He and a few of the guys were watching a Phillies-Mets game and shooting the breeze when the alarm went off and the men sprang into action. Ninety seconds of frenzied activity later, Mickey was on a truck racing down Pond Street, the main drag that dissected the town, and praying that drivers approaching at the cross streets would hear the sirens and stop. He remembered the efficiency of the firefighters when they arrived on the scene. Questions needed to be answered quickly. Were there people or pets still in the building? What was stored on the property? How should the firefighters be deployed? How should traffic be rerouted? Should nearby structures be evacuated? To outsiders the scene may have looked chaotic as station chiefs barked orders and additional trucks arrived. But within minutes the situation had been assessed, hose was laid, hydrants were opened, and the flames were being doused.

Fortunately, the fire was out in a half hour with no injury or loss of life.

"This was an easy one, kid," one of the members had told Mickey as they packed hose later. Maybe, Mickey thought. But the experience had been both terrifying and exhilarating. He was exhausted, but felt a tremendous sense of satisfaction, more so than in anything he had ever done.

Mickey turned his thoughts to the meeting that was about to begin. As chief of the hosting community, Borough Fire Chief, Andy Bidlingmaier, opened the meeting. "I want to welcome you to Bristol Borough and congratulate you on this great turnout. I also want to thank the members of American Hose, Hook and Ladder for making their room available."

Everyone clapped.

"I'm told our hosts have a keg tapped for the visitors when our meeting is over."

The men cheered and someone called out, "Hot dogs too."

"Business first," Bidlingmaier said. "But I hope you stick around. It isn't often that we get to be in the same room. We should do it more often."

Few felt that way, but they clapped politely.

"Okay, let's get started. As you are well aware, the country experienced a trauma in New York last month, six deaths and over a thousand injuries."

A voice in the back hollered, "Seven deaths, Andy. One of the victims was eight months pregnant."

The room got quiet and Andy said somberly, "Okay, seven deaths." Then he added, "I shudder to think about what could have happened if that tower went down."

"I'd like five minutes with the bastards," someone shouted. Others joined in with amazingly creative expletives, and Andy waited until they settled down.   .

"We all feel the same way. But here's the good news. We can use this tragedy as an opportunity to reexamine our emergency management practices on every level to make sure we're prepared and the public is informed."

There was general agreement on that.

"We all know the score in the fire service. The public appreciates us when there is a disaster and pretty much forgets we exist when things are quiet. Now that we have everyone's attention, we should take advantage of it."

The chief checked his watch and said, "You're not here to listen to me, but before I turn this meeting over to the county, I want to share a quick story for you guys from out of town. On the morning of the World Trade Center bombing, one of the factories in town received a bomb threat. We followed procedure, and it turned out to be bogus. An hour or two later the WTC blew. You can imagine what we were thinking."

He paused. "The FBI investigated but came up empty. In retrospect, we know it was all a big coincidence. But my point to you is what if it wasn't? What if the place had blown? Or what if a major facility in *your* town blew? What if the building stored explosives or toxic materials? Would you be prepared? What if people needed to be evacuated? What if there was a school or hospital or nursing home nearby?"

He paused and scanned the audience. "I know you guys have plans in place in your towns, plans you've worked hard on. Now is the time to revisit those plans to make sure that all of your emergency services personnel, especially the new ones, are familiar with them. Now is a good time to meet with elected officials, school principals, hospital administrators, and any other key players to put everyone on the same page."

Heads nodded.

"I know none of us likes to have someone tell us how to do our business." He smiled and added, "The fact is, some of you guys are pretty damn hard headed."

"Damn, Andy," someone shouted, "Your head's like a friggin' anvil!"

Everyone laughed, and the chief joined them. "That's because I know I'm always right."

A couple of guys booed jokingly.

The chief laughed and held up his hands. "Okay, enough of this bullshit. The point is that the county has done a lot of work on this and is here to help. So I'm gonna turn this over to Mitchell Clark from the Bucks County Fire Marshall's office. Mitch is going to run us through a check list, a task analysis of all the things we should be doing in our municipalities. "

The men clapped, and Mickey's thoughts drifted as Clark made his way to the front of the room. From the day when Mickey and Johnny saved Old Man Lombardi, Mickey had been taken by the idea of helping others. His respect for emergency services had grown during his training. Now he saw an even bigger picture when it came to disaster management. What happened in New York could happen anywhere. One of his instructors had said that all emergencies are local. He was right.

Mickey scanned the room and noticed John Doster. John was somewhat of a legend in the fire service. He was 75 years old and had been fighting fires for forty-eight years. He'd been a chief in nearby Bristol Township and had once used his home as collateral to help his company secure a mortgage for a new firehouse. In 1972 he entered a burning building to rescue a three year old boy. Five years later he repeated the feat, this time rescuing a mother and her young child. The heart attack he suffered as a result ended his firefighting career but couldn't keep him away from the fire service. While others might have considered retirement, he devoted himself to training firefighters and working with the fire police.

When Mickey was in training, one of his instructors had said that every young firefighter needs an experienced person to look up to, someone to emulate. For Mickey, that person was John Doster. He had led a purposeful life and was old enough to be sitting on a park bench somewhere swapping stories with old men. But instead, he was where he belonged, sitting with his fellow firefighters and searching for ways to protect others.

Mickey knew for certain that this was what he wanted to do with his life.

43- Game 5

October 21, 1993

The Pac Men stood at the south gate of Philadelphia's Veterans Stadium, waiting for the others to arrive.

"Nine World Series tickets!" Bobby gushed. "Nine! How did you do it?"

Brian shrugged. "Just lucky, I guess."

"No way," Mickey said. "This isn't luck. What's up with these tickets?"

"My stock broker," Brian confessed, smiling. "The guy can be resourceful when a two million dollar customer gives him an assignment."

"You are definitely the man," Tommy said.

"Hey, the Phillies haven't won a World Series since 1980," Brian replied. "I told my broker I didn't care about the cost, just get me the tickets."

"Nine!" Bobby repeated.

"So how much was it?" Mickey asked. "We're all chipping in or we're not going." The other guys nodded their agreement.

"That's the beautiful thing," Brian said. "They're free."

Mickey wasn't buying that. "Nobody gets World Series tickets for free."

"Trust me," Brian said. "My guy got us seats in his corporate box. It took a lot of effort, but I squeezed him pretty good."

"Those boxes serve free food," Tommy said excitedly.

Bobby changed the subject. "Where is everybody? I want to see batting practice."

Brian checked his watch. "Relax. They'll be here soon."

Mickey said to Brian, "If it wasn't for you, I don't know if we'd ever get the guys together. Thanks again."

Brian nodded. The Pac Men hadn't seen each other since a brief gathering over the summer, and Brian knew the Series would draw them like a magnet. Bobby, Mickey and Tommy, who had finally flunked out of Slippery Rock, had driven down from Bristol. Brian had taken the train from Boston, and Johnny was driving in from Penn State. Knowing what fans the guys at the deli were, Brian also invited Mr. Marzo and Johnny's adopted uncles, Nick, Jimmy, and Big Frankie.

The crowd filing into the stadium was a sea of red, with Phillies chants coming from all directions and everyone caught up in the excitement. Bobby saw the men from the deli approaching and called to them. Jimmy spotted him and steered Angelo, Nick and Big Frankie in their direction.

"Hey, guys," Nick said. "It's a beautiful night for a ball game." They all shook hands and exchanged greetings.

A blind man nearby, wearing sunglasses, a red hat, shirt and pants, started playing an amplified guitar and thanking fans as they dropped change in his tip cup. "God bless you. God bless the Phillies. God bless us all," he said over and over.

Angelo shouted above the noise, "Where's Johnny?"

"No sign of him yet," Brian said, struggling to be heard as well.

They moved away from the performer, and Angelo said, "We would have been here sooner, but Big Frankie made us stop at Tony Luke's."

Brian looked disappointed. "You guys ate?"

Angelo shook his head. "I told these guys there'd be food in the box, but…"

"Look," Frankie said. "You can't go to a game in Philly without stopping at Tony Luke's for roast pork, provolone, and peppers. How do ya pass that up?"

"Big Frankie ate two gigantic sandwiches," Jimmy said. "I don't know where he put them"

"In his mouth," Nick interjected. "Which is more than I can say you did. Look at your Phillies shirt. Stains all over it."

"It was juicy," Jimmy protested. He examined his shirt and looked disappointed. "Do you think they'll come out? I paid good money for this shirt."

"No," Nick said. "You're screwed. Throw it away."

Brian laughed. He really enjoyed these guys and was glad he was able to include them. He wished his father could be there too, but he was away on business.

Big Frankie put his arm around Brian and said. "I've never seen a World Series game in person. Thank you."

Tommy added, "I haven't either, but the Phillies haven't been in any since I was seven."

"Well, that's gonna change tonight," Brian said. "I'm glad we could all get together."

They heard a familiar voice scream, "Go Phillies!" and turned to see Johnny approaching.

"There he is!" Jimmy said rubbing his hands together. "Now we've got a ball game."

Johnny hugged his dad and exchanged greetings with everyone else. Then he said, "This is for you, Pop." He handed his dad a Phillies hat that matched his own. Angelo put it on and said, "Thanks, Son. It's good to see you." They hugged again and Johnny said, "I can't wait to see Mom."

"She'll be waiting up for us. She's thrilled that you're staying over tonight."

"Hey," Bobby pleaded. "How about some batting practice?"

"Let's do it," Brian said.

They entered the stadium and were escorted to the corporate box that had a fully stocked bar, complete with a bargirl that could have been a super model, and a food table with a generous spread.

Brian's financial advisor greeted them and Brian introduced him to everyone.

"It's our pleasure to have you with us," the stockbroker said. He looked like he actually meant it. "Please help yourselves to the food."

"If you insist," Big Frankie said smiling. "I'm starving."

"I just have one request," their host added. "The seats are numbered, so please sit in the seat that corresponds with your ticket number. Others will be coming and we want everyone comfortable."

They took their seats just as the Toronto Blue Jays were finishing batting practice and the Phillies were about to begin theirs.

Nick and Jimmy were sitting next to each other. Two years earlier Jimmy had the improbable luck of winning a pickup truck at a Phillies game by sitting in the lucky seat. What should have been a happy occasion resulted in near warfare when Jimmy learned he had to pay tax on the value of the car. He did, eventually, but it nearly cleaned him out.

Everyone knew Jimmy was a little slow, and Nick loved him like a brother and had protected him since grade school. Nevertheless, every once in a while, Nick liked to have some harmless fun at Jimmy's expense.

"Hey, Jimmy," Nick said loud enough for the other guys to hear. "I heard they're giving a car away tonight. Don't forget, if they call your seat number, you have to pay taxes."

"Ah, shit," Jimmy said. "Not that again."

"Just so you know," Nick added, winking at Big Frankie.

Frankie jumped in. "I heard they raised the tax rate too."

"No way," Jimmy said. "I can't afford to pay anything."

"Well, let's just hope you don't win because I don't want any trouble like last time," Nick said.

Jimmy looked nervous. "Do you think I'll win?"

Frankie was enjoying this and said, "You can never tell, but maybe not. There're a lot of people here."

"Thousands," Jimmy said. "Somebody else will probably win."

"I don't know, Jimmy," Nick chimed in. "Ever since you sat down I've just had this feeling about that seat."

"What kind if feeling?"

"I can't explain it," Nick said. He shot Frankie another look and said to Jimmy, "Kind of like it was a lucky seat or something."

"Really," Jimmy said, sounding more anxious. "You have a feeling?"

"It's probably nothing," Nick said. "Don't worry about it."

Nick pretended to focus on batting practice. "Look, Lenny Dykstra's batting. I bet he hits a few out."

Dykstra had three home runs in the series thus far, including two in game four, which the Phillies lost by the incredible score of 15-14. They found themselves behind the Blue Jays three games to one and needed a win tonight to avoid elimination. A coach was lobbing them in and Dykstra was spraying balls around the field.

From the corner of his eye Nick could see Jimmy fidgeting in his seat. Dykstra hit a massive shot just foul and Nick hollered, "Okay, Lenny, straighten it out."

Jimmy tapped him on the shoulder. "Hey, Nick."

Nick didn't respond. "Let's go, Lenny. Pop one."

"Hey, Nick," Jimmy said louder. "Can I ask you a favor?"

Nick looked at him. "Did you say something?" Nick could see Frankie struggling not to laugh.

"Nick," Jimmy said. "Would you change seats with me?"

Nick feigned surprise. "Why?"

"I…I don't want the lucky seat. I'm afraid I'm gonna win again. I can't afford it."

With that Big Frankie broke out laughing and Jimmy got angry. "What's so funny, Frankie?"

"Nothing," Frankie said, trying to get under control. "I was just thinking of something that happened yesterday."

"Bullshit," Jimmy said. "You're laughing at me. Maybe I should switch seats with you since you're a big time carpenter and make plenty of money. You can win the damn car and pay the taxes."

Angelo was sitting on the other side of Frankie and had heard most of the exchange. He leaned in and said, "Will you guys knock it off and give the guy a break?" Then he said, "Jimmy, they're not giving a car away. These guys are just bustin' your chops."

Jimmy looked at Nick. "Son of a …"

Nick put his hands up. "That's not true, Jimmy. I really thought they were giving a car away. It was an innocent mistake, right Frankie?"

"That's right," Frankie said, "an innocent mistake."

"You guys are a pain sometimes," Jimmy said. "I'm gonna get a soda."

He stepped over Nick and headed for the bar, and Nick called to him, "Hey, Jimmy, don't spill the soda on your shirt."

The fans were insane when the game started, screaming and waving their white towels. Curt Shilling was on the mound for the Phillies, and he retired the Blue Jays in the first inning. Now the Phillies were up and they started off well. Dykstra got on base and eventually John Kruck drove him in for a 1-0 lead. The Phillies pecked away in the second inning as well, when doubles by Darren Dalton and Kevin Stocker resulted in another run. After that, Schilling and Toronto's Juan Guzman settled into a pitcher's duel with the Phillies leading 2-0.

Johnny was sitting next to Brian, and they used the time to catch up. Brian told Johnny about his work with Dr. Blake. The guy was a genius who spent most of his time on his government consulting work. He liked Brian and brought him in on several projects. Recently, Blake had suggested that Brian consider a career in the technical end of the intelligence field when he graduated.

"You mean, like a spy?" Johnny asked.

"I'm thinking about it," Brian said.

Then the conversation turned to Johnny and, of course, Carrie.

"Things are good," Johnny said, "but not great. It was hard being away from her this summer, and things got a little stressful."

As part of his ROTC requirement, Johnny had spent a month in the Army's Leader's Training Course at Fort Knox, Kentucky, and Carrie used the time to return to Germany to be with her parents.

"So what was the training like?" Brian asked.

"It was great. I had one of those typical sergeants you see in the movies. He was constantly on our backs, but I loved it. The physical training was tough, but I liked the challenge. We did what they call adventure training in the field and combat water survival. We practiced repelling down a mountain and scaling cliffs. I thought about the guys at Normandy when we did that.

"We practiced marksmanship with M-16 rifles. It was pretty cool."

"Sounds that way," Brian said.

"The toughest part was the urban combat simulation. It's scary as hell. You move through streets in tight surroundings with windows and alleyways everywhere, and you don't know where the bad guys are. You think things are okay and wham, a bad guy pops out of nowhere and hits you with a kill shot. They use these paint ball devices, so when you're hit, you know it.

"But I'll tell you what, you learn in a hurry that training can save your life."

"Are you sure this is what you want to do?" Brian asked.

"Positive," Johnny said. "I haven't told you the most important part yet. This program is more than just making me a soldier. It finally sunk in that I'm training to be an officer. Once you truly understand the dangers involved and realize that someday you'll be a Second Lieutenant in charge of your own squad or platoon…" Johnny paused. "Once you realize that soldiers' lives will be dependent on you, you grow up fast."

"You're a natural leader," Brian said. "You always have been. People follow you because you're good at it."

"Yeah," Johnny said. "But that was kid stuff. Now, when you're in training and simulated rockets are exploding around you and tracer bullets are sailing over your head, you think to yourself that someday your squad will look to you and say, 'What do we do now, Lieutenant?' It's a pretty sobering thought. The army says it brings out the real leader in us. I hope so."

Both the Phillies' and Blue Jays' bats went silent as Schilling and Guzman plowed through inning after inning. Johnny was always amazed by the ironies of baseball. Incredibly, the teams had scored a combined twenty-nine runs the day before, and now, the score remained 2-0 in the seventh. Both pitchers looked stronger as the innings progressed. Johnny had taken a break to share a sandwich and some conversation with his dad near the bar before they returned to their seats for the final three innings.

When he got back, Brian said. "So you mentioned some tension with Carrie. What's that all about?"

"Things are great in most ways. They really are. I'm crazy about her. We spend most of our free time together, and there's no doubt we love each other. She's fun, she's upbeat, and everybody likes her."

"But?"

"But there are a few problems. Carrie really doesn't like the military and is upset that I made a commitment. She tells me it's not too late to get out. Give up the scholarship and do something else with my future."

Brian looked at him. "If it's the money you're worried about, my tuition offer is still good. I mean that."

"Thanks, but that's not it. I made a commitment and, like I said before, I like the Army. Carrie and I are gonna work things out, but it'll take some time."

"What does she do when you're in training at the college?"

"She volunteers. I swear she's involved in more causes. Now she works for the Red Cross, which is nice. She runs blood drives on campus. She's really a terrific person."

"You don't have to tell me," Brian said. Then he added, "So how does she like Penn State?"

"Well, that's another thing. She likes it, and we have a great time. But every once in a while I can tell she's hungry for something. I think she misses Europe a little too. She wanted me to go with her to see her parents last summer and was mad that I couldn't because of my training. She said we could have had a great time. I guess she had a point."

"It would have been nice," Brian said.

"Yeah, anything I do with her is nice. She wants me to fly home with her for part of Christmas vacation."

"I hope you're going."

"I am. I just have to break the news to mom tonight. I'll promise her we'll both be home for Thanksgiving."

A little while later Brian said, "Just make sure you hold on to that girl, Johnny. Whatever it takes."

"That's the plan," Johnny replied.

Johnny turned his attention to the game as the Phillies were six outs away from keeping the series alive. Mickey and Tommy were debating whether or not Schilling should pitch the ninth or reliever Mitch Williams should be brought in to close. Jimmy and Big Frankie were already analyzing the pitching match ups for the next game. Jimmy was on his third hot dog and Brian noticed some new mustard stains on his shirt. Everyone was having a good time, everyone except Brian.

Brian scanned the stadium. The place was electric. He saw little kids in Phillies caps, wearing their baseball gloves in the hope of catching a foul ball. He saw young girls with their long hair pulled through the back of their hats, holding on to their boyfriends and praying for a win. He saw old men who remembered the famous Phillies Whiz Kids of the 1950's. There were 62,000 fans at Veterans Stadium, and everyone seemed happy.

Brian thought of a book he read once, a novel titled *Black Sunday*. The book was about a Middle Eastern terrorist group called Black September that planned to kill thousands of Americans at a Super Bowl in Miami by using a blimp with an explosive device.

Brian scanned the crowd again and imagined the carnage that could take place in such a gathering. He shook off the image and told himself that things were fine. Everyone was safe. It worked a little.

Schilling was taking the mound for the ninth inning and the crowd was on its feet. The noise was deafening as the Pac Men and the guys from the deli were whooping it up. Brian caught Nick's eye and Nick gave him a thumbs up. Brian smiled and shouted, "Let's go Phillies!"

Schilling seemed to be stronger in the ninth than he'd been the whole game. The crowd roared after each out, and when Schilling retired the last batter, the fans erupted.

The series was now 3 games to 2 and the Fightin' Phils had survived to fight another day.

44- March Madness

March 17, 1996

Johnny called Carrie at her off campus apartment before she left for her morning class. The NCAA tournament was in full swing and he thought it would be fun if they caught some of the regional games at a sports bar in State College. They were big basketball fans, especially during March Madness.

"I have a better idea," Carrie said playfully. "I just found out that my roommates will be away for the night. Why don't you come here? I'll make tacos and we'll have a little party."

"I'll be over in ten minutes," Johnny teased.

"No you won't," she said firmly. "You'll go to your classes and come over at seven."

"How about four o'clock?"

"Seven!" Carrie said laughing.

Johnny feigned disappointment. "Fine. I'll come at seven and I'll bring some salsa and chips for our little Mexican party."

"That's okay; I already have some."

"Then I'll bring refried rice."

"I have it."

"How about if I bring us two of those big Mexican sombreros?"

"No hats. They mess up my hair."

"How about a Mexican guitar like the guys in the movies play outside the window of the pretty girl?"

Carrie laughed. "You don't know how to play."

"I'd learn for you."

"That's sweet, Johnny Marzo, but I've heard you sing, so skip the music."

"Okay, my last offer. I have some old Geraldo Rivera videos. I like the one where he's opening Al Capone's…"

Carrie giggled. "Knock it off or I'll be late for class."

Johnny got quiet.

"If you want to be helpful, why don't you stop at the liquor store and pick up a bottle of tequila and some margarita mix."

Johnny liked the idea. "Have I told you lately that you're perfect?"

"Not since yesterday, but that's okay."

Johnny was excited. "I'll see you at 6:59 tonight."

"There's one more thing, Johnny."

"What's that?"

"Bring your toothbrush."

She hung up before he could reply.

Johnny clapped his hands and jumped up to touch the ceiling. No one ever gave him the emotional lift that Carrie did. He'd given a lot of thought to their future lately. They'd be graduating in three months, and it was time to resolve what they would do next. Johnny's full time military commitment would begin, and he knew it would be a problem. They'd avoided the topic like the plague, but it was always the elephant in the room, the issue they tried to ignore but could never escape. It was time to face reality and sort things out.

Johnny showed up at 6:45. When Carrie opened the door he said, "Sorry I'm late. I was held up by the border patrol."

He had cut a hole in the center of a large brown towel and was wearing it as a poncho. Carrie laughed out loud. He was holding two bags. He handed her the smaller one and said, "This is a little something for you."

She opened the bag and found a cinco de maya refrigerator magnet. "It's beautiful," she said smiling. "How did you know I wanted one?"

"I think it means I love you in Spanish."

Carrie shook her head. "You're better at languages than I am, and you know that's not what it means. You're crazy, Johnny Marzo, but I love you anyway."

She put her arms around his neck and kissed him- He loved it when she did that.

When they parted he gave her the other bag and said, "And this is for us."

The bag contained the tequila, margarita mix, bar salt and two margarita glasses.

"Wow," she said. "We're doing this right."

"This will have to do until we make it to sandy beaches and beautiful sunsets of Cancun."

"That sounds nice."

"Or, we could go during hurricane season. We'd save money and, if we're lucky, we'd have to barricade ourselves in our hotel room to ride out the storm. There wouldn't be much to do, and it would just be the two of us."

Carrie smiled. "That sounds nice too."

"Or," Johnny added. "We could go during the good season, and barricade ourselves in our room anyway."

Carrie knew that Johnny might go on forever, so she said, "How about if you take off that silly towel and start mixing us some margaritas, and I'll work on the food?"

They moved to the kitchen and Johnny made the drinks. Johnny said, "Temple's playing Cincinnati tonight. Who do you like?"

"I like Duke."

"Sorry, Babe, but Duke's been eliminated."

"I know, but they're still my favorite team."

"That's because they win a lot and you're a front runner."

"Not true. I just like them."

Johnny handed her a margarita and said, "Cheers."

They clinked glasses and drank. Carrie said. "This is very good."

"Thanks," He said. "Now let's get back to basketball. I don't think you can like a team unless you can spell its coach's name. Can you spell the coach's name?"

Carrie smiled. "Sure I can. M-I-K-E."

Johnny laughed. "That's cheating. Try his last name."

"No problem. It's spelled K."

Johnny shook his head. "The full name."

"They call him Coach K, so it's spelled K."

"You know his name is Krzyzewski, and I know you can't spell it."

"Okay, you win. I'll change teams."

"Great. So why not cheer for Temple since they're the hometown team?"

Carrie's smile faded. "I don't have a hometown, remember?"

Johnny gave her a hug. "Someday you will. We'll settle down somewhere."

Carrie looked at him and said, "We?"

Johnny kissed her forehead and said, "Let's sit down a minute."

"The food is cooking."

"Just turn down the heat for a while. We need to talk. Bring your drink."

They returned to the living room and sat on the sofa. Johnny said, "Carrie, I think we know how we feel about each other. I love you more than anything."

Carrie smiled nervously and said, "I feel the same way about you."

"We're graduating in three months. I think it's time we face our future."

Carrie nodded warily.

"I know this isn't the most romantic way to put it, but I'm prepared to make a commitment, and I hope you are too. I think we should get engaged. In fact, I've never understood the whole engagement thing, so maybe we should just get married."

"Married," Carrie said softly. "Wow. That's quite a surprise."

"I know that sounds impulsive, but I've been thinking about it all day."

"All day! And that's not impulsive?"

"That's not what I meant. I've known since you got here that I want us to be married. But this morning I thought, why wait?"

Carrie didn't respond.

"I know it's a lot at once," Johnny said. "But why fool around?"

Carrie took a sip of her drink. "Johnny, I can't see myself spending my life with anyone but you. I hope you know that."

Johnny sensed something bad coming, but tried to stay positive. "I think I do. So let's make it happen."

She turned to face him. "How can we do that under the circumstances?"

"Do you mean the army? That doesn't have to be a problem."

"Listen, Johnny. You're about to begin a four year commitment with the military. What am I supposed to do during that time?"

"There are thousands of army wives. Once my training is over we can be together."

Carrie put her head down. "Can you really see me living on a base in some God-forsaken place in Georgia or South Carolina? I'd die, Johnny. I'm a little antsy just living in a college town. I need some excitement. I need museums and concerts, cultural things."

Johnny started to speak, but Carrie held her hand up for him to stop.

"There's more. You've picked your future, and I know you made the decision when I wasn't around, so I don't blame you. I wish you didn't do it, but I don't blame you. But what about my future? I'm only twenty-one. I have interests too."

"What do you want to do?"

"Go to graduate school, for one thing. And travel."

Johnny looked surprised. "Travel! You've lived around the world."

"Here's the thing. As much as I hate the fact that I don't have any roots or a spot to call my hometown, I do enjoy seeing the world, and there are places I'd like to visit."

Johnny was trying hard to be understanding. "Like where?"

Carrie was reluctant to answer. She swallowed hard and said, "Africa."

"Africa!" Johnny exploded. "My God! Why Africa?"

"There are people there who need help. There's an AIDS epidemic and malaria and droughts and food shortages. Civil wars create thousands of refugees. The list goes on."

Johnny respected Carrie's commitment to people, but this idea sounded crazy. He said gently, "No offense, Carrie. But aside from making a donation, what could you possibly do to help with those problems?"

Carrie took another sip of her drink and put her head down.

Johnny went on. "There are some problems in the world that we just can't do much about. Maybe if you…"

Carrie interrupted him. "Johnny," she said softly. ""I'm thinking about working for the International Red Cross. There's a headquarters in Kenya that I'm interested in."

Johnny was stunned. He sat back on the couch, took a deep breath and exhaled slowly. When he spoke it was barely above a whisper. "Jesus, Carrie. Kenya?"

Carrie remained silent.

Johnny said, "Talk about impulsive. What's this?"

Carrie sat closer and draped her arm through his. She looked as if she might cry. "Ever since I got here I've thought about what would happen when we graduate and you go away. I've tried not to be mad at you, but it was hard sometimes. So I told myself that I had to respect your decision no matter how much it hurt."

"But you said yourself that I made that decision when I thought you were out of my life," Johnny said.

"But you could have broken your commitment when you were a freshman, and you didn't. That hurt, Johnny, and I've been trying to find a way to cope with it."

Johnny closed his eyes. "Senior year seemed so far off then."

"Well, it's here, Johnny. And like I said, I'm not mad at you. But the only way I can tolerate you being in the army for four years is for me to pursue my own dream. I have to survive."

"By going to Africa?"

"At least I have an idea where I'm going. You have no idea where the army will send you."

Carrie snuggled closer. "This could actually be romantic."

Johnny shook his head. "You'll have to explain that one."

"You are my man, and I'll be waiting for you. And if your feelings for me are what you say they are, then you'll be waiting for me too. We'll share our love from exotic places. When you're on leave, we'll rendezvous in cities we can't even think of yet. I'll fly to meet you and we'll barricade ourselves in our room, you me and a bottle of wine. We won't take each other for granted because our time together will be precious. And when your tour is over, I'll quit the Red Cross and we'll get married. We'll have kids and grandkids and tell them of the love we shared from across continents."

Johnny looked at her and smiled. "You're a little crazy, aren't you?"

Carrie smiled sheepishly and said, "It beats the heck out of belonging to the Army Wives Club at Fort Bragg, North Carolina."

When Johnny spoke, he sounded resigned to Carrie's plan. "I have to say this isn't the plan I envisioned for us."

"Life's never what we plan, Johnny Marzo. We just have to roll with what it sends us." Then she drained her glass and said, "Now are you going to kiss me or not?"

45- Career Path

September 1996

Brian walked down the long corridor to Dr. Blake's office, eager to get his take on the events of the day. The U. S. Attorney's office for the Southern District of New York, considered by many to be the most prestigious prosecutorial district in the nation, had just won a conviction against three terrorists who conspired and took substantial steps toward blowing up twelve United States passenger airliners in mid-flight over the Pacific Ocean in 1995. If successful, the plot could have resulted in as many as 4000 deaths.

The jury returned guilty verdicts against Ramzi Ahmed Yousef, also believed to be the mastermind behind the 1993 World Trade Center bombing, Abdul Hakim Murad and Wali Khan Amin Shah.

News of the plot had especially hit home for Brian because of his Uncle Ray's death aboard Pan Am Flight 103. So while Brian was horrified by the destructive potential of the plot, he was elated that the perpetrators were brought to justice.

Brian had been Dr. Blake's intern for all four years at M.I.T. At graduation, he applied for and was accepted into an accelerated doctoral program at M.I.T. that combined a Master's Degree and Doctorate into one intensified course of study. It was Dr. Blake who sponsored his admission into the program, and it was Blake who now served as Brian's doctoral advisor. But Dr. Blake had long ago become much more than an academic advisor to Brian. He was a mentor who watched over and guided his protégé. He was highly impressed by Brian's intellect, and he used his considerable clout to open doors for him whenever possible.

Brian entered Dr. Blake's office and the professor rose to greet him. He was beaming. "Come in, Brian. Have a seat."

"Good morning, Dr. Blake. I came as soon as I heard your message."

"This is a great day for America. We should celebrate. How about a coke?"

"Thank you, sir."

Blake opened the small office refrigerator and removed two bottles. He handed one to Brian and sat on the edge of his desk. He raised his bottle to Brian in a toast and drank. Then he said, "Have you ever heard of Mary Jo White?"

"Not until today."

"Well, put her name in your memory bank because I believe she is one of the toughest and most capable U.S. Attorneys in the country. And we all owe her a debt of thanks today for her work."

Brian nodded, and Blake went on. "Her office put together a masterful case to win the convictions, a complicated case. This Ramzi Yousef was a highly dangerous and elusive individual. We know he masterminded the World Trade Center bombing in '93 and fled the country immediately afterward. This is the same guy who was also planning to blow up the Lincoln and Holland Tunnels, the Statue of Liberty, and the United Nations building."

Brian shook his head at the thought.

They may have pulled this airline plot off if it weren't for a fire that broke out last year in the Manila apartment they were using to mix chemicals. The Manila police moved quickly, but even then Yousef was able to flee the country and ended up in Islamabad, Pakistan, where he was apprehended by authorities and extradited to the United States. The extradition itself was no small accomplishment. The U. S. Attorney General's office worked closely with the Department of State to pressure Pakistan to release him."

"Well," Brian said, "It looks as if all the hard work paid off. Maybe I should become a prosecuting attorney," Brian said.

"Maybe," Blake replied. "But remember, Mary Jo White did an excellent job with the prosecution, but a prosecutor is helpless without the evidence supplied by law enforcement or intelligence agencies."

Brian nodded.

Blake knew that protecting citizens was Brian's chief motivation and added. "And even more important than prosecuting these criminals is the ability to uncover their plots before anyone gets hurt."

"Exactly," Brian said.

"That means the FBI, or groups like the Joint Terrorism Task Force in New York, or the CIA abroad. It also means Special Forces units working on clandestine missions in countries we don't acknowledge a presence in. Their job is to find the worst threats, take them out quickly and secretly, and leave."

Brian had heard this speech before and agreed with it.

"This is where the war on terror... I should add it's a war the United States still doesn't fully understand we're in. This is where the war on terror will be fought and won. Many of our leaders still think in terms of large scale combat. That may work when you're fighting a conventional war against a conventional army. But that's not what this is all about. What we need is intelligence gathering and small, highly trained Special Forces units that can infiltrate foreign countries and surgically remove the cancers that plot and train there."

Blake was preaching to the choir because Brian understood and agreed. .

The professor took a long pull from his soda and then looked at Brian. "I've been thinking about your career path."

Brian smiled. "So have I, sir."

"I see three avenues you could pursue. You could get a law degree, become a prosecutor, and help put the bad guys in prison."

Brian nodded.

"Or you could join the army and eventually apply for Special Forces training, although I frankly don't see that for you."

"Probably not," Brian said.

"Or you could work in the intelligence community, using state of the art equipment to gather vital information, the kind of work you've been helping me with here."

"I like this work," Brian said. "And you know how much I've appreciated the opportunity to work with you."

Blake smiled. "Do you want to turn things up a notch?"

Brian was intrigued. "How do you mean?"

"I didn't call you here to discuss the airline plot conviction. That was just good news that happened to break today. I want to discuss your future."

Brian sat a little more erect.

"Your doctoral program has an internship component that requires students to have hands-on experiences in the real world, either corporate or government. Normally, we expect students to find and apply for positions on their own, but with your permission, I'd like to help."

"Thank you, Dr. Blake. I welcome all the help I can get."

"I'm glad to hear it because I've taken the liberty to recommend you for an internship with the CIA. Your security clearance is already in place. They've examined your record and my recommendation and informed me this morning that they're prepared to bring you in."

Brian sprang out of his chair. "Are you serious? That's incredible."

Dr. Blake laughed. "You'll have to go through a battery of tests, but I'm familiar with them and I'm confident they won't be a problem."

Brian was ecstatic. "Thank you so much, Professor. I can't believe this." Brian loved the research and lab work he'd been doing with Dr. Blake and was fascinated by the potential of the equipment and programs Dr. Blake pioneered, but he'd grown eager to see them in practical application.

Blake smiled. "You've earned it. In fact, they're as pleased to have you as you are to be with them. Now just keep your feet on the ground and do a good job."

46- Nairobi

The pilot announced they'd be landing in Nairobi in thirty minutes. Carrie looked out the window at the central Kenyan landscape and willed herself to be strong. She'd had serious doubts about her decision to go to Africa ever since she landed in Khartoum the day before. There was a long layover before her flight to Nairobi, and it proved to be the worst three hours of her life. The temperature on the tarmac was 105 degrees, and the stark, concrete terminal was hardly a welcoming sight for visitors. The Sudanese customs officials rummaged through her baggage and gruffly questioned her travel plans as they checked her passport. Inside, the rest room facilities were squalid, and Carrie endured two hours of discomfort before surrendering to the need to use them. There was little in the way of food or beverages in the terminal, and she didn't trust what she saw. But she'd been warned about dehydration, so she reluctantly purchased a bottle of water to wash down the protein bar she had in her bag.

She thought back to her last days with Johnny. Following their trip to Bristol, the two of them went to Long Beach Island, New Jersey for Memorial Day weekend. It would be their last chance to be alone for a long time. The weather was warm and the beaches were beautiful. During the day they took long walks, jogged, rented bikes, and visited shops. They had taken a small suite on the top floor of a bed and breakfast on Center Street near the ocean. On the first night, Carrie suggested dining at a nice restaurant, but Johnny refused.

"No way," he said. "We don't have a very good track record at restaurants, and I'm not taking any chances." He was right, of course. Carrie smiled at the thought of it. Instead, they ordered take-out and dined and drank wine on their balcony. There was a pleasant breeze, and they could hear the waves crashing against the jetty and the sound of soft music in the distance. They talked and laughed and seemed to appreciate each other more than ever. They were about to embark on separate adventures, and the thought that their love affair would span continents was exciting and very romantic.

On the final evening, after they shared ample amounts of wine, Johnny tried to sing a few lines from the song, *Somewhere Out There.* He was able to get out, "...even though I know how very far apart we are, it helps to think we might be wishing on the same bright star," and then he burst out laughing.

"Sorry," he said as he dripped wine down his shirt. "I was trying to be romantic."

"It was sweet," Carrie had said.

"It was cornball," Johnny said, still laughing. "Too much wine. Don't ever tell the Pac Men I did that. They'd eat me up."

"It'll be our secret."

Johnny turned serious. "You know, corny or not. It's true. We'll be apart, but we'll share the same sky. And every time I look at the stars I'll think of you."

A tear ran down Carrie's cheek. "I love you, Johnny Marzo, and we're gonna prove that this is a much smaller world than people think it is." She leaned over and kissed him.

"These have been the best three days of my life," Johnny said. "Promise me you'll be careful."

Carrie smiled. "You're going into the army and you want *me* to be careful?"

"You're going to Africa!"

"I guess we're both a little crazy." Then she added. "We'll be fine, and like the song says, 'Love will see us through.'"

Carrie was jarred from her thoughts when the stewardess asked her to buckle her seat belt for landing.

She looked out the window again and could see Nairobi in the distance. From her reading she learned that it was one of the most modern and westernized cities in sub-Sahara Africa. She took some consolation in that. Even though she wouldn't be stationed in the city, she looked forward to at least one comfortable night in a hotel after her travel ordeal.

After forcing herself to be strong for the past two days, she finally admitted to herself that she was frightened, not for her safety, but for her emotional well being. What in the world had she gotten herself into? She loved excitement, but she feared this little adventure might turn out to be far more than she bargained for.

She scanned the passengers as they prepared to leave. The vast majority were African. Most were well dressed and obviously traveling on business. There was a decent number of foreigners, maybe one in five, and most of them looked to be American or European. She reassured herself that English was the principal language of Kenya, at least in the urban areas. That would help. And, of course, the Americans maintained an embassy in Nairobi. She'd be fine. She steeled herself for what might come next and made her way to the exit.

She was pleased to see that the Nairobi airport was head and shoulders above Khartoum. It was cleaner and more modern with courteous employees. She followed the crowd to the baggage area and waited with the other passengers. Her bag came, and she winced as she pulled it from the conveyer. Her arm still hurt where she had gotten her immunization shots, and she shuddered at the memory: Hepatitis A and B, typhoid, yellow fever, rabies and tetanus-diphtheria. The ordeal had been enough to make her re-think the whole trip, but she toughed it out, although at times her imagination ran wild about why she would need a rabies shot.

She moved through customs and found the officials to be conscientious but polite. Finally she was cleared and walked to the entrance of the main terminal. She had been assured that someone would meet her and was relieved to see a young man, a rather handsome young man, holding a sign with her name on it. He spotted her, flashed a big smile, and walked in her direction.

"Miss Boyle?"

"How did you know?"

"They gave me the photo from your application. I must say, you weren't difficult to pick out." Carrie noted a heavy British accent.

He extended his hand, "I'm David Ward from the Nairobi office of the International Red Cross."

She took it and said, "Carrie Boyle. Thanks for picking me up."

He eyed her briefly and said, "Believe me; it is my pleasure. I hope you had a good trip."

"It was awful," Carrie said bluntly.

Ward laughed. "I appreciate your honesty."

"I was told to ask for identification."

"Yes, of course." He produced his wallet and showed her his I.D. Then he reached for her bag and said, "Please allow me." Carrie noticed that his hand touched hers a little longer than was necessary, and she hoped David Ward wasn't going to be a problem.

He left her at the curb while he retrieved the Land Rover and was back quickly.

"I hope I can show you Nairobi sometime," he said. "But we have a two hour drive to the camp and I'd like to do it in the daylight."

"Camp?

"Yes. We're doing malaria vaccinations west of here and we've set up camp for about two weeks."

Carrie's heart sank. She needed a warm bath and a bed just one more night before beginning her work.

They drove in silence for a while and then her driver said, "I'm sure you've read your orientation manual."

"I absorbed what I could in the time I had. It was extensive."

"Indeed it is. So then you know some of the statistics. Seven percent of the adult population of Kenya has HIV/AIDS, and there are 1.2 million people living with the virus now."

Carrie knew that.

"I want to caution you. There is a very high risk of food and waterborne diseases: like bacterial and protozoal diarrhea, hepatitis A, and typhoid fever. I know you've had your shots, but do not drink *anything* that hasn't been boiled or isn't bottled, and don't eat anything that hasn't been provided by the agency."

Carrie knew that too.

"Our major emphasis right now is combating malaria in the countryside.

Climate changes and a growing resistance to older vaccines have resulted in a new outbreak. I know that people around the world are into the whole mosquito net thing, and that's good. The nets help, but what the people really need is immunization and treatment."

Carrie knew that too, but she appreciated the chatter because it helped to pass the time. After a while Carrie said, "So how long have you been here, Mr. Ward."

Ward laughed and said, "Almost three years. And please call me David."

Carrie nodded.

"May I call you Carrie?

"Of course."

The roads were less well paved as they traveled farther from the city, and the Land Rover was kicking up dust. Carrie coughed and David smiled. "You can cover your nose and mouth with a bandana if you like."

"I'm fine," Carrie said even though she wasn't.

David returned to his travel guide mode. "Almost half the population of Kenya is under fifteen years of age, and only two and one-half percent live past 65. People die young here, but we're working on it."

Carrie felt miserable, and the more the Land Rover rocked on the uneven road, the worse she felt. She saw workers in a field and said, "What are they doing?"

"That's a tea plantation. You'll find them all along here now. Tea is one of the most important products of Kenya. It's a labor intensive crop and the commercial plantations employ a lot of people. It makes our job easier, because the corporations ensure a healthy workforce by providing immunization and proper medical treatment."

David took a bottle of water from a cooler between their seats and handed it to Carrie.

"No thanks," she said. She felt queasy already and really didn't want to risk putting anything in her stomach right now.

"It's not optional. If you don't make a conscious effort to drink you'll be dehydrated in no time."

"Thanks," Carrie said. "I guess you're right."

She had gotten a bad vibe from David at the airport and had been intentionally cool ever since. But he was pleasant enough and she didn't want to be rude to the only person she knew in Kenya. She said, "So what's your job here, David?"

"I'm a physician's assistant. I spent two years in medical school before I got a little stir crazy and decided to find out if medicine was really what I want to do with my life. I've been here ever since."

"They use physician's assistants to make four hour round trips to the airport? I'd think they could make better use of your skills."

David laughed. "Ah, you got me. Actually we have drivers who normally do that sort of thing. But when I saw your photo I lobbied hard to get the job. Our supervisor, Dr. Graham, owed me a favor."

Carrie decided it would be best not to reply. They drove the rest of the way in silence and arrived in camp at dusk. Dr. Graham was

African. He greeted her warmly and welcomed her to Kenya. "I'm sure you're tired and hungry. David will show you to your tent. Dinner is in one hour, so you'll have some time to get situated and rest beforehand. Later we'll discuss your duties." He smiled. "I hope you find your work here fulfilling."

Carrie thanked him and assured him that she was looking forward to helping in any way she could.

David took her elbow and gently guided her toward the tent. She'd had enough of him by now and was anxious to be alone. "You'll have three roommates, or tent mates I should say. They're not here now, but you'll meet them at dinner. There are twelve of us in all on the team. You'll meet everyone at dinner. *Always* close the flap or mosquito net on the tent or your roommates will be very unhappy." He thought a minute and added, "The lavatory facilities are just beyond the tents to the right. If there is anything you need, please ask." He smiled again and added, "You'll be fine here."

"Thank you, David. I'm sure I will." She turned and entered the tent. It was stark but well organized. Her roommates were obviously neat. She determined which cot was hers and placed her bags next to it. Then she collapsed on the cot, exhausted. She thought about what she had done, and then she cried.

47- Ranger School

January 1997

Johnny had dreamed of joining the Army Rangers since his first year of ROTC, but for the past several months the dream had become a nightmare.

The elite corps of airborne infantry could be deployed anywhere in the world at short notice, to any climate or terrain, and they needed to be trained for any eventuality. The Ranger Instructors used the rugged area near Fort Benning, the Blue Ridge Mountains of Northern Georgia, the swamps and coastline of Florida, and the parched terrain of Northwest Texas to drill trainees in amphibious landings, air assaults, jungle warfare and desert survival. They scaled cliffs, rappelled mountains, and traversed large expanses in hostile environments with little food and even less sleep.

At first Johnny soared through the requirements. He attacked each challenge in the Army Physical Fitness Test and excelled. But the course took a heavy toll on him and the others. Rangers were trained to survive on two meals a day or less and three and a half to four hours sleep. He'd lost twenty-two pounds, had a persistent case of trench foot, had suffered from dehydration twice, had shin splints, and his muscles and joints ached constantly. But worst of all was the effect of sleep deprivation that impaired his ability to recover from the strain of the training.

On average, about 60 percent of the candidates failed the program and only 20 percent made it through without having to repeat a phase. Johnny was physically and emotionally drained, but he was determined to finish and do it right the first time.

He remembered his last visit to Bristol. His parents were so proud. Nick and Jimmy, veterans themselves, had tears in their eyes as they wished him good luck, and Big Frankie, well, he was just Big Frankie, as strong and supportive as ever. He thought of Mr. Lombardi and the sacrifices he had made. There was no way Johnny could face any of the people back home if he washed out. He simply wouldn't let that happen.

If pride was his antidote for fatigue, it was thoughts of Carrie that gave him emotional strength. They wrote each other as often as they could, and her letters sustained him. She'd been down at first and confessed that Africa may have been a mistake. But gradually her letters became more upbeat as she adapted to her surroundings and saw the value of her work.

It had been eight months since they'd seen each other, but if all went well he'd complete his training in sixty days and be eligible for leave before he began his deployment. He knew they would both be different people when they met again, with amazing stories to tell, and he was certain their experiences would draw them closer than before. Her letters said as much.

But while she was as loving and sensitive as ever, he still detected something in her writing that betrayed her continued uneasiness with the military. He respected her views, but he didn't back away from sharing his experiences. Instead, he wrote extensively about what he was doing in the hope that she'd appreciate it more.

He was between training sessions now, with two precious days to rest. He had just read another of her letters and finished composing his reply. He stretched out on his bunk to read it once more before sending it off.

> *Dear Carrie,*
>
> *It was great to hear from you, as always. I've been in the field for two weeks and received your most recent letter today. It sounds like you're still doing amazing work, and I'm glad you're still getting satisfaction from it. I admire what you're doing and hope that someday I can visit Kenya with you as my guide.*
>
> *I'm about to enter the most demanding challenges of Ranger school, and I hope I'm ready. I'll have to run 1.6 miles in full gear and then attack the infamous Malvesti Field Obstacle Course. The course has the standard obstacles like a cargo net climb and overhead vertical bars, but it also has heavy mud, complete with leeches, barbed wire, and a large worm pit that we have to travel through. The pit is exactly what the name implies, with more worms than I've ever see in one place. It's supposed to build our mental toughness. I told the guys that after my experiences with you, the worm pit should be a breeze. Just kidding.*
>
> *We'll also make parachute landings from low altitude in very tight spaces. It's a harder jump than anything we did in airborne school, but it should be okay.*
>
> *Remember those long walks we took on the beach at LBI? You better. Anyway, I have to complete a 21 mile march at night in full gear and engage in simulated combat at the end. Then there's the water combat test. We'll toss our gear out of a helicopter and then jump out ourselves from twenty feet into a body of water while in full uniform. Then we have to retrieve our bags, swim to shore or inflate a raft, and prepare for an assault. Luckily, we have warm weather. I'm told they do the exercise as long as the water*

temperature is above 39 degrees! There's a part of my anatomy that wouldn't handle that too well.

There's so much more, but I think you've got the picture. It has been and will be grueling. Of course, all of what I just described is designed to help us get to the target. I haven't gotten into the training we receive in the use of weapons, close combat, communications, first aid, and all the rest.

They keep us motivated by asking us to visualize the situations that might require our deployment. We may have to rescue an ambassador in an urban setting, or destroy a drug factory in a South American jungle, or take out a terrorist cell in the Middle East.

I've made a lot of friends here. Most are great guys, dedicated to protecting their country, but a few are crazy and can't wait to get into combat. I don't see things that way. I hope we'll never fight, but I plan to be totally prepared if we do.

There's one guy here from Kansas named Chet Stoudt who I've become especially close to. We've been assigned as team partners for these final tests. The way it works is that we take the tests together and neither of us passes unless we both do. That goes for each exercise. It certainly builds a buddy system and gives soldiers a sense of responsibility. I've heard stories of guys who carried their partners the last couple of miles to finish the course. That kind of brotherhood reinforces the Ranger motto, "Never shall I leave a fallen comrade."

There's one good thing about all of this training. It keeps me occupied, which is a blessing, because I miss you so much that it drives me crazy when I have time to think about it. I want to sit on a balcony again with you on Long Beach Island, or Brooklyn, or Nairobi, or any place we can be together. I want to hear your voice again, hold you, and plan our future. I love you Carrie, and I pray for you every day. Please be careful and write as often as you can.

Johnny

48- Nairobi Countryside

March 1997

Dr. Harold Graham was remarkable. Trained in Tanzania, he had dedicated his life to humanitarian missions sponsored by the World Health Organization, the African Relief Fund and, most recently, the International Red Cross. He was an efficient manager who demanded that his team adhere to strict medical standards, even in the adverse conditions of the field. He asked a lot from his employees, and they willingly followed his lead.

On their current operation, Graham intended to set up camp in the Narok district, a couple of hours west of Nairobi. The area was largely populated by the Maasai, a semi-nomadic ethnic group indigenous to southern Kenya and northern Tanzania. Graham tried to visit the area once every three months to provide medical checkups.

Carrie had taken David Ward's advice and wore a bandana around her neck on long road trips. Now, as the convoy moved west, she raised it to shield her nose and mouth from the dust. David was driving the second Land Rover in the convoy with Carrie across from him and two African nurses in the back.

"After you're here a few years you'll get to ride in the lead vehicle," David said smiling. "Less dust."

Carrie doubted that would happen. She valued her work, but had no intention of spending several years in Africa.

"So how much do you know about the Maasai people?" David asked.

Carrie lowered her bandana and said, "Nothing. What can you tell me?"

Carrie was more relaxed with David now. After rebuffing his persistent advances for months and telling him of her commitment to Johnny, David had finally given up, and the two of them settled into an easy friendship.

"In the village they speak a language called Maa, but many understand some English and Swahili. So communication today shouldn't be too much of a problem. They rely heavily on cattle herding, but they're also pretty adept at farming in arid areas. The government tried to dissuade them from their nomadic practices but is beginning to realize that climate change is part of what keeps them on the move. It's a problem the western world is just beginning to understand."

Carrie already did and thought back to her involvement with environmental groups in Europe.

David continued. "As you can imagine, their diet is limited. They eat some meat, but rely mostly on cows' milk and maize. The milk pretty much gives them the protein they need, but Dr. Graham fears they're deficient in some essential vitamins. He dispenses what he can when he's here and explains how to use what he leaves behind."

"Are they receptive to our help?" Carrie asked.

"They love Dr. Graham. Once he won over the tribal elders, we were good to go. Their god, Enkai, takes two forms. Enkai Narok, the black god, is kind, and provides the essentials like rain and sun. Enkai Nanyokie, the red god, is vengeful. I think they see Dr. Graham as a gift provided by the Enkai Narok."

"Whatever works," Carrie said.

"There's one more thing," David added with a wink. "They occasionally drink cows' blood. Not everyone, and not that much. I'm not even sure who gets to do it and why, but it is done."

Carrie cringed. "Thanks for sharing that."

"I just didn't want you to see it and be caught off guard," he said, laughing.

They reached their destination and began to set up camp. A group of villagers gathered as the team worked, and David said, "Wait and see how the crowd grows as word spreads that Dr. Graham is here."

He was right. By the time their tents were pitched and tables were set up, village leaders had spoken to Dr. Graham, and people were lining up for examinations.

"It looks like they know the routine," Carrie said.

"They do," David replied.

Graham divided his team into three groups with a physician's assistant at the head of each. The visitors were funneled into the three lines where the teams performed initial exams to determine if any significant ailments existed. They dispensed medicine and administered immunization shots to children who needed them. Those deemed to have more serious conditions were sent to Dr. Graham's tent for further examination. Carrie, the remaining member of the team, was prohibited from performing any medical tasks. Instead, she raced from team to team, keeping inventory, recording medications used, and dispensing supplies.

As the day wore on, the lines grew. Mothers with newborns, fathers with toddlers in tow, and the elderly all waited patiently in the scorching sun for their turn. Carrie watched David and was struck by his demeanor. As she had seen so many times before, he greeted each visitor with a smile. He knew some limited Swahili and used it if he had to break the ice before switching to English. He took his time with each patient, checking their throats and their breathing, examining their eyes, probing their stomachs, and looking for rashes and other signs of illness. He was especially caring with the children, easing their fears and often taking the time to make them laugh before their examination.

Carrie considered the contrast between him and Johnny, and the paths they had followed in their young lives. Johnny had chosen to protect people by serving in the military. She found it ironic that in order to defend his countrymen, he needed to learn to harm others. That was a harsh assessment perhaps, but one that she felt was fairly accurate. David had chosen a different path, one that knew no national allegiance. He was thousands of miles from his native country, helping people that the world had forgotten or didn't know existed. He did it without seeking recognition or material gain. And his help came in the form of healing.

It was dusk by the time the last patient was seen, and the team was exhausted. As a non-medical employee, preparing dinner was one of Carrie's duties, and she laid out the food they had packed for the evening. Dr. Graham was elated by the success of the day and produced a few bottles of wine to celebrate.

"Everyone did an exceptional job today," Graham said. "We saw more patients than I dreamed would be possible. Most important, we have reinforced their confidence in us, which will serve us well if a serious outbreak of something develops. You should all be proud."

Carrie was. She was bone tired, her skin was covered with sweat, her hair was matted, and she tasted dust each time she took a bite of her food. But she felt enormously proud and privileged to know the people she was working with. Of all the rewarding experiences she'd had with the Red Cross in the past months, this was by far the most satisfying. She wasn't quite sure why, but today she felt like she was finally a member of the team.

It was dark by the time they finished dinner, and one by one team members dragged themselves to their tents. Soon Carrie and David were the only ones left at the table, and David said, "I'm still too wound up to sleep."

"I know what you mean," Carrie said. "I keep thinking there's more to do."

"I'd say you've done enough for one day," David replied. "You were great."He reached for the remaining bottle and said, "More wine?"

Carrie laughed. "No thanks. I've had enough."

David filled his glass. He drank and Carrie said, "You're good at this work."

"Thank you," he said modestly. "I enjoy it."

"I can tell." She studied him briefly. He looked just as worn out as she felt. Then she said, "I want you to know that I admire what you do."

David smiled and raised his glass. "And I admire you. Anytime a beautiful girl gives up an easy life to spend months in Eastern Africa, she earns my respect."

"Does it happen often?"

"Never, "David said.

"How do you know I had an easy life?"

"Mostly from what you've told me," he replied. Then he eyed her up and down and smiled. "Besides, you don't look like you were a farm hand in Nebraska. Although today you do, just a little."

Carrie laughed. "I guess I'm a mess."

David turned serious. "You're even more beautiful this way."

A cool night breeze replaced the oppressive heat of the day and Carrie sighed. "That feels so good."

"The temperature can drop quickly in this part of the valley."

Carrie was silent. She was aware that David had slid closer to her on the bench. She had to admit that she had started to feel attracted to him recently. There was a lot to like. He was handsome, intelligent, gentle, and obviously selfless in his desire to help others. In an odd way, she had missed his advances once he stopped them. But now she sensed a different vibe coming from him, a renewed interest.

He said softly, "You know Carrie, even with all of this work to occupy us; it can get terribly lonely sometimes."

"I know," Carrie whispered. Sometimes the loneliness was oppressive. On a few occasions she had feared a panic attack coming on as she allowed herself to think about where she was and how long she had been there.

He stroked her arm gently and said, "It doesn't have to be that way."

"I know," Carrie said again. The fatigue and the wine had finally hit her, and she was feeling... oddly vulnerable.

"I know why I'm here," David said, still stroking her arm. "I came searching for meaning in my life and found the work I love." He paused and said, "But I wonder about you. Why are you really here?"

That was a good question, Carrie thought. Why was she here?

She turned to face him and David leaned in to kiss her. She hesitated for a moment and pulled away. She smiled and said, "It's been a wonderful day, and I'm glad I was a part of it. But I'm very tired and I think I'll call it an evening."

David leaned back and smiled graciously. "Of course," he said. "Let me walk you to your tent."

"Thank you," Carrie replied, standing now. "But I'm fine and I prefer to be alone."

It was a clear night. As she walked back to her tent she looked up at the sky and saw a brilliant array of stars. She smiled and wished Johnny good night.

49- Sweet Sorrow?

Carrie arrived at the mess tent early the following morning. It was her job to prepare breakfast, and the plan was that they would break camp and head back to Nairobi after everyone had eaten.

She'd had a fitful night, tossing and turning with thoughts about Johnny. She was proud of herself for resisting David's latest advance but also felt guilty because she knew that she'd been attracted to him. She tried not to be too hard on herself, deciding that her attraction had been perfectly normal under the circumstances. She hadn't seen Johnny in over eight months, and she'd been isolated in a hostile environment that whole time. The more she'd gotten to know David the more she realized that they shared the same humanitarian interests, and she liked that. Add the fact that David was an appealing figure, and it was indeed understandable that she'd come close to straying. What mattered was that her senses prevailed, and she'd remained true to Johnny.

She told herself that the whole event was actually a positive thing. It was difficult to maintain the spark in a long-distance relationship that is limited to letters, photos, and an occasional phone connection. Passions recede over time and memories become less vivid. In a strange way, what happened the previous night rekindled the images that drove her relationship with Johnny in the first place. Coming close to violating her trust somehow made her commitment even stronger.

The team began to file in, and Carrie braced herself for David's arrival. He'd been a gentleman the night before, and she appreciated that, but she still feared their meeting today would be awkward. The team was still feeling the effects of their exhaustive work, and everyone was more subdued than usual. Most of the team was seated, but David hadn't arrived yet. She moved from table to table serving coffee, juice, toast and fruit preserves and making small talk.

It had been a productive trip, but everyone was anxious to get back to Nairobi to enjoy a good meal, a hot shower and some clean clothes. Most ate quickly and returned to their bunks to pack, but there was still no sign of David.

Dr. Graham was one of the stragglers and Carrie said, "Should I save something for David before I clean up?"

"That won't be necessary," Graham said. "David won't be coming."

Graham noted her quizzical expression and added, "He stopped by my tent last night and asked permission to head out at daybreak today. He had some personal business to attend to before our next field operation. You'll ride back with me in my vehicle."

Carrie nodded and tried not to appear too surprised.

"He asked me to give you this." Graham pulled an envelopee from his pocket and handed it to her." Then he smiled. "You did a good job on this trip. It's good to have you around."

"Thank you," Carrie replied nervously. "It's an honor to work with you."

Graham turned to leave and said over his shoulder, "Try to pack as quickly as possible. We need to move on."

She waited until she was alone to open the envelopee and read the note inside.

> *Dear Carrie,*
>
> *I apologize for not telling you this in person, but I just can't. When Dr. Graham returns to Nairobi later today, I intend to ask for a transfer to another team. I feel myself falling in love with you and can't imagine continuing to work together without pushing myself on you again in the future. I don't want to do that, so I feel it's best that I move on.*
>
> *I love my work, but there's much to do elsewhere, and I should be placed easily. I'll miss Dr. Graham, but I think another experience will be just as rewarding.*
>
> *Of course I will miss you terribly. I was infatuated from the first time I saw you, but my feelings have grown into something much, much more. I admire your commitment to someone else and I have to respect that. He must be a very special person to be blessed by such loyalty. I hope he appreciates what he has.*
>
> *If you ever need me for anything, I'm sure I can be reached through the Red Cross Headquarters. I wish you*

*the very best, Carrie, and will always dream about what
might have been.*
   All my love,
   David

Carrie swallowed hard and folded the envelopee. She knew she
should feel relieved, but she felt saddened as well. David had become
something special to her, and even though she'd never given in to his
advances, it was somehow nice knowing that he was interested. And
she certainly had grown to depend upon his companionship. Suddenly,
she felt very much alone.

She tore the letter into small pieces, threw it in the trash, and began
clearing the dishes. It was time for the team to move on.

50- The Swamp

June 1997

Johnny still hadn't gotten used to the oppressive heat. The swamp
that was south central Florida was no place to be in late June, which was
why the Rangers picked it for this phase of the training. Chet Stoudt
sat across from him in the MH-60 Blackhawk as they flew low over
the everglades. The Blackhawk was ideally suited for covert insertion
missions like the one they were on now.

It was the Blackhawk that had been used in the Battle of Mogadishu
in 1993. Two of them had been brought down with rocket propelled
grenades fired by militia fighters of Somali war lord, Mohamed Farrah
Aidid. The downed Rangers were quickly surrounded and grossly
outnumbered. They engaged in a fierce, eighteen hour firefight under
urban conditions. By the time reinforcements arrived to extract them,
eighteen Americans had died and more than seventy were wounded. The
trapped Rangers had defended themselves gallantly and had inflicted
considerable losses on the enemy. The entire event, the original mission,
the crash, the firefight, the rescue extraction and first aid administered
in the field, became a case study in Ranger training. Johnny wished
tonight's mission was in an urban setting instead of the swamp, and he
hoped they'd have more success.

It was a moonless night, and Johnny could barely see Chet with his blackened face and camouflage uniform. For the rest of the mission their code name would be Tropical Gemini, and they had already won each other's confidence.

Johnny reviewed his mental checklist for the tenth time and was sure Chet was doing the same. The chopper would slow to twenty knots, and they'd enter the water from twenty feet. Twenty knots! Johnny smiled at the thought. He would have preferred that the chopper hover nicely in a fixed position until he made his exit, but that wasn't how it was done. He also got a kick out of the "enter the water" phrase because looking outside he couldn't tell what was below them. A twenty-foot jump into anything but water would be nasty. He had to trust the pilot.

Toss, pause, jump- Johnny had practiced the rhythm countless times. He had forty pounds of gear packed in a watertight rucksack. With the chopper traveling at roughly thirty feet per second, he didn't want to be swimming in the dark looking for the sack before he made his way to shore. The sack was attached to his wrist by a long flexible cord. He had to toss the bag, pause a half second and jump. If he jumped too soon he could be ensnarled with the bag and cord and have a problem. If he jumped too late the cord could yank his arm out of its socket. Toss, pause, jump. Chet would follow, and the same timing would apply.

There were plenty of reasons to get out of the water as soon as possible, and he mentally reviewed his survival skills. A good place to shoot an alligator was above the eyes at the base of the skull, although an alligator's brains were small and he'd need a direct hit. But his firearms were packed in the sack anyway, so that option was out. The only weapon he'd have available when he hit the water was the six inch shank he had attached to his belt. Don't waste time stabbing a gator in the flesh, his RI had said, because that would only piss him off. A gator's eyes were especially vulnerable, and that would be an effective place to strike. Johnny wasn't sure he could do that, but didn't plan to be in the water long enough to find out.

A crew member motioned Johnny to the opening. Johnny winked and gave Chet a thumbs up. Then he shouted, "See you in the slime."

Chet smiled. "Keep your mouth shut when you hit the water."

Johnny sat at the opening prepared to jump. Below him was nothing but blackness. The tap on his shoulder came and Johnny tossed, paused and jumped. He held his feet together, and was relieved when they sliced the water. He went under and came up quickly. The water was warm and slimy. Airbags in the rucksack kept it afloat and he pulled it toward him. He could hear Chet doing the same. They swam toward each other and used what little light there was to get their bearings.

Chet said, "Let's get out of this sewer."

They swam quickly, pulling their sacks behind them. Finally they were out of the water and dragged their gear over ten yards of swampy mush to firm ground.

"Sweet Jesus," Chet said, wiping slime from his arms. "That was nasty."

They checked each other for leeches. Chet was clean, but Johnny had one attached to his neck. The little bastard hadn't taken long to find its new host, and Johnny hadn't felt it. That was the thing about leeches. Their suckers release an anesthetic that prevents the victim from knowing the leech is there. Earlier in their training Johnny had one attached a few inches below his armpit and didn't know it until another squad member noticed.

Pulling the leech off the body was out. It could result in the mouth remaining attached and becoming more difficult to remove. Chet opened his sack and was relieved to see that everything was dry. He took out a pack of cigarettes and matches. He lit a cigarette and told Johnny to stay still. He singed the leech and it fell to the ground. Leeches also released an anti-clotting enzyme with their bite to keep the blood flowing, and Johnny's bite continued to ooze a stream of blood. Chet applied an antibiotic as best he could and covered it with a bandage.

"You're the prettiest nurse I've ever had," Johnny said.

"Just don't get your ass infected on me," Chet said. "We've got work to do."

They removed the contents of their sacks and got busy. Within minutes they assembled their weapons, emptied and cleaned their boots, applied dry socks and prepared to move out. They had twelve miles to cover in full gear, through dense vegetation, in a little over three hours. It was a pace they'd trained for, but it wouldn't be easy.

Johnny thought back to his training manual. There were forty-one snakes indigenous to Florida, but only six were venomous- only six! Those weren't odds that Johnny liked. They had anti-venom serum in their sacks, but they knew that the most effective way to treat venomous bites was with a serum specific to the species. They'd have to be careful, but it was hard to look for snakes when he could barely see in front of his face.

After a while the clouds cleared and visibility improved. Their mission was a simulated raid on the outer defenses of a cocaine factory of a South American drug cartel. The outpost was designed to provide advance warning to the cartel if it detected approaching helicopters. The warning would give cartel sentries ample time to use their state-of -the-art shoulder-fired stinger missiles that are deadly against choppers. The Rangers' job was to cover the twelve miles, find the outpost, take it out quickly and efficiently, and radio the command post that the raid was good to go. The key was for the choppers to strike quickly and without warning. It was Johnny and Chet's job to make sure the warning never came.

They moved at a steady pace and were making good time. Johnny often found himself in the bad habit of thinking about Carrie during these long marches, and this one was no exception. Their mission was one of the final hurdles they had to clear before graduation from Ranger school. Graduation meant leave time, and leave time meant time with Carrie.

He forced those thoughts from his mind for now. They'd been warned that the areas closest to the target may be booby-trapped and he needed to focus. Any slip-up would doom their mission and they'd be recycled back to the beginning of jungle training. He wasn't about to do that. He'd trained in the frigid mountains of Georgia in February, the parched plains of Western Texas, and the semi-tropical swamps of Florida. All were grueling, but Florida was by far the worst of the three, and he had no intention of staying.

They had jogged and walked, depending upon the vegetation, for over an hour and stopped briefly to drink. They were perspiring profusely and, if there was one thing the army was adamant about, it was remaining hydrated. Nothing saps the strength like dehydration.

They each had four bottles of water and they sat and drained one now.

Chet studied the handheld GPS, one of the army's latest toys. It had a data base capable of storing vector graphics and topographical data and gave the men reliable information about their location and distance to target.

"We're making good time," Chet said,

Johnny nodded. "Let's keep making it. Never can tell what lies ahead. I'm not carrying your Kansas ass over the finish line."

"Not a chance, Marzo," Chet said smiling. "You just worry about yourself."

They were up again and moving. Their code name for the assault was Tropical Gemini and they'd use that term for any transmissions to base, which would be minimal.

Johnny thought about his training. He remembered his first mile and a half run carrying a loaded rucksack. He had completed it with no trouble and remembered how proud he felt. But that first event was minor compared to what came next. They endured impossible physical and psychological demands, and men washed out every day.

The Ranger Instructors constantly told the team that only a third would finish the program without being recycled at least once. Each time Johnny had heard that he grew more determined not to fail.

The twelve mile runs came next. He'd attacked them all and made sure his partner did too. Now they faced a major test. Completing the twelve miles in the allotted time wasn't the test. It simply put them in position to do what they came for. The test was taking out the observation post successfully.

Johnny felt up to the challenge. He'd never been in better shape in his life. In fact, he'd never dreamed he'd be able to accomplish the physical demands that he had mastered. Building confidence was a hallmark of Army Ranger training, but so was guarding against overconfidence. They were constantly reminded that this wasn't Hollywood movies, where the bad guys were hapless idiots easily overtaken. He was taught to expect the enemy to be as well trained as he was. Overconfidence could be deadly against such an adversary.

When the GPS indicated that they were a mile away they stopped to review their strategy. To make the simulation as authentic as possible, the guards stationed at the outpost were army personnel who had been placed there between one and fourteen days earlier. They knew an assault would come at some time, but had no idea when. By stationing them so long in advance, the army was allowing for the fatigue factor present in all sentry assignments. Regardless of how hard they tried, soldiers on guard duty had a drop off of attention span the longer they had the assignment. Johnny and Chet hoped this wasn't the first day for the guards on duty.

This raid was what the men in the unit jokingly called a Sherman-Williams assault because the army used to provide paintball ammunition. But they had recently switched to wax bullets that provided more accuracy from a greater distance and still left a mark on the uniform. Wax bullets could hurt like hell and leave a significant bruise, and a shot to the face could do serious damage. For this reason, both teams wore flack jackets and protective goggles, and were encouraged not to aim for the face.

To simulate hand to hand combat, the army equipped the participants with knife- like gadgets with collapsible blades that injected a paint cartridge when pressed against the skin. The rules of the war game were clear. If you were hit you dropped.

At 200 yards they stopped, and Johnny used the field glasses to survey the area. The outpost was built like a small bunker designed to withstand an air assault. It was made of cement with openings for a door and two windows. There was no back entrance or window. There was one guard outside and no one else around. They had no idea how many were inside, but whoever was there would be trapped if they pulled off the element of surprise. The assault would have to be quick with everyone taken out simultaneously. If even one sentry survived briefly, he could alert the main building two miles away, the stingers would be ready to fire, and the air assault would be aborted. Worst of all, their training would be recycled.

The plan they devised seemed too easy. They would crawl as close as they could to the building. Johnny would move to the west side and Chet to the east. The sentry was pacing back and forth in front of the building, probably to relieve his boredom. When the sentry turned his back, Johnny would spring at him from behind and take him out quietly with the spring loaded knife.

At that moment, Chet would sprint to the open doorway, and toss in two paint ball grenades while Johnny followed. They would both spray the room with wax bullets until everyone was "dead." They reviewed the plan several times before deciding it was a go.

They went in their opposite directions and crawled slowly to their places. Johnny had been trained to move like a snake, and he did. A broken twig or ruffled leaf could blow the whole operation. Slowly and silently, he guided himself over the ground. God, he hated the tropics. How could so many lizards be harmless when they looked like God-damned dinosaurs? He prayed that when this was over he'd never be assigned to jungle warfare. Let someone else get the drug lords. He'd take the mountains or the desert.

He got in position and waited, knowing that Chet had a longer distance to cover and would need more time. He thought he felt something crawling on his pants but was reluctant to move. What the hell was it? An insect? Maybe a spider? He felt it now on the small of his back, and it was really starting to piss him off. There was a space between his shirt and his flack jacket. He wondered if the spider would crawl between the two. Jesus. Then it turned, walked along the edge of his belt, jumped off his body and scurried away, running right by his face. It was a small mouse, or whatever other rodent they had in this God-forsaken section of Florida.

Johnny eyed his watch. It was three a.m. The sentry looked tired. That could be good and bad. Of course a tired sentry was a good thing, but it could mean that a shift change could happen any minute. Probably not though because there were no lights on in the bunker. Johnny decided he'd take him out on the next trip. He hoped Chet was watching closely because there would be no signal other than Johnny's move toward the guard.

The sentry turned for his next approach when suddenly another guard emerged from the building. He was carrying a roll of toilet paper and was obviously heading for some privacy. He stopped to joke for a minute and offered the sentry a cigarette. They both lit up and the guy with the toilet paper stepped away. Where the hell would he go? Would he end up near Johnny or Chet? He moved away from Johnny, in Chet's direction.

Shit, Johnny thought. How close would he get? And how much longer would they have to wait. Luckily Johnny could follow his lit cigarette and knew Chet could too.

The sentry continued to walk back and forth, not interested in the friend in the woods. After all, who would be?

Now what? Johnny wondered. He didn't have to wonder long. He was watching the cigarette when, suddenly, it fell to the ground. Johnny looked back to the sentry. He was still smoking. It was too short a time for the other guy to have tossed his smoke. He returned his gaze toward Chet's position. Someone had picked up the cigarette and was using it to give a signal. He hoped it was Chet. Whoever it was, cupped it to hide it from view and then showed it. Cupped it and showed it. Chet must have been saying he took the guy out. That had to be it. Maybe he was spotted and had to do it. Johnny didn't know. But if Chet took him out, Johnny would have to move quickly. If the crapper took too much longer the sentry would call to him, which would wake up the others in the bunker.

Johnny needed to make a decision and decided to go. He realized if he was wrong the Tropical Gemini team would be screwed. The sentry was coming his way again. He waited for him to turn and then he sprang. The guard just started to turn when Johnny reached around his neck, cupped his hand over the guy's mouth, inserted the spring knife to his back and said, "You're dead, Chico."

The guard had just placed the cigarette in his mouth before Johnny cupped it, and Johnny burnt his hand as he crushed the cigarette against the guy's lips. "Ah, shit," the guy muttered as he dropped to the floor.

Chet was already bounding for the door, grenades in hand with the pins pulled. The guy who had left for the visit to the john had closed the door behind him, but Chet knew it wouldn't be locked. In one fluid motion, he kicked in the door, tossed the grenades, and stepped aside to shield himself from the blast.

There was commotion inside as the sleeping men were awakened by the noise and found themselves splattered with paint. Johnny and Chet crashed into the room and sprayed the place with wax bullets. They stopped quickly as they noticed that the men were already covered with paint and weren't wearing flack jackets. Bullets fired from that close range would hurt like hell.

"Son of a bitch," one of the guards had yelled. We're dead, man. We're dead."

"Bastards," another said.

Chet smiled. "Just doing our job, guys. You're supposed to wear your flack jackets."

"Screw you," one of them said.

Just then the other sentries walked in, one rubbing his burnt lips and the other pulling up his zipper.

Chet laughed and said to Johnny. "I think we're going home bro. We're going home.

They stepped outside and Johnny got on the secure line. "This is Tropical Gemini to base. This is Tropical Gemini."

"This is base, the voice said."

"The outpost is secured with five hostiles KIA. He looked at his burned hand. No causalities to the team. You're clear to take out the target. Over."

"Good work, Gemini. Move to rendezvous point for extraction."

"Over." Johnny smiled. They were leaving the swamp.

51- Eilat

December 1997

Graduation was held at Ft. Benning, Georgia, and Johnny's parents insisted on flying down for the ceremony. They weren't alone. Nick, Jimmy, and Big Frankie made the trip with them, and Johnny was touched by their presence. He hadn't seen any of them in months, and within minutes they had him in stitches.

The ceremony was held in mid December near Victory Pond, the site of much of the Ranger combat training. The commanding officer spoke glowingly of the caliber of the graduates and explained that only 92 of the 240 candidates who began the program completed it. Johnny caught Chet's eye and nodded. Chet nodded back. The speaker went on too long, and Johnny's thoughts drifted to Carrie. With his training over, Johnny had leave time coming and he couldn't wait to see her.

The Bristol gang beamed as Lieutenant John Marzo's name was called and Angelo stepped forward to pin the black-and-gold *Ranger* tag on his son's left shoulder. Ever since Johnny was a young boy, Angelo had sensed uneasiness between them over his decision to go to Canada during the Vietnam War. Angelo still felt he had made the right decision, but times were different now, and Angelo and Donna supported their son's decision to join the military.

"I'm proud of you, son." Angelo said. "I couldn't be prouder."

"Thanks, Pop," Johnny said. "It means a lot to have you here today." Angelo wiped his eyes as he left the stage.

Later, they found a place in town that served pizza, sandwiches and cold beer. Everyone ordered a sandwich except Nick and Jimmy, who decided to split a pizza. The waitress watched in amazement as the two men argued over the topping and finally settled on sausage and extra cheese.

The food came, and they ate and laughed and brought Johnny up to date on Bristol gossip. It was like old times again at the deli. They talked about the Philadelphia Eagles and their prospects for the next year. The Eagles were in the middle of a dismal season, and everyone hoped they'd lose enough games to ensure a high draft pick. Next year's college draft was rich in talented players and the deli guys wanted one. A new fight broke out over which player they should draft. Angelo, Big Frankie and Nick wanted Tim Couch, a quarterback from the University of Kentucky. Jimmy wanted Texas running back Rickey Williams, and Donna wanted Syracuse quarterback Donovan McNabb.

"No offense, Donna," Jimmy said. "But women don't know jack about the NFL." Donna smiled, and Johnny just took it all in. He'd hadn't been this relaxed in a long time. Finally, Angelo looked at his watch and said, "Well, son. We have a plane to catch tonight."

"I know, Pop. I'm sorry you can't stay. Not that there's much to do around Ft. Benning."

"You know your father," Donna said. "He has to open that damn store."

"Gotta pay the bills," Angelo said.

"Oh, my God," Donna said, bringing her hands to her mouth. "I almost forgot." She opened her purse and brought out two envelopees. "Mickey dropped this off at the deli for you, and this FedEx from Brian arrived yesterday. I think it's about your vacation."

He put both envelopees in his pocket. Everyone exchanged tearful good- byes, and Johnny told them he'd spend some of his leave time in Bristol. "That's bull," Nick said jokingly. "You're gonna spend it all with that honey of yours, and I don't blame you."

Johnny laughed. "Most of it," Johnny admitted. "But I'll be home too."

Everyone left, and Johnny missed them immediately. He was glad they'd been there to share the day and glad his uncles came too. He thought about how lucky his parents were to have life-long friends like that and hoped the Pac Men would last as long.

The waitress came and he ordered another beer. He opened Mickey's letter and read.

> *Johnny*
> *Sorry I can't be there, but I'm proud as hell of you. Lieutenant Johnny Marzo, U.S. Army Ranger and all around bad-ass. Sounds good.*
> *Everything here is pretty good. I'm making thirty-five emergency runs a month and I'm visiting schools to talk about fire safety. I love the fire service and can't see myself doing anything else. Bobby is doing well too. He just landed a mechanic's job at McCafferty Ford and is making decent money. I swear, the guy's not happy unless his head is buried under a hood. I hear from Brian once in a while. He's probably running the damn CIA by now, or at least telling them how it should be run. I can't believe you guys, a spy and a super soldier. Impressive.*
> *I'm a little worried about Tommy. He's drinking more and not looking too good. He's working at the book warehouse, but he's not happy. He says it's temporary, but right now he seems lost. Well, congrats, buddy. I'll see you when you get home.*
> *Mickey*

By the way, I don't have a girl yet, but I'm still looking. So what's up with Carrie?

A lot, Johnny thought. He made a mental note to find out more about Tommy and opened Brian's FedEx. Johnny had four weeks leave coming before his unit would be deployed to Bosnia for peace keeping operations, and he planned to spend most of it with Carrie. She had over a year remaining on her Red Cross commitment in Kenya, but had some time off coming. Brian had been writing to both of them and had called Johnny a few days earlier with an idea.

"Listen, Johnny boy. My supervisors say I've been a little too intense lately, and I need some time off. They're right. I have been, and I do. So here's an idea. Jenny and I have been going pretty strong while you've been doing your John Wayne thing, and I'd like to take her someplace. I'm thinking, Carrie's in Kenya and you'll have to end up in Bosnia when your leave is finished. Why don't I do some research and find you a nice place midway between both of you, and Jenny and I can join you for a vacation? Don't worry, we'll give each other plenty of private time, but I think it'd be fun to spend some time together."

Johnny was reluctant because he wanted to be alone. But the more he thought about putting the arrangements together, the more he realized he needed Brian's help. Besides, it would be fun. "Okay," Johnny had said. "But no Kelly handouts. I've got money saved, and I'll take care of our expenses." "Sure, Johnny," Brian had said. "Whatever you say. Let me do some research, and I'll send you and Carrie the information." Now, Johnny opened the envelopee. He could only imagine what was inside. He found a letter, a hotel brochure, and a ticket. He opened the letter.

> *Dear General Marzo,*
> *Congratulations! I hope graduation went well. Was President Clinton there? Al Gore? You can tell me all about it when we get together.*
> *I checked around and decided that a good mid-way point between Bosnia and Kenya is Eilat, Israel, a beautiful resort city on the Red Sea's Gulf of Aqaba near the Negev Desert. It's the Israeli version of South Beach, Miami and Palm Springs rolled into one. I've booked us rooms at the Crown Plaza, a real nice place that overlooks the water. You're on the tenth floor and we're on the twelfth, so we*

won't be on top of each other. The rooms have private balconies, Jacuzzis, and fully stocked bars. If we don't like the ocean, there are three pools to choose from. I hope this sounds good.

    Enclosed are your plane ticket, flight arrangements, and hotel reservations-- don't worry, we can square up later. After you visit your parents, get your butt to Philadelphia Airport for your flight on January 10. You'll have a stopover in Tel Aviv and then fly south to Eilat, where we'll relax and party until January 17. I've sent Carrie the same information and her ticket. Jenny and I can't wait to see you guys.

    Brian

52- Israel

January 1998

Johnny flew from Philadelphia to Frankfurt where he had a one hour layover before flying to Ben Gurion Airport in Tel Aviv. As they began their descent, he could see the Mediterranean shoreline and the white beaches lined with hotels. It was a welcome sight compared to the places he'd seen over the past several months.

They landed easily and Johnny had to change planes for the short flight to Eilat. He was grateful for the opportunity to stretch his legs after the long journey. As he moved through the airport, the first thing that struck him, other than the Hebrew and English signage everywhere, was the level of security. Things had been tight at the Frankfurt airport, with extensive baggage checks and personal screenings for anyone heading to Israel. But at Tel Aviv there were heavily armed police and Israeli Defense Forces everywhere.

Johnny tried to relax on the short flight to Eilat, but he couldn't. It had been thirteen months since he'd seen Carrie, and he was apprehensive. He wondered what a year in Africa had done to her, and he wondered how she would view him after a year of what he'd been through. He thought back to the time in her apartment when she told him she was going to Kenya and they talked about what their time apart would be like. Neither expected that time to be so long, but he remembered her words:

"We'll share our love from exotic places. When you're on leave, we'll rendezvous in cities we can't even think of yet. I'll fly to meet you and we'll barricade ourselves in our room, you me and a bottle of wine. We won't take each other for granted because our time together will be precious."

Well, the time was here, and he prayed that things would go well.

He exited the plane and walked to the baggage area, expecting to see a driver with a sign or some other display of Brian's impeccable planning. Instead, he saw Carrie scanning the crowd. She was standing on her tiptoes to get a better look. At least he thought it was her. She was only fifty feet away, but her skin was much darker from months in the African sun and her hair much lighter. She was leaner too. She wore a lightweight bush jacket with the sleeves rolled up and khaki shorts. She had the hardy look of someone who had traded a life of indoor comfort for something far more rigorous, and she looked more beautiful than ever.

Johnny was thinking about the perfect thing to say to her, but she spotted him before he had it right. She screamed his name and raced to meet him. Without a word she ran into his embrace, locked her arms around his neck and kissed him, long and passionately, without regard for anyone in the room. When their lips parted, she put her head on his shoulder and held him tightly. Neither spoke for a long time until Carrie whispered, "You're here. You're finally here."

Johnny saw tears on her cheeks when they separated, and he gently wiped them away. He looked into her eyes to confirm that they still sparkled. They did, but her face was different, in a good way. She had matured far more than one would expect in a year, and her features had a character and depth that made her even more appealing. Gone was the perky, youthful innocence he had known. Carrie was a woman now.

She flashed her familiar smile and said, "Well, Johnny Marzo, are you going to say something?"

He stammered briefly and then said, "I didn't think we'd ever get together. I love you and I'm glad you're here."

"That's good enough for me," she said brightly. "Let's go. We have some catching up to do." She draped her arm through his and was surprised by the firmness of his muscles. "My, Lieutenant, haven't you become quite the iron man."

Johnny shrugged. "I thought I always was."

Carrie smiled. "In my eyes you were." Then she stopped and playfully eyed him up and down. "But not like this. I hope those army guys developed your brains as much as your body."

He smiled. "We read poetry and listened to Mozart every night."

"I bet."

Johnny retrieved his luggage, and they walked to the exit. There were armed soldiers everywhere, and Carrie said, "I can't believe the security here. It makes me uncomfortable."

"We're safe," Johnny said. "The Israelis know what they're doing."

"I know. But I just don't like seeing people with guns."

"If you've been through what these people have been through, I think you'd feel differently."

"Maybe," Carrie said.

Johnny knew there was no maybe about it, but he didn't want to go down that road. Not now. He changed the subject. "So where's Brian?"

"He's back at the hotel talking to the concierge about dinner reservations. We thought maybe at seven."

"Sounds great," Johnny said.

"He already checked everybody in, and I saw the room. It's lovely and has a nice balcony that overlooks the gulf. And there's a wonderful beach."

"I'm not gonna let Brian pay for this," Johnny said.

"I know. I told him the same thing when we checked in, but he just winked and said, 'sure.'"

Johnny shook his head.

They hailed a cab for the short ride to the hotel. It got quiet for a minute and Carrie said, "Jenny seems very nice." She sounded a bit sheepish.

Johnny looked at her. "It was nothing," he said. "We dated during our senior year. She's a real nice girl and we had a good time, but there was never anything beyond that…"

Carrie interrupted him. "Brian told me all about it. I just wanted to bring it up to let you know I like her and I'm fine with her being here if you are."

"Why wouldn't I be?"

"Well," Carrie said shyly. "I just wouldn't want you getting confused about who your girl is."

He put his arm around her and said, "That will never happen."

"Good," Carrie said, removing his arm playfully. "Because I'd hate to have to throw her into a fountain."

"Very funny," Johnny said, sounding a little embarrassed. "I'd rather not talk about that whole scene."

"Fine," Carrie said. "But I want you to know...I never told you this, but I want you to know that while I always had feelings for you, it was at that moment that I knew you'd be the one forever."

"That's good to know," Johnny said. "Maybe I'll dunk someone every now and then just to keep you interested."

"That won't be necessary. I'm interested. So how about you?"

"Me, of course I'm interested. I just flew..."

"No, Silly," Carrie said teasingly. "I mean when did you know I was the one?'

Johnny replied without hesitation. "The first time we met in front of Bristol High."

Carrie slapped him on the arm. "I'm serious. When did you know?"

"I'm serious too, and I just told you."

"You're sweet," Carrie said. "My sweet iron man."

They arrived at the hotel, and Johnny whistled when they entered the lobby. "Not bad."

"Wait until you see the room," Carrie gushed.

They rode the elevator to the 10th floor, and Carrie ushered him in.

"Wow," Johnny said sarcastically. "It's pretty much what I've gotten used to over the past few months."

"Me too," Carrie said, taking him by the hand. "Check out the balcony."

It was a scene from a postcard, with clear blue water, smooth beaches, and people swimming and sun bathing. Johnny noted the clear, sunny sky and said, "It looks like a bad storm is brewing."

Carrie didn't catch on at first until she saw Johnny's smile. Then she said, "Do you think we'll have to barricade ourselves in our room?"

"I'm sure of it," Johnny replied. He led her back into the suite and she said, "I told Brian you'd probably be tired when you arrived and that we'd call him when you were feeling better."

Johnny checked his watch. It was 1 p.m. Israeli time. "I might be okay by dinner."

Carrie smiled.

They met in the lobby at 6:45, and Carrie and Jenny watched as Brian and Johnny hooted, hugged, and slapped each other on the back. It seemed more like a reunion of brothers, which of course, they considered themselves to be.

"Look at you, man, double-o-seven," Johnny said. Then in his best British accent he added, "Kelly, Brian Kelly."

Brian laughed and punched Johnny's shoulder. "Yeah, I'm double-o-seven and you're Rambo. You look great, Johnny."

They hugged again and then turned to the girls. Brian jokingly said, "Johnny, have you met Jenny?" Everyone laughed and Johnny said, "Hi, Jenny, it's nice to see you again." He gave her a peck on the cheek. "It's nice to see you, Johnny. And it was nice meeting Carrie this morning."

"Great," Brian said. "I just wanted to break the ice. So everyone's cool?"

They all nodded. "Then let's move out. I've booked us at a Japanese restaurant not far from here. It should be good."

As they left the lobby, Brian fell in next to Johnny and said, "Hey, Lieutenant, did you get enough rest this afternoon? You look tired."

Johnny laughed and gave him a shove.

Dinner was a blast, and the chef was a great showman. The couples were seated at the grill and he chopped the food, tossed and juggled his utensils, and kidded like a pro. Toward the end of his cooking, he flipped baby shrimp in the air for the diners to catch with their mouths. Carrie and Jenny were good at it, and the table cheered each time someone caught one. Brian caught a couple, but Johnny missed six tosses in a row. Finally, with great fanfare, the chef leaned over and placed a shrimp on Johnny's tongue.

They ate slowly and, at one point, Johnny said, "Using these chopsticks is torture. After what I've been eating lately, I just want to dig in."

"You and me both," Carrie said. "We didn't exactly feast in Africa." Then she leaned closer and said, "We have a lot of catching up to do, don't we?"

"I thought we gave it a good start today," Johnny teased.

"You know what I mean," Carrie replied. "I want to know everything you've done since I last saw you. The letters aren't enough."

"Me too," Johnny said. Carrie nodded absently as she thought about her time in Africa.

The rest of the week was a whirlwind of activity. They snorkeled, went parasailing, and rented speedboats. Each time Johnny pulled out his credit card to pay, the cashier quietly informed him that payment arrangements had been made in advance.

They alternated nights dining as a group and as separate couples. On two of the evenings Johnny and Carrie dined on their balcony, recreating their last time together at Long Beach Island.

On their last afternoon together Carrie and Jenny went shopping while Brian and Johnny relaxed on the beach. A cute waitress with long dark hair approached and asked if they needed a drink.

"Absolutely," Brian said. "What do you recommend?"

The girl thought. "Well, they're all good."

"It's early yet," Johnny said. "Make mine a Bloody Mary."

"Ohhh. We have a drink called a Sangre de Maria. It's the rum version of the Bloody Mary. They use spiced vanilla rum and some other dark rums."

"Sold," Johnny said.

"Make it two," Brian added.

"Gotcha," the waitress winked and started to leave. Then she stopped and said, "Are you guys Americans?"

"Yup," Brian replied.

"I thought so. My name is Sarah. I'm from just outside of Philadelphia."

"No kidding," Johnny said. "So are we."

"I saw you guys yesterday with your wives... or whatever, and I wanted to ask, but this wasn't my assigned area."

"So how did you end up here, Sarah?"

"Well, I just graduated from Penn State..."

"Penn State!" Johnny interrupted. "I'm from Penn State. I graduated almost two years ago."

"Really," Sarah beamed. "Gee, with only forty-thousand students, you'd think we'd know each other."

"You graduated? You look pretty young, Sarah," Johnny said.

She rolled her eyes. "I know. I get that all the time."

"So how'd you end up here?" Brian asked.

"Well, I'm Jewish. And young adults are encouraged to make a pilgrimage to the homeland of Israel, to visit the Holy City, the Wailing Wall, the center of our religion. I offered a Kvitlach at the Wailing Wall. It's a very moving experience."

"Kvitlach?" Johnny asked.

"It's when you write a prayer, a special intention, on a piece of paper and place it in cracks in the mortar."

Brian knew that and asked, "Jerusalem is 150 miles north of here. How'd you end up in Eilat?"

"Well, my parents encouraged me to make the pilgrimage, like all Jewish parents do. But, like all parents, they worry about the danger... suicide bombers, rocket attacks, mortar attacks, kidnappings."

"So you came here instead?" Brian asked.

"No. I spent two weeks up north and especially in the Holy City. But when my time was up, I wanted to stay longer. It's the fiftieth anniversary of the birth of Israel, and I wanted to be here for it. I'm young. I don't have a job yet. I'm a teacher by the way, or at least I will be. I'm not attached. So I thought I'd stay a while and soak up the culture."

"But your parents were concerned," Johnny added.

"Scared stiff, especially because of the anniversary . . . They wanted me to come home. So we compromised. The south is much safer, so they said I could stay in Eilat for a month." She spread her arms to point out the beach and surroundings. "Not a bad deal, I'd say."

"Good for you," Brian said. "It sounds like a great experience."

"It is," Sarah said. Then her smile faded. "I'm amazed by the country. This has been a garrison state for fifty years. It's been under siege. Young people here see sacrifice as a way of life. They accept compulsory military service without question. It's not about preference; it's about survival. At dance clubs or at pizza joints, people have fun, but in the back of their minds they're looking for people with bulky coats or loose fitting clothing, wondering where the next suicide bomber might strike."

"That's pretty sobering," Johnny said.

"It is," Sarah added. "Americans, especially American students, have no idea how good they have it and the dangers that are out there."

No idea, Brian thought. No idea at all.

53- Going for a Run

Sarah brought their drinks and left, and Brian said, "She's right you know, about people having no idea of the threats out there. She's right."

"I guess you ought to know," Johnny said. "So what do the spy boys have you doing? Or can't you tell me?"

Brian smiled. "I can't tell you much. But basically I work with a team on threat assessments."

Johnny took a sip of his drink and said, "Not bad, but I should have had a beer. So what does threat assessment mean?"

"We have agents and informants all over the world, gathering information and sending it in. Sometimes the threats are obvious, and we kick them upstairs for further attention. That's the easy part. The hard part comes when you try to put small pieces together. There are literally thousands of things that might be a problem. The key word is might. We couldn't possibly react equally to all of them, and we shouldn't. So we have to decide which ones require the most attention."

"Sounds like a lot of pressure," Johnny said.

Brian nodded. "If we're wrong just once, or if we fail to connect the dots on one seemingly small thing, a major problem could result. Lives are at stake. Plus, there are other agencies involved. If our intelligence leads us to believe that a plot is taking place within the United States, that there are bad guys right here, we have to pass things over to the FBI because we're not allowed to spy on Americans. Sometimes, the two agencies don't share information as well as they should. That can be a problem."

"That's hard to believe," Johnny said.

"Sometimes you work hard to cultivate a source, and it's very delicate. You might be reluctant to pass something on for fear the other agency might screw things up. There's a lack of trust on both sides, but we work on it."

Johnny changed the focus. "So, career wise, how are they treating you there?"

"They're treating me well. Apparently, I really kicked ass on their entrance tests, and Dr. Blake has opened some doors for me. Then I did some work that impressed my superiors and it's been good. Let's just say that I have a lot more responsibility than a person my age and with my experience would normally have. It didn't hurt getting my doctorate early."

"It was pretty quick," Johnny said.

"That was Dr. Blake again. He was my advisor. I sailed through the coursework, and he let me use my work at the CIA for my dissertation. It was titled "Threat Assessment Utilizing Advanced Electronic Surveillance.""

Johnny laughed. "Remind me to read it sometime."

"Blake liked it so much that he sent it to some higher ups in the agency. I think that's what helped move my career along."

"Blake has really been a sugar daddy for you."

"We think alike," Brian said.

Johnny knew what that meant. "Well, Brian, you've come a long way for a Bristol boy."

Two lovely bikinis came walking by and Brian and Johnny took a minute to enjoy the view.

Johnny smiled when they were gone and said, "Our girls top them."

"That's true," Brian replied. "But those two were a close second."

"There weren't many women where I've been for the past few months," Johnny said. "So it's hard to have a perspective." They laughed, and Johnny added, "So how's Jenny?"

"Terrific. I mean, we click real well. She understands my time commitments and is okay with them. I'm thinking about asking her to come to Washington to move in with me."

"Wow," Johnny said. "That's a jump."

"She's the only girl I've ever dated," Brian said. "And I'm starting to think she's the only one I'll ever want." Then he asked, "So what about you? What's up with Carrie?"

Johnny smiled. "This has been the best week of my life. Now granted, my life has been pretty miserable lately, but every time we get together, it's like we never parted. I've got to hang on to her."

"You better," Brian said.

Another group of girls walked by and both guys sat up to take notice.

"Damn," Brian said. "Is there a beauty pageant or something here this week?"

"It certainly looks that way. You picked a good spot, Brian. By the way, I owe you money and I want to square up. We can't keep doing this."

Brian sighed. "Not this again. Listen, I haven't touched a dime of Uncle Ray's money, and I never will unless it's to fight terrorism. That's what I said, and that's what I'll do. But I told you before; I've done well investing it, very well. Plus, now I have a good job. When I'm not with you or the Pac Men, I'm in my cubical at the agency and I'm not spending money. So just shut up about this and let me have some fun."

"Okay, you win," Johnny said.

Brian was eager to change the subject and said, "So what's going on with you and the army?"

"Well, I'm a Second Lieutenant and an Army Ranger now. I'll join my unit in a little over a week, and we're heading for Bosnia for peacekeeping operations. I'll command a platoon and be in line for a promotion to First Lieutenant."

"Bosnia's a nasty place. Those people would slaughter each other if given the chance."

"That's why we're there."

"The question is, how long do we stay? What's to stop them from killing each other again once we leave?"

Johnny shrugged. "That's for somebody else to figure out."

It got quiet, and Brian seemed to be thinking. Then he said, "I don't see this for you."

"See what?"

"I don't see you spending your career patrolling the streets of Sarajevo hoping Bosnian Serbs and Croatian Muslims don't kill each other. I see something bigger for you."

"Carrie and I have been talking. I have a little over two years left on my commitment and that might be it. She'll be out of Africa by then, and maybe we'll start normal lives."

"I'm not sure you can do that," Brian said. "I mean, I'm sure you'll end up together, but I'm not sure about the normal life part."

"We've both had our share of adventure. I think we need some normalcy."

"Maybe," Brian said.

It got quiet again and Johnny said, "What did you mean when you said you see something bigger for me?"

Brian looked as though he was struggling with something. Then he said, "Look, here's the part I shouldn't tell you, but most people suspect it anyway. Often, when we recognize a threat in a foreign country, I mean when we're sure something is about to go down, we act on it."

"Act on it?"

"Yeah. We identify a target, plan an operation, and send a covert team, either CIA or Special Operations Forces in to do the job, quickly. They're in and out in minutes or days depending on the operation, and no one else knows what happens"

"Which foreign countries?"

"Potentially any that we deem necessary."

"And the White House approves it?" Johnny asked.

Brian was evasive. "There are some things that have to be done that really make a difference, like short, surgical operations that can save lives. You've already gone through Airborne training, you're an

Army Ranger, you've got smarts, and you have an aptitude for foreign languages. With your background, you'd be a prime candidate for Special Operation Forces. Become a Green Beret, or hop over to the CIA. I think you should give it some thought."

Johnny didn't answer. He was already giving something else a lot of thought.

The girls returned and they all went to the hotel lobby for a drink.

"So what did you guys buy?" Brian asked.

Carrie winked at Jenny and said, "I bought a beautiful pair of spiked heels and some silk blouses. I think they'll be perfect in the African bush."

They all laughed. "We just window shopped," Jenny said. "But we had a good time, and we're getting to be good friends."

"Good," Brian said, "Because we should do this at least once a year."

Everyone agreed.

"Actually," Jenny said. "We found a nice jewelry store on the promenade. Carrie tried on a beautiful necklace and looked stunning in it."

"She'd look stunning in anything," Johnny said.

"And it would go perfectly with the heels and silk blouse," Carrie joked. Then she turned serious. "I'm not really looking forward to going back, but go back I must for one more year."

"Hey, come on," Brian said. "No downers. We have one more night. Let's make the best of it."

"Absolutely," Carrie said.

"You're the chairman," Johnny said to Brian. "So what's on tap?"

"Well, we need one last celebration, and I'm sure we'd like some time alone. So how's this? Let's have an early dinner at the steak house we saw the other night and then do our own thing afterward."

"Sounds like a plan," Johnny said.

Carrie said, "If we're having an early dinner, I need to get back to the room to get ready. I'm a mess."

"Me too," Jenny said.

"And I'm gonna recharge my batteries with a power nap," Brian said.

As they walked back to the room, Johnny said, "I need to get in the groove again. I'm gonna take a short run. I'll be back by the time you're out of the shower."

Johnny got back just as Carrie was drying her hair, and he took his turn in the shower. He came out with his towel wrapped around him and stopped in his tracks. Carrie was wearing a red silk spaghetti-strap dress, and she looked breathtaking.

"Do you like it?" She asked sheepishly.

Johnny couldn't answer.

"Jenny and I lied about not buying anything. I wanted to look nice for our last night together." She looked like she might cry.

He stepped toward her and they kissed. He wanted to rip his towel off and ease her out of the dress, but he didn't. "This is not our last night together. It's just our last night together on this vacation."

"Promise?"

"I swear."

Then he said, "Stay right here a minute. I have something that will go well with that.

He opened a drawer and took out a small bag. "I lied too. I didn't go for a run, I went shopping while you were in the shower."

He handed her the bag, and she noticed the name of the jewelry store she had visited. "Oh, Johnny, you bought me the necklace?"

"Not quite," Johnny said.

He opened the bag, took out a small box and silently handed it to her. She opened it and saw a diamond ring. Johnny smiled and said, "Will you marry me?"

54- The American Embassy

August 7, 1998

Carrie sat in the Red Cross mess tent sipping tea and thinking about Johnny. She had been engaged for eight months and was still coming to grips with not having seen him once since getting her ring. Everything had happened so fast. Johnny had offered her the ring, which she readily accepted, and twelve hours later, he was leaving to report for duty in Bosnia, and she was on a flight back to Africa.

Spending the week with Johnny and receiving the ring had made her happier than she could imagine. But as she endured the long months in Nairobi that followed, the euphoria wore off as she thought about the things they should have resolved.

Never accept a ring from a handsome, sculptured man wearing a towel, she thought, at least not until you've thought it through. It had to be one of the most impulsive proposals and acceptances ever. He had purchased the ring while she was in the shower! She smiled at the memory. There was no doubt she loved Johnny and hoped to spend her life with him, but there were still commitments they had to honor and issues they had to work out. She had another year left on her promise to the Red Cross, and Johnny had at least two years in the Army. Although he had hinted that he'd leave the service when he finished his obligation, she wasn't so sure. He loved the military and might change his mind. She still couldn't see herself as an army wife, but she also knew that it might seriously harm their relationship if she forced him to leave the service. She took another sip of her tea. She loved Johnny, and they'd work it out. Besides, she was the one who had gushed about romantic relationships that spanned continents and exciting rendezvous in exotic cities. Be careful what you wish for, she thought, smiling again.

She and her team were in a village ten miles west of Nairobi, testing the water supply and distributing medications. It was simple work and she was grateful for the easy transition back to her duties. Because they were working so close to the city, they were able to return to Nairobi each night and sleep in normal beds. They were scheduled to leave the following week for another swing through the countryside.

She finished her tea and was about to leave when Dr. Graham came rushing in. "Come quickly," he said breathlessly. "There's been a terrible explosion at the American Embassy in Nairobi. There are reports of massive injuries and bodies buried in the rubble. The Red Cross needs everyone we can provide. We're packing whatever emergency supplies we can and leaving in ten minutes."

Carrie raced to the supply tent where she found the others already loading the trucks. She fell in beside Barika, a native Kenyan who had been with the team since before Carrie arrived in Africa. Barika was crying as she worked, and she told Carrie that her brother, Chiumbo, was an employee at the embassy.

"I have to make sure he's all right. His name is Chiumbo Kufuor."

Soon they were in their Land Rovers racing to Nairobi. Dr. Graham instructed them as he drove on how they would operate at the scene. "Every available Red Cross employee has been summoned. We have to make sure our work is organized. I expect you'll see things you're not used to seeing. You must steel yourselves against emotion and focus on finding victims and saving lives."

He looked at Carrie and Barika in the back seat and wondered whether Barika was up to the task. She read his mind and said, "I'll do my job, Doctor. Just get us to Nairobi."

The city was in chaos when they arrived. Traffic was at a standstill as pedestrians swarmed the streets making their way to the bombing site, anxious to learn the status of scores of Kenyans employed there. Dr. Graham sat on his horn, and people moved when they saw the Red Cross symbol on the truck.

Four Kenyan policemen armed with automatic weapons were rerouting all traffic within two blocks of the embassy. Dr. Graham's caravan stopped and guards approached the vehicle. "Everyone out!" A guard barked in English. Dr. Graham was incensed by the delay. "Can't you see we're with the Red Cross?" "I don't know who you're with. Get out of the vehicle so we can search it."

"This is an outrage," Graham said. "We're wasting valuable time. I have documentation. He began reaching for his wallet, and the policeman raised his weapon. He spoke slowly, but in a menacing tone. "It is a common practice of suicide bombers to detonate a second bomb after rescue workers have arrived on the scene. This truck will not pass until it is searched. Get out of the vehicle, now!"

"I'm sorry," Graham said. "I didn't realize…"

"Move!"

They all got out and Graham told the passengers in the other vehicles to do the same. The policemen searched them and the contents of their storage areas quickly. When they were finished, the lead policeman said, "You're free to go. Thank you for your help."

They arrived at the scene and got out, and Dr. Graham went to find someone who would give them instructions. As they waited, Carrie couldn't believe what she saw. There were emergency vehicles everywhere and people being carried on stretchers. Some of the bodies were fully covered with sheets, and she heard Barika stifle a sob. Victims sat on curbs, their faces and clothing soaked with blood. Others, covered with dust, wandered in a daze. Carrie looked up at what had been the American Embassy. A large part of the seven story structure was gone. Windows were shattered, and parts of the building were still smoldering. Adjacent buildings were damaged as well. Rescue workers walked through the rubble looking for bodies and listening for the cries of the injured.

Two workers approached carrying a stretcher with a covered body. One of the workers shouted to her, "You! Take this end while I go back to search for more." A moment later Carrie found herself straining under the weight of the stretcher. Her hands were shaking uncontrollably. She tried to avoid looking at the covered corpse by focusing on the African man carrying the other end. He was dressed in a suit, and Carrie supposed he was an embassy employee pressed into service just as she had been. His eyes were glazed. They moved to a morgue truck that held several stretcher racks, and workers there helped them glide the body in. It wasn't the first. Then she and her partner went back to the rubble and repeated the task. They worked wordlessly, too numb to speak. Carrying the injured as they cried out in pain was almost as difficult as carrying the dead, and she lost count of the trips. At one point she saw Barika walking amid the rubble, and Carrie said a prayer that her brother was alive.

She worked until she could work no longer and then dropped to a curb in exhaustion. Her partner wandered off without a word, and she sat sobbing with her hands covering her face. Then she remembered what the guard had said about suicide bombers detonating a second after a new group of potential victims arrived. Suddenly she saw everyone as a possible murderer, and she wanted to flee. Her heart was racing and she tried to get up, but she lacked the strength. Then she forced herself to control her panic. She couldn't leave. There were people who desperately needed her help, and she would help them as soon as she could summon enough strength.

She didn't know how long she sat there when she felt the presence of someone who had sat next to her. A man put his arm on her shoulder and handed her a bottle of water. She turned to thank him and saw that it was David.

"David, my God!" She collapsed into his arms and sobbed. "Why did this happen? What kind of monsters could do this?" She shook her head. "So many innocent people. My God."

David didn't have an answer. He was too shaken himself. He rubbed her back soothingly, trying to calm her. Then she covered her face with her hands again, and David noticed her ring.

In Boston, Dr. Blake viewed the television screen as President Clinton addressed the nation. Casualty information was still sketchy, but it appeared that 11 Americans and   63 Kenyans had died, and as many as sixteen-hundred people were wounded. Property damage was extensive. The American Embassy in Dar Es Salam, Tanzania had been bombed at the same time, and information about causalities there was still forthcoming. Clinton vowed to find and punish the people responsible. Blake pounded his fist on his desk. Why couldn't we head this off?

In Washington, Brian sat in front of his computer screen and cursed under his breath. The State Department received an estimated 30,000 threats a year against embassies, consulates, and American corporate offices around the world. It was impossible to track them all, but he searched the database for anything that may have been overlooked, anything that could have averted this disaster, but could find nothing actionable.

Then he examined the latest intelligence on who might be responsible. He found it frustrating that the Agency would come up with suspects *after* attacks occurred. A name that kept surfacing was a Saudi Arabian named Osama Bin Laden and the terrorist group al Qaeda that he headed. Brian studied Bin Laden's photo for a long time. It was a face he didn't want to forget.

Johnny had called him when he heard the news. Communication in Nairobi was disrupted, and he was terrified that Carrie may have been near the blast. Brian accessed the State Department list of dead and injured, and he scanned the list one more time to ensure that Carrie wasn't on it. He exhaled deeply and rubbed his temples. He needed to decompress. Then he picked up the phone to call Johnny and tell him that Carrie wasn't on the list. There were other things he wanted to tell him as well.

55- The Plaza Hotel

Carrie wanted to rejoin the rescue efforts, but David stopped her. She looked exhausted and deeply shaken, and he was concerned for her safety. "You're in no condition right now," he said. "You need to rest."

She scanned the rescue scene and said quietly, "I have to find Barika. She's looking for her brother." She seemed distant. David held her and tried calming her by stroking her hair. It was matted with perspiration. "Please drink some water, Carrie," he said, holding a bottle up to her.

She ignored him and said, "Where's Barika?"

"I don't know," David said. "But I'm sure she's alright. Nairobi is her home. She knows people and knows what to do."

"I want to help!" she shouted. Then she sighed and rubbed her forehead. "All those innocent people," she said weakly. "So many people."

It was late afternoon, and the curb was hot from the beating sun. David raised the water bottle to Carrie's lips, and this time she drank reluctantly.

"Our work is finished here," David said soothingly. "There's plenty of help and the authorities have things under control. Let me get you out of this sun."

David was right. Most of the bodies had been cleared and only a fraction of the rescue workers remained. They had been replaced by additional police and forensic teams combing the rubble for evidence.

David helped Carrie to her feet. She wobbled a bit, and he steadied her. Then with his arm around her shoulder, he guided her away from the scene.

Carrie was in a daze. "I have to join Dr. Graham and Barika," she mumbled. "Have to find them."

"No, Carrie," David said softly. "You need some fluids and food. We're going to the Narobi Plaza Hotel. Most likely they'll turn up there." The Plaza was a refurbished Holiday Inn that had seen better days. It was two blocks from the embassy and was moderately priced. It was used by Red Cross members when they stayed in town.

Carrie was too numb to disagree, and she moved along gingerly. They passed survivors, whose clothes were filthy from the blast, victims with minor injuries receiving first aid, and mourners grieving the loss of loved ones. Most spoke in hushed tones, but others cried out. David tried to move Carrie through the crowds as quickly as she could manage.

Finally, they reached the hotel. The lobby was only sparsely occupied, and David led Carrie to an empty table in the restaurant section. The room wasn't air conditioned, but it provided welcomed shelter from the sun. A waitress arrived and David ordered them bottled water and fresh fruit. Carrie slumped back in her padded chair and took a deep breath. An overhead fan offered a gentle breeze that seemed to relax her, and she closed her eyes.

David turned his attention to a television report on the bombing. He was waiting for a causality report that was sure to be dreadful. Something startled Carrie from her rest and she slammed her palm loudly on the arm of her leather chair. Then she screamed, "Why? Why did they do this? They're monsters!"

David slid his chair closer to hers and tried to soothe her. She was nearly hysterical now, sobbing uncontrollably. He held her without speaking and waited for her tears to subside.

The waitress returned with their order, and David coaxed Carrie into nibbling on some fruit. He offered her more water and she accepted it. She was coming under control now and said, "I'm sorry, David. It's just that..." She wasn't sure how to finish and said instead, "Thank you for being so kind."

David smiled. "No apology or thanks are necessary. This has been ghastly for all of us."

She smiled at the Brit's choice of words. "Ghastly. It certainly was."

They ate and drank some more, and Carrie's demeanor improved. "I'm not sure what I would have done if you hadn't arrived. I think I may have been in shock."

"You were a very brave woman today," he said.

"I only did what everyone was doing. I still can't believe it."

David looked at her and said, "Shouldn't you be calling someone?"

She wasn't sure what he meant, so he touched her ring and said, "You're in Nairobi, and it's all over the news there's been a major explosion. Someone must be very worried."

Carrie gasped. "Oh my God, yes. Johnny." She was on her feet. "I need to get to a phone."

"I've already tried my cell phone," David said. "What little service we usually have is unavailable. Let's try the front desk."

They tried the desk, and the clerk informed them that the phones had been jammed after the explosion and then went down altogether. They'd have to try later.

They were walking back to their table when Barika entered the lobby, led by Dr. Graham and another nurse from the team.

"Barika!" Carrie called.

Dr. Graham and the nurse looked her way, but Barika didn't respond. Dr. Graham walked toward Carrie and David as the nurse led Barika to the elevator.

"We were at the morgue," Graham said somberly. Barika just identified her brother.

56- They're in Our Garden!

Brian had pulled strings to arrange a phone hookup between Johnny and Carrie. He'd contacted the International Red Cross, which pointed him in the direction of the Plaza Hotel. Then he sent an embassy official to find her and take her to the makeshift office the embassy was using. They would call him back when they were ready, and Brian would patch her through to Johnny.

Brian had Johnny on the line and vented while they waited. Johnny had never heard him so angry. "We have to stop these bastards!" Brian shouted into the phone.

Johnny's main focus was Carrie. He was relieved to learn she was okay, but he wanted to hear her voice. "I know," he replied.

"The hell with tracking them down *after* they do something," Brian said. "We have to find them *before* they act and destroy them."

"I'm with you," Johnny said.

"No you're not, Johnny. You've been on some Boy Scout mission in Bosnia for months."

Johnny was offended and let Brian know it. "Hey, wait a minute. You have no idea what it's like here. It's ugly, and what we're doing is important, or Clinton wouldn't have sent us."

"Actually I do know what it's like there," Brian said, "and I apologize. "Those people have committed horrible acts against each other and would do it again. So let the Canadians or somebody else keep the peace. We're talking American lives here, Johnny. Somebody bombed our embassy for God's sake!"

Johnny didn't know what else to say, but it didn't matter because Brian thundered on. "Do you remember what Old Man Lombardi told us about Pearl Harbor?"

"Of course I do," Johnny replied.

Brian ignored him and said, "I can almost remember what he said word for word. He said, 'Your *country is like a tomato garden… If somebody tries to take your tomatoes you stop them. You protect what you have.* "In fact," Brian added. "He said, *'You fight like a son of a bitch. America is like your tomato garden. If some son of a bitch tries to hurt your country, you fight.'* "

"I remember," Johnny said.

"Well, these bastards are in our garden, Johnny. Are we gonna wait until they're in our damn house?"

Johnny took a breath. "I hear you, Brian, but what do you want me to do?"

"I want you to stop jerkin' around in Bosnia and apply for training in the Special Forces. Become a Green Beret, Johnny; that's what I want you to do. Then you can really do something!"

Johnny started to reply when Brian's other phone clicked. "Hold on," Brian said. "This may be Carrie. I'll patch her through if it is, and you and I will talk more, later."

"Thanks, Brian."

"No problem. Just think about what I said."

Carrie came on the line and said, "Johnny, are you there?"

"It's Brian, Carrie. I'm going to put you thorough."

"Brian! Thank you so much for doing this. The phones here are a mess."

"Just tell me that you're safe."

"I'm fine," Carrie said. "Still shaken, and very, very angry, but I'm fine."

"You're not the only one who's angry. Please be careful, love. Here's Johnny."

As soon as she heard Johnny's voice, she broke down again. "It was so horrible: the mangled bodies, the blood. People were screaming. My friend Barika's brother was killed. He was an interpreter, Johnny. That's all. She showed me his picture once. He was young, just out of school. He wasn't hurting anyone. None of them were hurting anyone."

"My God, I can't imagine how terrible it was for you, Carrie. I'm so glad you're safe."

"I know," Carrie said. "But I don't feel safe. I'm not sure if I'll ever feel safe."

Johnny tried to console her, but she interrupted. "There's something I have to tell you, and I want to get it out. I feel so guilty."

Johnny braced himself. What could she possibly feel guilty about?

"I owe you an apology for how I've acted. I'm so glad you're in the army. I was naïve before, but I realize now how important it is to do what you do. It's a dangerous world, and I'm proud of what you do to make it safer. I want you to know I'll follow you anywhere your service takes you. I love you more than ever, Johnny Marzo."

57- Special Operations Forces

October 1998

Johnny was torn. He appreciated the importance of the Bosnia peacekeeping mission, but he couldn't get Brian's words out of his mind. He knew what motivated his friend, but he'd never heard him so passionate before, or so angry. Johnny had always been intrigued by the Special Forces and the challenges the program presented, but taking that path had been out of the question. There was no way he could make such a commitment and hold on to Carrie. He was sure of it. But all that changed with one phone call from her. She'd been traumatized by the Nairobi bombing, and it seemed to have had a lasting impact.

He was shocked by her statement about his military career and convinced that it was her emotions speaking. He was fairly sure that she'd think differently once things settled back to normal. But she didn't. In subsequent conversations and letters, she'd been just as supportive, encouraging even. He appreciated her support, but feared she'd change her mind once he immersed himself in the demanding Green Beret regimen. Of course, he was getting ahead of himself because there was no guarantee he'd even be considered for the program or make it though the training if he was accepted. He decided to talk with his battalion commander, Lieutenant Colonel Flood. Colonel Flood liked him and treated him well, and Johnny valued his opinion.

"Your feelings are natural," Colonel Flood said. "You want a bigger challenge, which is commendable, but you're not sure you're up to the task."

"It's not that I don't think what we're doing here is important," Johnny added. "We're preventing a bloodbath, and things could get nasty very quickly. I understand that. But I'm looking for something more than patrols and surveillance."

Colonel Flood leaned back in his chair and examined Johnny's folder. "You have an outstanding record, Lieutenant. You completed airborne school while in ROTC." Flood flipped the pages. "You were an honor grad at Ranger school. That's impressive. You completed the Infantry Career Captain's Course. You've been an excellent platoon leader. You are tactically and technically proficient and most importantly, you are highly respected by the troops in your company. This is the kind of background the army doesn't want to waste."

"Thank you, sir."

"But you feel wasted," Flood said. It was more an observation than an accusation.

"Yes," Johnny replied. "I suppose I do."

Flood returned to the folder. "I see you've got a good balance of brains and brawn. I'm looking at a strong academic record."

"I was a late bloomer, Sir. But I guess I came along."

"Blooming late is better than peaking too early," Flood smiled.

"Yes, Sir, I suppose you're right."

Something on the page caught the Colonel's attention and he sat forward. "Your record indicates a strong aptitude for foreign language."

"I always liked History, but midway through high school I learned that foreign languages came easily to me."

Colonel Flood folded his hands on his desk and looked Johnny in the eyes. "How serious are you about wanting something more out of the military?"

"I'm very serious, Colonel."

"Well, Lieutenant, I don't want to get your hopes up because an extremely small number who apply actually make it. But I think you would be a legitimate candidate for the Special Forces. You should apply."

Johnny paused. "I'm flattered, sir."

"You should be. And you've been in the army long enough to know what Special Forces entails, but let me clear up any misconceptions."

The colonel leaned back again. "When young studs like you first think about qualifying for the Special Operations Forces and wearing the Green Beret, they think about their physical attributes: their fitness level, their strength and endurance, their ability to handle weapons."

"I feel good about those areas, sir."

Flood shook his head. "You should. But let me make this clear, Lieutenant. Everyone who applies for Special Forces training is exceptional in those areas. Everyone, that's a given. But physical prowess merely scratches the surface of what the army requires from SOF candidates. The army wants highly intelligent, emotionally stable, and professionally mature people who can also perform at the highest physical level. And they want people of extraordinary character." Flood paused and then added, "I think you might be a good fit in all of those areas. Throw in your language aptitude, and you just might be of interest to them."

Johnny wasn't sure what to say. So far he had mastered everything the army had offered: basic course, jump school, ranger school, platoon leadership. He loved a challenge, but admission to the Special Forces was an enormous commitment that would keep him in the army for at least three more years.

"I'm flattered, Sir. I need to think about this further, but my inclination is that I'm interested."

"Good!" Colonel Flood replied. "Why not proceed as though you are? Now I want to be clear; I think you're an excellent candidate, but it's not my call. There are no guarantees you'll be accepted, but I suggest you call infantry branch and see what they have to say. I'm going to give you the number of a close friend of mine, a Special Forces combat commander. I want you to talk with him to fully understand what you're getting into. You'll be seeking admission to the Special Forces Assessment and Selection Program at Fort Bragg, North Carolina."

"I will, Sir." Johnny said. "And thank you." .

Johnny wanted to see Carrie and wished he could fly to Nairobi, but neither of them had free time coming less than two months after their last visit. He wouldn't be granted leave and she was scheduled to leave the city soon with Dr. Graham's team for another swing through the countryside.

Phone service had been restored in Nairobi, so Johnny called. He needed to make a decision and wanted to talk with Carrie one more time before he did. He knew he wanted to apply. Pressure from Brian and more detailed reports on the Nairobi and Tanzania bombings had pushed him in that direction, especially the reports of gloating from al Qaeda, the group that claimed responsibility. He was also encouraged by Carrie's letters. But he needed to speak with her. He needed to hear her say she'd support his decision.

Carrie came on the line and sounded more like the Carrie he knew. Her voice was crisp and she laughed and joked. They shared how much they missed each other and what they'd been doing. Carrie had been spending a lot of time with Barika and reported that she was doing much better.

They talked a while longer before Johnny told her he needed to make a decision about Special Forces.

"So what are you thinking?" Carrie asked.

"I'm thinking that I need to know what you're thinking."

"My thinking hasn't changed, Johnny. I was wrong before, selfish and naïve. I used to think that the military life was foolish and filled with yahoos who loved combat. I see now that the world truly is a dangerous place, and we need good people to protect us. You have a calling for this stuff, and you're good at it. If this is what you want, I won't stand in your way."

Johnny paused. Then he said, "Thank you. I'd like to apply for the program, but what I really want is to be happy with you. Saying you won't stand in my way is not what I'm looking for. I need this to be a decision that we make together."

"I'm sorry," Carrie replied. "That was a poor choice of words. So let me say this, and this will be the last time I say it," she chided him. "Are you listening?"

"I'm here," Johnny replied.

"Do I wish people didn't have to do the sort of things I imagine you will have to do in Special Forces? Absolutely. But I know now that someone has to do it, and it might as well be the person who is good at it and willing to serve. You know I want to lead a purposeful life, so I guess supporting you this is part of it. So here it is, Johnny Marzo. I love you. I will follow you. I will live in a dusty base town if I have to, which, by the way, I'm doing now quite nicely. Is that good enough?"

"It is," Johnny said. "But are you sure you're not saying this just to appease me?"

"Have you ever known me to be shy?"

Johnny smiled over the phone. "No. I can't say that I have."

"Then accept the fact that I mean what I'm saying. Now, I'm pretty sure I won't want you to make this a twenty-year career, but if you want to do this for the next few years, I'm all for it."

58- Special Forces Assessment and Selection

February 1999

Johnny stood shivering in a wooded area somewhere in the North Carolina countryside. It was mid-February and the temperature was twenty-six degrees and dropping. A thin layer of snow covered the landscape, but the air was dry and the sky was clear.

He'd been awakened at Fort Bragg's Camp Mackall at 0500 hours and assigned tasks that lasted all day. He'd been denied food until 1600 hours when he was brought back to his barracks, where he thought he'd finally eat and get some rest. Instead, he was told to grab matches, a survival knife and a poncho and board a military vehicle. It was then that he was blindfolded and driven to his current location.

He was told he was on an impromptu survival simulation. He'd be dropped off alone with orders to avoid capture during the night and move to a point twelve miles due north where he'd be extracted by helicopter at daybreak. Once he spotted the arriving chopper, he'd have seven minutes to make it to the landing zone for rescue. Those were the only instructions he had.

The Special Forces assessment was jammed with ordeals that tested a soldier's ability to handle emotional stress, and this was one of them. Mind games, Johnny thought. It was all about mind games, so he did what his training had taught him. He fought off panic and evaluated his situation.

He considered his hunger. He hadn't eaten since the evening before, almost twenty-four hours, and he had no food with him. He did a quick review of what he could eat in the wilderness. Hunting small game was too time consuming, so he went through his mental checklist of edible things he could scavenge like bird eggs, bugs and roots. But he dismissed them as well. It was February, and he doubted many birds were laying eggs. He decided to give up on food altogether. He'd survive another thirteen hours without it.

Water was a different story. He hadn't drunk all day, and dehydration would be a serious problem once he began hiking. With no streams in sight, he removed his waterproof poncho and spread it out on the ground under an evergreen. He shook the lowest branches until a decent amount of snow had fallen, then moved the poncho and repeated the process. When he was satisfied that he'd collected enough snow, he gathered the poncho by the corners and embraced it until the snow became a watery slush. Then he drank, careful to go slowly to avoid a brain freeze. He'd repeat the process every hour until he was rescued.

His next problem was land navigation. Under normal conditions, he could cover the twelve miles easily in four hours. But he'd be traveling in darkness, on unfamiliar terrain, and would have difficulty gauging the distance traveled. Still, he had plenty of time. The bigger problem was avoiding detection. He doubted that there actually would be anyone waiting along the route, and he considered that aspect of the simulation as just another Special Forces mind game. But he needed to err on the side of caution. He estimated that if a trap were in place, it would be somewhere on a direct line between his current location and the landing zone, so he decided to head east for two miles before turning north.

As for gauging distance, he decided to pace off the first mile. He'd travel his seventeen-hundred-and-sixty yards counting each step along the way and would measure the distance against the time it took to cover it. After that, he'd keep the same pace and judge distance traveled by time lapsed. It was the best he could do.

He sat against a tree, drew his knees to his chin, and closed his eyes. His body shook from the cold, and he had to guard against hypothermia, but he was tired, very tired, and he needed to rest for a few minutes if he were going to tackle the ordeal ahead of him.

His thoughts drifted to Carrie. Things had happened quickly since he applied for the Special Forces. He'd been accepted into the Assessment and Selection process in mid December and given two weeks leave before having to report to Fort Bragg. But the selection process was only the first phase. If he made it through, he'd be admitted to the Qualifying Course, or Q course, as it was commonly called, which would last a year.

Knowing this could be their last chance to be together until his training was over, Carrie requested and was granted a transfer to Europe for the balance of her Red Cross commitment, and took a week off to be with Johnny.

This time they met in Rome. Johnny flew in from Bosnia and Carrie from Nairobi. Incredibly, it was the first time they'd seen each other since their engagement. It was also the first time Johnny saw her since the embassy bombing. It was obvious that the bombing had changed her world view, and she was still frightened and angry. She wanted to know what the world, or at least the United States, was doing to track down the people who were responsible. She'd read widely about al Qaeda, Osama bin Laden, and radical Islam. She asked about the Clinton administration's cruise missile attack on a pharmaceutical plant in Sudan believed to be manufacturing weapons of mass destruction and sites in Afghanistan suspected of harboring Osama bin Laden. Most importantly, she was far more interested now in Johnny's training and peppered him with questions.

She seemed more emotionally vulnerable than he'd ever known her to be, and her vulnerability strengthened their bond. For Johnny, Carrie had become the personification of everything he was trying to protect, and Carrie treated his military commitment with a new-found appreciation.

Their week in Rome was wonderful. It was the Christmas season, and they took long walks through the city and the Vatican in the December cold, dined in small side-street restaurants, fell in love with the local wines, and spent glorious nights by the fireplace in their room.

On Christmas Eve they waited hours to attend midnight Mass at Saint Peter's Basilica and followed Mass with a two a.m. dinner at a small restaurant near Saint Peter's Square. Carrie's cheeks were still pinkish-red from their long wait in the cold, and her eyes sparkled in the candlelight.

There was no menu. A waiter greeted them with an antipasto plate, coarse bread, and a bottle of red table wine. They nibbled on cheese and olives as an old man played a small accordion in a corner. Others arrived from Mass, and by three a.m. the restaurant was filled with happy patrons singing and wishing each other Buon Natale. The entrée of rigatoni with cherry tomato sauce and assorted fishes arrived, and Carrie oooed with delight at the first bite.

The pace was slow, and the dinner, dessert, and sing along lasted for hours, until they found themselves sipping Limoncello as the winter sun inched over the horizon. It was the most relaxing and serene setting either had experienced in a long time, and surely a stark contrast to

289

the tension and devastation Johnny had witnessed in Kosovo or the primitive countryside Carrie had see in Kenya.

Johnny smiled as he recalled their conversation.

"Can you believe we're here?" Carrie had said softly. "This is so perfect."

Johnny agreed. "You don't want to know what I think of your dumb Hollywood notion of our crazy long-distance relationship when I'm on some miserable exercise in a God-forsaken place and haven't seen you for months. But I have to admit, these times together are pretty damn special. They DO NOT make up for our time apart, but they come damn close."

Carrie nodded. "The time apart is awful." Then she reached across the table and took his hand. "But it reminds me of how much I love you. I know that when all of this is over and we're together, we'll never take each other for granted."

"Bet on it," Johnny said.

"We'll have a nice house and three or four kids," Carrie declared. Then she added, "You do want kids, don't you?"

"Are you kidding? Of course I want kids!" Johnny said. "Two boys and two girls. The boys will be athletes, studs like their dad, and humble too. And the girls will be like their beautiful mom."

"It almost sounds too good to be true," Carrie said, wistfully. Then she added with more conviction, "But it will happen. I know it will."

"You can bet on that too," Johnny said.

Carrie's smile faded. "It concerns me that we've never talked about kids before. It reminds me that there's so much we haven't talked about."

"We don't need to talk about anything," Johnny replied softly. "We want to spend our lives together. Anything else can be worked out."

They fell silent and Johnny seemed to drift. Carrie noticed and said, "What are you thinking?"

Johnny sipped his Lemoncello and said, "I'm thinking that I'm in a great restaurant in Rome at five o'clock in the morning on Christmas Eve, or day, or whatever it is, with the most beautiful girl in the world, the girl I've loved since the first time I met her. That's what I'm thinking."

Carrie looked out the window at the rising sun and said, "I think it's officially Christmas."

"I guess you're right," Johnny replied. Then he raised his glass and said, "Merry Christmas."

"Buon Natale," Carrie said. They clinked glasses and drank. Carrie's eyes filled and she said, "I love you."

Johnny reached into his pocket, pulled out a small box and handed it to Carrie.

It was a medal of Mother Theresa that hung from a silver chain. "It was blessed by the Pope," he said.

"It's beautiful," Carrie said. She opened the clasp and put it around her neck.

Johnny turned serious. "You've been through a lot in Africa, and I know how the bombing affected you. But I don't ever want you to lose sight of the wonderful work you do for people, and I don't want you to stop doing it. This is still a good world, Carrie, a good world with some evil people in it. Don't let them take that sparkle from your eyes."

Carrie's smiled bravely and said, "I won't. I promise." Then she brightened and said, "I'm embarrassed. I don't have your gift with me. You're early you know. The custom in Italy is to exchange gifts on January 6, the feast of the Epiphany. Children receive their toys from a kind but ugly witch named Befana. She flies around on a broom instead of a sled."

"You're putting me on, right?"

"No," Carrie laughed. "There's some story about the Three Wise Men telling her to visit the Baby Jesus, but she got there late. Just a silly custom I guess."

Johnny thought about what he had read in the Special Forces orientation manual about understanding and respecting customs. He'd have to learn the language and traditions of a particular part of the world as part of his training. He wasn't sure if his language placement would be Chinese, Russian, Spanish, Arabic, or if he'd qualify at all, but his work would require a good working knowledge of the language and customs of the indigenous population.

Carrie interrupted his thoughts. "I have a harder job selecting your gift, you know. What in the world do you buy the man who's about to train for a year in Special Forces?"

Johnny laughed. "A sympathy card, maybe?"

"Anyway, your gift is back at the room," she said with a wink.

"You're damn right it is," Johnny said. "And I want to collect it right now. Let's go."

That night they set a date for their wedding. It was to be late January of 2000, as soon as Johnny earned his Green Beret. Johnny smiled at the memory.

A chill brought his thoughts back to the problem at hand. He knew he needed to get moving. He stood and shook off the snow. He needed to cover twelve miles before daybreak without being detected. He checked the matches in his pocket. More Special Forces mind games, he thought. A fire would be nice to keep warm, but who lights a fire when he's trying to elude capture? He tossed the matches in the bushes. "Screw your games and emotional tests," Johnny whispered to himself. "I'll be at that landing zone waiting when you arrive." He checked his bearings by the setting sun and headed east.

59- The Cold

February 1999

The weather worsened as the night wore on. A biting wind developed from the northwest, blowing snow from the trees into Johnny's eyes and slowing his progress. The temperature continued to drop and Johnny tried not to think about what the wind-chill index must have been. He was wearing the best winter gear the army offered, but it wasn't enough, not for the bone-chilling cold he was feeling now.

His body ached from the long grind over uneven terrain, and his muscles began to tighten. He knew dehydration would cause cramping, so he continued the painful routine of adding what amounted to ice water to his already freezing body.

He cursed the army, the Special Forces, Colonel Flood, Brian, and his own stupidity for signing up in the first place. He considered the possibility of dying before the night was over and wondered how the army would report his death. He was sure the story would be whitewashed.

He worried about his location. He'd been unable to maintain the pace he originally calculated and had to make several adjustments along the way. He hoped his calculations were right, or at least close.

He thought about the warnings of an enemy team being part of the simulation and hoped his initial thoughts about them were wrong. He now hoped he would run into one because he wanted to beat the crap out of somebody. He'd take out his frustrations with the army on any poor bastard they tried to send his way. Then he thought better of it. He was so weak he doubted he could take on anyone.

The moon peeked through the clouds, and the additional light helped. He stopped repeatedly to check the moss at the base of the trees to make sure he was still heading north. He was. He checked to make sure he still had his knife and told himself if he saw a small animal, any animal, he'd kill it and carry its carcass inside his jacket until it lost its body heat; then he'd kill another. But animals had long since bowed to the brutality of mother-nature and abandoned the landscape. He thought of Carrie and the warm fire of the hotel room they shared in Rome. He thought of the life they'd promised each other. "Bet on it," he had said to her. He pushed on.

He'd been walking for eight hours. He estimated that he'd covered three miles in each of the first two hours, and that his pace had slowed to less than half of that for the next two. Factoring in stops for drinks and directional checks, he estimated that he'd traveled about seven miles by midnight. At that point he decided to count out the paces again and measure them against the time lapsed to cover a mile. With the wind in his face and his body resisting every step, he was surprised to learn that his pace had slowed to just about one mile per hour. Still, if he could continue that pace, or something near it, he'd cover the twelve miles with ample time to spare.

He cursed the army again. He had run ridiculous distances in record times in his past training and gone on long marches carrying a fifty-five pound rucksack without exceptional difficulty, but never in the dark, in freezing temperatures, with blinding wind and without water. He wondered what kind of sadist dreamed up this routine.

The Special Forces training credo was, "Always do your best." He was, damn it. But how could he be expected to find a rendezvous point when his only instructions were to head twelve miles north and look for a chopper at daybreak? This whole ordeal was insane.

He felt himself beginning to panic. He knew self doubt was his worst enemy, but he couldn't shake the fear that he'd be drastically off in his calculations and that he'd be far away from the landing zone at daybreak. Maybe he'd overshoot it, or undershoot it, or maybe he had drifted a mile east or west of the site. His body found it harder to walk when his mind was telling him the effort might be in vain.

He stopped by a tree and took several slow breaths to gather himself. Maybe his calculations were wrong, but he had no choice but to assume they were correct. What else could he do? He checked his watch. It was two a.m. if he walked at the same pace, he'd be at his destination in two hours. He moved on.

His feet were numb and the tips of his fingers ached. It was time to consume more slush, but he couldn't bring himself to do it. In the moonlight Johnny saw a raccoon twenty feet ahead in his path. It was lying on its side and it eyes were wide open staring at him. Johnny pulled his knife and approached slowly, but the 'coon didn't move. When Johnny got close enough, he kicked it and it moved without bending a limb. It was frozen stiff.

He pressed on until his watch read four a.m. This should be the spot, he thought. He scanned the area as best as he could see, and his intuition told him it wasn't right. The chopper would need a clearing to land, at least a small one. The woods here were still thick. He said a prayer. He'd said several during the night when he wasn't counting steps. His prayers had been simple: Let me live, God. I'm trying to do what I think is right. Let me live, so I can do it, he had said.

This time he prayed for guidance. He needed to adjust his location; he could feel it. But he didn't know in which direction. He stood still and listened to the wind. It seemed to be whispering his demise. He fought off that thought and waited. Something was drawing him forward, and he willed himself to go on.

Each step was agony now. He walked for another fifteen minutes when he found a clearing. It wasn't a large one, but it was the largest he'd seen thus far and certainly large enough for a helicopter to land. He stopped. This was his spot, or at least he hoped it was. There was no sense in going on. He checked his watch again. It was just shy of 0430 hours. It was still another ninety minutes to two hours before daybreak. The wind was even stronger now. He couldn't just stand there for two hours, nor could he walk in circles to keep his blood flowing. He was exhausted.

He decided to move away from the clearing in case there was an enemy team searching for him. Then he went to work making a lean-to shelter. He found two trees spaced closely together that each had limbs that formed a "Y" about three feet off the ground. He cut a cross branch and laid it across the limbs. Then he cut several full branches and rested them against the cross branch on a forty-five degree angle to block the wind. He was exhausted, but the work gave him purpose and was a welcome change from the continuous walking he'd been doing. He cut several more branches and wove them as carefully as he could with his shaking hands. Finally he removed his outer poncho and used it as a tarp to cover the branches. Then he crawled inside.

The wind break lessened the cold, and he pulled his knees to this chest again to ease his shivering. He knew he shouldn't fall asleep, so he struggled to keep himself occupied. He thought of his last trip home to Bristol to see his parents. It was just after his week with Carrie in Rome. He was able to visit for a few days before his due date at Fort Bragg. He decided to pass the time by recreating as much of the trip as he could.

He had landed at Philadelphia airport at mid morning, took a train into the city and then transferred to the SEPTA R-7 for the final leg home.

As the train pulled away from the Bristol station, Johnny stood on the elevated platform and took in the sights of his hometown. Directly in front of him stood the fourteen story Grundy clock tower, the town's most recognizable landmark. To his left, in the distance, was the lagoon of the old Delaware Canal, dug by Irish immigrants almost one-hundred and fifty years earlier. Behind him, barely visible over the rooftops of row homes was the cluster of ball fields where Johnny had spent so much of his youth. Seeing the town again reminded him of how much he had missed it.

He took the steps and passed through the tunnel that ran beneath the tracks to the other side of the station. The graffiti covered walls reminded him of the stories his father told of how, as teenagers, he and Johnny's adopted uncles would sing in the tunnel at night. Johnny missed those guys and couldn't wait to see them.

At the end of the tunnel he saw some kids playing whiffle ball. They stopped to do a double take of his uniform. Johnny smiled and walked by. He was supposed to call the deli for a ride as soon as his train arrived but decided to walk home instead. He slung his rucksack over his shoulder and headed east on Washington Street.

Much of the gritty, blue-collar town looked the same as when he left it, but it was Disneyworld compared to places he'd been.

The deli came into view and Johnny's eyes began to fill. Most of the people he loved would be in the store waiting for him. He thought of Carrie in Europe and Brian in Washington and wished they'd be there too. Of course, they wouldn't.

He reached the door, took one last breath to prepare himself for what would happen next, and walked in.

Jimmy saw him first and yelled, "He's here!"

Johnny's mother let out a scream and ran to her son. His father vaulted the counter and joined her.

"I won," Jimmy said to Big Frankie. "I said 3:45. I'm closest."

Frankie handed Jimmy five bucks.

"Look at you," Johnny's mother said. "You look so handsome in that uniform. She kissed his cheeks and his forehead over and over until Johnny's father said, "Can I get in here?"

Angelo grabbed his son by the shoulders, and they embraced.

"It's good to see you, Son."

"It's good to be home, Pop."

"Why didn't you call?" Johnny's mother said. "We had a ride waiting."

"Yeah," Jimmy said. "I was gonna pick you up in the truck."

"Thanks, Uncle Jimmy. But I felt like walking. It was nice to see the town again."

"You look great, kid," Big Frankie said, reaching out to shake hands.

"Thanks," Johnny said. "You do too. Everyone does."

Then Johnny's eyes met Nick's. Nick had been standing quietly in the background. "Look what the wind just blew in," Nick said. He limped slowly to Johnny and gave him a long bear hug. "I'm so proud of you," he whispered. Johnny could see that Nick's eyes were filling up.

"Special Forces," Nick said proudly. "I can't believe you're gonna wear the Green Beret."

"Easy, Uncle Nick. I haven't even qualified yet, and it's a tough course. No one knows that better than you."

"It's a damn tough course," Nick said. "I think it's even tougher than when I qualified. But there's no doubt in my mind you'll make it."

"How are you feeling?" Johnny asked.

"I feel great," Nick said. "Never felt better."

Johnny knew that was a lie. Five years in a North Vietnamese prison camp had taken its toll on the former Special Forces Sergeant, and the pronounced limp meant that this was an especially painful day.

Johnny played along. "Glad to hear it."

"You must be starved," Johnny's mother said. "Let's eat."

They had pulled some deli tables together to form one long one and everyone sat.

"Your father prepared a feast," Donna Marzo said.

"No doubt," Johnny said smiling.

They sat down to eat and Donna asked, "So how was Rome?"

"Terrific," Johnny said. "It's an unbelievable city."

"Lots of fountains in Rome, right?" Nick asked with a playful look on his face. Brian had told the guys about the episode in Berlin. "Was there any juicy action involving a fountain?"

Johnny laughed. "Nah, Uncle Nick. Things were pretty quiet."

Jimmy started to say something about the Roman ruins, but Donna cut him off. "If I want to learn about Rome, I'll buy a travel book. What I meant was how was *Carrie* when you saw her in Rome?"

"Oh," Johnny teased, smiling. He cleared his throat and said, "I have some news."

Jimmy blurted out, "Am I going to be a Great Uncle?"

Big Frankie smacked him in the head and said, "Let the kid finish."

"I was kidding," Jimmy said, rubbing his head..

"Well?" Donna said, looking at her son. "We're waiting."

Johnny told them that he and Carrie had set a date, and the room erupted.

They sat for dinner and feasted on sausage smothered with onions and peppers, meatballs, pencil points, mozzarella and tomatoes, and fresh Italian bread. The conversation flowed from the wedding plans, which were non-existent, to the war in Kosovo, to Bristol gossip, to sports, and Johnny was reminded of how much fun it was to be in the deli.

For a time, Johnny felt warm and full until he awakened with a start and realized he'd been dreaming. He wasn't warm at all; he was freezing and his body was shaking uncontrollably. His watch read 0515 hours, and he looked for a glow in the east, for any sign of dawn breaking, but there was none, nor would there be for another hour at least. Johnny wasn't sure he would last that long. He started to pray.

Within minutes he heard what he thought was a chopper. He wasn't sure if he was dreaming again or not because it was still too early. He left his shelter and scanned the sky. It was still too dark to see, but the sound of the rotor was growing louder.

A chopper turned on its search lights and headed for the clearing and Johnny's heart leaped. He had carved himself a staff to help him navigate the final miles, and he used it now as he limped to the landing area. He had never felt such conflicting feelings before. He was elated that he was rescued, but he wanted to unleash the rage that was building inside him toward the first military person he saw.

The downward draft of the blades kicked up particles of dirt and snow that felt like needle pricks as they struck his face. He shielded his eyes with his forearm and moved ahead. Two crew members were sitting by the opened door and offered Johnny a hand. Johnny fantasized about stabbing them with the sharpened end of this staff, but he took the hand instead. One crew member shouted to be heard above the motor, "Congratulations, solider. You made it."

"Screw you!" Johnny shouted in return. The crew member grinned.

The chopper felt warm compared to where Johnny had been, and he welcomed the change as they removed his poncho and wrapped him in a warm blanket. Someone handed him a hot coffee from a thermos and said, "Just sip." He took the cup with two shaking hands and savored the warmth as it entered his body. He took a few deep breaths and then exploded. "Are you friggin' guys out of your minds? Is the whole God-damned army out if its friggin mind?"

A guy with Master Sergeant stripes said, "Go easy solider. It's over and you made it. You did a great job." Under normal circumstances, Johnny outranked the sergeant. But officers vying for Special Forces selection held no rank during training. Johnny knew he should hold back but was too angry to care.

"Bullshit!" He thundered above the rotor noise. "That wasn't a training exercise; it was a God-Damned suicide mission. I could have died and no one would have known it. You call that training? Was that supposed to build my trust in the service?"

The sergeant spoke more sternly now. "Be quiet, Marzo, before you say something I won't overlook. Then he said to one of the crew members, "Get his shoe."

The crew member leaned forward and started to untie Johnny's boot. Johnny protested, but didn't resist. "What the hell…"

The sergeant interrupted. "I understand what you're feeling, Marzo. We all do, because we've all done it. But make sure you know what you're talking about before you criticize the Special Forces."

The crew member handed the sergeant the boot, and the sergeant snapped off the heel to reveal a small chip the size of a nickel. "This is a tracking devise," the sergeant said. We've been able to track your progress ever since you were dropped off. We were concerned about the weather but felt that you were okay as long as you kept moving, which you did, remarkably, for over ten hours. When you stopped at 0430 hours, we thought something was wrong and we activated the pick up early."

Johnny didn't know what to say, and the sergeant went on. "You can bitch all you want about what we put you guys through, but don't ever, I mean ever, think the Special Forces would abandon one of its own."

Johnny nodded.

"We were prepared to pick you up at every step of the way if we had to. Remember that."

"I will, Sergeant," Johnny said weakly.

"The purpose of this mission was to test your physical and emotional strength." The sergeant gave his best impression of a smile and added,

"You were outstanding. The conditions were as bad as some you will face when you do this stuff for real. You adapted well. You improvised. You covered more ground than we expected you to."

"I was afraid I was far off the mark for the rendezvous point," Johnny said weakly.

The sergeant laughed. "There was no rendezvous point. We don't expect anyone to travel a straight line in the dark for twelve miles without instruments to calculate distance. But," he added, "if we drew a line twelve miles due north from the point where you were dropped off, you made it to within a mile and a half from that spot. Remarkable."

"Thanks," Johnny said.

"We thought we had a real loser when you started off in the wrong direction," one of the crewmen said. "You headed east for roughly two miles, and we thought we'd have to take you out early. But then you turned north and stayed on course."

The sergeant said, "You took that course to avoid an ambush, right?"

Johnny nodded again.

"Perfect," the sergeant said.

"Thank you, sir," Johnny replied.

"You've got a long way to go, soldier, but I think you're gonna be a hell of a member of the Special Forces."

Johnny smiled.

60- Dr. Blake's New Office

March 1999

The 1998 Nairobi and Dar es Salaam Embassy bombings had shaken the intelligence community and infuriated the Clinton administration. The FBI had placed Osama bin Laden on its Ten Most Wanted List, and the CIA had searched furiously for actionable intelligence to go after the perpetrators.

The President had vowed that justice would be served and within days ordered a cruise missile attack on a pharmaceutical plant in Sudan owned by an associate of Osama bin Laden and believed to be manufacturing weapons of mass destruction. Cruise missiles were also launched at sites in Afghanistan suspected of harboring Osama bin Laden.

At first the American public applauded the attacks, but as time passed doubt was shed on the reliability of the intelligence that prompted the bombing of the Sudanese factory. In the rush to demonstrate bold, decisive action, the President may have relied upon faulty information from the CIA. News agencies reported no evidence of chemical weapons at the bombed plant, and the world press had increasingly referred to the factory complex as merely an "aspirin factory." In the months since then, the United States was having difficulty producing convincing evidence to the contrary.

Clearly, the United States needed to thwart terrorist attacks before they happened and, at the same time, have reliable intelligence before striking suspected terrorist facilities. Clinton's National Security team wasn't pleased with the progress on either front, and they let CIA Director George Tenet know it.

Tenet felt the criticism was unfair. They had done the best they could with information they obtained on the ground and passed on their recommendations with some reservations. As with any CIA activity, intelligence successes are generally shielded from public view while failures are plainly seen. Tenet felt the Agency was doing a good job in the face of enormous pressures, but he needed to be proactive in addressing the administration's frustrations. He assembled his closest assistants and empowered them to come up with something extra, something more than what was already being done.

Dr. David Blake was contacted at his MIT office and invited to come to CIA headquarters for a security discussion with agency heads. They wanted to establish another layer of intelligence analysis, an office that would operate independently from the existing offices and would review raw intelligence as well as conclusions reached by other analysts. They wanted an outside team with a fresh perspective that would do some out-of-the-box thinking and deal with the often incomplete and sometimes contradictory information the agency received and try to make sense from it. Given the circumstances, the new office would have a generous budget, and they invited Blake to head it.

Organizationally, Blake's team would be part of the Office of Intelligence Analysis. His team would review information from three related offices: the Office of Near Eastern Affairs, which included countries in North Africa, the Middle East, India, Pakistan, and Afghanistan; the Office of Terrorism Analysis; and the Office of Political Islam Strategic Analysis.

Blake had been incensed by the Nairobi bombings. He was deeply concerned by the increase of seemingly unrelated attacks around the globe that Blake felt were, in fact, related. He loved the academic life as well as the financial rewards of his outside consulting work, but he loved his country even more. He accepted the position without hesitation and agreed to take an extended leave from the college. He had one condition, however. He wanted input on the selection of his team, and he wanted Dr. Brian Kelly to work with him.

61- Sergeant Blanchard

March 1999

Master Sergeant Ike Blanchard was an imposing figure. He had the chest of a weightlifter, the stomach of a ballerina, and a name given by parents who obviously knew he was destined to become a Special Forces instructor. He had a strong chin, a booming voice, and the demeanor of a medieval executioner. He also had the abiding respect of anyone who ever worked with him. He'd conducted operations in Panama, Granada, Iraq, and places the United States Government would never acknowledge, and his prowess was legendary. In an era when non-commissioned officers formed the backbone of the army, Sergeant Ike Blanchard was one of the very best.

Johnny was seated with over two-hundred other candidates at the John F. Kennedy Special Warfare Center and School at Fort Bragg. They were beginning the grueling one-year Qualification Course. Johnny noted that only half the candidates who entered the Assessment and Selection Program six weeks earlier were still with him.

Blanchard addressed the group. "Welcome to the Q Course, and congratulations for completing Phase I. You've proven that you have the toughness and mental disposition necessary to be a member of the United States Army SOF." Blanchard grinned and added, "But now the hard part begins."

Blanchard liked that comment and let it sink in. "What separates the Special Forces from other outfits is a greater range of capabilities. The Q course is a year-long study of tactics, survival, language, and unconventional warfare. Over the next several months, each of you will master the skills of your Military Occupation Specialty, your MOS. Each of you will become an expert in either weapons, engineering and demolition, medicine, or communications, and all of you will be cross-trained in the other areas.

"Some of you are commissioned officers," Blanchard said neutrally. "As you learned last month, you check your rank at the door in Special Ops training until you earn your Green Beret. At that point you will renew your rank and take command of an 'A- Team.'

"We'll discuss the 'A-Team' structure later, but first I'd like to read you a quote by Major General Sidney Shachnow, the former commander of the Warfare Center here at Fort Bragg. General Shachnow said, 'A Special Forces guy has to be a lethal killer one moment and a humanitarian the next. He has to know how to get strangers, who speak a different language, to do things for him.'"

Blanchard scanned the room again before resuming. "When we venture into a foreign country, our job is to help the good guys, kill the bad guys, and win over the hearts and minds of those who are undecided. We need to be able to work with indigenous forces who want to cooperate. Therefore, it's vital that we speak their language. Whether we're helping the Columbian government deal with drug lords, eradicating poppy production in Afghanistan, tracking down known terrorists in the Middle East, searching for loose nukes in the former Soviet republics, or rescuing a downed American pilot in Southeast Asia, it's imperative that we can speak the native language. That's why we administered the Defense Language Aptitude Battery and informed you of your language placement. Everyone in this room will learn a language. Everyone!

"You will study your assigned language for the entire year you're at Fort Bragg, and continue to do so after you've completed the Q Course. Depending upon your placement, some of you will go through as many as fifteen weeks of intense, day-long study, after which you will continue your language study during the other phases of your training. So while you're learning your demolition skills, you'll study your language. While you're learning to operate sophisticated communications equipment, you'll study your language. You'll study as if your life depends on it, because it will. You'll also study the culture of your assigned area. In fact, you'll fully immerse yourself in it."

Johnny knew that was true. Candidates with the highest battery scores were assigned the most difficult languages. Johnny had obviously done quite well because he'd been assigned Arabic and told he would also be exposed to Pastun and Dari, the principal languages of Afghanistan. So far his head was spinning.

"Now let's address some other issues," Blanchard said. "First, you need to know that it gives me a royal pain in the ass when civilians call us Green Berets. You are not training to become a Green Beret," Blanchard thundered. "A Green Beret is a God-damn hat! You're training to become a member of the United States Special Forces, the most elite military outfit in the world. You'll *wear* the Green Beret proudly, that is if you make it through the year, but you'll *be* a member of the Special Forces."

Johnny didn't see what the big deal was, but if that was the way Blanchard saw it, then as far as Johnny was concerned, that's the way it would be.

"Now, another thing," Blanchard said. "Get rid of any of that John Wayne, Hollywood bullshit you may have in your head about how we conduct ourselves. There will be no heroes in this room, at least not in the public sense. You'll do heroic things, plenty of heroic things, but the public will not know about them, and you won't be able to enlighten them.

"We are quiet professionals. We receive our orders, execute our assignments quietly and effectively, and return home to wait for our next assignment. There will be no ticker tape parades down 5th Avenue at the end of our missions. In fact, our government would not even acknowledge most of our missions. You'll have to be content with the personal satisfaction of knowing you did your job and made your country just a little safer."

Johnny had already read everything Sergeant Blanchard was telling them, but hearing it from him gave it added significance.
Blanchard grew quiet for some time before going on, "Now I said we'd discuss the A-Team structure. Again, we're not talking about that

stupid show on television a few years back. Who was that guy, Mr. T, or something like that?" Blanchard actually smiled and the men laughed.

He turned serious again. "When you complete your training, you'll be assigned to a Special Forces Operational Detachment- A or an 'A-Team' as it is commonly called. A twelve man 'A Team' forms the foundation of Special Forces operations. Each team will have a captain, a warrant officer and members who have exceptional operations, weapons, engineering, medical or communications skills. As I said before, there will be two members on each team trained in each MOS, but everyone will be cross trained. The team will use these capabilities to organize, train, equip, advise, direct and support indigenous forces friendly to the United States or to engage in unconventional warfare, special reconnaissance, counterterrorism and search and rescue.

"Never underestimate your training. Someday you may find your ass in the middle of an Iranian desert trying to rescue a downed American pilot, or on a frozen tundra trying to separate the Russian mafia from a nuke they're trying to sell to the highest bidder. When you do, it's your training that will keep you alive."

Everyone in the room understood.

Blanchard's voice got softer as he delivered the next piece of news. "As you know, you'll be shut off from the outside world for a couple of months. We'll approve a letter now and then, but you'll be in the field and there will be no phone contact and no personal meetings. I know this will be difficult for many of you who have wives, girlfriends, or children. But there's a reason for this. Once you've become a member of the Special Forces, there's a possibility you could be deployed for several months at a time, with absolutely no contact with loved ones. This is a warm-up to see if you can make it and if they can make it."

Johnny knew this would be the part that he'd hate the most. He could handle the physical training and the mind games. He'd study the language and the advanced courses, but the separation from Carrie would be tough.

Blanchard closed his remarks by saying, "So, we'll learn our MOS, master our assigned language and culture, and do physical training like sons-of-bitches for another year. When you're finished, you'll wear the Green Beret and maybe do some good in the world. Good luck."

62- Arabic

May 1999

Brian sat at his desk reviewing old reports and searching for links between the Khobar Towers bombing of 1996, the Nairobi Embassy bombing, and other terrorist attacks. He studied materials and methodology, security lapses, and reports from agents in the field. He needed a link, something he could use to predict and prevent future attacks.

The towers were part of a housing complex located in Khobar, Saudi Arabia, near the headquarters of Aramco, the Saudi national oil company. The eight story building that bore the brunt of the attack housed members of the 440th wing of the United States Air Force, holdovers from the Bush administration's Operations Desert Shield and Desert Storm in 1991.

Mecca and Medina, Islam's holiest shrines, were located in Saudi Arabia, and   Islamic extremists had been incensed that American "infidels" had a military presence on sacred land. They had warned through al Jazerra six months earlier that they would attack the complex if the American military did not leave the country, and in June of 1996 they made good on their promise.

The terrorists used a tanker truck filled with explosives equivalent to 20,000 pounds of TNT. They parked the tanker near a security fence less than one hundred feet from the building. Minutes later the truck detonated with astonishing force, killing 19 Americans and wounding almost 400 people of various nationalities also housed at the complex. The American losses would have been higher were it not for a sentry who had witnessed the truck's suspicious arrival and began to rouse the sleeping airmen from their beds and evacuate the building.

Brian stopped reading and closed his eyes. He rubbed his temples, took a deep breath, and emptied his lungs slowly. The job was stressful and yielded few results. Lately, he found himself unable to escape his work, even at home, and sleep was becoming more and more difficult. The tension and fatigue were affecting his performance, and Dr. Blake had spoken to him about it.

"I picked you for the team because I admire your ability, and because you're passionate about our mission," Blake had said. "Everyone here appreciates your intensity, but there's a point after which people begin to lose effectiveness. You need to keep your perspective. You can't do it all, and you can't do it all at once. I want you to ease up and take a couple of days off, and I want you to do it soon."

Brian knew he was right. Jenny had told him the same thing, and Brian smiled at the thought of her now. Having her move in was the best thing that ever happened to him. Dr. Blake had insisted they run a background check on her, which disturbed Brian at first, although he knew it was sound procedure. Following her clearance, Blake had helped her get a job. She'd been a Communications major in college, and she ended up at the Museum of American History writing promotional material and doing event planning.

At first she enjoyed her work and enjoyed Brian even more. They shared a townhouse in Georgetown that Brian had purchased soon after he moved to the city. It was an overpriced place on Wisconsin Avenue near the restaurant district, and they loved the area. Georgetown always seemed so alive, Jenny had said. They discovered a pub called Walker's that was frequented by mostly a professional crowd, and Brian and Jenny ate there often. It was an old building with an elaborate mahogany bar and brass light fixtures. It boasted of the best crab cakes in town, and the inside walls were lined with photos of dignitaries who had eaten there. Images of Henry Kissinger, Ted Sorenson, and United States Senator Arlen Spector overlooked Brian and Jenny's favorite booth. Brian enjoyed the photo of the Pennsylvania senator most because it made him feel at home. He often missed Bristol and his parents.

The front wall consisted entirely of multi-paned windows that swung up and outward during good weather to give the place an airy, outdoors feel.

Jenny was perfect for Brian, and he knew it. She understood what motivated him, and she valued his work. She realized there were classified things he couldn't share but provided a willing ear for things he could. More importantly, she offered Brian a much needed release. She knew how to have fun and could make him laugh easily. They'd discovered the joys of martinis and had sampled every concoction Walker's bartenders offered. Eventually she settled upon the apple-flavored while he stuck with the more traditional Grey Goose with three olives. Their parting words after their morning coffee were often, "Let's meet at Walker's after work."

It felt good to have a place where they felt at home. The bartenders knew their names and drink preferences, and Jenny's outgoing persona made it easy for her and Brian to befriend some of the regulars.

But recently, Jenny's exuberance was fading, and Brian knew why. "I'm worried about you," she had said over drinks. "You're much too tense. You're restless in your sleep, and you seem to be distracted lately when we're together. I know you're under a lot of pressure and I try to make you smile a little, but too often your thoughts seem far away."

She'd been right, of course. His thoughts were quite far away. They were in the Persian Gulf, and Iraq, and Egypt and East Africa; anywhere that day's work had taken him. It saddened him to hear her concerns because the last thing he wanted was for her to be unhappy. He promised her and himself that'd he'd try to separate things. He'd do his job as best he could at Langley, and then leave his work and worries at the office. He even agreed to let her look into a vacation for them.

Nevertheless, he was driven by the knowledge that a missed clue or an overlooked connection in the terror reports could cost lives in the future. He exhaled deeply and returned to his work.

He was reviewing the types of explosives used in the bombing and how they were acquired when he received a call on his private line. It was Johnny.

"Hey, super sleuth, what going on?"

Brian smiled. He needed a break and Johnny sounded like he was in a good mood. "Just trying to keep America safe, my friend. How about you?"

"I'm missing my woman like crazy." Johnny said. "At least we're in from the field now, and I have some freedom, but it's been five months since Italy."

"I don't know what made you join the Special Forces anyway," Brian kidded. "I get to go home to Jenny's warm embrace every night."

Johnny laughed. "I'm gonna kick your ass real good when I see you again."

"Careful," Brian said. "I have all kinds of gadgets that can kill a person in three seconds."

"You're gonna need them when you see me."

Brian laughed and changed the subject. "So how is Carrie?"

"She's great, I guess. She's enjoyed the opportunity to be with her parents for a few months while she finished her Red Cross commitment. The commitment just ended, so I'm hoping she can come to the states."

"That would be nice," Brian said. "So what else is hot?"

"I'm bustin' my ass in North Carolina. This qualification course is a bear."

"That's bull," Brian kidded. "From what I've read the Q course is a cakewalk."

Brian knew better, and Johnny laughed again. "Cakewalk! You're the guy with the desk job."

"Believe me, Johnny. There are times when I'd rather be out there with you doing the Rambo thing. At least if you get mad you can take it out on someone."

"So wrestle the guy in the next cubical."

"I'll think about it," Brian said. "So how's the language study?"

"Its murder," Johnny said. "Six hours a day for fifteen weeks. My head is spinning."

"Poor guy," Brian deadpanned. "Are you learning anything?"

"Yeah," Johnny said. "I'm learning a lot. But..."

"Listen, Rambo, you lucked out with the language placement. Anybody can pick up French easily, and Spanish will land you in South America fighting druggies. The Russians have gone quiet since Reagan kicked their ass, at least for now anyway, so nobody cares about Russian. But ninety percent of the problems that cross my desk have Arabic names. You need to learn to speak their language so you can say good-bye in Arabic before you blow them away."

"I'm trying," Johnny said.

Brian changed the subject. "So I hear Carrie's doing well. She and Jenny e-mail each other almost every day. I'm glad to see the ladies becoming good friends. "

"Me too," Johnny said. "Carrie has bounced around so much that she's never really developed close friendships, and she likes Jenny a lot."

"Jenny feels the same way. She came to D.C. not knowing anyone but me, so writing to Carrie has been good for her too."

"Speaking of the girls, Carrie called yesterday and said she had a giant surprise for me. Surprises make me nervous, especially Carrie's, so I'm wondering if maybe Jenny knows the secret and let you in on it."

Brian remained quiet for some time and then said, "Maybe I do and maybe I don't. But I'm in the CIA, so I can't divulge secrets anyway. Sorry, Johnny boy, but you'll need a different source."

63- Make Mine a Bud

August 1999

Johnny found them relaxing in side-by-side Queen Ann chairs in the lobby of the Marriott Courtyard, just outside of Fayetteville, North Carolina. Brian was scanning the *Fayetteville Observer,* and Jenny appeared to be absorbed by a paperback. Two half empty drink glasses sat on the small table that separated them.

Johnny hadn't seen either of them since Israel, and his impulse was to call out across the lobby. Instead, he walked quietly around the periphery of the room and came up behind them. When he got to within five feet he said, "You can't fool me. I've got you pegged as CIA all the way."

They turned toward his voice. Brian yelped when he saw him, sprang to his feet, and came around the chair to meet him. They exchanged a bear hug and some boyish banter for a few seconds until Johnny turned to Jenny and said, "And you are obviously the beautiful girl that every Hollywood spy has hanging on his arm."

Jenny smiled and said, "Hardly." They embraced and she gave Johnny a kiss on the cheek.

"No really," Johnny said as he took a step back but held on to her hands. "You look terrific, both of you."

Jenny still had long, straight dark hair which she had pulled back. She wore a tank top, jeans and sandals. "I'm still a mess from the drive," she said modestly. "Traffic from Washington was awful, and it's hot down here."

Johnny released her hands and said, "Being where I've been for the past few months gives a guy a whole new appreciation of women. If I say you look great, then you look great." He slapped Brian on the shoulder and added, "And she's obviously just what the doctor ordered for you. You look like the world's at your feet."

"Bad choice of words," Brian said as he made a playful face in Jenny's direction.

"That's right," Jenny added. "Brian's not happy with the world at all right now, and he's working way too hard to fix it. So we're not talking about the world in any way during this little vacation."

Johnny smiled. "That's good by me. I've got a three day leave and I'm thrilled you guys are here, although there's got to be a better place for you to vacation than beautiful downtown Fayetteville."

"Not when my best friend is here," Brian said. "Besides, like I said, this is a business trip."

"Yeah," Johnny said, looking perplexed. "What's that all about?"

"My accountant says I should diversify, get into real estate a little. He said the Carolinas are a hot market right now and should be good for another five to seven years. So I thought, why not look at a small place near Fort Bragg, just to get a start. So here we are."

Johnny grinned. "You're nuts, Brian." Then he turned to Jenny and said, "You know he's nuts, right?"

Brian put his arm around her and said, "She knows I'm nuts about her."

"That's right," Jenny said and gave him a kiss.

They sat, and Johnny took a chair facing them. Brian said, "Since this is a business trip, I'll claim entertainment expenses, so the drinks are on me. How do you say martini in Arabic?"

"Haven't learned that yet," Johnny said. "But it doesn't matter because Muslims don't drink."

"Atta boy," Brian said. "Know the language and know the culture."

"Stop it," Jenny said abruptly. "No shop talk."

Johnny put his hands up in mock defense. "Hey, I'm off duty for three days, and I wore civilian clothes today. It's your boyfriend you need to straighten out."

A waitress arrived and said to Johnny, "Can I get you anything?"

Brian sat up. "Ah, Leighann. I want you to meet our very dear friend, Johnny Marzo, Lieutenant Johnny Marzo, actually. Johnny this is our friend, Leighann. We just met, but we feel like we've know each other forever. She's been very helpful, right Leighann?"

The waitress winked and Brian continued. "She's an elementary school teacher in Fayetteville, and she serves drinks here in the summer for extra cash. She's also the friendliest person we've met since we left Washington."

Leighann flashed Johnny a big smile. "Nice to met ya, Lieutenant."

"It's nice to meet you, Leighann." Johnny said. "What grade do you teach?"

"Third," she said. "And I love it."

She was perky and attractive and Johnny could picture her in the classroom. He thought of Witch Watson back in grade school and shuddered.

"Johnny copied off of me all the time in third grade," Brian said. "Fourth, fifth and sixth too. As a matter of fact…"

"Wait!" Johnny interrupted. "We didn't even know each other until fifth grade."

"Well, I'm sure you copied off of someone before you met me."

Leighann laughed. "Looks like he turned out all right. He's a Lieutenant."

The Fayetteville area had deep military connections with Fort Bragg and the adjoining Pope Air Force base just eight miles away. "Are you from Ft. Bragg or the airbase?" the waitress asked.

"Fort Bragg," Brian answered for him. "He doesn't fly the planes; he jumps out of them."

Leighann faked disappointment and said with an exaggerated southern drawl, "All us girls 'round here want to marry us a pilot like Debra Winger did in that movie, *An Officer and a Gentleman*."

"Well," Johnny said, playing along, "I hope a pilot comes in here one day and sweeps you off your feet."

Leighann smiled and said, "For now, all I want is a good tip. Now, how about that drink order?"

"I'll have a cold Budweiser," Johnny said.

"Budweiser!" Brian roared. "What's happened to you? Nobody drinks Budweiser."

Johnny shook his head. "I'd like to remind you that we're in North Carolina, and that NASCAR is the biggest sport around here besides hunting, and the Museum of the Fayetteville Motor Speedway is just miles from here." He looked back at the waitress and said, "Yankee snob. Please forgive him and make mine a Bud."

Brian looked at Jenny and shrugged. "What the heck, bring us all a Bud."

"Three Buds," Leighann confirmed. Then she looked at Jenny with a mischievous smile and asked, "Are you ready for the rest of your order?"

Jenny grinned. "What do you think?"

"I'd say you are," Leighann said, stifling a giggle.

"Bring it with the beer," Brian said.

"You got it," Leighann replied and disappeared.

"What was that?" Johnny asked.

"Just something we thought would go well with the drinks," Jenny said. Then she said, "So how are things with you? How's Carrie doing in Berlin?"

"Great, as far as I know," Johnny replied. "She's finished with the Red Cross, but I've been isolated in the field, so you probably know more than I do."

"Well," Jenny said. "I know she enjoyed spending a few months with her parents."

"Yeah," Johnny agreed. "The girl certainly gets around. I'm sure Africa was a great experience, but I think she needed to decompress a little."

They got quiet, and at some length Johnny added, "She said once that she could never spend her life as an army wife near some military base. Then later she said she could. I hope she still means that."

"I'm sure she does," Jenny said reassuringly. "She accepted your ring."

"I know," Johnny said. "But when you're in the field, isolated from everyone for months, you get to think a lot. Then you start to worry. I just hope she feels the same way, that's all."

"Then why don't you ask her?" Brian said.

"I plan to," Johnny replied softly. "We talked a few days ago. Right after my field training ended, and I didn't want to bring it up so soon. She said she had some business to attend to with her parents and that she'd be free in a few days. I'm gonna call her then."

Brian laughed and fixed his gaze over Johnny's shoulder. "I mean why don't you ask her right now?"

Johnny followed Brian's eyes and turned and saw Leighann holding a tray with four Budweisers. Leighann winked and said, "I brought an extra beer in case you need it. Someone else is coming right about now." She motioned to the elevator doors. Seconds later the doors opened and Carrie stepped out.

64- Woodland Estates

They headed west on Route 24 toward Fort Bragg. Brian drove and Jenny sat in the front with him, while Carrie and Johnny laughed and smooched like teenagers in the back seat.

"I can't believe you're here," Johnny said.

Carrie beamed. "Were you surprised?"

"Are you kidding? I was floored. How did you plan this?"

"Jenny and I have been e-mailing, and when Brian learned you were going to get some time off after your field exercises, we put it together. I was going to come sooner or later as a surprise anyway, but you know Brian. Once he got involved, things happened pretty fast."

"I know Brian," Johnny deadpanned. Then he leaned toward the front seat and said, "Thanks for doing this."

Brian nodded and Jenny turned and said, "I haven't had this much fun in a long time."

Johnny sat back and said to Carrie, "So tell me about your trip."

"Well, I flew into Philadelphia, rented a car, and drove to Bristol."

Johnny looked surprised, and Carrie said, "I just had the urge to see the town. Even though I only lived there for a year, I feel like it's an important part of my past. I don't have many roots, you know."

Johnny nodded and said tenderly, "You will. Some day we'll own a house on the river and sit in the back yard while our kids play. We'll watch the sailboats go by and use binoculars to look for eagles on Burlington Island."

"Someday," Carrie said wistfully. Then her mood brightened and she said, "Guess where I stayed?"

Johnny thought for a minute, but Carrie answered for him. "I stayed in the home of Mr. And Mrs. Angelo Marzo."

"No way! My parents were in on this?"

"Yup." Carrie said. "I called your mom and told her I'd be passing through on my way here, and she insisted I stay overnight. I can't believe how much fun I had. Your parents are great, and your uncles are wacky but lots of fun."

Johnny grinned. "They're certifiably insane, but in a good way."

"Of course, your dad cooked a great meal and everybody was over. We ate in the store instead of the dinning room."

"You ate in the store?" Johnny said, obviously surprised.

Brian interjected, "That's an honor, you know."

"I know," Carrie said proudly. "Your mom started to set the dining room table, and I said you told me about the great dinners in the store, and the next thing I knew, we were all sitting at card tables having a blast. Nick and Jimmy argued about which one would sit next to me, and Big Frankie had to change his seat so they could sit on either side."

Johnny shook his head and got quiet. Then he said, "I miss them. I've got to get up there soon."

"Well, make sure you take me along," Carrie said.

Johnny perked up again. "So tell me what else you did."

"I arrived in Bristol on Saturday, and we had that dinner. On Sunday, we all went to church, and then the whole gang went to the Italian Festival at Lions Park."

"You're kidding!" Johnny said. "Did you see anybody?"

"Tons of people," Carrie said excitedly. "It was a beautiful day and the place was packed."

"Who'd ya see?"

"Well, for starters, I think I saw Mr. Lombardi."

"You think?"

"He was standing by the Italian Mutual Aid 5th Ward booth. They were selling veal and pepper sandwiches. But by the time I fought my way through the crowd to say hello, he was gone. I think it was him though."

315

"Too bad you didn't catch up to him. I wonder how he's doing."

"From what I saw he looked okay. You should write him."

Johnny agreed. "He's on the list."

Carrie continued. "The big news is that I saw the Pac Men. Mickey was selling chances for the fire company. He looks great. He said he really likes what he's doing and told me to tell you to get your butt up to Bristol as soon as you can. I like Mickey; he's nice."

Johnny smiled. "What about Bobby?"

"Bobby looked good too. He was hanging around with Mickey. He's working at a car dealership and hopes to have his own garage some day. He sends his best."

"And Tommy?" Johnny asked guardedly.

Carrie shook her head. "Tommy wasn't there. Mickey said he's not doing too well. He's drinking a lot. Bobby seemed pretty worried about him."

Johnny knew that from letters he'd received from Mickey.

Brian called over his shoulder, "We'll have to do something about that."

Johnny nodded.

Carrie changed the subject. "I drove to Washington Monday and visited Jenny at the museum. I hung around until she finished work; then we met Brian at Georgetown and had a great dinner. I spent the night at their place." She tapped Jenny on the shoulder and added, "Your house is beautiful, by the way." Jenny turned and smiled and Carrie continued. "Then we got up early this morning and drove here."

Johnny sighed contentedly. "Last week I was in the field cross training in combat and communication skills, and now I'm sitting in the back seat with my girl, who's looking better than ever, driving who knows where with my best friends."

Brian said, "I told you, I'm going to look at an investment property. In fact, we're almost there."

Johnny shrugged. "Whatever, man. I'm just happy to be here."

Jenny spotted the sign, Woodland Estates, and directed Brian to turn. They entered a small development of modest townhouses with brick facades. "We're meeting a REMAX agent here," Brian said. "What's the address again?"

Jenny checked the printout. "It's one-twenty-three Mulberry Street."

They parked at the address and saw a woman in her early thirties standing in front of the property. She was wearing a tee shirt, running shorts and sneakers. She had a slender build with well toned arms and legs. A leashed dog stood by her side. They looked as if they'd just finished a run.

Everyone got out of the car and the woman glanced back and forth between Brian and Johnny and said, "Mr. Kelly?"

"That's me," Brian replied.

"Hi, I'm Gretchen," she said as she reached out her hand and stepped toward him. "We spoke on the phone."

Brian shook hands and introduced Johnny and the girls. Then he said, "Thanks for seeing us today."

"Oh, it's my pleasure," she said. "Please excuse my appearance. As I said on the phone, Tuesday is my day off and I…" She looked down at the dog and said instead, "and *we*, went for a run."

"Multi-tasking," Brian said. "I like that."

"What a beautiful; dog," Jenny said. "He looks pure boxer."

"He is," Gretchen said proudly.

"May I pet him?" Jenny asked

"Sure, his name is Sherman."

The Boxer had a marvelous brindle coat with a white chest. Jenny and Carrie knelt beside the dog and stroked him gently. Jenny cradled his face in her hands and said, "Sherman, you're such a handsome dog."

Gretchen thanked her and said, "Should I tell you about the house?"

"I'm not sure," Brian said. "I think Jenny's more interested in the dog."

"Well, Sherman's not for sale," Gretchen said playfully. She turned to Brian and said, "You specified a furnished house, and that limited our choices somewhat, but I think you'll find that we're lucky to have this one available. The owner was a Major at Fort Bragg who was transferred last month. His wife said if she had to move again and uproot the kids, then she wanted new furniture, new everything in fact."

Gretchen paused and then asked, "You said on the phone you wanted an investment property. Is that correct?"

"That's right," Brian said. "We're beginning our real estate empire. You'll be happy to know that Woodland Estates is ideally located between Fayetteville and Fort Bragg, about four miles from the base, which puts it in high demand for both sales and rentals. The development is currently ninety-eight percent occupied, and properties move quickly. Shall we go inside?"

"Let's do it," Brian said.

Gretchen tied Sherman's leash to the handrail and worked the lock box combination until she produced a key. Then she opened the door and led everyone inside. The foyer opened to a spacious living room and a kitchen-dining area that was separated from the living room by a breakfast counter.

"As you can see, the owners wisely chose neutral colors for their floors and walls and the furniture is traditional and nice," Gretchen said.

"Good move," Johnny said.

She opened the kitchen cabinets to reveal dishes, glasses, pots and pans. "Everything you see comes with the house, including the curtains and bed coverings. As I said, the Major's wife was upset about moving. Instead of paying a mover she intends to buy everything new."

"Now there's an assertive woman," Carrie said.

Jenny agreed.

Gretchen showed the couples the powder room and laundry room that opened to a small patio and backyard. Brian noticed a gas grill on the patio. "Does that work?"

"The owners certified on their disclosure form that everything works."

She led them upstairs to three bedrooms and a bath. One of the bedrooms had been converted to an office. Then they went back downstairs and Gretchen said, "Any questions?"

Brian looked at his friends. "What do you guys think?"

"I love it," Jenny said.

"It's very, very, nice," Carrie added.

Johnny shrugged. "It looks good to me."

"How much?" Brian said.

"It's listed at $165,000."

"I'll go $145,000," Brian said.

Gretchen though a moment and said, "Just between us, the owners authorized me to accept $157,000 without going back to them for approval."

"Sold!" Brian said, without hesitation. "I'll want a termite certification and some other inspections, but you can draw up the agreement."

Gretchen was taken back by the quickness of the sale and said, "Great! I'll prepare the paperwork and we should be able to go to settlement within thirty days."

"That's fine," Brian said. "But I need the place starting tonight."

"That's impossible," Gretchen said. "The paperwork takes time..."

"I'll rent it for $500 a month until we go to settlement," Brian said.

"Done," Gretchen said cheerfully. "I can be back with a simple lease agreement in a couple of hours, and I'll have the agreement of sale prepared by tomorrow."

Johnny turned to Brian and said, "What's your hurry? You don't even have a tenant yet?"

"Yes he does," Jenny said smiling.

Johnny didn't get it. "Who?"

"Me," Carrie said. "I'm moving in."

65- 123 Mulberry Street

Gretchen left with Brian's deposit check and promised to return with the paperwork. She closed the door behind her, and Brian let out a loud whoop as Carrie and Jenny hugged and broke into a dance in the middle of the room. Johnny laughed and took it all in, still not sure what had just happened. When the celebration subsided he said, "Would somebody please fill me in?"

Carrie put her arms around his neck and said, "That's easy, Lieutenant. I, Carrie O'Brien, am moving into this townhouse so I can be near my man, Johnny Marzo. I told him once I could never do that, but I was wrong. I've traveled the world and seen incredible sights, but there's no place I'd rather be than right here in NASCAR country, where the men hunt and their women skin and cook what they kill, where the town folk dance to shit-kickin' music on Friday nights. I wanna be right here, midway between the magical city of Fayetteville, North Carolina and the famous Fort Bragg."

She kissed him long and tenderly, and when they parted she said softly, "And I mean that, Johnny. I'm here if that's okay with you."

Johnny smiled and lifted Carrie off the floor. Brian and Jenny clapped as Johnny spun Carrie around until they both got dizzy and collapsed on the couch laughing.

He looked at Brian and said, "Okay, get the smug look off your face and tell me how all of this went down. And make it the short version. We have some celebrating to do."

Carrie said to Brian, "You go first."

"Okay, Johnny boy. The short version or what we call in the CIA, the executive summary. Pay attention."

Johnny laughed and said, "Just tell me."

Brian said to Jenny; "Help me out, Babe, if I miss a point."

"I'm here," Jenny said.

Brian sat down, cleared his throat, and said, "The following facts crossed my desk at Langley in recent weeks.

"Fact: First Lieutenant John Marzo has completed a long field training exercise and will return to base where he'll have much more freedom of movement as he proceeds to the next training phases.

"Fact: Electronic correspondence was brought to my attention which indicated that one Carrie Boyle has been communicating extensively with one Jenny Ryan.

"Fact: After extensive code breaking and analysis, it seems apparent that one Carrie Boyle has spent several enjoyable months with her parents in Berlin and was now desirous of moving back to the United States.

"Fact: One Carrie Boyle has expressed a strong interest in locating in proximity to the man with whom she has had a long-standing romantic relationship and to whom she is engaged.

"Fact: Lieutenant Marzo's unit will remain stationed at Fort Bragg even after he earns his Green Beret unless or until he is deployed overseas.

"Fact: One Carrie Boyle wanted to maintain an element of surprise.

"Fact: Real Estate experts see the North Carolina area as a growing market with enormous potential.

"Fact: A well capitalized investor and undying friend of all the aforementioned parties, one Brian Kelly, wanted to diversify his investments.

"Fact: CIA agent-analyst, Brian Kelly, can pull off just about anything on short notice, and he did!"

Brian sat back smugly in his chair and said, "That just about sums it up, Johnny boy."

Everyone laughed and Jenny said, "Put another way, Carrie decided about six weeks ago that she was ready to come back to the states. We talked about it and she said she'd love to surprise you. I've been bugging Brian to take some time off to unwind a little. So Brian got his wheels turning and suggested we combine a vacation with helping Carrie get settled here. He called REMAX and got the ball rolling, and here we are."

Johnny shook his head in amazement. He was thrilled that Carrie was there but uneasy about how quickly things went down.

"So you bought a house, just like that. We've talked before about you and your money."

Brian smiled. "First of all, I appreciate your concern, but I'm a big boy, and my money is none of your business. But if it helps set your mind at ease, last year I earned $120,000 just in interest and dividends. That doesn't count my salary at the agency. Plus, Jenny works. And my accountant really did say I should have some tax write-offs, and Carrie isn't living here for free. We agreed in advance that she could afford five hundred a month in rent."

Carrie jumped in. "My parents want me to do this. They're helping until I get a job."

"So," Brian said. "I'll keep the house for a few years, depreciate it, build some equity, and sell it when I'm ready."

Johnny shook his head and smiled "Sounds like a plan," he said. But he had deeper concerns than Brian's finances. He turned to Carrie and said, "Listen, I know this all sounds exciting now, but will you be happy here? What will you do with yourself while I'm in training or on duty?

You're a person who likes to be involved. How will you get fulfillment? I don't want you ending up unhappy here."

Carrie and Jenny exchanged smiles, and Jenny said, "Brian isn't the only one who's been busy planning."

Carrie said excitedly, "Do you want the short version?"

"I can't wait to hear this," Johnny said. He sat back and said, "Yes, the short version, please."

Carrie sat up straight and folded her hands on her lap. "While I was in Berlin, my parents asked me what I planned to do career-wise after my Red Cross commitment was over. It was a great question because, when you come right down to it, I really don't know how to do anything."

Johnny started to disagree, but Carrie cut him off. "I'm not putting myself down; I'm just stating a fact. I'm a good student, I've certainly traveled a lot, and I think I'm fairly intelligent, but I don't have a marketable skill. I thought about it, talked things over with my parents, and I'm happy to announce that I've been accepted into the graduate School of Journalism at Fayetteville State University, about five miles from here."

Johnny was stunned. He shot forward and said, "That's a terrific idea."

"It's not on a par with the Columbia School of Journalism," Carrie said. "And I wish it were Duke or the University of North Carolina, but they're too far away. But FSU is part of the North Carolina State University System and has a good reputation." She smiled proudly and added, "I'm going to be a journalist."

"Fantastic," Johnny said. "You did all of this already?"

Carrie continued. "The admissions office liked my undergrad record and flipped out about my travel and living experiences. I submitted a writing sample, and they said they were fairly confident they could place me as a part-time writer with the *Fayetteville Observer*. It has a wider circulation than you'd expect, and the school thinks the paper would be interested in some articles about East Africa, so I'll be earning some money too."

"This is almost too good to be true," Johnny said. "And you're a great writer, although I don't think we should publish your letters to me."

Carrie looked embarrassed. "No, I don't think we'll want to publish those."

Brian looked at Jenny and said, "Wow that sounds intriguing."

Jenny laughed and said, "Better drop it."

"Anyway," Brian said to Johnny. "Did we explain things sufficiently for you?"

"I hate to say it," Johnny replied. "But...her clothes?"

Brian shook his head and said to Carrie, "The guy's anal."

Carrie laughed and said to Johnny. "I don't have much. I lived in Africa for almost two years, remember? But I have suitcases in the car and a few boxes I shipped to Jenny's place last week that didn't fit in the SUV."

"And we're gonna ship them here when we get home," Jenny added.

"Okay," Brian said. "That's it, no more questions. Now come with me to the SUV to get some things."

When they were alone outside, Johnny stopped and said. "Thanks for doing all of this. I just hope Carrie knows what she's getting into."

Brian looked at him. "She and Jenny talked several times about it, and I talked with her too. She wants to be with you, and you're here so..."

Johnny nodded. "I just hope she still feels that way a month or two from now."

Brian understood Johnny's concern. "What's your remaining training schedule look like?"

Johnny shrugged. "There's some good news there. For the next few months I'll be in a language classroom more than I'll be in the field, and I'll be free to leave the base. But we will go out again, maybe two months total. I still have SERE training to do."

"SERE?"

"Survival, Escape, Resistance and Evasion."

"Sounds like fun. I thought you did that when you almost froze to death a while back?"

"That was when I was going through assessment. This is the real thing."

Brian raised his eyebrows and said, "Better you than me."

Johnny smiled and punched him on the arm.

"Anyway, it won't be a problem," Brian said.

They walked to the car and Brian said, "The real good news is that after you earn the Green Beret, the home base of your Special Forces Group will be right here at Fort Bragg. You guys will be fine."

Brian opened the back hatch to reveal a stack of suitcases. "Forget those for now," he said. He pointed to a large cooler and said, "First things first, grab an end."

They brought the cooler into the house and found the girls in the kitchen going though the cabinets.

"Party time," Brian said. He opened the cooler to reveal a case of beer on ice and a bottle of champagne. He pulled out the champagne. "We need to toast Carrie's new abode. Are there any glasses in those cabinets?"

Jenny produced four long, fluted glasses and said, "I guess the major and his misses knew how to party."

Brian filled the glasses and passed them out. Then he raised his and said, "To Carrie's new home."

They drank and complimented Brian on his selection. Then Johnny said, "To Carrie's new career," and they drank again.

Carrie checked the bottle, poured everyone equal amounts of what was left, raised her glass and said, "To the best friends in the world."

They cheered and drained their glasses.

Brian said, "Okay, so what's the party plan?"

Jenny said, "Carrie and I were talking while you guys were at the car. It's four o'clock now and we thought it might be good if we all took a nap for an hour and then planned dinner."

"A nap," Brian objected. "We're just getting started. It's time to…." He stopped in mid sentence when he caught Jenny's eye.

Jenny said, "Carrie and Johnny haven't seen each other in a long time, and the excitement has made her tired. I think we could *all* benefit from a nap."

Johnny and Brian got it at the same time and fell all over each other agreeing.

"A nap," Brian said. "Makes a lot of sense."

Johnny grinned. "I was going to suggest that myself."

"Well you didn't," Carrie said, taking him by the hand. "I did. Now let's go."

They lay in bed together, relaxed by the champagne and engulfed in each other's embrace. It had been months since they had been like this in Rome, months since he'd felt the softness of her skin or stroked her hair. They explored each other's bodies as if they were together for the first time. They whispered to each other the same words they had whispered to themselves during the lonely nights when they were half a world apart. When they finally made love, they did so with an energy and passion that surpassed all other encounters. And when they had spent themselves, Carrie drifted off to sleep snuggled against him with her arm across his chest.

Johnny stared at the ceiling, as his thoughts swirled with emotions he had never anticipated when he left the base that morning. Seeing her so unexpectedly and learning she'd be there to stay seemed almost illusory, a dream from which he would awaken disappointed. But their last hour together had made it all quite real. He should have been happier than ever, and he was. He was certain of that. He had loved this girl since the first time he met her and had found her perfect in every way. But there was something nagging at him beneath the surface that made him uneasy. It was more than the common affliction some have when things are going well, like the belief that things were too good to be true. There was a sense of foreboding, a premonition that something still needed to be resolved.

He pushed those thoughts from his mind and lay perfectly still, listening to Carrie's light breathing and allowing himself to drift to the dreamy state between sleep and consciousness.

It wasn't often he could feel so relaxed. His body constantly sent him reminders of the grueling demands he put it through, and they were often amplified when he was at rest. This time was no different as his peacefulness was disturbed by his newest aches and pains. He felt his legs begin to cramp lightly as they always did, and a bruise on his arm throbbed.

Carrie stirred in her sleep, and he turned his head to face her. The fading sun found its way through gaps in the drawn curtains and cast shadows across the room. A ray of light illuminated her face and hair, and she looked angelic, like an innocent child.

Johnny thought of the contrasts between his life at Fort Bragg and what it would be like here. Two days earlier he'd been in a heavily wooded area, engaging in combat tactics, recon, and the never-ending land navigation. He had run, crawled, fired weapons, and engaged in hand to hand combat drills, and now…now he had this.

It was that thought that brought him to the realization of what had been bothering him. It wasn't the time he'd be away and Carrie would be alone. She said she was prepared for that. And it wasn't life near a military base. She seemed genuinely enthused about her schooling and new job opportunity. It was her proximity to the life he had chosen that worried him.

She'd always had philosophical reservations about the army, and he believed her when she said she had a new appreciation for what he'd committed himself to after she witnessed Nairobi first hand. But now, with her living so close, he wondered if she'd feel differently about *him* as she became more aware of his work. He could speak in generalities about the work Special Forces did in providing protection, training troops to liberate themselves from oppressive tyrants, or interdicting foreign drug traffickers in their countries of origin. But he wondered how long it would take before she reached the understanding that in addition to those duties he was trained to find bad guys and kill them. It was an obvious part of his job. In the harshest sense, he was becoming a trained killer. The cause would always be just, at least he hoped it would, and the outcome would be a safer America. But he wondered what it would be like for both of them when he returned from a mission and tried to resume a normal home life. He feared their relationship might not survive those kinds of strains.

She stirred again and was beginning to awaken. He stroked her hair and she kissed his shoulder and said sleepily, "What time is it?"

Johnny checked the clock. "It's a little before six."

"Do you think Brian and Jenny are up yet?"

"Not sure," Johnny said. "I haven't heard them." She seemed fully awake now. Johnny kissed her on the forehead and said, "I'm gonna take a quick shower before we go downstairs."

He started to ease himself out of bed and Carrie pulled him back. "No way, Lieutenant Marzo," she said playfully. "I'm not finished with you yet."

66- Pizza Toppings

Johnny and Carrie showered and went downstairs where they found Jenny and Brian sitting at the kitchen counter finishing a beer.

"Now it's party time!" Brian said.

Carrie's hair was still damp and she had it pulled back into a pony tail. "Hi guys," Carrie said. "Have you been up long?"

"Only about fifteen minutes," Jenny said. "Gretchen stopped by for Brian to sign the lease, and she gave him the agreement of sale. So you're all set."

"Great," Carrie said. "Thanks again."

Brian moved to the cooler and said, "Okay, Johnny boy, you guys have some catching up to do. We have Sam Adams Boston Lager in honor of my M.I.T. days, and some Hacker-Pschorr for the lady from Berlin if she so desires. We also have some good old Coors Light, a favorite everywhere."

Johnny asked for a Coors and Carrie said, "Me too. I need a break from Germany if you don't mind."

"Not a problem, young lady. We have plenty of each," Brian said handing them the bottles. Jenny placed two beer mugs on the counter compliments of the Major's wife, but they both opted for the bottles.

"Let's drink again to Carrie's new home," Brian offered.

They drank deeply and Carrie said, "This place is really nice, Brian. It's going to be perfect here."

"Glad you like it. If you have any problems at all, take them up with my property manager, Miss Jenny Ryan. I'll give you her number."

Jenny laughed and Johnny suggested they drink to Jenny's new promotion. They drained their bottles, and Brian promptly produced another round. "We better slow down," Carrie said. "We haven't eaten yet."

With that Brian said, "Jenny and I were thinking that maybe we should eat here tonight, kind of christen the place for Carrie and make it feel lived in."

Johnny and Carrie looked at each other and Johnny said, "Sounds good to us."

327

"Well," Brian said jokingly, "I'm thinking Johnny and I could find the Major's gun, go out and shoot something, and drag it home so you girls could skin it and fix it up real good."

The girls shrieked and Johnny said, "How about if we go buy some steaks instead and cook them on that grill we saw?"

"Pizza," Carrie interjected. "I feel like pizza."

"Great idea," Jenny said. "I crave pizza whenever I'm in a good mood."

"Pizza's good by me," Brian said and then he mimicked an exaggerated southern drawl. "I wonder if they have dee-livery 'round these parts?"

"Knock it off," Johnny said. "North Carolina is much more progressive than you think. It's not like we're in the Mississippi backwater. There's Duke University and major research facilities, and ..."

Brian stopped him. "Easy man," he said smiling. "I'm only kidding. The fact is, North Carolina's per capita income last year was $26,000, only two thousand below the national average."

Carrie shook her head in disbelief. "You're kidding, right? I mean you don't really have those numbers memorized?"

Brian grinned. "You're hurting my feelings. Look 'em up if you don't believe me."

"Don't bother," Johnny said laughing. "I'm sure he's right."

"Ya gotta feel sorry for me, guys," Jenny interjected. "I have to live with this human encyclopedia. It's a good thing he's so loveable."

"Damn right," Brian said. He slid off his stool to get another round of beers. Then he said, "Jenny brought in her CD player. How about if you guys put on some music while Johnny and I search for a phone book?"

Jenny shuffled through the CD's and Carrie said, "The phone book's in that drawer under the microwave. I saw it earlier."

Brian found it and flipped through the yellow pages until he found what he wanted. "Here we go. I see two places that deliver. One's called Tar Heel Pizza and the other is called Luigi's."

"Just pick one," Johnny said.

"Okay, Tar Heel Pizza has the menu printed right on the page. They have pizza, stromboli, wings, salads."

"I'm starved," Carrie said.

"Me too," Jenny added. "Get some of each."

"What kind of toppings do we want on the pizza?" Brian asked.

Jenny opened the cap on her fresh Coors Light and said, "Read us what they have."

"Let's see," Johnny deadpanned. "They have pepperoni, mushrooms, olives, onions, possum, and squirrel brains."

That got another laugh and Jenny threw the bottle cap at him. "Talk about a northern snob!"

Brian held his hands up in defense and said, "Last joke. I promise."

"Just order, Brian, and surprise us." Carrie said.

Brian pulled out his cell phone and Jenny fiddled with the CD player. Soon Bon Jovi's "Living on a Prayer" was playing, and the girls sang along. Carrie was feeling giddy and grabbed a large spoon to use as a microphone. Jenny did the same. In an instant they were screaming rock stars on stage.

" *...We've got to hold on to what we've got...*"

The girls bent their knees and threw their heads back as they sang, and Johnny couldn't believe how terrible they sounded.

"We've got each other and that's a lot. "

They were shrieking now, and Jenny had the CD at full volume.

"...For love - we'll- give- it- a- shot!"

The noise was deafening and Johnny hit the off button. He pointed to Brian on the phone and used him as an excuse.

"Killjoy," Carrie said.

"I guess he doesn't appreciate our talent, but we know we're good." Jenny added.

The girls clinked bottles and took another swig. .

Brian got off the phone and said, "I got two pizzas, one plain and one with everything. But I told him to hold the ..."

"Stop!" Jenny shouted, and Brian smiled. "I was going to say garlic. I also got two strombolis, an order of wings and two salads. Sound like enough?"

"For an army," Jenny said.

Brian said, "The pizza should be here in twenty minutes. What should we do now?"

"I know," Jenny said brightly. "Let's play a drinking game."

"I'm in," Carrie said.

Jenny instructed everyone to grab their beer and proceeded to explain a drinking game called categories that made little sense except for its requirement that everyone drink for just about anything that happened. They played for at least a half hour and the game had taken its toll on all of them. Finally, the doorbell rang and Johnny said, "Must be the pizza."

"Or the cops," Carrie said.

"Or the Klan," Jenny offered.

"Listen to you!" Brian retorted. "What a stereotype. You should be ashamed."

"Not my fault," she slurred. "Been drinking."

Johnny moved to the door, and Brian stood and reached in his back pocket for his wallet. "Put that away," Johnny said sternly. "I've got this, and I mean it."

Brian shrugged and sat down.

Johnny came back with a high stack of food and put it on the counter. The girls found plates and utensils, and soon they were at the table again, feasting.

"Starved," Carrie said.

"Munchies," Jenny added.

They ate ravenously for a few minutes until Carrie broke the silence. She turned to Johnny and said, "I just remembered that job you had that one semester at Penn State."

Johnny smiled, "You mean the pizza delivery job."

Carrie nodded and said to Brian and Jenny, "Johnny had this job delivering pizza at Penn State. The neat thing was that the place was called 'Peace of Pizza' and they used an old Volkswagen Bus as the delivery vehicle. And it had a large pizza on top sliced in the form of a peace sign."

"Cool," Jenny said.

They resumed eating and after a while Carrie said. "It's pretty ironic."

"What is?" Brian asked.

"Never mind, it was nothing," Carrie said quietly. She took another bite of pizza.

"Come on, Babe, no secrets," Johnny said smiling. "What was ironic about the pizza job?"

Carrie looked at him as she chewed her pizza. No one spoke. At length, Carrie said, "It just seems ironic that you, of all people, used to drive a VW bus with a peace sign on it."

Johnny's smile faded. "What's that mean?"

Carrie wished she hadn't brought this up. "Sorry," she said. "That was the beer talking. Forget it."

"What did you mean by me 'of all people?'"

"You know," Carrie said, stroking his arm. "You get up every morning and train for war. You train to…"

It got quiet again and Johnny said softly, "You still have a problem with that don't you?"

Carrie averted his gaze and said, "I'm conflicted."

Brian shifted in his chair and gave Jenny a concerned look.

Johnny placed his hand on Carrie's and said gently, "Talk to me, Babe."

Carrie looked up and they could see that tears were forming in her eyes. She spoke haltingly. "Of course I have a problem with that. . . Who wouldn't? How can someone be comfortable knowing the person they love is in this kind of work? And I'm frightened. I'm frightened for your safety, and I'm frightened for my own ever since Nairobi. I'm just a little screwed up about all of this. So much has happened today." Then she put her free hand over his and forced a smile. "But I love you, and I'm fine."

No one spoke. Johnny and Carrie held each other's gaze. Brian sat back in his chair and stared at the ceiling, and Jenny put her elbows on the table and rested her head in her hands.

It was quiet for a long time and then Jenny said abruptly, "You're not fine. None of us are fine." They looked at her waiting for more.

"Look," she said. "We've been drinking and sometimes that makes people a little more emotional. But I've always believed that true feelings surface when we're half gone. So let me tell all of you what I'm thinking."

She took another swig of beer and said, "Every time we're together, either the four of us or when we're alone as couples, the proverbial big, fat elephant is in the room with us, and we try to ignore it. Obviously, that doesn't work."

She looked at her friend across the table. "Carrie, our men are involved in dangerous business. My guy doesn't violate any state secrets, but I know that he tracks skillful, fanatical killers all over the globe. It makes him a different person sometimes. And you know what? If he had the chance to send a missile their way, he would in a minute. If he's successful, they'd be dead. That's a fact. The stress of the job and the knowledge that if he fails good people will die, eats at him. Now that's not easy for me to live with, and it sure as heck isn't easy for him. But that's the reality, and there's no pretending it isn't so."

Carrie nodded and Brian and Johnny remained silent.

Jenny continued. "Your guy is in a similar line of business. Only sometimes we can't send a missile to kill the bastards, we have to do it up close and personal. That's a large part of what Johnny Marzo trains for. Does that trouble you? It should. Is his job dangerous? You're damn right it is. But here's the thing. You saw more in Nairobi than most people have seen. So you know what happens if we don't get these guys before they do their evil deeds." Then she turned to Brian. "And no one has felt the personal loss that Brian felt when his uncle was murdered. So there's no doubt in any of our minds that the job has to be done by someone."

She paused and looked around. Jenny had the floor and no one made any move to take it away from her. "So here's the question?" she said. "Why us? Why does it have to be us who carry the ball? Why does Brian have to live his life under such horrific responsibility and pressure? And why does Johnny have to literally put his life on the line as well as carry the psychological weight of his actions? And what about you and me, Carrie? Why, with all the guys in the world, do we have to love and be with guys who put us through this?

"We have a decision to make. And I don't just mean you and me, Carrie. I mean Johnny and Brian too. Both of you could have a very good life in some other line of work. You can get out. Brian can quit, and Johnny can finish his current commitment and get out." She looked at Carrie again. "And you and I can leave. We can just tell these wonderful guys that we love them, but we can't live this kind of life."

She sat back and exhaled deeply. She was sweating and she wiped the moisture from her brow. She scanned their faces slowly and said, "So it's time that all of us cut the bull and make a decision. We're either in and fully committed, or we're out."

No one spoke or moved for a long time, and the room was totally silent. There were no ticking clocks, humming compressors, or creaking floors. Finally, Carrie looked at Johnny and said, "I'm in."

Johnny sighed and said, "Are you sure?"

"I'm in if you want to be," she said.

"I'll quit and sell insurance if you want me to," he replied.

She shook her head no and Johnny said, "Then I'm in."

Jenny looked at Brian. And Brian said, "There's nothing I'd like more than to get out and spend an easy life with you, but you know I can't."

"I know," Jenny said. "That's why I'm in."

"Then we're all in," Brian said. "Just like in Texas Hold 'Em, only the stakes are much higher."

67- Rules of Engagement

January 2000

Brian stood among the crew members watching as the attractive young woman raced her speed boat back and forth along the starboard side of the USS Pennsylvania, a guided missile cruiser docked for refueling in the Persian Gulf port of Aden, in Yemen. Even from a distance of forty yards, it was clear the woman was striking, with long dark hair and olive skin.

The boat pulled a male water skier, and the sailors cheered as the skier jumped the waves formed from the speedboat's wake. The woman acknowledged the men with a playful wave and broad smile. On their next pass she stood while steering, and the sailors roared their approval of her bikini-clad body.

Others heard the cheers and joined the crowd. It was their first day in port after a month at sea, and the show was a welcomed break from their routine. But Brian felt uneasy. Something wasn't right.

On the next pass the woman slowed, waved to the men one more time, turned and began to speed away from the ship. She drove about a hundred yards before she turned back and headed toward them at full throttle. She was flirting now, and the sailors cheered.

Still, there was something Brian didn't like, and he struggled to put his finger on it. The boat got closer, eighty yards, seventy. Brian turned to the gunner manning the M-60 next to him and said, "Aim your weapon." The gunner looked at him as if he was crazy, and Brian noticed that it was his friend, Tommy Dillion, from the Pac Men. "That's an order, sailor. Aim your weapon," Brian barked, and the gunner did.

The boat closed to forty yards when Brian realized what was wrong. The life jacket on the skier was bulky, much too bulky, suicide bomber bulky. "Prepare to fire," Brian said.

"But, Sir, the rules of engagement…" the sailor protested, but Brian interrupted. "Damn it, Tommy, do something right for once. Prepare to fire."

The boat was closing fast and the driver's smile was gone. She was looking up to the sky.

"Fire!" Brian screamed. "Fire! Fire!"

Brian awakened in a sweat. His sheets were soaked and he was disoriented. The clock on the nightstand read three a.m. He was breathing heavily and his heart was pounding as he tried to calm himself. His work at the CIA demanded that he be mentally sharp, but his constant nightmares were ruining his sleep. This one had been especially vivid, and Brian knew what prompted it.

Yesterday an informal report with unconfirmed backchannel information crossed his desk about an attempted attack on the USS Sullivans, a guided missile destroyer named for the five brothers who perished in a Japanese torpedo attack against their ship, the USS Juneau, in 1942. Allegedly a Yemeni informant of unconfirmed reliability had passed on information about an aborted attack on a United States warship. The report stated that the USS Sullivans was docked at the port of Aden in Yemen when a small boat loaded with explosives began making its way to the ship in an attempt to destroy it. However, the attack boat was so overloaded that it began to sink, and the attempt was aborted. No one could confirm the report, but Brian thought it had value anyway because the methodology could be utilized in the future.

Brian was a wreck. Suicide bombers on small boats- what would they think of next? The Navy had been fortunate this time, but the alleged incident raised serious issues about the vulnerability of American vessels in foreign ports, especially ports in the Persian Gulf. Brian followed procedure and sent his assessment up the chain of command, hoping that someone would take it seriously enough to alert naval commanders around the world.

He moved to his dresser and searched for his pack of cigarettes. He'd only recently started smoking and wasn't happy about it. He lit one, took a deep drag and coughed. It tasted awful. He stuffed the cigarette out in the ashtray, crumbled the rest and tossed them into the waste basket. He had enough problems without taking up smoking.

He went to the kitchen and put on a pot of coffee. It was Sunday morning, and Jenny was away visiting Carrie in North Carolina for the weekend. Johnny had finally gained Special Forces status and was wearing the Green Beret. But his training was on-going and he was currently out on field exercises.

Carrie had been assigned by the *Observer* to cover some municipal meetings in Fayetteville as a stringer and had done a good job. The editor rewarded her with an assignment to do a human interest piece on the work of the International Red Cross in East Africa. She'd been allocated sixty column inches, and the editor liked what she submitted. The article was scheduled to appear in the Sunday Magazine section of the paper, and Jenny drove down to have dinner Saturday night and be there when the article hit the newsstands on Sunday. Brian was grateful that Jenny wasn't there to see him on edge.

The coffeemaker was still brewing when Brian pulled the pot from the heating element and poured a cup. Coffee continued to drip through the filter and splashed on the countertop. Jenny hated it when he did that, but he was half asleep and needed the caffeine in a hurry. He made a note to buy the new type with an automatic shutoff.

He carried his cup to the kitchen window. He still marveled at the majestic scene of the nation's capital, illuminated in the distance in the early morning darkness. He needed to see it every once in a while to remind himself of where he was. At work, he spent countless hours isolated in a cubical, and there was nothing glamorous about that, so it was important to remember that he was living in the epicenter of the most powerful country in the world.

He grabbed a yellow pad and pencil from the drawer, shuffled to the breakfast counter, and took a seat. The coffee tasted almost as bad as the cigarette, but it was strong and he appreciated the jolt it gave him.

He'd been under extraordinary pressure for the past two months because of what the media had labeled Y2K or the turn of the new Millennium. Doomsayers had speculated that all hell would break loose at midnight, January 1, 2000. Their fears were based on the belief that the electronic clocks would fail in the massive computers used by banks, insurance companies, payroll firms, pension funds, and countless other corporate and private entities, causing the world to be thrust into economic chaos. They feared that the inability of some computers to "understand" that the numbers 1-9-9-9- would be followed by 2-0-0-0 would mean that credit card companies wouldn't be able to function, automatic payroll transfers wouldn't take place, and computerized shipments would be disrupted. There were even reports that some alarmists liquidated their assets and put the cash under their mattresses. Others, less willing to buy into the fears, nevertheless took prudent steps to stockpile bottled water and non-perishables just in case. Most Americans, however, took a "screw it" approach, hoping that whatever needed to be done to address the problem would be. Of course the fears were grossly overblown, but the CIA wisely ran a series of time- consuming computer drills just to be safe.

Y2K also posed a serious security problem. The intelligence community feared that al Quada was planning a series of dramatic hits to mark the turn of the new Millennium. Counter-terrorist teams worked feverishly to follow leads, and Brian took pleasure in helping to foil three plots the public would never hear about.

The most dangerous involved a Times Square New Year's Eve plot to lob mortar shells capped with deadly sarin gas into the dense crowds gathered at Times Square. The CIA uncovered the plan in Islamabad, tracked the shipment of the mortars and shells to Canada, and monitored the flight of the plotters to Toronto. In a joint effort between the Canadian Royal Mounted Police and the FBI, the terrorists were arrested as they attempted to enter the United States at Niagara Falls. It was an excellent example of international and inter-agency cooperation, and Brian felt good about it. But he was still constantly obsessed by other schemes he might be missing.

He'd come a long way from Bristol, Pennsylvania, and he often missed it. He thought about his parents and reminded himself to call them later.

He went back to the counter, sat in front of the notepad and thought about his dream. He didn't buy the whole dream interpretation thing, but he did believe that they often provided a window to the subconscious, and he wanted to make sure he wasn't missing anything. That was Brian's nagging problem, the fear that he had the answer to questions right in front of him, perhaps subconsciously, but failed to see them or make connections.

In the dream he'd been a naval officer, which, of course, he wasn't. Brian thought about that and dismissed its significance. Obviously, the dream was prompted by what he'd just read in the USS Sullivans report. He thought about the relaxed crew cheering the girl on. There was an obvious message there. The men were too relaxed, which was understandable after long stretches at sea, but nevertheless, their guard was down and that shouldn't ever happen.

He considered the water skier, the potential suicide bomber. There was nothing new there. A bulky life jacket was little different from a bulky coat, but it was a clever approach on water skis.

Then he considered the girl. That part of the dream didn't fit. She was stunning and highly sexual, with a revealing bathing suit that flaunted her voluptuous body. Fundamentalist Islam, especially the type practiced by the radicals, would never condone such a breach of morality, especially by a woman. Or would they? They had twisted the Koran to justify the slaughter of innocent women and children. Maybe they could justify any behavior if it served their goals of Jihad. The CIA had already made the paradigm shift to include women as potential suicide bombers, and Brian made a note to discuss the possibility that future female attackers may not fit the profile of women wearing berkas.

Then there was the issue of Tommy Dillon. Why was he in the dream? It probably meant nothing. In fact, he could easily attribute it to a letter he'd received from Mickey indicating that Tommy's drinking problem was getting worse. More than likely that was what placed Tommy in his subconscious, but something kept telling Brian there was more to it. He closed his eyes and tried to recall the dream's dialogue. He'd ordered Tommy to aim his weapon, and when Tommy resisted, Brian had told him to do something right for once. Brian could easily attribute that comment to his belief that no matter how many highly competent, dedicated and courageous people we had in the intelligence service and the armed forces, we also had our share of incompetents. That thought continued to concern him. Still, he felt there was more.

He took another sip of his coffee. It had gotten cold, and he pushed the cup aside. He took a deep breath and massaged his temples. He pushed his chair away form the counter, grabbed his cup and walked to the sink, where he poured out the contents. He was about to pour a fresh cup when it hit him. Tommy had been reluctant to fire when Brian first gave the order. Brian allowed that thought to formulate until he made sense of it. Tommy was reluctant to fire because the rules of engagement precluded him from doing so.

The Navy, the State Department and the Department of Defense were highly sensitive to the potential fallout from a political incident in a foreign port, especially a port in a country whose people were lukewarm at best toward the United States. To avoid an incident, the rules of engagement stipulated that American forces may only fire upon foreigners if fired upon first or when an attack was imminent.

Brian exhaled deeply. That was it. That was the area of vulnerability. He knew the navy had procedures in place to deal with potential threats short of opening fire as a last resort. He wrote himself a note to recommend a reassessment of those procedures. Then he tore off a handful of paper towels and wiped the spilled coffee from the counter.

February 2000

68- The Inside Scoop

Angelo's deli had been converted to a makeshift interrogation room. Big Frankie had flipped the door sign to "closed" and dimmed the lights. Nick was seated at a card table in the center of the room, surrounded by Donna, who sat across from him, and Jimmy and Big Frankie, who stood silently by her side. Angelo watched from behind the counter as he filled cannoli shells.

"I think you're bluffing," Nick said nervously.

"Don't bet on it," Donna said.

"You'd throw me out in the cold, just like that?"

"In a heartbeat!"

"After all these years?"

"In the dead of winter," Donna replied without hesitation.

"For life?"

"Until you die a cold, miserable death."

Nick mustered some courage and looked Donna in the eye. "You can't break me. I've been through worse than this, and I can take whatever you can dish out."

"It's February, Nick," Donna said without emotion. "It's twenty two degrees outside. You won't last long out there."

Nick gulped and tried a different angle. "You know I never brag, but I have a medal. I'm a combat veteran. I have rights."

Donna glanced at the wall clock and flashed a menacing smile. "If you don't tell me what I want to know in ten minutes, your ass will be out of here."

Nick looked past her to Angelo behind the counter. "You'd let her?"

Angelo laughed. "Let her? Since when do I let Donna do anything? Donna does what she pleases. I think you'd better tell her what she wants to know."

"I do a lot around here for free," Nick said. "How would you get by?"

Angelo shook his head. "I lose money on you every day. The Cokes alone cost me a fortune, not to mention the free food. It's good business sense to get rid of you."

Nick needed an ally. He looked at Jimmy for support, but Jimmy said, "I'm real nervous for you, Nick. I think they mean it."

"Damn right we mean it," Donna said to Nick. "And if you go," she motioned to Jimmy, "your sidekick here goes with you."

That took Jimmy by surprise. "Me! Why would I go?"

"Because with Nick gone you won't have anyone to talk to, and I'm afraid you'd talk to us. We couldn't have that." Then she called over her shoulder, "Right, Angelo?"

"Whatever you say, sweetheart," Angelo said, licking the last of the cannoli filling from his fingers.

Jimmy was sweating now. "Better tell them, Nick. This sounds real bad."

Nick turned to Big Frankie as his last hope, but Frankie offered zero support. "I want to know this as much as they do. Just tell her and get it over with."

"It's not my place to tell her," Nick said. "Johnny should."

"Eight minutes," Donna said impassively.

Nick was having fun and didn't want the charade to end, but he was getting hungry and knew he wouldn't eat until he talked. "I need some food," he said. "Even the Geneva Convention guarantees prisoners of war…"

Donna cut him off. "You'll eat after you talk."

"Anything I want?"

Donna nodded reluctantly.

"I want it now," Nick said.

Donna leaned toward him and whispered slowly, "After you talk."

Nick needed to save some face. He sat back in his chair, folded his arms and said defiantly, "Angelo starts getting it ready while I talk. That's my compromise."

Donna waited a long time and then nodded her approval.

Nick licked his lips and said, "I want a meatball sandwich smothered with melted mozzarella on a twelve inch roll. I want a large order of onion rings, extra crispy, a bag of salt and vinegar chips and a Coke. Two Cokes actually. And I want…"

"Shut up, Nick," Donna said.

"Can I just add two Snickers bars for dessert?" Nick asked sheepishly.

Donna was considering the request when Angelo shouted, "Just give him the damn candy bars and get started."

Donna said okay, and Nick smiled and sat forward. "Then I'm all yours."

Big Frankie and Jimmy pulled up chairs and Angelo said, "Talk loud so I can hear while I'm making your damn sandwich."

Nick turned serious and said to Donna, "I have ground rules."

"Okay," Donna replied.

"I don't talk about Nam or tell war stories."

"I understand," Donna said kindly. "We all respect that."

Everyone in town knew that Nick was a Vietnam War hero and a former Green Beret who operated deep in enemy territory, well above the DMZ. On one occasion, after leading a mission to liberate a downed American pilot from a North Vietnamese village, he ordered his team to carry the injured pilot to safety while he went back to help a fellow Green Beret who'd been wounded in the rescue. In an ensuing firefight, Nick received neck wounds that left him unconscious. He was taken prisoner and brought to Hanoi, where he was tortured, isolated, and denied standard medical treatment for five years. Upon his release he was awarded the Army Distinguished Service Cross for extraordinary valor. He was also classified as eighty-percent disabled by the Veteran's Administration and given a modest pension. Since then he had endured years of medical procedures that did little to relieve his chronic pain. He never spoke about his ordeal and devoted his life to advocating for other veterans who'd been denied benefits.

With the exception of young Brian Kelly, Nick was the brightest guy anyone in the deli knew, but he coped with his emotional scars by adopting a goof- ball persona from which he departed rarely.

"And, believe it or not," Nick added, "there are some things about the Special Forces that I just can't tell you."

"Agreed," Donna said.

"I also want to say that Johnny should be telling you this stuff instead of me. That's why I've been reluctant."

"I'm his mother," Donna said. "And I need more than the Disney version he'd give me. It'll be better for me if I know the truth than if I let my imagination run wild."

"Okay," Nick said. "Ask your questions."

Donna looked relieved. "I'd like to know what he'll be doing as a Green Beret and where he'll be doing it."

Nick smiled. "Well, first of all, and I know you've heard this before, a Green Beret is a hat. Johnny belongs to the United States Special Forces, and they *wear* the Green Beret. But since everyone calls them Greenies, we will too.

"Your son is one of the most highly trained individuals in the United States Army. Consider what he's done: ROTC in college, graduated as a Second Lieutenant, completed jump school and earned his Airborne Wings, completed the Advanced Course for officers, led a platoon in Kosovo, and was promoted to First Lieutenant. He was flying high."

Angelo brought Nick's food and Nick immediately stopped speaking and dug in. Angelo returned with sandwiches for Big Frankie and Jimmy and brought Donna a yogurt from the dairy case. Everyone began eating as Angelo came back with a six pack of beer and passed it around. "Thought you might prefer this," he said as he pulled up a chair.

Nick was devouring his sandwich and had a string of cheese hanging from his chin. He said, "Delicious. I'm telling ya, you could open a chain selling this stuff."

"Yeah," Jimmy agreed. "Call it something like 'Angelo's Meatballs.'"

"Catchy name," Big Frankie said with a mouthful.

"I could be your east coast sales manager," Nick added.

Jimmy said. "We could open places from Bristol all the way to the east coast."

Everyone just looked at him and he shrugged. "You know what I mean."

Nick shoved a full onion ring into his mouth. It occurred to him that he should offer onion rings to everyone, so he said while still chewing, "Does anyone want an onion ring? I'm sure Angelo wouldn't mind making you some."

"You're pushing me," Angelo said.

Nick smiled and said, "Okay, back to the story."

"No offense," Angelo interrupted, "But you haven't told us anything new yet."   Nick looked exasperated and said to Jimmy, "These people don't understand the value of context. I'm putting things in context for them."

Jimmy nodded knowingly and said to Angelo, "Nick's giving you context."

"Just get to the Green Berets," Donna said, handing Nick a napkin.

Nick wiped his mouth and continued. "Okay, so things were going smoothly, and then Johnny got a bug up his you know what to become a member of the Special Forces."

"That's the part," Donna said impatiently.

Nick continued. "As you know, he applied for the Special Forces Assessment and Selection Program and went through a grueling thirty-day assessment that challenged his physical, mental, and emotional capabilities under extreme conditions."

"We know all that," Donna said.

"Context," Nick said. Donna rolled her eyes and Nick continued. "Next, Johnny was admitted to the Qualification Course and the real ordeal began, with another full year of extensive training.

"Johnny's a tough kid," Nick said. "But plenty of guys are tough. The thing that got him into the Green Berets was that, in addition to his extraordinary physical attributes and emotional toughness, he has high intelligence and an exceptional aptitude in foreign languages."

"I know that," Donna said. "He's my son. Now tell me what he'll be *doing*."

"For the past year he and his team have trained in tactics, weapons, engineering, demolition, communications, medical treatment, the whole bit. Plus, he's been fully immersed in his assigned language and culture. Johnny must be pretty damn smart because they assigned him to learn Arabic, Arab culture, Islam, and the geography and topography of the Arab world and South Asia."

"We know that," Angelo said. "Get to something new."

"At Fort Bragg, Johnny and his team will continue to train and study languages until they are deployed."

"The team," Donna said anxiously. "That's what we want to know about."

Nick nodded and smiled, "Now that you have some context, I can tell you." He took a long pull of his beer and continued. "The key division of the Special Forces is something the army calls Operational Detachment Alphas or A-Teams for short."

Nick looked squarely at Donna and said, "Special Forces A-Teams are the most highly advanced combat and operational entities in the world. There are twelve guys on a team that are commanded by a captain. That's why Johnny was promoted to Captain when he finished the Q Course. He will command his own team."

"Damn," Jimmy said. "That's unbelievable."

"The team will also have a Warrant Officer who runs the day to day operations and directs the men. Warrant officers are the heart and soul of the army, and I'm sure Johnny will have a good one."

Nick took another drink and finished his beer. Big Frankie reached for another bottle and handed it to him.

"The remaining ten guys are highly trained experts in specific areas: Two in operations, two in weapons, two in engineering and demolition, two in emergency medical treatment, and two in communications. Plus everyone is cross-trained in all five areas.

"When it comes to language, while Johnny has basically learned Arabic, he told me he has also been exposed to Pashto, a language of Afghanistan. Other guys on the team have learned Dari, another Afghan language, and Farsi, the language of Iran.

"Now these are tough languages, and you don't learn them in a year or two. But you keep training and learn enough to get by.

Nick folded his hands behind his head and stretched his back before continuing.

"So what we have is a group of twelve very bad-ass guys, who speak another language, understand the culture, can operate advanced weapons, can build or blow up bridges, provide medical care, and communicate by using our most sophisticated equipment."

Donna looked concerned. "I don't think I want my son playing shoot 'em up in South Asia or the Middle East like the stuff you see in the movies."

"Neither does the army," Nick said. "These guys are too valuable to use recklessly. The most successful Special Operations missions are the ones where the A-Team's are in and out before the other country even knows they were there."

Donna nodded.

"The Special Forces are kind of like America's Swiss Army knife. They are small, easily concealed, and can be used in so many useful ways."

"Give me examples," Angelo said.

Nick gathered his thoughts and said, "We may deploy Special Forces to a country in trouble to signal our determination that we're there to help. We train them, equip them, and teach them tactics. Or, we train rebels we like, to help them overthrow an unfriendly government. A-Teams are called force multipliers because by the time their work is finished, the people they work with are stronger than they were before."

Donna's eyes were saying she wanted more, and Nick continued.

"The Special Forces guys learn the language indigenous to the area because they have to work with the locals. They have to win the hearts and minds of people we want to be on our side."

"Don't sugar coat stuff, Nick, " Donna said. "Sounds like a heavily armed Peace Corps. Get to the other stuff."

Nick went on reluctantly. "Sometimes it gets nasty. Suppose a country has some type of facility we don't want it to have. We may slip a team in to eliminate it."

"Eliminate?"

"Yeah, blow it up. That's why they have engineering and demolition experts on the team."

Donna stayed quiet and Nick continued. "Sometimes we use A-Teams to paint targets for the munitions carriers too."

"Put that in English," Donna said impatiently.

"Special Forces are the eyes and ears of the military. We use teams to infiltrate an area, get up close to identify high priority targets not easily seen from the sky, and 'paint' the target using sophisticated laser technology. That way the cruise missile, bomber, or carrier aircraft, whoever is carrying the bombs, can put its spot on it and deliver the payload. After the air attack, the A-Team delivers its damage assessment report."

"This all sounds very dangerous," Donna said..

"I'm not gonna bullshit you, Donna; it is extremely dangerous. But let me make something clear. They are trained to navigate hostile terrain without being detected. Johnny could be standing ten feet from you and you'd think he was a tree. They're the best at what they do, but there's obviously danger."

"I appreciate your honesty," Donna said. Then she paused and asked, "Is that the most dangerous thing they do?"

Nick waited a long time to reply. Then he said, "The most dangerous would be the search and rescue or search and destroy missions. That's when they play 'shoot 'em up,' as you call it, up close and personal. They're the best at it, Donna. But it can get nasty."

Donna looked at the scar on Nick's neck and understood.

69- Breaking Tradition

April 2000

Jenny warmed the Chinese food in the microwave. It was nine-forty and Brian had just called from the office to say he was heading home. She checked the beer mug she had placed in the freezer, and it was covered with frost, just the way Brian liked it. She poured herself a glass of Pinot Grigio and sat on the sofa to relax. She'd reported to work at 6:00 that morning for a thirteen hour day, and she was worn out.

Jenny's responsibilities at the National Museum of American History were expanding, and she'd recently been placed in charge of special exhibits. She'd been working on her first display for two weeks, and it was scheduled to open the following day. It had been well publicized and was expected to draw thousands. It was an exhibit of mementoes left at the Vietnam Wall, or the Vietnam Veterans Memorial as it was formally called.

Visitors had been leaving items at the base of the polished black onyx panels since the wall's dedication in 1982. The National Park Service usually allowed items to remain there for a day or two before collecting them and placing most in storage. The memorial was now the most visited site in Washington, and there was always a new supply of mementoes left each day.

Recently the Park Service selected some of the most moving objects and made them available to the museum on loan. It was Jenny's job to examine the items and determine the best way to exhibit them. She supervised the arrangement, the security encasement and the written narrative that would accompany each section.

She sipped her wine and reflected on some of the more poignant mementoes she'd seen, like letters left from mothers, wives, or girlfriends who'd lost their loved ones. One that especially moved her was from a daughter who had never met her slain father. She was conceived before he left for Nam and born after his death. The sense of loss the letter conveyed to the father she never knew was heartbreaking. Jenny had read a novel about that subject once and had cried for days. Other daughters had left prom and wedding pictures, photos of events in their lives that their fathers never got to see.

There were painful good-bye letters from devoted widows about to remarry and move on after years of grief. There was a first baseman's glove left by a minor league baseball player who'd been taught to field and hit by his young father. There were ribbons and medals left by children who'd won them in spelling bees and science fairs. Tragically, each told a story of joy and emptiness, of people longing to share their most important experiences with someone who was taken from their lives.

Perhaps the most painful items of all were those left by soldiers who had served with the deceased. Their words captured the torment of guilt-ridden men who wondered why they had been spared while so many were taken. Some spoke in gratitude to the men who gave their lives in the act of saving others. There were packs of cigarettes, and six packs, and copies of sports magazines left at the memorial. Each item spoke of simple things once enjoyed by the men whose names were etched on the black panels and served as stark reminders of experiences cut tragically short.

It was heart wrenching for Jenny to review them all, but the depth of their stories and the grief they conveyed had inspired her to display the items with the quiet dignity and honor they deserved.

In the end her supervisors said the exhibit was brilliantly conceived, but instead of gaining satisfaction from her work, Jenny was humbled by it. The assignment had been emotionally draining, and it opened her eyes to the sacrifices made by previous generations. Though humbled, she wasn't pulled down by the experience. Instead, she was bolstered by it. It reminded her to appreciate the joys of life with the loved ones she had. She was glad to be alive.

She'd been waiting to ask Brian something very important for the past few days, but they had both been so busy. Now, she'd decided there would never be an ideal time, so she might as well ask him tonight.

She heard Brian at the door and got up from the couch to meet him. She was barefooted and wore cut off sweatpants and a faded University of Maryland T-shirt. She smiled when she saw him and gave him a kiss. When they parted, he stood back and held her shoulders at arms length. Her hair was casually pinned up and loose strands fell over her forehead into her eyes. He smiled and said, "I'm crazy about you."

She grinned and replied, "You should be, Spy-boy." Then she draped her arm around his and led him toward the kitchen. "I've got cold beer and warm Chinese waiting for you."

"That sounds good," Brian said. "But I prefer a nice warm Irish girl named Jenny Ryan."

Jenny laughed. "We've got that too."

He noticed the set table and said, "No dinner in front of the TV tonight?"

"Not tonight." She struck a match and lit the two candles on the table.

"A candlelight Chinese dinner?"

"Yup. At first I thought it would be dumb. I mean who eats Chinese out of a box by candlelight? But then I thought, what do young Chinese couples do? And I thought what the heck."

"I think it's great," Brian said.

She led him to a chair and got a beer and the frosted mug from the freezer. She poured it for him and said, "You must have had a grueling day."

"Forget my day," Brian said. "What was your day like? Are you all set for the exhibit?"

"I'm bushed," Jenny said as she took a seat and poured herself another glass of wine. "But we're all set, and Dr. Patterson was very complimentary about the display."

Brian leaned over and gave her a peck on the cheek. "I'm proud of you. You must be pumped. I read the PR piece you wrote, and I bet the place will be packed tomorrow."

"I hope so," Jenny said. "Not just because I did it, but because it's something people should see."

Jenny and Brian had talked about the emotional impact of the display all week, and he knew what she meant. He said softly, "I'm looking forward to seeing it myself tomorrow."

"Tomorrow?" Jenny said brightly. "What about work?"

"I'm taking off. That's why I worked extra late tonight." Brian rarely got home before seven, but it was rare that he got home as late as he did tonight.

"Now I'm really excited," Jenny said. "I just assumed you were having an affair with your secretary."

"That would never happen," Brian said. "Besides my secretary is old enough to be my mother, and I keep her way too busy."

"I'm so glad you're coming. It's so thoughtful. But are you sure it's okay?"

"Positive," Brian said. "This is a big day for you and I want to be there. And I made reservations at the Old Ebbitt Grill for a late dinner. Is that okay?"

"Terrific!" Jenny said. "You know it's my favorite."

Brian smiled and dug into his food, and Jenny watched him eat.

"I'm starving," Brian said. "This is good."

"There's a new place around the corner called Mao's Little Red Cook Book. I thought the name was cool so I gave it a try."

"Well, Mao's a keeper." Then he looked at her plate and said, "Aren't you going to eat?"

"I am, but I want to ask you something first. I was going to wait until later, but…"

"If it's about painting the bathroom again, forget it. I told you I'm not doing it. I hate to paint. And I don't think you should either. You're a terrible painter. I mean, I love you and all, but you're sloppy and you'll get it all over that priceless Italian tile you picked out. Just hire someone. Pick any color you like. You have great taste, Jenny, but you're an awful painter."

Jenny laughed and tried to stop him, but Brian wanted to drive home his point. "Remember when we painted the closet in the bedroom…"

"Stop!" she shrieked. "It's not about painting!"

"Oh," Brian said softly. "Then it shouldn't be a problem. Shoot."

Jenny took a sip of her wine and said abruptly, "Will you marry me?"

Brian dropped his chopsticks. He looked at her and squinted as if she were out of focus. "What did you say?"

"I said, 'Will you marry me?' It's a new millennium and the world is changing fast. So I thought it was time to toss out the antiquated custom of boy asks girl. So I'm asking you."

Brian smiled. The girl was audacious, and he loved it.

"So," Jenny repeated. "Will you marry me or not?"

"Of course I'll marry you!" They leaned in to hug and Brian knocked over his beer mug. He tossed his napkin on the mess and said, "Does this mean we're engaged?"

"Yes!" Jenny said, beaming.

"So now what? Do you give me a ring?"

"Absolutely not," Jenny said. "That's one custom we're not tossing out."

"So I still give you one?"

"The sooner the better."

Wait here, Brian said. He left the table and went into the bedroom. When he came out, he was holding a small box. He held it out, and she saw that it was from Tiffany's. "I've been saving this for next month when I was going to ask you the same question on your birthday."

He opened the box and revealed a ring that took her breath away. It was a traditional round cut of moderate size with a simple, but tasteful, setting. "They said we could exchange it if you prefer something else."

"No," Jenny said, slipping it on and admiring it on her finger. "It's perfect."

"When I told them money wasn't an issue, they showed me some much larger and more elaborately set rings. But I thought they weren't you."

Jenny was still admiring the ring. "This one is me. It's perfect." Then she looked up and said, "And you're perfect."

Brian smiled. "I think I'm supposed to pick you up now and carry you into the bedroom."

Jenny turned serious. "Can we sit a minute?"

"Sure," Brian said.

She filled her wine glass and Brian said, "Mind if I get another beer first?

"You better unless you want to lick this one off the table."

Brian took a beer from the fridge and checked the freezer for another frosted mug.

"Sorry," Jenny said. "I only put one in."

"Some wife you're gonna make. First you drop the ball on the beer. Who knows what'll come next."

"Wife," Jenny said. "That has a nice sound to it."

"Yes, it does," Brian said. He kissed her on the forehead and sat.

"Are you okay with all of this?" She asked.

"Couldn't be better. Are you?"

"I've never been happier."

"Great," Brian said. "The bedroom's this way." He started to stand, but Jenny told him to sit and he slid back in is chair.

"Are you okay that I asked you first?"

Brian laughed. "Sure I am. It took the pressure off because I didn't have to worry about what you'd say when I gave you the ring."

Jenny smiled. "It's nice that you had the ring because I'd always wonder whether you were ever going to ask me."

"So it worked out perfectly."

"Perfectly," Jenny agreed.

"So why do you look like you have something on your mind?"

Jenny sighed. "I'd just like to take a minute to tell you how important this is to me."

Brian nodded and took a gulp from his beer.

"Back in Bristol there are two wonderful people who live on Wilson Avenue. Their names are Tim and Bridget Ryan."

Brian laughed. "Yeah, your parents."

"Exactly. I adore them, and I know you like them too."

"Very much," Brian said.

"They have always supported me in all of my decisions."

"They're great people," Brian agreed.

"When I told them I was moving in with you, they were happy for me, but I could tell they were hurt. Not because they don't love you, because they think you're terrific. It's just that their values are different."

"I can understand that," Brian said.

"To tell you the truth, I felt a little bit the same way. I know it's cool among people our age to say rings and ceremonies don't mean anything as long as people are committed to each other, but I guess I'm a little old fashioned. I can't wait to tell my mother that we're engaged to be married."

"Trust me; I can't wait to tell mine. You're not the only Irish Catholic in the room, you know. My dad rolled with things okay, but my mom raised some eyebrows too when I told her you were moving in. She loves you, but I could tell she was uncomfortable."

"This is great," Jenny said.

Brian turned serious. "So now the world will be right with our parents," he said. "But that's not why we're doing this, right? We're doing this for us."

"Absolutely. It all started when I visited Carrie. She was talking about their wedding plans, and I realized how nice it would be to have that in our future."

Brian nodded. "I was disappointed when their wedding was postponed."

"Me too," Jenny said. "But it's only for three months and it was for good reasons. Johnny's training will be less intense by then; Carrie will finish her Master's degree, and she'll be able to have a full church wedding. Since she doesn't really have much of a family beyond her parents, she wants to have it at St. Theresa's in Bristol where Johnny's crowd can come. And most important of all, it will give her dad the chance to finish a major corporate project he's working on in Europe.

Her parents plan to come for a couple of weeks, and her mom wants to help her plan everything. It's exciting."

Jenny watched Brian's eyes widen. It happened whenever he had an idea, and his wheels seemed to be turning now. "So the wedding is moved back to March 2001?"

"Right," Jenny said.

"That's almost a year from now."

"Eleven months to be exact."

Brian took Jenny's hand in his and said, "Then why don't we make it a double ceremony?"

70- Making the Rounds

June 2000

Johnny and Carrie took a flight from Fayetteville to Philadelphia International Airport, and Brian and Jenny were at the gate to greet them. Johnny had a three day weekend pass, and the four of them had business to conduct. They drove north on Route 95 toward Bristol while the girls sat in the back discussing Carrie's next writing assignment.

Carrie's article on East Africa was so well received that her editor invited her to pitch another story idea. After talking with Jenny about the success of her museum exhibit, the girls decided the display, and the public's reaction to it, would make for a great story line. Carrie's editor agreed, and the girls were mapping out the shape of the story. On Sunday night Johnny planned to fly back to Fayetteville alone while Carrie drove to Washington with Brian and Jenny to visit the exhibit and conduct interviews.

They took the Bristol exit from Route 95 and headed south on Route 413 for the short ride to town. Brian spotted the Grundy clock tower first and said, "There it is; we're officially home."

Carrie hadn't been to Bristol since she graduated from Penn State, and she got a little misty over it. "I've lived all over the world," she said. "But for some reason nothing gives me a feeling of home like this little town. Can we drive around for a minute?"

"Sure," Brian said "It's a homecoming for us too."

They turned onto Mill Street and headed for the river, and Carrie noted the King George II Inn. "I'll never forget our dinner there," she said to Johnny.

"You told me you were moving to France," Johnny said. "It was the worst night of my life."

"Our lives," Carrie corrected. "But I remember a nice part of the evening, when you told the piano player to play something from Les Mis and he played 'On My Own.' It was so beautiful."

Brian looked in the rearview mirror and winked at Johnny. Johnny said to Carrie, "Yeah, I'm sensitive that way."

They turned left onto Radcliffe Street. After a few blocks they passed the house where Carrie had lived, and she felt some pangs of nostalgia.

"The place looks good," Jenny said. "I wonder who owns it now."

"My parents still own it," Carrie said. "They never know where my dad's work will take them, so they held on to it just in case. A local realtor manages the property, collects the rent and makes the repairs. He sends them photos of the place every year."

"Cool," Jenny said.

They continued down Radcliffe and turned left at Cesare's Ristorante. "There's a good memory," Johnny said.

"Let's promise that before the weekend is over we'll share a pizza at Cesare's," Jenny added.

"I'm in," Brian said. "But let's make it two."

They drove through the Harriman section of town, down Green Lane and Wilson Avenue until they came to Bristol High School.

"Drive by the football field," Jenny said.

Brian turned and they drove slowly by the field and Carrie said. "So this is where the great Johnny Marzo kicked butt against all opposition."

"This is the place," Brian said.

"And this is the place where Brian Kelly delivered an incredible commencement speech," Jenny added.

Brian smiled in the mirror again. "I was afraid Mr. Baxter would yank me off the stage."

Jenny said, "That was the day, you know."

"What do you mean?" Brian said.

"You winked at me as you walked to the podium and then delivered a speech that left me in tears. A little voice inside told me that you were something special."

"Keep listening to that voice, Honey," Brian said over his shoulder.

They continued down Wilson Avenue until they reached Jenny's house, and Brian slowed. No one was outside, but Jenny rolled down the window and playfully called out, "I'll be home in a minute, Mom."

"Okay," Brian said to Johnny. "Let's review the plan. We'll drop you and Carrie off at the deli so you can visit with your folks while Jenny and I take our parents to lunch. This is the big post-engagement meeting of the two families, and we're going to the King George. After lunch we'll drop off our parents, pick you up and we'll meet with Father Morris at St. Theresa's to plan the wedding. Our appointment is at three o'clock."

"Sounds good," Johnny said.

"And while you're at lunch, don't forget to ask the King George about using their back room for a reception," Carrie added. "And see how many people the room holds."

"Right," Jenny said. "The room should be fine. I think it holds about a hundred and twenty."

Brian continued, "After we meet with Father, we'll drop you guys off at the Grundy Library to work while Johnny and I attend to some things with the Pac Men. Then we'll spend the night with our families."

"That's the plan," Johnny said.

The day went well. Johnny's parents and the guys at the deli were excited to see them, and they joked, laughed and ate like there was no tomorrow. The luncheon at the King George was also a big success. Both sets of parents were ecstatic about the engagement and hit it off nicely. The banquet room was available on the wedding date and was the ideal size for the gathering they were planning. At the rectory the meeting with Father Morris went smoothly. The girls gave no indication of becoming bridezilla's, and Father was very accommodating about their desire for a double wedding.

They were finished by four o'clock, and Brian dropped the girls off at the library with a promise that he and Johnny would be back in two hours. The girls told them not to rush and that they would walk to the deli when they were finished.

Brian and Johnny drove to the Number 3 Firehouse on Swain Street where Mickey was waiting for them out front. It had been over a year since he had seen either of them on one of their brief trips home, and he greeted them with a broad grin.

"The Pac Men reunite," Mickey shouted as they got out of the car. They hugged and exchanged back slaps and Brian said, "You're looking good, man. You look like you've trimmed down a little."

Mickey nodded and padded his stomach. "You should have seen me six months ago. I looked like a blimp. There wasn't much to do between emergency runs except eat. Then the chief told everyone they were getting fat, so he converted an extra room into a small gym. Now we lift and use the treadmill every day. Plus I watch what I eat."

"It's paying off," Johnny said. "You look real good."

"What about you, soldier?" Mickey said, giving Johnny a light punch on the arm. "You goin' to the Olympics or what? You're built like a rock."

"I guess they keep us moving a little," Johnny said.

Brian changed the subject. "So what's new?"

"Not much that we haven't said in the letters and e-mails," Mickey replied. The three of them had always kept in frequent contact over the years.

"Bullshit," Johnny said. "You can't just end an e-mail with, 'by the way, I have a girl,' and expect that to be enough. So tell us about this girl in your life."

Mickey looked embarrassed. He had never dated in high school. He looked at the ground and said, "I met her here. She's an EMT like me. We trained together, became good friends and one thing led to another."

"So when do we meet her?" Brian asked.

"You guys around tonight when I get off duty?"

"We're gonna spend some time with our parents," Johnny said. "Maybe about ten? We'll bring our ladies and everyone can meet."

"Ten sounds good," Mickey said. "Maybe we can grab a beer at Phinny McGee's."

They all agreed and Brian changed the subject again. "Should we go pick up Bobby?"

Mickey checked his watch. "He's meeting us here after work. Should be any minute. Let me introduce you to some of the guys while we wait."

They shook hands with the firemen hanging around and exchanged small talk. Soon Bobby arrived, and the Pac Men repeated their greetings.

Then Brian said, "So how's work?"

"Real good, sort of," Bobby replied. "I love it and I'm good at it, but I'm getting frustrated working for other people. It's a big place and I can do things just as good and twice as fast as the other mechanics, but we're unionized, so it doesn't matter. It seems like nobody wants to work anymore. Someday I'll have my own place and make some real money."

"Sounds like a good goal," Johnny said.

Mickey checked his watch again and said, "I guess we should do it."

Brian and Johnny nodded.

Bobby asked, "Are you sure you made all the arrangements?"

"Everything is done," Brian said. "The room is reserved; we're paid in advance, and they're waiting for us. All we need is…" His voice trailed off.

Mickey said, "Then let's get it over with."

71- Tough Love

They piled into the SUV and drove a few blocks before Mickey directed Brian to park in an ally near a tire repair shop. Brian didn't see any dwelling units around and gave Mickey a quizzical look.

"He lives in a two room dump above the repair shop," Mickey said. "Two hundred bucks a month. I doubt the place is legal but I didn't report it in because I don't know where else he'd go."

"Parents?" Johnny asked.

"They tossed him out months ago," Bobby added. "Broke his mother's heart to do it. It's real sad."

The building was severely run down, and Brian wondered out loud whether the rickety outdoor steps would support their weight. Johnny shrugged and said, "We'll find out," and began to climb. The others followed.

There was a small landing at the top, and a lidless trashcan sat by the door. The tattered window shade was drawn. Johnny took a breath and knocked. There was no answer. He knocked again louder, and Mickey said, "He hardly ever answers the door."

Johnny took out his cell phone. "Do you know his phone number?"

"He doesn't own a phone," Bobby said sadly.

Johnny put his phone away, put his hand on the doorknob, and was about to open the door when he turned back and asked, "Dog?"

Mickey shook his head. "Couldn't afford one.

The door was unlocked, and Johnny opened it a crack and called in. There was still no response. He stepped in, and the others followed.

The room was a combined kitchen and living area. Johnny looked around and shook his head at the squalor he saw. Behind him Brian whispered, "Sweet Jesus." It was a scene out of bad trailer park movie. Dirty dishes were piled in the sink, a milk carton and the remains of a meal were on the table. Trash and debris were everywhere, and a foul smell dominated the room.

Mickey motioned to an open door at the far end of the room and said, "Bedroom's in the back."

They entered the bedroom and were hit with the stale smell of body odor, alcohol and cigarette smoke. There was a pile of clothes in the corner, and fast food wrappers littered the floor. On the bed was the sleeping figure that scarcely resembled the Tommy Dillon they once knew. At least they hoped he was sleeping. Next to him was an empty pint bottle of Jim Beam, and Johnny wondered whether bourbon was Tommy's only addiction.

Mickey stepped forward, listened for his breathing, and nodded to the rest of the guys. He nudged him slightly without a response. He shook his shoulder, and Tommy snorted, but continued to sleep.

"This guy is really out," Mickey said.

Johnny was stunned. "I knew he was bad, but…"

"It's worse than I ever imagined," Brian mumbled.

"He's gotten progressively worse," Mickey said. "Another month or two like this and …"

Brian interrupted him, "There won't be another month or two, or even a day or two. Let's wake him up."

Mickey shook him harder and shouted his name. Brian joined him and shouted, "Hey, Tommy. Wake up, man."

Tommy stirred but turned away from him. Johnny said, "I've had enough of this crap." He left the room and returned with a full glass of water. "Isn't this what they do in the movies?" The guys stepped back and Johnny tossed the water into Tommy's face. Tommy was awakened with a start and began to cough, then he started to dry heave, and Mickey looked for a waste basket thinking Tommy might retch. He didn't. Gradually the heaving stopped and he managed to say, "What the hell!"

He sat up rubbing his eyes. He scanned the room and said sarcastically, "Jesus, the Pac Men are here. What the hell's the occasion?"

No one replied.

He looked at Brian and Johnny and said, "I see Bobby once in a while, and Mickey stops in now and then, but you guys," he shook his head. "You might as well be ghosts."

"We've been a little busy." Brian said.

"Yeah," Tommy replied. "You guys are real important, can't stop by."

"You never answered my letters," Brian said.

"I delivered them," Mickey said. "Brought them here from his parents' house."

"Maybe I've been busy too," Tommy said, searching for a cigarette on the night table.

"But you cashed the checks I sent, " Brian replied.

Tommy laughed. "Yeah, I spent the money on fresh vegetables and reading materials."

Johnny looked at him in disgust. "What the hell is all this, Tommy? What's going on?"

"Nothing is going on," Tommy said indignantly. "Things are fine."

"Bullshit," Johnny thundered. "You don't have a job, you live in a pig sty, and you're a drunk."

Tommy glared at him and tried to stand but couldn't. He sank back to the bed and said bitterly, "Who the hell are you to judge me? You guys have cake jobs without a care in the world. You come in here from your cushy lives and get all indignant with me. Beat it. I never liked you guys anyway."

Johnny smacked him hard across the face and Tommy almost fell off the bed. Mickey stepped in front of Johnny, but Johnny said it wasn't necessary. "I just wanted to get his attention," Johnny said.

Tommy rubbed his face and said, "Bastard."

Brian squatted in front of Tommy and said coldly, "We've leaving now, Tommy."

"Good," Tommy said. "Don't let the door hit you in the ass when you go. I hope you don't mind if I don't say goodbye."

"No," Brian said. "I mean we're all leaving. You're coming with us."

"I'm not going anywhere," Tommy said. "I'm happy right here."

Brian sighed. "We got you a rehab place in Jersey, right over the bridge. It's run by nuns."

Tommy shook his head, but Brian continued. "They're gonna clean you up and dry you out. Get you on your feet again."

Tommy sat motionless for a while, as though he was considering the possibility. Then he started to whimper. It was pathetic to watch.

Brian waited briefly and then said, "Let's go."

"Can't do it," Tommy sobbed. "Can't."

Johnny knelt by the bed and stroked Tommy's back. "Yes you can, Tommy. You can do it, and we want to help. The place is real nice and it's already paid for. All you have to do is sign yourself in."

Tommy threw his arms around Johnny's shoulders, and Johnny steeled himself against the smell. "Won't work," Tommy sobbed. "Not worth trying."

"Yes it will," Brian said. "But you've got to be tough."

"Bobby and I will visit you all the time," Mickey added.

Tommy sat straighter on the bed and wiped his nose on his sleeve. Then he said, "My life's already over. Don't waste your time with me."

Johnny looked at the weak, pitiful figure Tommy had become and it broke his heart. It remained quiet until Brian said, "I wish we could just let Johnny beat the crap out of you until you agreed to come, but we can't. The rehab facility won't take you unless you go voluntarily."

Tommy nodded his understanding.

"You've got a life to live," Brian said. "We need you to stand up and walk out of here with us. Walk away from this place and never come back."

Tommy didn't answer, but a single tear ran down his face.

"Will you do that for yourself, Tommy? Will you stand up and walk out of here with us?"

Tommy looked at their faces and then the room around him. He nodded slightly and tried to stand. Johnny and Mickey clutched him under each arm and helped him up. They waited until he had his footing and then led him gently out of the room.

When they reached the kitchen door, Tommy paused, looked back, and shook his head in disgust. Then he smiled faintly and said, "Pac Men."

72- Pick the Biggest One

It was nearly seven o'clock when Johnny and Brian returned from the rehab center. They dropped off Mickey and Bobby and promised to meet up with them at Phinny MeGee's at ten. They were emotionally drained and didn't feel much like partying, but they wanted to meet Mickey's girl.

Brian parked in front of the deli, and he and Johnny could hear laughter coming from inside before they even opened the door. When they walked in, they found Carrie and Jenny surrounded by the guys.

Nick looked their way and said, "Hey, here come Thunder and Lightning."

The boys looked at them, and Jimmy added, "We named your girls Wind and Rain." The boys knew that Nick was unable to begin a conversation without a reference to the weather.

Brian smiled and said, "Which is which?"

"I'm wind," Carrie hollered cheerfully.

Jenny raised her bottle and said, "And I guess that makes me Rain."

"Wind and Rain," Johnny said. "We'll have to remember that. I guess we're a little late for this party."

"Nah," Big Frankie said. "We just got started."

"We were telling the ladies how we used to pick up girls at Seaside when we were younger," Jimmy said.

Johnny looked around and asked, "Where's Mom and Pop?"

"They're making a delivery for a party. Should be back in an hour," Nick said. "Big Frankie's in charge if you want to buy anything."

"Yeah," Jimmy said dejectedly. "Your dad never leaves me in charge."

"Maybe someday," Johnny said. "You have to prove yourself."

Jimmy shrugged. "Been hangin' here for almost thirty years."

Johnny winked at Nick and said to Jimmy, "Some things take a long time," "That's what I told him," Nick added.

"Yeah, I suppose you're right," Jimmy said.

Brian looked at Jenny and said to the group, "I hate to break up a good party, but Rain's parents are expecting us."

"Same here," Johnny said. "Wind and I have a stop to make."

Nick said to the girls, "You'll come around tomorrow before you leave, right?"

"Definitely," Carrie said.

Jenny and Carrie gave each of the men a big hug, and Thunder, Lightning, Wind and Rain left the store.

Brian offered to give Johnny and Carrie a ride, but they opted to walk. They agreed to meet at Phinny's at ten and went their separate ways.

Johnny led Carrie down Pond Street until they reached the Lafayette Street alley.

"I'm excited," Carrie said. "I hope he likes me."

"That won't be an issue," Johnny said. "The issue is whether he'll like you too much."

"How do you mean?" Carrie asked.

"You'll see," Johnny said. "Just brace yourself and, no matter what happens, know that he has the best intentions. Oh, and by the way, I hope you didn't have too much beer at the deli, because you'll definitely be drinking some wine here."

"I'm fine," Carrie said. "But I think I'll just have water anyway."

Johnny smiled knowingly and said, "Oh, ok."

They reached the back gate and found it unlocked. Johnny opened it, and they took the narrow walkway to the house. The garden was in full bloom, and Carrie marveled at the tomatoes, squash, and other vegetables in various stages of growth. The garden was obviously well cared for and Carrie said, "Shame on you, Johnny Marzo, for violating this beautiful place."

Johnny held a hand up and said, "Please. It was a long time ago and I suffered enough."

"Well, you should have," She said.

Johnny knocked loudly and it was several seconds before Old Man Lombardi came to the door. He opened it, smiled broadly, and said something in Italian. Then he bellowed, *"Mr. President, Captain Marzo, my friend, what do I call you? Vieni, Vieni. Come."*

Johnny stepped into the kitchen, and Lombardi gave him his customary bear hug. His grip was strong, but not the vice hold it used to be. Lombardi let go and Johnny turned to introduce Carrie who had followed him in. He was able to say, "Mr. Lombardi, this is…" before Lombardi pushed him aside and said, *"Oh Dio mio, tanto bella."* She smiled at him and he said, *"So beautiful."* He locked her in an embrace, and she looked at Johnny as if she needed help. Johnny laughed.

Lombardi freed her and took a step back. He pinched her cheek lightly and said, *"You even more beautiful den da picture."*

Carrie smiled shyly and said, "Thank you. It's so nice to meet you."

Lombardi ignored that and said, *"Look."* He pointed to a 5 x 7 photo Johnny had sent him of the two of them. He had it prominently displayed on the kitchen counter. Aside from a photo of his wife and a print of the Blessed Mother, there were no other photos in the room. Lombardi said, *"When I see da photo I say to myself, 'Mista President, you do good."*

Carrie kept smiling.

He turned to Johnny and gave him a playful smack on the back of the head. *"One year you no visit! Where da hell you been?"*

Johnny laughed. "I've been busy. I told you in the letters."

"I know," Lombardi said. *"I understand, I kid you."* Then he said proudly, *"Big shot captain. Where's da uniform?"*

"I'm on leave," Johnny explained. "I'm relaxing."

"Send me a picture in da uniform." Then he added firmly, "Soon!"

"I will," Johnny said. "As soon as we get back."

"Look at me," Lombardi said to Carrie self consciously. He was wearing his customary sleeveless undershirt. *"I should have worn da shirt."*

"You look fine, Mr. Lombardi," Carrie said.

Lombardi grunted and said, *"I get da wine."*

He put a glass in front of Carrie, and she said, "Thank you, but I think I'll just have some water."

"Bullshit da water," Lombardi replied without hesitation. "We celebrate."

Carrie looked shocked and Johnny almost fell out of his chair laughing.

Lombardi apologized when he realized what he had said and Carrie said, "I'd love to have a glass of wine with you."

Lombardi cut some cheese and joined them at the table.

They sipped their wine and talked about their lives. They talked about Johnny's training and career, Carrie's writing ambitions, and news about the town. Eventually the conversation turned to Mr. Lombardi's wife. It was obvious that even after all the time that had passed the pain of her loss had barely subsided, and his eyes filled as he spoke of what she meant to him. He told Carrie about the day that he insisted Johnny visit Carrie in Europe to tell her in person what she meant to him. Carrie had heard the story before, but it meant so much more coming from the old man. Lombardi told Carrie that he hoped she and Johnny would have as much happiness as he had shared with his beautiful Angelina, and Carrie's eyes filled as well. Then he said, *"You Catholic?"*

Carrie said that she was, and Lombardi said, *"I be right back."*

He left the room, and Carrie said to Johnny, "He's such a sweetheart."

"I love him like a grandfather," Johnny said.

Carrie wondered out loud where he went, and Johnny said he had no idea.

Lombardi came back shortly holding two medals on chains. He gave the first one to Johnny. *"Dis is da Sacred Heart. If you ever go to war, you wear dis."*

Johnny was moved and said, "I will Mr. Lombardi. Thank you."

Lombardi said to Carrie. *"Dis medal of da Blessed Mother belong to my Angelina. You wear dis to protect da captain."*

Carrie felt a lump in her throat. She said, *"Thank you, Mr. Lombardi, but I can't. It's important to you and you should keep it."*

"Please," Lombardi said softly. *"It belong on a beautiful girl. Not in da drawer. Please wear; it make me happy."*

Carrie stood and walked around the table to meet him. She bowed toward him, and he gently slipped the chain over her head. She grasped the medal and looked at it for time, then she gave him a long hug. When they separated she said, "Thank you so much for this. I'll cherish it. And thank you for sending me Johnny."

Lombardi looked tired and said he needed to rest. He walked them to the door and made them promise they would visit whenever they could. He looked much older now, and Johnny wondered if he'd ever see him again. They said their good-byes and walked down the steps.

Lombardi called to them. *"How you like my garden?"*

"It's beautiful," Carrie said. "The tomatoes are fabulous."

"Please, pick the biggest one for yourself."

Carrie seemed reluctant, and Lombardi said, *"Please."*

She stepped into the garden and Johnny followed her until Lombardi roared, *"Not you captain. You leave da tomatoes alone!"*

73- Bush-Gore

September 2000

Johnny's unit was back from two weeks of desert training in Western Texas, so he and Carrie took advantage of a weekend pass to drive to Carolina Beach. Carrie surprised Johnny with a rented convertible for the weekend, and they were cruising along with the top down.

Carrie sat with her arms raised above the windshield and the wind blowing her long, blond hair. "I love it," she said. "Sand, sun and ocean, here we come."

Johnny smiled. "I like the ocean part, but I think I've had enough sand and sun for a while."

Carrie cuddled his arm and put her head on his shoulder. "My poor baby out in the barren wasteland for so long. Maybe you should sell insurance instead."

"Speaking of which, did you pay the bills while I was gone?"

Carrie sat up again. "Yup, I paid the bills, called the cable company, put Draino in the clogged sink..."

"We had a clogged sink?"

Carrie grinned. "While you were off roasting marshmallows by the campfire, I had some real problems to take care of, but all is well. So you have nothing to worry about this weekend except having a good time and keeping me happy."

"I think I can handle that," Johnny said. Then he added, "Did you start your article about the election?"

Carrie's mood suddenly dipped and she said, "Killjoy. Why'd you have to bring that up?"

Johnny took on a fatherly tone. "Don't tell me you haven't started it? Your editor wants it in..." He thought for a moment and added, "In two weeks."

"I'm stuck," Carrie said. "I sit in front of the keyboard and can't get going."

"Why not?"

They were approaching a drive-through fast food joint and Carrie said, "Can we get something to eat?"

"No," Johnny said with mock sternness, "You're avoiding the question. We'll be at the beach in a half hour and I'll buy you a great lunch. Now tell me about the article."

"My editor wants me to write a nice, balanced piece about both candidates and add a fluffy, human interest aspect to both men."

"Sounds simple," Johnny said. "So do it."

"I can't," Carrie insisted.

"Why not?"

"Two reasons. I'm tired of doing feature articles, especially fluffy ones. I've written about the Fourth of July parade, Civil War Monument restorations, the North Carolina State Fair. I want to do some hard news reporting, some real analysis. I think I've proven myself and deserve the chance."

"Sounds fair enough. So do a good job with this one and then make your case with the editor."

Carrie thought about that and Johnny said, "What's the other reason?"

Carrie looked at him. "I can't write a balanced article because I think Bush is a dope."

Johnny laughed and said, "Wow. That's pretty strong."

"I call it like it is," Carrie replied. "Everyone knows he was a dunce and a clown at Yale. You've heard his 'young and reckless' answer to questions about his alleged drug use. And his policies... don't get me started." She was animated now and kept going anyway. "You know how I feel about the environment and poverty and health care. He's gonna be against everything I stand for."

Johnny nodded and said, "Probably."

"Not probably," she said. "Definetly."

Johnny laughed at her zeal, but it just made her more animated. "So what about you, soldier boy? Who do you support?"

Johnny hesitated. "That's a tough one. I was raised a democrat. My parents, my grandparents, the guys at the store, every adult I knew was a democrat. I'm sure they'll all vote for Gore."

"I hear one of those gigantic "buts" coming."

He nodded and said, "The military feels that republicans are more supportive of the armed forces, more willing to increase military expenditures. So..."

Carrie shook her head vigorously, and Johnny laughed. "Calm down, Babe. You asked."

She took a breath and said, "I hope you're not implying that democrats would leave the country weak."

"No. Not intentionally. But you'll understand if I want the best equipment I can have in the field. Besides, you see him as dumb; I see him as decisive. I think he has a way of boiling things down to the simple issue like Reagan did."

Please don't get me started with Reagan," Carrie teased. Then she smiled and said, "I love these arguments."

"I'm not arguing," Johnny said happily, "You are. I'm just cruisin' to the beach."

"Me too," Carrie said. "Anyway, of course I want you to have the best equipment possible. It's just that I'm convinced that republicans will pay far more for it because they're in love with the big corporations. Then they'll cut valuable programs to pay for it. Maybe I should write a piece about that for the paper."

"Better not," Johnny said. "I bet that half the people who read the *Fayetteville Observer* either work for the army or have businesses that benefit from their proximity to Fort Bragg and Pope Airbase. Besides, North Carolina has voted republican in every election since Fred Flintstone took Wilma to the prom. You might want to think about those things when you select the angle for your article."

"I know," Carrie said glumly. "I've already decided to do a piece on Bush and Gore's pets. You can't get any fluffier than that."

"Now you're talkin'," Johnny said. "Sounds like a Pulitzer if you do it right."

She rested her head on his shoulder again and said, "Let's go have a good time."

They drove a few minutes, and then she whispered in his ear. "I wonder if I can find a photo of Bush and his dog."

She sounded mellow, and Johnny was relieved. "I'm sure you can find one on-line," he said.

"Great," she said playfully. "The caption will read, 'Which has the higher I.Q.?'" Johnny hesitated and said, "That remark, sweetheart, just cost you lunch."

74- The Curse of Cassandra

October 13, 2000

Everyone on the Threat Assessment Team looked shaken, especially Dr. Blake, as more information came in about the deadly attack on the USS Cole in Aden Harbor in Yemen, the Persian Gulf. The Cole had been docked for refueling when it was approached by a small boat. Early reports indicated that the crew believed the vessel was a garbage service boat and allowed it to draw near undisturbed. Soon after, suicide bombers detonated their explosives and blew a forty foot square hole in the side of the guided missile destroyer killing seventeen American sailors and injuring over thirty others. At last report, the crews were working to stem the flooding of the ship which appeared to be under control.

Blake had the disheveled look of someone who hadn't slept all night. His face was flushed and his voice cracked as he spoke. "We have the FBI and our best forensic teams in route to the Cole, and we'll follow every lead we can get: the type of explosives used, the boat manufacturer, or anything else that can give us information. Osama bin Laden's al-Qaeda has already claimed responsibility. Our job will continue to be to track down as many of these bastards as we can and prevent further attacks." Blake continued, "From the information we have thus far, we believe…"

Brian had been seething all morning and chose this time to interrupt him. "Excuse me, sir," he said tersely.

Blake shot him a look of surprise and annoyance. He wasn't used to being interrupted. Brian respected him immensely and was often amazed by his skill and work ethic, but there was something he had to get off his chest. Without waiting to be recognized, Brian said, "We should have seen this coming, Sir. This could have been prevented."

Blake glared at him and then looked at the others seated at the conference table. Then he spoke calmly. "Do you or did you have information we didn't have?"

"Nothing hard," Brian said. "But in January I passed on information an agent in Yemen filed from an untested informant about an unconfirmed plot to destroy American vessels using suicide bombers in small boats. The report even said that there had already been an aborted and undetected attempt upon the USS Sullivans in January. We should have known, Sir."

The room got quiet. Everyone at the table was charged with recognizing and preventing potential attacks, and they were understandably on edge. Saying an attack that cost American lives could have been prevented was very serious stuff.

Dr. Blake waited several seconds to reply. Then he cleared his throat and said, "I appreciate your anger. We're all angry. But we get thousands of reports a day; you know that. We make on-the-spot decisions about which ones to move forward. Unconfirmed plots from untested informants don't receive as high a priority as others deemed more actionable. You know that, too."

Brian held his ground and said, "Yes, Sir, I do. But this is different. It didn't matter that we lacked actionable facts. Once that unsubstantiated report hit my desk I knew that such an attack was possible. Some obscure agent in Yemen did us a favor because he brought an obvious possibility to our attention. From that moment on an attack like this became foreseeable."

Dr. Blake nodded. "You make a valid point." Then he paused and said, "Can I assume you still have your initial report?"

"Absolutely," Brian said.

"You know that once our threat assessments are passed on, other levels of the agency decide what to do with them."

"I've always been painfully aware of that, Dr. Blake. The navy should have received this information and should have changed its procedures. The rules of engagement should have been tightened. Maybe that boat in Yemen should have been blown out of the water when it got to within a hundred yards of the Cole. Maybe all approaching service boats should be intercepted, boarded, and searched while they're well away from the main ship. I don't know. But there are seventeen dead sailors…"

Brian was getting more emotional and Blake interrupted. He said softly, "Give me that report and I promise you I'll have it tracked. I don't know who may have dropped the ball, or even whether it was CIA or navy. I doubt we'll ever hear who did. But I'm confident the exercise will make the process better next time."

"Thank you, Sir," Brian said.

"In the meantime," Dr. Blake said, "Keep your chin up, all of you. This is exceptionally difficult work. We'll continue to have successes and failures, and we'll continue to do our best."

That night Brian and Jenny went to their favorite tavern in Georgetown, but the only things Brian ate for dinner were the olives in his martinis. Jenny knew there was no use trying to console him at times like this. It was better to tread lightly and let him do the talking when he was ready. But he seemed more distant than ever, and after some time she said gently, "What are you thinking?"

"I'm thinking about Cassandra," he said.

"Cassandra," Jenny said. "Sounds familiar."

"She's from Greek Mythology. There are different versions of her story, but one says that she had the gift of seeing into the future. She tried to warn people about the destruction of Troy and the whole Trojan horse thing. "

"Interesting," Jenny said.

"It became a curse though," Brian added.

"And why is that?" Jenny asked.

"Because no one would listen to her."

75- Recount?

December 12, 2000

The guys at the deli were having a heated discussion as they awaited the CNN broadcast of the Supreme Court ruling in Bush v. Gore which was expected to be announced at any minute. Angelo shouted from behind the counter, "If you guys don't quiet, down I'm gonna toss you out."

"Come on, Angelo," Jimmy said. "This is history. We've been waiting over a month for a new President. There's a lot of tension in the air."

"The Supreme Court's gonna screw over Gore anyway," Angelo quipped. "I don't know why you're bothering to watch."

"I know they're gonna do it," Nick said. "I'm just interested in how."

"Doesn't matter how," Angelo said. "You're gonna have Bush as President, and then we're all gonna get screwed over."

"I told you guys before; I like Bush," Big Frankie said. "They say he did a good job in Texas. Besides, Gore's a little too pompous for me."

"I can't believe you voted for Bush," Nick said. "You're a democrat. You voted for Clinton twice. You always vote for democrats."

"Not this time," Big Frankie said.

Nick wouldn't let it go. "You're a union carpenter. Who did your union support?"

"Gore," Big Frankie said. "But I do what I want to do. I just don't like Gore."

"That's the trouble with people," Nick said. "They don't vote like they should."

"You can't decide how people are supposed to vote," Big Frankie said. "After Clinton's impeachment trial, Gore put his arm around Clinton and said that he would go down as one of the greatest Presidents in modern times."

"Yeah," Nick said. "And he was right."

Big Frankie shook his head. "I think what Clinton did with that Monica girl was wrong. He disrespected her and he disrespected his wife, and that was it for him in my book. Then, when Gore said that nice stuff about Clinton, it was over for him too."

Nick held his throat and pretended to be gagging until Big Frankie rolled his eyes. Then Nick said, "That's exactly what Bush's cronies want you to do. You're a hard working guy, a union carpenter. You'll definitely benefit by democratic polices toward unions and be hurt by republican policies, and you vote for President of the United States on the basis of Billy Clinton making hanky panky with the chubby intern. It's crazy."

"Not to me," Big Frankie said.

"Nick's right, Frankie." Angelo said. "Republicans trick people into voting for side issues while they take us to the cleaners on the big stuff."

"Side issues?" Big Frankie said.

"Yeah," Angelo explained. "Gun control, abortion, prayer in schools, gays getting married, keeping the words 'Under God' in the Pledge of Allegiance."

"Those things are important," Big Frankie said.

"Sure they are," Nick said. "And nobody's gonna do much about them, but the republicans get people like you all fired up about them to get your mind off the things like health care and social security. They'll whack the little guy every time."

Big Frankie shrugged. "I think Bush will do a better job with national security too. That Cheney guy seems to know his stuff. And Bush is gonna use Colin Powel too."

Nick was about to respond when Jimmy said, "It looks like they're going to announce the decision after these commercials."

Then Jimmy said to Nick, "I still wish I understood what they are deciding."

Nick sighed. "We've been through it a hundred times, but it boils down to this. It doesn't matter *what* they're deciding. What matters is *who* is deciding. The majority of the Supreme Court is republican. You can figure it out for yourself, but I think we're gonna get Dubya and his national security team."

76- I do, I do

December 15, 2000

It was after dark when Johnny arrived home, and he found it strange that Carrie's car was parked outside, but no lights were on in the townhouse.

They had set aside tonight to review the wedding guest list because Carrie wanted to mail the invitations for their March ceremony right after Christmas. She and Jenny had been talking and e-mailing almost every night, and plans were moving ahead nicely. Carrie's mom was going to come in February to be a part of the planning and help Carrie pick out a dress. In the meantime, the girls had developed a long checklist of things that needed to be done, and Johnny had agreed to set aside the evening to review it with her. He and Brian were grateful that both girls wanted a simple wedding and had opted to skip the traditional showers and bachelorette parties. The girls had even flown to Bristol together to meet with Father Morris again to attend to some details. Given their location, Father had agreed to allow them to complete an on-line version of the Pre Cana sessions required by the Catholic Church.

Johnny assumed Carrie was visiting one of the neighbors or taking a nap. Still, it wasn't like her not to leave any lights on. He parked the car and walked to the front door. It was unlocked. He walked in and flipped the light switch and was startled to see Carrie awake and sitting in an armchair. She barely flinched when she saw him.

"Hey, sweetie," Johnny said. "Cutting back on the electric?"

Carrie didn't respond. When he got closer, he noticed her eyes were puffy and her lap was filled with crumpled tissues. She seemed distant.

He knelt beside the chair and said, "What's wrong? Are you sick? You look like you've been crying."

She managed a barely audible, "Hi Johnny," but that was all.

He put his arm around her and said, "What the heck's going on? How long have you been sitting in the dark?"

She sniffled and said, "Dad called today."

Johnny's concern grew. "Did he call from Germany, or is he in the states?"

"Germany," Carrie mumbled.

"What did he say?" he asked gently.

She turned to him and said, "Mom's sick, Johnny. She's real sick." With that she began to sob and buried her head in his shoulder.

He held her and let her cry for a while before saying, "Tell me everything."

She straightened and said, "Mom found a lump on her breast three days ago."

Johnny's heart sagged.

"Naturally, it frightened her," Carrie said. "She went to the doctor immediately, and he performed a biopsy. They're still waiting for the full results, but at this point, the doctor is certain it's cancer." She shuddered at the word and then went on. "The doctor said additional tests will determine whether she'll need a lumpectomy or a full mastectomy. She's terrified."

Johnny's head was spinning and he was at a loss for words. He managed to say, "I'm so sorry."

Carrie looked at him and said faintly, "I know. Thank you."

Johnny took her hand and led her to the couch so they could sit together. She seemed more composed now, and Johnny asked, "How's you father taking this?"

"He's devastated. He's a scientist who's usually very matter-of-fact about things, but he was a mess. It was awful to hear him sound that way on the phone. I've never heard him like that before."

Johnny nodded. He tried to imagine hearing the same news about her, and the thought sent a chill through his body.

Carrie went on. "The good news is that she'd just had a mammography five months earlier that was negative. So the doctor is very optimistic.

But he also wants to follow an aggressive treatment protocol depending upon the lab results."

"Of course," Johnny said.

"She's going to need months of chemotherapy or radiation or both, depending…"

Johnny could see the whole picture.

"She's going to be sick from the treatments." With that Carrie broke down again, and Johnny rubbed her back while she cried.

Finally, she stiffened and looked at him. She looked awful and Johnny's heart ached for her. She said, "I have to go to her."

"Of course you do," Johnny replied.

"We have no family. I can't let her go through this alone."

"I agree," Johnny said.

"My father won't be able to handle this by himself."

Johnny nodded.

"I feel so guilty. They're my parents and I've been away from them for years."

"You have nothing to feel guilty about," Johnny said.

"I think deep inside I've been angry with them because of the life they've chosen and the impact it had on me. I mean I love them like crazy, but I think I've been angry with them too, and that makes me feel even guiltier."

"It's understandable, but you shouldn't feel that way," Johnny said again.

"Do you understand that I have to go?"

Johnny looked at her and said, "Of course I do. You've changed your whole life to accommodate mine. How can I not understand?"

"I'll probably be gone for months depending upon the treatment option."

"Then that's the way it will be," Johnny said tenderly. "You know I'd be gone for some of that time anyway. I'm already scheduled for a three week field exercise in January. We'll get through this, Carrie. Right now you should just worry about your parents"

Carrie said, "I suggested they come back to the states for the operation and treatment, but Dad said no for several reasons. They have a lot of confidence in Mom's doctor and the hospital associated with the university there. Dad has connections there, and she'll receive the highest care. He also doesn't think it would be best for her emotionally to be uprooted in the middle of all this. Plus, they can't just throw out their Radcliffe Street tenants on a moment's notice, so they'd be living in a strange environment."

"That all makes sense," Johnny said softly.

Carrie sobbed and said, "Mom was coming in a month to stay until the wedding. We were going to shop for a dress together and get caught up in what mothers and daughters are supposed to do with each other."

"And you will someday," Johnny said soothingly. "She'll get through this, you both will, and the two of you will be closer than ever."

Carrie said, "Based on the test results, the doctor's schedule and pre-surgery preparation, my dad said that whatever surgery they have to do won't happen for two weeks. That's how long I have to finish things up here, to talk to my professors and the editor at the paper."

Johnny nodded.

They both got quiet and after a long time Carrie said, "What in the world will we do about the wedding?

Johnny didn't know what to say. He started to speak, but Carrie went on.

"I can't do it without her. She always wanted a church wedding for me and was so excited about it. I can't have it without mom there. And I can't be here to get married when I should be with her."

Johnny didn't want to say the wrong thing, but it seemed like there was only one answer. He swallowed hard and said, "We'll just postpone the wedding a few months until your mom can enjoy it. We'll be fine."

"No!" Carrie said without hesitation. "I can't do that. We already postponed it once, and it was obviously bad luck. It was my fault because of my stupid Master's program and new job. We never should have done that."

Johnny shook his head. "First of all, nothing was your fault. We decided together. And second, your job and degree program are not stupid, and I had training commitments that were part of that decision."

"Still," Carrie said. "We shouldn't have done it."

Johnny decided to let that go and said as gently as he could, "So if we can't postpone it and can't have it without your mother, I'm not sure what to do. I'm also not sure what to do about Jenny and Brian." He thought for a minute and added, "This really is a mess."

Carrie was thinking too. They sat quietly, with his arm around her and her head on his shoulder. After a long time she said, "We have to tell Jenny and Brian to go ahead without us."

Johnny agreed. "It's only right."

It got quiet again until Carrie shot forward with an idea. "You and I will get married twice."

"Twice?"

"Yes!" She was animated now. "I don't want to wait any longer to be Mrs. Johnny Marzo, and I don't want my mom to miss planning and seeing a nice church wedding and reception."

"I got that part," Johnny said. "But I still don't get..."

Carrie interrupted. "We'll get married by a Judge now, before I leave for Europe, and we won't tell anyone. And when Mom is better we'll have a full church wedding with a reception." She seemed proud of herself, and Johnny was relieved to see her come out of her shell. "How's that idea?" she asked.

"Works for me," Johnny said.

77- By the Power Vested...

Carrie and Johnny briefly considered a military wedding at the Fort Bragg chapel, but Carrie wasn't in the frame of mind for it and opted instead for a simple civil ceremony at the Cumberland County Court House in Fayetteville. Johnny was relieved to learn that North Carolina had very relaxed marriage regulations. There were no residency or blood test requirements, and no waiting period. With fifty dollars cash and proper identification, a couple could obtain a marriage license and marry the same day.

Carrie had called Jenny to tell her everything that had happened, and the two shared a good cry. Jenny had graciously offered to postpone her wedding to Brian as well and knew Brian would feel the same way, but Carrie insisted she not do that. In the end, Jenny asked Carrie to delay the wedding for a couple of days until she and Brian could clear their schedules and fly down for the ceremony. Carrie was thrilled to have them present and asked if they would serve as Best Man and Maid of Honor.

Brian and Jenny arrived three days later, and Johnny and Carrie met them at the Fayetteville Airport. The jovial exchanges that characterized their past reunions were replaced by somber exchanges of sympathy and support for Carrie.

Johnny was in full dress uniform, complete with the Green Beret, and Brian and Jenny realized they had never seen him dressed like that before. Somehow the uniform added to the formality of their meeting.

They fell silent for a minute and then Carrie said, "Hey, this is my long-awaited wedding day. So let's all cheer up and go to the courthouse. Johnny made reservations at a nice place in town and we'll enjoy a pleasant dinner after the ceremony."

"Sounds wonderful," Jenny said.

"Are you sure you have to fly back tonight?" Johnny asked.

"Afraid so," Brian said. "I have a staff meeting first thing tomorrow. I had to shuffle some things to get today off; it's complicated."

"I understand, but we really appreciate all the trouble..." Johnny said.

"We wouldn't miss this," Brian replied.

They left the terminal and Jenny and Carrie walked arm in arm to the car. Jenny asked Carrie how she was feeling. "Pretty nervous," Carrie said. "This is all so different from what I always dreamed."

"I know what you mean," Jenny said. "Just keep in mind that being married to Johnny is the most important thing. As for the ceremony, the delay is temporary. You'll walk down that aisle some day, just as you always dreamed you would."

"I hope so. I'm so happy for you though," Carrie said brightly.

Jenny smiled and said, "So am I."

The day had a surreal quality to it. This was a group that wasn't accustomed to being subdued. They made small talk on the way to the courthouse, and everyone seemed nervous. They arrived at the front doors and entered the main hallway. It was a stately old building, but it had a bureaucratic feel to it that disappointed Carrie. They passed offices for the Water and Sewer Department, the Department of Licenses and Inspections, and the Animal Control Officer. They finally reached the Marriage License Bureau, and Carrie stepped to the window while the others hung back. An elderly woman with a pleasant face said, "May I help you?" The nameplate on her desk read, "Mrs. Emily Lyons."

"Yes," Carrie said nervously. "We have an appointment with Judge Barner for a three o'clock marriage ceremony."

Mrs. Lyons flashed a big smile. "Wonderful. Let me see. We have a few weddings this afternoon in different courtrooms." She scanned a list and said, "Yes. The Kelly-Ryan wedding?"

"No," Carrie said, "They're the Best Man and Maid of Honor. This is the Marzo-Boyle wedding."

The woman looked confused and checked the list again. Then her smile returned and she said, "Oh heavens, this is the double wedding. Marzo-Boyle and and Kelly-Ryan. This is so exciting. Is Mr. Ryan here?"

Now Carrie looked confused. Jenny stepped to the window behind her and said, "I hope you don't mind sharing your special day, but Brian and I are getting married too."

Carrie was stunned. She shot Johnny a look and he said, "I'm just as surprised as you are."

Brian grinned and said, "Mrs. Lyons and I spent a lot of time on the phone the past two days, and we're ready to go. She's been very helpful."

Carrie's eyes began to fill and she looked at Jenny. "You can't," she said. "It's not fair to you."

Jenny hugged her and said, "I could never be happy walking down that aisle in March knowing you should be there too. It wouldn't feel right."

Carrie shook her head and Jenny continued. "The invitations hadn't been sent out yet. So we talked to our parents and explained everything. They were disappointed, but they feel we're doing the right thing. Everything is fine."

"Then your parents should be here for your wedding," Carrie protested.

"We didn't tell them that part," Brian said. He checked his watch and said, "In a little over a half hour, we'll all be married and no one will know except the four of us, the judge, some people in the court room, and my new friend, Mrs. Lyons."

Mrs. Lyons gushed. "It all sounded so romantic that I asked Mr. Kelly if I could attend. In all my years here, I've never seen a double wedding."

Jenny said, "When the time is right we'll have that wedding at St. Theresa's for our family and friends, and we'll do it the right way with a priest. Until then, we'll be married, and that's the most important thing."

Carrie laughed and cried at the same time, and Johnny was thrilled to see her happy. Earlier, everything seemed cold and impersonal, but this surprise added something personal that was missing, and she seemed more like herself. Johnny grabbed Brian by the shoulder and said, "This is terrific, man, thanks."

There was an awkward silence for a while and then Brian said, "Hey, Jenny and I are getting married in a few minutes. Shouldn't you guys congratulate us?"

They all laughed and exchanged hugs and kisses.

"Your paperwork is in order," Mrs. Lyons said. "Please go down the hall to Courtroom 3 and Judge Barner will join you shortly." She winked at Brian and he said, "See you at the wedding and thanks again.

They walked down the dimly lit hallway arm in arm. Carrie still wished her marriage wouldn't be taking place in such a drab building, but her spirits were high. Brian opened the door to the court room, and the girls were stunned. The room was awash with floral arrangements, and the aisle that ran from the door to the railing was covered with a white runner. White bows were affixed to the railing. In the corner a musician sat behind a portable organ, and a woman who was obviously a soloist, stood by his side.

A smartly dressed woman stepped forward and said to the group, "Mr. Kelly?'

"That's me?" Brian said.

"I'm Judy Robinson. We spoke on the phone."

"Several times," Brian said smiling.

Judy panned the room and said, "I hope everything meets with your approval.

"Looks great," Brian said.

Judy retrieved two bouquets from a nearby table and gave them to Jenny and Carrie. "They're beautiful," Carrie said.

Jenny turned to Brian and said, "You did all of this?"

"Actually," My good friend, Mrs. Lyons, put me in touch with Judy and cleared everything with the judge."

Mrs. Lyons had entered the room and said in a conspiratorial tone, "This is highly unusual, but Judge Barner is a former Green Beret, and I talked him into it."

Judy Robinson said, "There is a trial in progress next door that will recess for the day at 3:00 o'clock. At that time the organist will begin playing."

Brian said to Jenny and Carrie, "I found the song list you guys had been working on, and I faxed it to Judy. I hope that's okay."

"This is so nice," Carrie said. Jenny agreed and gave Brian a hug.

Carrie draped her arm around Johnny's and said, "Okay, soldier boy, are you sure you still want me?"

"More than ever," Johnny said.

Judy Robinson reviewed the procedures of the ceremony with the couples and Judge Barner entered the courtroom. The introductions were made and the ceremony was set to begin. Johnny and Brian were positioned at the rail and Carrie and Jenny stood side by side in the aisle at the rear of the courtroom.

The organist began playing Pachelbel's Canon, and the girls started their walk down the aisle.

Mrs. Lyons stood at the back of the room and cried.

78- Make Time for God

January 2001

Carrie sat at the kitchen table of her parents' apartment, poured herself a glass of Riesling and opened her laptop to check her e-mail. Johnny's last letter was dated January 6, 2001. She had read it before and was hoping something more recent had been sent. She opened it and read it again.

Dear Carrie,

I just received word that our unit is shipping out within two hours, and by the time you receive this I will have already been deployed. It seems the field exercise I told you about has turned into the real thing. I would have phoned to tell you this, but it's 3 a.m. your time and I didn't think your family needed that type of disturbance.

As you know, I can't tell you where we're going, how long we'll be gone, or what we'll be doing when we get there. I can tell you that I promise to be careful. Remember that we spend countless hours training to do our jobs safely and effectively. You have so much to deal with right now without having to concern yourself about me, so please don't.

I was hoping to hear from you about your mother's most recent tests. I hope the news was encouraging. Write when you can. You know we can't correspond from the field, but I'll read your letters and reply as soon as I am able.

With all my love to you and your parents,

Johnny

Carrie took a sip of her wine and ran her fingers through her hair. Johnny was right; she did have a lot to worry about, but she certainly couldn't dismiss the concern she felt for him now. She tried to imagine where he'd been deployed. She watched the news every day, and as far as she could tell, there was no crisis brewing. The best she could hope for was that he was on a mission to train friendly forces in some God-forsaken place. At least that would be better than a combat assignment.

She hit reply on the screen and began to write.

Dear Johnny,

It was good to finally hear from you, and I'm not going to lie and say I'm not worried about you because I am. But I do take some comfort in knowing you are good at what you do. Besides, by the time you read this, you'll be safely home.

I have so much news to tell you, and it's a good emotional release for me to write it, even if you're not there to read it.

The news about mom is mixed. The doctor performed a lumpectomy, and did a frozen tissue biopsy. The cancer is definitely confirmed, but it hasn't spread significantly. Without getting too technical, I'll just say that her cancer is stage 1 and has not metastasized. The doctors are very confident that she'll make a full recovery, but she has a difficult road ahead of her. They estimate she'll need a month to fully recover from the surgery. During that time we'll meet with oncologists who will asses her overall physical condition and determine her regimen of radiation treatment. Once the radiation begins, it will last about two months. Everyone reacts differently, but doctors say we should expect her to be weak. She'll be busy with an assortment of blood tests and medical appointments along the way. But her overall health is good, so we can only pray that her road to recovery will not be too severe.

Both mom and dad's spirits are much better. I think having me here is part of the reason, but I think it's also because the health care professionals have been great. They've helped mom understand what she faces, and the explanation is much better than the fear of the unknown. They provide you with an Oncological Breast Help Navigator, a person who counsels us through all of the steps we'll go through and point us in the right direction. She's been wonderful. They tell me the program is copied from an approach the Americans take.

By the way, here's a warning. I'm glad I'm married to a Special Forces stud, because you and I will be running in every breast cancer marathon we can find. Jenny is going to run too. Of course she was a runner in high school, but she said she'll help me train. She hopes she can get Brian out from behind his desk to do the same. We'll see.

I miss you terribly, but I want you to know that I'm glad I'm here. Mom and I always had a nice relationship, but we are bonding now in a way we never did before. Helping her get through these times is easing the guilt I've felt from being away from her for so long.

Occasionally, I get the urge to shout to the world that I'm your wife, but I won't because I really want to have that special ceremony in front of my parents. I'm confident that day will come soon. In the meantime, they'll have to think we have the longest engagement in history.

On, another note, my professors at Fayetteville have been great. As you know, I was able to complete the semester before leaving and need only to complete my dissertation for my degree. My advisor has agreed to allow me to do my work by correspondence from here.

I want to continue my newspaper writing if I can, and my dad is working through an associate to land me an interview with an English language paper. I won't have time to do much, but writing an occasional article would be nice and add to my resume.

Jenny and I correspond often and she's been a Godsend. Speaking of God, I pray frequently. I know people wait until a crisis hits before they take the time to turn to God, but if there's anything positive to come out of this whole ordeal with mom it's that we've been reminded of the importance of our faith.

I've been e-mailing Father Morris at St. Theresa's, and he's been wonderful. He said it's very common for people our age to drift away from our habits of worship, and what's important is that we recapture the importance of them. He said young people feel they're invincible and that life will go on forever. He knows the hectic lives we all lead and understands. His suggestion is to work hard, play hard, but set aside time for God. Mom and I have been going to daily Mass, and it feels great. In a way it helps me to face the challenges and joys the day may hold.

Don't worry, I'm not planning to drag you to Mass every day, but I am saying that I hope we can make church a more important part of our relationship. I've been thinking about our visit to Mr. Lombardi's and the wonderful relationship he and his wife must have shared. I feel as though it wasn't a coincidence that he gave us those religious medals.

You and I have a good life together, Johnny. I hope we will always have a greater appreciation of the gifts God has given us and show our gratitude more often. I wear Mr. Lombardi's medal every day and hope you do too.

I love you and can't wait to 'barricade myself in a room with you again.'

Carrie

Carrie hit the send button, closed the laptop, and went into the living room to check on her mother.

79- Turkey anyone?

January 2001

Captain John Marzo sat on the matted floor across from his Kurdish counterpart, Bazi Abdoli. They were thirty miles north of the Iraqi border in Eastern Turkey, sharing a meal of roasted lamb smothered with a crushed cucumber and cream paste and served with flatbread. It was good, actually, and reminded Johnny of the Gyros he and Carrie liked to share on the boardwalk.

With them were Abdoli's aid, whom he introduced simply as Hewar, and Richard DiLeo, a CIA field agent assigned to accompany Johnny's A-Team. DiLeo was a long time veteran of Central Asia, with a specialty in Kurdistan. He spoke decent Kurmanji, a primary dialect of the people they'd be dealing with, but he also carried a duffle bag of American money to dispense for services rendered to the United States. His language skills weren't necessary because Bazi and Hewar spoke perfect English, but the cash would be crucial to the success of their discussions.

Johnny and his team had flown aboard a C-130 transport to Ramstein Air Force Base in Germany where they met up with DiLeo for another flight to the base at Incirlik in southern Turkey. From there they traveled east by helicopter and truck over two hundred miles of rugged terrain toward the current location.

The Kurds are fascinating people. They are the largest ethnic group in the world without a country to call their own. Their people span international borders and encompass sections of northern Iraq, eastern Turkey, eastern Syria, and northwestern Iran, all of which have brutally suppressed their Kurdish minorities throughout history. The most notable example is Saddam Hussein, who had resorted to using poison gas on them.

Following the 1991 Persian Gulf War, the United States helped establish the Kurdish portion of northern Iraq as a semi-autonomous region, and Kurds enjoyed a degree of freedom denied to people in other parts of Iraq. It was a situation Saddam wanted to change, and the United States wanted to preserve.

The Americans had worked with the Kurds for years, and Johnny and his team were deployed to eastern Turkey as part of an on-going program to continue their military relationship. Their mission was to meet with the tribal leader that Dileo provided; nurture the friendship the United States enjoyed with him; train Abdoli's men in combat techniques, the use of American weapons, and the latest electronic equipment; and form the groundwork for whatever services America might need in the future. Because the mission would take several months, the Pentagon and Langley liked the idea that another highly trained team of Americans would enjoy the benefit of being fully immersed in the language and culture of the region without having to tread on enemy territory.

Turkey was a NATO ally, and the work would take place there because training Kurds on Iraqi soil would create an international embarrassment if Americans were captured there. The assignment was compounded by the Turks' wariness of the Kurds who had a long-term goal to establish a Kurdish homeland partly on Turkish land. The United States had to convince its ally that the Kurds were being trained for a potential conflict with Saddam, not Turkey.

DiLeo had recruited Abdoli after a long and careful vetting process. They wanted someone they could trust, which wasn't an easy thing to predict. There were competing, and at times warring, political parties in Iraqi Kurdistan, notably the Patriotic Union of Kurdistan (PUK) and the Kurdistan Democratic Party (KDP), and while the United States cultivated relationships with both, it didn't fully trust the loyalty of either. Bazi Abdoli, on the other hand, was an independent tribal chief with a deep hatred for Saddam's regime, and an equally deep love of American dollars.

In order to blend in with the indigenous population, the Americans dressed in the traditional garb of rural Central Asian men, and they hadn't shaved since they were made aware of the mission while at Fort Bragg.

Captain Marzo scanned the spartan surrounding of Abdoli's tent and knew the money Dileo carried would mean a lot to him. The captain was handed a drink of cold water mixed with yogurt. It wasn't awful, but it wasn't as good as the lamb. "You are a gracious host, Bazi," Johnny said. "Our government is appreciative."

"The Americans are good friends of the Kurds," the tribal chief said. "It is our pleasure to help."

Johnny knew that Abdoli didn't mean that entirely. It was the Americans who had encouraged the Kurds to revolt against Saddam after he was driven back from Kuwait in 1991. In the eyes of the Kurds, the U.S. didn't do enough when Saddam used the poison gas on the insurgents. Americans took a different view, especially since United States Special Forces rescued tens of thousands of Kurds and led them to safety during Saddam's attack. Regardless, Kurdish hatred of Saddam far surpassed any resentment the Kurds held toward the United States.

"We realize you have considerable expenses in providing the men we need to train," Johnny added.

Abdoli nodded. "The men have families. They cannot work elsewhere when they are helping the Americans."

"My government understands that and wants to compensate you. Richard DiLeo has brought along a generous payment that I'm sure you will find satisfactory. The two of you will meet often, and he will explain other services his superiors need." DiLeo passed the bag to Hewar, who accepted it without looking at the contents.

Bazi Abdoli did not acknowledge the transfer and sat expressionless. Johnny continued. "Of course, additional payments are possible. You and Mr. Dileo will discuss the conditions of that later."

"There are great dangers to us if we're discovered cooperating with the Americans," Abdoli said. "But my men will do everything possible to assist."

Johnny said. "As you know, we've brought weapons and equipment for you and your soldiers."

Abdoli smiled and said, "Which we will gladly use against Saddam if the opportunity presents itself."

Johnny continued. "If all goes well, we'll be here at least until the spring. We'll camp in the countryside and your men can join us."

"It will be good," Abdoli said.

Johnny thought of the terrain his team had just traveled and imagined living there for the next four months. He nodded and took the warlord's extended hand.

80- Going Home

March 2001

Carrie opened her laptop and checked her e-mail. There were messages from Jenny, Brian, her academic advisor, the editor of the newspaper she'd been working for, and some on-line catalogues advertising sales, but there was nothing from Johnny. She read the messages from Jenny and Brian first, hoping they had some news, but they didn't. She'd been tempted to ask Brian to pull some strings to inquire about Johnny's status, but she didn't. She knew that if there was something Brian could do he would offer. She decided to ignore the other messages, clicked the compose button instead, and began to write.

Dear Johnny,

It's been more than two months since I've heard from you, and I pray that you are well. I know you're not permitted to communicate when you're in the field, and I tell myself that if something were wrong I would know by now. I pray every day for your safety, and I try not to let my imagination run wild about what you're doing.

I keep writing in the hope that somehow you'll have the opportunity to check your messages. You'll notice that I try to keep the letters short and limit them to once a week so you won't be overwhelmed when you finally open them.

I'll limit this message to four quick pieces of news arranged from least to most important: First, I'm writing articles for a local English language newspaper and enjoying it very much. The topics are still shallow, but it gives me something to do. Second, my advisor in North Carolina likes my dissertation, and I should receive my Masters in Journalism by May. Now for the real important stuff: Mom is responding well to the radiation. There have been virtually no side effects, and her interim blood tests, especially a test called a CEA, have been good. She finishes her regimen in two weeks, and the doctor is optimistic about her progress.

Mom and I are closer than ever. When she feels up to it ,we go to the theater, visit museums, enjoy lunches at fancy restaurants, and take long, leisurely walks. We certainly have tons of things to talk about. During one of our outings we had a good cry over the time we've been apart from each other. Now here's the kicker: when all of this is over, my parents are moving back to the United States!

This came totally from left field. Mom told Dad a week ago that she had wanted to move back for some time but didn't want to tell him because she knew he loved his work here. He said he would be happy to move back and thought it was she who wanted to stay because she loved Europe so much. Anyway, the lease on the Radcliffe Street house expires in April, and Dad told the realtor to inform the tenants it wouldn't be renewed. The tenants asked for a three month extension and my parents agreed. Dad's work will be finished by then, and we'll be moving back to Bristol in August! Mom's doctor sees no problem with it. In fact he has a good friend at the Department of Oncology at Thomas Jefferson University Hospital in Philadelphia and has already made arrangements for Mom to transfer her care there.

I guess something good has come of this after all. I'm so excited.

All my love,
Carrie

81- Two Plus What Equals Four?

August 15, 2001

Brian and Dr. Blake sat in a small conference room in the CIA Building drinking coffee. Brian said, "I'm canceling my vacation next month."

"If you do, you're fired," Blake said. "You're a mess. You work harder than anyone on the team, and sometimes it takes a toll. You need your batteries recharged. Take a vacation, or find another job."

Brian ignored him. "This increase in terrorist chatter is troubling." For two weeks the CIA had monitored a spike of coded transmissions believed to be linked to al-Qaeda that suggested a planned hijacking or hijackings. Then the chatter stopped just as quickly as it started."

Blake took a bite of his sticky bun and said, "It's more than troubling; it's terrifying."

Brian said, "Remember the report we read, the one that was written back in the mid 1990s? It said we should consider the danger of planes being used as missiles? Remember those guys in Algeria who wanted to hijack a plane and fly it into the Eiffel Tower? And remember when Ramsi Yousef was captured? He boasted of a plan to fly a jetliner into this very building and the Pentagon. And then there was …"

Blake interrupted. "I know all that, Brian. That's what makes this latest red flag very important."

"And that's why I'm not going on vacation," Brian retorted. "We need to find out what's going on."

"We're on top of this as much as we can be. The director assures me this will be part of the President's daily briefing, if not tomorrow, then the next day. We're going to throw everything we can at this. "

Brian knew Blake was right about a vacation, but he still felt uneasy taking time off. "We need to step up surveillance on incoming flights, ask the countries of origin to step up security."

Blake nodded. "I'd like to do that, but you know as well as I that we need more to go on. We can't cry wolf too often or the other countries will lose interest."

"What if it's not an incoming flight?" Brian said. "What if it's a domestic flight?"

"That would increase the problem exponentially," Blake said.

"I wonder what the FBI is doing. We should talk more."

Blake agreed. "I've been assured that we'll pass our concerns directly to them."

"And what about them? Brian asked. "Do they pass their information to us?"

Blake exhaled deeply and said, "Yes." Then he amended it to "usually," and finally settled on "Let's hope so."

"Our two groups don't communicate as much as they should," Brian repeated.

Blake was growing weary and raised his voice, "Do me a favor today, Brian. Tell me something I don't know, okay? We can't change the whole damn bureaucracy by ourselves."

Brian felt officially chided and replied, "Sorry, boss."

Blake took another bite of his bun and washed it down with a sip of coffee. Brian studied his mentor for a while. He admired the gruff old man and knew Blake was doing everything he could. He always did. Brian said, "I guess I could use a little time off."

Blake pointed a finger at him. "You're outta here on the Friday of Labor Day Weekend, and I don't want to see you again until mid September. Two weeks. Take them or you're fired. I mean it."

"You win," Brian said. "Actually, this could be good. A friend is moving back to the states in a week. You've heard me talk about my Special Forces buddy, Captain Marzo."

Blake nodded.

"It's his wife, or I should say fiancé, who's moving back. He recently returned from a long overseas mission and has some leave time coming. He's saving it for when she gets here. Maybe Jenny and I will drive up to Bristol to visit them. Maybe we'll all go to the Jersey shore."

"There you go, Brian. Sounds like just what you need."

Brian smiled and said, "Yeah, maybe so." Then he added, "What about you, Doc? I think you could use a little R and R."

"Soon as you get back," Blake said. "I'm taking the next two weeks. I hope things are quiet by then."

82- The Park Bench

Johnny had landed in Philadelphia from Fayetteville that morning and took the train to Bristol. The town looked better than ever to him, especially after his months in Turkish Kurdistan.

He left Central Asia in May, returned to Fort Bragg and underwent a month of debriefing and additional training. Knowing Carrie would be coming to the states in August, he remained at Bragg for the summer and deferred his block leave until now. He wasn't due home for a few days, but he decided to surprise Carrie with an early appearance. He'd surprise his parents and the guys at the deli too, but a long visit would have to wait. He needed to see Carrie.

He walked home again, following the same route as before, and entered the deli to the same fanfare. The whole gang was there, as they were every day, and Johnny felt great seeing them. He couldn't leave without eating, so he agreed to sit for a while. Finally, after they'd eaten, he said to his mother, "Well, if you don't mind, there's a certain lady I need to see."

"I guess you do," his mother said. "And you better marry her while you're at it. She visited a few times since they moved back. Her mother is doing very well."

"I know," Johnny said. "I spoke with Carrie this morning, but she still doesn't know I'm coming."

"I like it," Nick said. "Surprises are good."

"Not always," Jimmy said. "How about that time somebody keyed my truck? Put a long scratch in it. That was a surprise but…"

"Shut up, Jimmy." Big Frankie said.

Johnny was still in uniform as he walked down Radcliffe Street to Carrie's home. His heart beat a little faster as he approached her porch. He hadn't seen her in eight long months. He remembered calculating once how much they'd been apart in the five years since they graduated from college. It more than tripled the time they'd been together. Theirs was certainly an improbable relationship. But just as Carrie had predicted, it was one in which every moment together was precious and neither took anything for granted.

Johnny knocked, and Mr. Boyle came to the door. He greeted him with a broad smile and warm handshake.

"Welcome home," Mr. Boyle said. "We didn't expect you until…"

"Welcome home to you, sir. It's good to see you."

Mr. Boyle shook his head and said wistfully, "We should have done it a long time ago."

Boyle invited him in, and Johnny inquired about Mrs. Boyle. "She's great," Mr. Boyle said. "She's a little tired now because the radiation has a cumulative effect. She's upstairs napping. But she's coming around, and the doctors are pleased."

"That's wonderful," Johnny said. "It must be such a relief."

"We're very fortunate," Mr. Boyle said. Then he said, "I could offer you something, but I suppose you'd like to see Carrie."

"It crossed my mind,' Johnny replied.

"She's at the Grundy Library. She's working on an article and has taken to writing drafts while sitting outside on the benches by the river. You'll find her there."

Johnny thanked him and left.

The library was a beautiful facility down the street from Carrie's house. It was situated on the Delaware River and had a rear glass wall that offered a full view of the water. Outside was a peaceful park area with benches and lighting that faced Burlington Island, New Jersey. The river was narrow there, and the island was less than 200 yards away.

Johnny saw Carrie sitting on one of the benches with her back to him. She had a yellow legal pad on her lap, but her attention was drawn to the river. Johnny walked up behind her as quietly as he could and said softly, "I used to sit here with my girlfriend when we were in high school."

Startled, she turned, and he said, "I'd walk her home, and we'd stop here to do our homework."

Carrie's jaw dropped, and she brought her hands to her mouth. She stood to face him, and Johnny went on. "We didn't do much homework though. We'd just sit here and talk for hours."

She smiled and her eyes began to fill.

"She looked a lot like you," Johnny said.

Carrie managed to say, "You look a lot like a boy I knew back then too. Only you're more handsome."

Johnny smiled. "We didn't have a care in the world. We talked about everything under the sun, but mostly, we talked about being together forever."

"We are," Carrie said tearfully.

They were still separated by the bench, with him behind it, and Carrie dropped her pad and stood on the seat to face him. She was taller now and she bent awkwardly to kiss him. They laughed at the attempt, and he put his arm behind her back, grasped her legs with his other arm and gently lifted her over the bench. She felt like a feather as he cradled her in his arms. He held her there, and she draped her arms around his neck kissed him.

An older woman three benches down stopped her knitting to take in the scene of the handsome, uniformed solider, smartly dressed and wearing a Green Beret, kissing the happy, pretty girl. She had the urge to clap or take a picture. But she just smiled and watched instead.

83- Long Beach Island, NJ

September 6, 2001

They met at Buckalew's Tavern at the intersection of Bay Avenue and Center Street in Beach Haven on Long Beach Island. "This is terrific," Jenny said. "The Labor Day crowd has cleared out. It's almost like we have the shore to ourselves." "September is the best month at LBI," Brian said. "Warm days, cool nights, water temp in the low 70s..." "And the bars and restaurants are still open," Johnny added. Brian went to the bar and returned with drinks for everyone. Carrie offered a toast, "To a wonderful two weeks." They drank and Jenny said, "I hope I can keep Brian pinned down for that long." Carrie looked at Johnny and Brian and said, "God knows you two deserve a long vacation." "And what about you," Jenny said to Carrie, "After what you've been through." "It was all worth it," Carrie said smiling. "Things are so good now. Mom's in good shape, and my parents are living back in Bristol." She motioned to Johnny and said, "I hated to be away from this guy, but it turns out he was gone anyway." Johnny nodded. "We had a four month golf outing at Pebble Beach. It was nice." Brian jumped in. "See, Carrie, and you were worried. I told you he was fine." Carrie smiled and said, "He is now, and that's what counts."Brian put his arm around Jenny and said, "Speaking of earning a break, I just want to say in front of everyone how much I appreciate the crap that Jenny puts up with from me. You guys only see the lovable side of me." Then he winked and added, "And I know there is a lot about me to love."The girls booed and Johnny said, "He's so humble!" Brian put his hand up for quiet and said, "Come on. I'm trying to be serious here." They quieted down and Brian went on. "I know you all think I'm wonderful, and I do too, but Jenny gets to see another side of me when I come home from work, and believe me, sometimes it isn't pretty."

Jenny shrugged and said, "I understand, and it's fine. Sometimes I wish you worked in a shoe store or something, but I love you for what you do." Johnny said, "Careful for what you wish for, Jenny. Working in a shoe store has its benefits." "Really?" Carrie asked. "Like what?" "Like checking out the legs of every female customer, and maybe tickling the feet of the really nice ones." Carrie slapped him on the arm and Johnny said, "I'm serious. I bet Brian could pick up more girls working at a shoe store than he could telling girls in a bar that he works for the CIA." Carrie smiled and said, "Can I remind you guys that you're married. There won't be any need for pick up lines." "There never was a need," Johnny said. "Girls used to pick us up. Right, Brian?" "It was terrible," Brian said. "We never had any peace." Jenny laughed and said sarcastically, "Carrie and I are soooo very, very fortunate to have two awesome studs like you. Aren't we, Carrie?" "We're blessed," Carrie said.

Jenny added, "Speaking of being married, now that things are back to normal, Carrie and I are thinking about visiting Father Morris to plan that wedding we never had." "I think that would be great," Johnny said and Brian agreed. "Our parents will be thrilled," Carrie said happily. Brian said, "Since we tend to do things differently, let's make this our honeymoon." He took a stack of brochures from his pocket and tossed them on the table. "We have parasailing, deep sea fishing, spas, happy hours, bicycle rentals, sailing lessons, hundreds of restaurants. Where should we start?" Their waitress arrived wearing a big smile and said, "My name's Julie, and I'll be your server. Did you guys just arrive?"

"This afternoon," Jenny said. "We're here for two weeks." "Terrific!" Julie said. "Why not begin your week with a nice dinner?"

84- Before we get started

September 7, 2001

They had an early breakfast on Wednesday and piled into the SUV for the trip to the parasailing site on the bay. They had a ten a.m. reservation, and Carrie asked that they leave by 8:45 because she had a surprise stop she wanted them to make first.

They drove five miles north in the direction of the causeway when Carrie said, "Slow down Brian, the turn is just head on the left."

"Where?" Brian said. "I don't see any streets."

"Right there," Carrie said, pointing to her left. "The parking lot."

The sign read SAINT FRANCIS OF ASSISI CATHOLIC CHURCH, and Brian looked confused, but he turned and parked. Everyone looked at Carrie.

She smiled sheepishly and said, "We've been through some difficult times."

They nodded but remained silent.

"And when we get together we party hard and have a great time."

"That's for sure," Brian said.

"There's a daily Mass here at nine a.m. I saw it in the newspaper. I just think it would be nice if we begin our vacation by taking some time to catch our breaths and say thanks for what we have together. Do you mind? We don't have to if ..."

"I think it's a great idea," Jenny interrupted.

"Me too," Brian said. "I have to admit it's not how I'd plan to begin my vacation, but I think it's real nice."

"Especially since we're going parasailing later," Johnny joked. "I hear it's dangerous and I'm afraid of heights."

Brian laughed and said, "Hey, big guy, you're a paratrooper, remember?"

85- September 11

September 11, 2001

Dr. Blake was seated at his computer consol when it was first reported that an aircraft had struck the North Tower of the World Trade Center at 8:44 that morning. The early speculation was that the accident involved a small private plane and was probably the result of pilot error. But Dr. Blake knew instinctively that this was a terrorist attack, and a sick feeling permeated his body. He thought of the FBI report he had seen on Zacarias Moussaoui, a man who had come to the Bureau's attention when he enrolled for flying lessons and was acting oddly. Blake had also read FBI reports about the boasts of captured terrorist Ramzi Yousef that al-Qaeda would crash hijacked planes into American buildings one day.

Blake broke into a cold sweat as he searched his consol for information. Soon there was a live video feed of the North Tower. By then it was confirmed that the plane had been a commercial liner, and Blake watched in horror as the upper floors of the building burned. When a second plane hit the South Tower at 9:03, Blake bent over and vomited into his trashcan. He wiped his mouth with his handkerchief and searched his cubicle for water. He rinsed his mouth and spit into the can.

Questions swirled in his mind. How many more planes were there? Have we grounded all aircraft? Have we scrambled fighter jets? Should we authorize American pilots to fire on hijacked planes filled with innocent people? He worked the phones and monitored his e-mail until he received word that a third hijacked aircraft had struck the Pentagon at 9:37. Within minutes the FAA grounded all commercial aircraft and ordered all flights in progress to land at the closest airport. Foreign flights headed to the United States were diverted to other locations. Soon the President authorized the military to shoot down any additional hijacked planes it encountered.

The atmosphere at CIA headquarters could best be described as bedlam. There were unsubstantiated reports of other unidentified aircraft approaching Washington with the White House, the Capitol

Building, the State Department, and CIA headquarters as possible targets.

Blake felt helpless. The CIA wasn't structured as a rapid response organization. It was an organization that gathered information over time, analyzed it and made long range plans. It was almost powerless to do anything in real time. Blake began to monitor transmissions regarding who might be responsible for the attack. He felt this was foolish, of course, because he had no doubt that it was Osama bin Laden. Nevertheless, he did what he was trained to do in the hope that he would uncover something useful.

At 9:59 the South Tower collapsed, and Blake pounded his fist on his desk so hard that his coffee spilled. Four minutes later still another commercial airliner crashed in Western Pennsylvania. Soon it was announced that CIA Director George Tenet had ordered the building evacuated, but Blake refused to leave. Eventually, the head of the Counter-Terrorism Center and Blake's direct superior convinced Tenet it was vital that certain units of personnel remain to monitor information from human assets around the world, information that could provide a clue to more attacks.

Shortly before 10:30 the North Tower collapsed, breaking the hearts of Americans even further and blanketing Lower Manhattan with a gray-white dust. At CIA headquarters, after the initial shock of the attack subsided, the brief state of bedlam it had created was replaced by an eerie calm, and workers went about their duties with a deep seeded anger, but a strong sense of professionalism. They had a job to do.

At 10:45 Dr. Blake finally had a chance to take a breath. He drank some water, splashed some on his hands to rub on his face, and dried his fingers in the hair. Then he reached for his phone and dialed Brian's cell number.

In Bristol, Mickey sat in stunned disbelief as he and the other firefighters of Goodwill Hose Company Number 3 watched CNN's coverage of the tragedy. It had been said that over four hundred firefighters had converged on the World Trade Center after the planes struck. Now, commentators reported in subdued tones that there were hundreds of first responders either inside or in the vicinity when the South Tower fell. Mickey's fellow firefighters cursed. Some thrashed about the room, punching walls and kicking furniture. Some left to be with their families. An assistant chief cried openly.

Across town, in Angelo Marzo's Deli, Donna watched the scenes unfold like a low budget disaster movie with a terribly improbable script. She knew the men around her were ranting, crying and carrying on, but she tuned them out. Like so many mothers across America, she grieved for the victims and their families and was terrified over what the implications of the attack would mean for her son.

Johnny, Brian, and the girls rose early, finished breakfast, and drove toward Holgate on the southern tip of Long Beach Island in search of the wildlife refuge located there. Its brochure boasted of a two and one-half mile stretch of beach and marshland rich in exotic animal, plant and marine life.

They left their towels, beach bags, and coolers on the beach near the park entrance and set off on a long morning walk, armed with nothing more than binoculars and maps of the refuge. It was a beautiful spot, where the ocean and inlet converged. Johnny and Brian weren't much in the way of nature lovers, but even they were fascinated by what they saw. The area was virtually deserted, and the couples enjoyed the solitude.

At eleven o'clock Johnny said, "If I wanted to hike for hours, I would have stayed at Fort Bragg. Let's head back for a swim."

They walked back to the spot where they'd left their things and began to strip down to their bathing suits when Carrie said, "Did anyone bring a cell phone? I'd like to check on my mom."

"Sure," Brian said. "I have mine." He fished in his bag until he found it. Flipped it open and froze.

86- "What works best for me is…"

They sped back to their shore house and threw their things in their bags as CNN replayed the horrific images of the planes hitting and the towers coming down. They saw the films of ghost-like figures walking the streets covered with gray-white dust. They heard a senator from the intelligence committee say he wasn't surprised by the attack, but he was surprised by the nature and extent of it. That about summed it up, Brian thought. The intelligence community knew of the possibility but didn't know when, where or how. Of course, they had a pretty good idea about who planned it.

The girls were barely able to move as Brian and Johnny led them to the SUV. Soon they were on the causeway leaving the island, and traffic slowed as other vacationers joined the exodus. It seemed that everyone needed to be someplace else once they heard of the disaster. They tuned to KYW News Radio and began the drive.

Brian's thoughts were reeling. Blake had sounded shaken in his message, and service was down when Brian tried to return his call. Blake had said to get back as quickly as possible, as if Brian needed that encouragement, and he added that all flights were grounded.

Brian said to everyone, "I think our only choice is to drive to Bristol and drop off the girls. It's on the way." He looked at Jenny and said, "There's no way you're going to Washington. It's not safe." Then he turned to Johnny and said, "Should we try to get you a ride on a military transport flying out of McGuire or what?"

Johnny shook his head. "Can't risk the wait. I don't know what will be flying when."

"Then we'll drive to Washington, and you can take my car on to Fort Bragg."

Johnny nodded and checked his watch. "That should get me there by midnight." He visualized the scene at Fort Bragg as personnel raced to report to their units. Things would be hopping. He tried his cell phone, but the system was still overloaded.

They drove in silence through the Jersey Pine Barrens with everyone lost in their thoughts. Each had a pretty good understanding of what this would do to their lives for the foreseeable future. Brian thought about Blake's phone message. Blake had said that they did their best within the system to protect the country. He said everyone did. He told Brian there was no time for second guessing. He should report to work prepared to be productive. Brian knew he was right. Carrie wanted to hold on to Johnny, but the look on his face told her the time wasn't right. He was transforming into someone different right before her eyes. She took out a yellow pad and began to write. Jenny sensed a migraine coming and slumped down in her seat and closed her eyes. Johnny looked at Carrie and remembered a conversation he'd once had with one of his training sergeants. Johnny had asked the sergeant how to deal with thoughts of loved ones when going into combat. The sergeant replied that thinking about loved ones in a war zone was a very bad idea. It made a soldier tentative; it slowed his reactions and could get him killed. The sergeant went on to say, "What works best for me is, when I go into combat, I tell myself that I'm already dead. It helps."

87- The Northern Alliance

Dr. Blake, Brian, and other members of Blake's team huddled around a television monitor as President Bush addressed grieving and angry rescue workers at New York's Ground Zero. He was standing on a pile of rubble next to a fireman and was using a small megaphone. When a worker in the crowd called out, "We can't hear you," Bush replied, "I can hear you, the rest of the world can hear you and the people who knocked these buildings down will hear all of us soon."

Hopefully that was true, Blake thought. Amid all the grief, a profound sense of anger was swelling in the American people as they watched firemen and other workers sift through the rubble, day after day, looking for survivors or human remains. While driving in that morning, Blake saw a large white sheet hanging from an overpass. Painted on it in uneven lettering was the message, "Hit someone, Mr. President- Hard!" There were isolated reports of Americans mistreating not only Muslims, but anyone from central or southern Asia who looked different. The mood of the nation was ugly.

The CIA had been working feverishly to provide the President and his cabinet with the information they needed to formulate an appropriate response. There was little doubt that Osama bin Laden had masterminded and funded the attack and that his al-Qaeda network was firmly entrenched in Afghanistan. There was also no question that the Taliban who ran Afghanistan were protective of al-Qaeda. Any attempt to go after al-Qaeda and bin-Laden would require an all-out effort to overthrow the ruling faction in Afghanistan as well.

The task would be difficult. The Soviets had fought a protracted war there that ended in a Soviet defeat. That war had come to be regarded as Russia's Vietnam.

Fortunately, not all Afghan people supported the Taliban. The Northern Alliance was a loose coalition of warlords who often feuded among themselves. But they hated the Taliban and could, if the price was right, be united to fight against them. The CIA had been formulating a contingency plan long before 9-11 that would utilize the Northern Alliance as the main ground force in a war against the Taliban, assisted by American Special Forces teams and massive American bombing.

It was the plan being sold to the President now. It would require covert CIA paramilitary teams to be dropped into Afghanistan to meet with the various Northern Alliance leaders, pay them large sums of money, and assure them of massive American air support if they moved against the Taliban.

Brian knew that if the plan was approved, Johnny's Special Forces team would be sent to Central Asia to fight side by side with the Northern Alliance and direct air strikes against the Taliban. It was what he'd been trained to do.

88- Remembering

October 14, 2001

The CIA's courtship of the Northern Alliance worked, and a war plan was put into effect. In the first phase, the United States would initiate a bombing campaign to soften Taliban placements around the cities of Kabul, Jalalabad, and Kandahar. In the next phase, positions in the countryside would be bombed. Finally, the Northern Alliance would launch its ground assault against the enemy's weakened defenses.

American Special Forces would be crucial to the Northern Alliance's success. They would be at the front lines using lasers and other equipment to provide target information and coordinates to the American command and control centers.

The bombing began a week earlier, on October 7, and now it was time for Captain Marzo's team to join the ground action. They sat on the tarmac in Tashkent, Uzbekistan, waiting to begin the first leg of their flight to Afghanistan. Unlike their training assignment in Turkey, this would be a combat mission, and Marzo knew the men would perform well. Instead of the typical Hollywood rah-rah atmosphere, the men conveyed a sense of quiet professionalism. Each man's specialty would be vital to the mission's success, especially the communications experts who would guide the air assault by painting the targets.

He thought about the Afghanistan fact sheet they had studied. The country was the size of Texas and had a population of thirty-three million, facts that would make it difficult to control once it was defeated. Eighty percent of its people were farmers, and yet it was a barren place, with less than twelve percent arable land. Afghanistan's per capita domestic product was only one-thousand dollars and Afghans had a life expectancy of just forty-four years.

Most Afghans were Sunni Muslims, but twenty percent were Shia. The largest ethnic groups were Pashtun and Tajik, and the official languages were Dari and Pashto. While Johnny's Arabic training would be helpful in this cross cultural environment, he would rely heavily on the six team members who had training in the indigenous languages.

In short, Afghanistan offered a convergence of cultures in a most inhospitable place, with a harsh, unforgiving climate that produced bone chilling winters and scorching summers. It was where Captain John Marzo and his team would be for the next few months until the Taliban was overthrown, al-Qaeda was crushed, and Osama bin-Laden was killed or captured.

Captain Marzo looked at Rip Duncan sitting next to him. As the A-Team's Warrant Officer, Master Sergeant Duncan was an essential asset to his much younger Captain, and the two men had developed a strong bond. With eighteen years under his belt, Duncan was the most experienced member of the team. He had the answers to Marzo's questions before Marzo asked them, and he enjoyed the Captain's complete confidence.

Duncan was a man of few words, but at one point he leaned toward Johnny Marzo and said, "That was quite a film you showed, Captain."

"I thought so," Marzo replied.

Prior to shipping out, Marzo had received a videotape from Brian and a short message that read, "You and your men may find this useful. Be safe and get the job done."

Johnny had reviewed the tape expecting to see more footage of the towers falling and engulfing Lower Manhattan in smoke and soot. What he saw instead was far more disturbing. It was footage the networks had shied away from out of respect for the victim's families. It showed the upper floor windows of the trade center, the floors immediately above where the planes had struck. Gradually, people emerged at those windows, people who were trapped by the rising flames and noxious flumes below them.

He watched in horror as some made the dreadful decision to jump to avoid the inevitable fate that awaited them if they remained. One by one they leaped from the building. The figures looked tiny in the distance, and the scene seemed surreal as they tumbled silently, with arms outstretched, to the street hundreds of feet below.

Johnny was sickened by the sight. He stared at the blank screen and began to tremble. He tried to imagine the anguish the victims must have felt sitting at the windows, knowing they would die, and deciding what form their death would take. He considered the final thoughts they must have had about their families. He considered the sheer terror they surely felt, and a renewed anger swelled inside him. He recalled a photo he had seen of people evacuating the towers while firefighters climbed the stairs shortly before the building collapsed. He concluded the obvious, just as Brian must have concluded, that this was the real message of 9-11. It was not the catastrophic destruction of the buildings, or the impersonal realization that many had died, but the very personal consideration of the horrific manner in which *individuals* had died, innocent workers and brave first responders.

He decided to show the video to the team. He assembled the men in front of a small television at the airbase and delivered a brief statement. "I know you don't need any additional motivation for this mission. In fact, as Special Forces, you don't need additional motivation for any deployment. But I want to show you this video anyway."

He inserted the tape and pushed play. The men watched in silence. The segment lasted less than five minutes. No one spoke when it was over. No one had to.

89- The Taliban Compound

Relying upon Afghan intelligence reports and drone aircraft photos, Captain Marzo's team was deployed to a village compound believed to be housing Taliban leaders. They were to assess the feasibility of a "strike and snatch," or direct the destruction of the compound by aerial attack if a ground assault was deemed impossible.

The compound was set back in a wide horseshoe-shaped ravine bordered by sixty-foot ridges on three sides. From a distance, the mud-brick buildings were barely discernable against the tan, almost colorless backdrop of the rugged landscape. It was mid afternoon, and Marzo had his team spread in a broad arc as they inched toward the compound.

At one-hundred yards, Marzo knelt behind a rock formation and Rip Duncan squatted by his side. Both men had their field glasses focused on the compound, and both were on edge. From this distance it would be a snap to paint the target for an air strike and obliterate the camp. But nothing was that easy. Central Command wanted to ensure there were no civilians in the area before ordering an air strike, and they didn't want to rule out a possible abduction of Taliban leaders too quickly.

Captain Marzo knew that Afghan intelligence had often been unreliable, or worse, untrustworthy. There was a good chance that no Taliban leaders of value would be present. Beyond that, there was also the remote possibility that the informants had been compromised, and the A-Team could walk into an ambush. After surveying the landscape, Marzo felt that neither prospect warranted a dangerous assault under such difficult tactical conditions. It was his assessment that putting his men into that horseshoe could be lethal.

Besides, the possibility of taking live prisoners was unlikely. Taliban and al-Qaeda were fierce soldiers who earned the reputation of fighting to the death. There were even reports of al-Qaeda fighters killing themselves with hand-grenades when capture seemed imminent.

"I'm not feeling real good about this setup, Captain," Duncan said. He never shied away from a well-planned fight, but he wasn't a cowboy either. Marzo trusted Duncan's tactical judgment, and he knew his warrant officer was right.

"Niether am I," Marzo said. "There's too much open space between us and the compound." He scanned the ridge lines fifty yards away that flanked him on either side and added, "Those ridges could expose us to serious cross fire if we got any closer. We're not going in there without air support."

Duncan nodded. "Good call."

Marzo looked to Bill Keen, his communications specialist, and said, "Get me headquarters." Then he said to Duncan, "I'm telling them we're staying put today. We'll keep an eye on who moves around in the compound. If we don't see any women or kids by morning, we'll request an air strike. If we kill some valuable leaders, then so be it. Maybe we'll nail bin-Laden and get an interview on CNN."

Duncan smiled. "Every soldier's dream."

"Getting on CNN?" Marzo asked.

"Hell no, Captain. Nailing bin-Laden."

Marzo shook his head and said, "I was only kidding. I'll bet bin-Laden took off as soon as the towers fell and that he's long gone. But we'll see. If he's in that compound, his ass will be dead tomorrow morning, and his DNA will be at the lab by lunchtime. In the meantime, spread the men out and get two teams of three up into those ridges to protect our flanks."

Duncan nodded and started to move when the first sniper shot caught Sergeant Keen in the chest and knocked him back. Then all hell broke loose as the ravine erupted with gun fire and RPG explosions. Duncan pulled the injured Keen closer to the rock formation while Captain Marzo screamed for his men to dig in. Intense fire was coming from both ridges and the compound directly ahead. It was obvious they had been lured into a trap, and judging by the amount of fire they were heavily outnumbered.

The Green Berets reacted quickly, returning fire in three directions. Keen's injury looked bad, and Duncan was calling for a medic. Soon Sergeant Ralph Mazilli came crawling toward them amid a hail of machinegun fire. Bullets were landing everywhere, kicking up dust, and spraying chips of rock on the crouching soldiers.

While Mazilli tended to Keen, Marzo reached for Keen's radio and got Ricky Bond. Bond was the team's other communications specialist and was positioned at the far end of the team's line, about fifty yards from Marzo. "We need to back out of here," Marzo yelled. "Radio our location and then begin pulling back. Once we get some space between us and the bad guys, I'll call in an air strike."

The men prepared for a controlled withdrawal, and then Marzo's heart sank as they started receiving fire from the rear. The enemy had slipped in behind the team and now had them completely surrounded. The battle intensified as the Americans formed two small perimeters and returned fire. Mortars fell dangerously close, kicking up more dust and sending shards of rock into the side of Captain Marzo's face.

Duncan was returning fire while Mazilli applied pressure to Keen's wound. Captain Marzo used the radio again to report their situation and call for air support. Help was on the way, he was assured, but it would be at least twenty minutes before Apache gun ships could arrive. Marzo directed the approaching air power to the compound and the ridges. The enemy in the rear was too close. An attempted strike there could kill more Americans than Taliban.

Twenty-minutes, Marzo thought. He hoped the team's defenses would last that long. He reached inside his shirt and briefly touched the Sacred Heart medal Mr. Lombardi had given him. Then he returned his attention to the battle.

Sergeant Bond was back on the radio reporting that Tim Dickson, one of the team's demolition experts, had also been wounded. That made two causalities on the fourteen man team.

The rear attack picked up in intensity with some Taliban fighters positioned less than forty yards away. Enemy fire was hitting all around them, "Get these bastards off our backs," Marzo yelled, and more firepower was directed to the rear.

Marzo was returning fire when Cosmo Farina, the team's weapons specialist crept to his position. "Bad shit, Captain," Farina said, looking wild eyed.

"Damn right," Marzo said. Then he pointed to the rear and said, "And that's the only way out of here."

Farina said, "Do you want me to lay some smoke?" Farina had smoke grenades that could provide a visual cover for a few minutes.

Marzo was surprised Farina even asked. "Negative," Marzo replied. "It wouldn't do much good now. We'll need smoke to cover the extraction when the choppers come. You just keep laying down suppression fire on the rear."

Another mortar exploded and Marzo felt a sharp pain on his upper arm. The explosion had sent a sliver of rock toward him, and it penetrated his bicep. It looked as if the tip of a spear had broken off and was lodged in his arm.

Mazelli looked at the wound and said, "I've got to get that out."

"It's okay," Marzo said grimacing. "You take care of Keen. I'll get this."

Mazilli was about to protest when Marzo grasped the rock by the edge and yanked it out. The pain was brutal. He saw black for a moment and felt nauseous, but he recovered to see that the three inch object was sharp rather than jagged and had entered cleanly. He tossed it aside and allowed Mazilli to tear open his sleeve. His blood was flowing, but the puncture didn't involve an artery.

Mazilli applied pressure to the Captain's arm, and Marzo said, "I'm fine. Take care of Keen." But Mazilli replied, "Keen is stable. We need to slow this bleeding so you can get us out of here."

Mazilli applied antibiotic and covered the wound while Marzo used his other hand for the radio. The choppers were just minutes out now, as was an Air Force F-16 Viper carrying two five-hundred pound bombs. Marzo directed Sgt. Bond to provide laser assistance to the F-16. He wanted both bombs dropped on the compound. Then he directed the Apache helicopters to lay suppression fire on the ridge lines. The rear action was too close, and he still feared anything but a precise assault there could accidentally hit his team.

A Taliban gunner on the ridge was directing steady machine gun fire at their position, and Marzo, Duncan, and Mazilli ducked under the barrage. Mazilli was covering Keen with his body as bullets ricocheted off the rocks and showered them with more shards. The noise was deafening.

Staff Sergeant Hector Perez, the team's best sniper, was twenty yards away from Marzo and Duncan. He'd been firing on the compound, but now he calmly turned his weapon to the ridgeline and adjusted his scope until he had the machine gunner in his sights. He considered the wind and distance to target and gently squeezed the trigger. A small red dot appeared on the gunner's forehead, and he fell. Perez smoothly shifted his scope to the man who'd been feeding the gun and fired again. The second man fell as well. Perez smiled, counted them as kills six and seven, and scanned the ridge for more targets.

The F-16 was the first to arrive, and Marzo could hear its approach in the distance. Duncan smiled at the sound, looked toward the enemy compound and hollered, "Twenty seconds to hell. Tell the seventy virgins we said hello."

The F-16 roared overhead, and in seconds the earth shook and there were two massive explosions at the compound.

"Yeah, baby," Duncan said, as the explosions sent smoke and dust high into the air. When it settled there was no more gunfire from the compound, but the ridge lines and the line to the rear continued their onslaughts.

Daylight was turning to dusk, and Captian Marzo knew the team's night vision goggles would give them an advantage. He also knew the Apaches' target acquisition capability and night vision made them highly effective in darkness. But Marzo was growing impatient. If anything, the explosions at the compound had intensified the output of the remaining Taliban and probably increased the likelihood of a suicide attack from the rear. He needed the choppers now.

Within minutes he heard rotor blades as two Apache AH-64s suddenly emerged like killer angels from behind the ridges and unleashed a relentless barrage of firepower on the Taliban positions below. Each chopper was equipped with a 30mm M230 nose cannon and a full payload of AGM-114 Hellfire and Hydra 70 rockets.

The team on the ground turned its full attention to the rear assault as the Apaches made run after run over the ridges, strafing the Taliban. In time the ridgelines fell silent as the remaining Taliban hunkered down and waited. Finally, the enemy halted its rear assault as well, and everything became eerily quiet.

Marzo and Duncan used the lull to take a damage assessment and plan their next move. Aside from the Captain's arm wound, Keen and Dickson were the only causalities, but both wounds were serious, and they needed to be airlifted as soon as possible. In the meantime, Mazilli and the others were giving them the best field treatment possible.

The team was secure for the time being, but extraction was impossible. Marzo had to assume that he was still surrounded by what he estimated to be one hundred and fifty Taliban fighters. Landing a helicopter in the horseshoe with a high level of enemy firepower nearby was far too dangerous. The Apaches had withdrawn to safer surroundings but were close enough if help was needed. Marzo contacted Command and Control and was told reinforcements were on the way. Two Special Forces teams and a platoon of Army Rangers were being flown in on UH-60 Black Hawk helicopters supported by more Apache gun ships. They would be dropped behind the Taliban positions that formed the rear assault. By daybreak the reinforcements would be in place, and they would encircle and destroy the enemy, allowing for the rear escape of Marzo's team. In the meantime, the A-Team had to wait and prepare for another possible assault.

Captain Marzo directed Sergeant Duncan to reposition the men, establish fields of fire and set up a rotating watch. He also cautioned them to conserve ammunition. Then they waited.

The temperature dropped considerably as the night wore on, causing Marzo's arm to throb. Mazilli kept a close watch on Keen and had inserted an IV, just as the other medic had done for Dickson. The morphine helped the men doze in and out of sleep, and both were stable.

After some time, Duncan said to Marzo, "We'd all be dead now if you would have led us into that ravine. Nice job, Captain."

Marzo shrugged. "It was an easy call."

"Still," Duncan said, "a more reckless commander may have taken the risk."

Marzo's arm felt worse now. He said softly, "Live to fight another day."

It got quiet again and then Marzo looked at Duncan and laughed.

Duncan smiled and said, "Clue me in, Captain."

"I'm just thinking about your name," Marzo said.

"My name?"

"Yeah. It's like your parents knew you'd grow up to be a bad-ass Green Beret NCO when they named you Rip. It's the kind of name a Hollywood editor would scratch out for being too trite. I mean, come on? Master Sergeant Rip Duncan! How did they know?"

Mazilli agreed.

Duncan laughed and said, "You've got it all wrong, Captain. My parents named me Eugene."

"Eugene!" Marzo said. "How'd you get Rip out of Eugene?"

"I was playing in a junior high football game. It was a big game, and I'm the middle linebacker. Late in the game, I make a tackle and my pants split right up my butt. There I am with half my ass hanging out, but there's no way I'm coming out of the game. We ended up winning 6-0, and I had a big day- twelve tackles, including three on the other team's final drive. In the locker room the coach presents me with the defensive game ball. He stands on a bench in front of the team and says, 'And the defensive game ball goes to Rip Duncan!' The guys went nuts, and the name stuck. Tell ya the truth, it beats the heck out of Eugene."

They all laughed.

Mazilli was the youngest guy on the team. Marzo watched him as he checked on Keen and then he said, "You did a good job today, Mazilli."

"Thanks, Captain," Mazilli said, glancing again at Keen. "I'd still like to get these guys out of here ASAP."

"Couple hours," Marzo said.

Mazilli scanned the darkness and asked, "Think they're still out there?"

Duncan replied first. "Truthfully? I don't think so. They know what's coming and they probably hauled ass. That doesn't mean we relax, but I think if they were going to hit us again they would have as soon as darkness fell."

Mazilli looked at the Captain and Marzo nodded his agreement. "I can think of three scenarios. One is that they're long gone like Sergeant Duncan says. Another is that they established new positions and are waiting to ambush the incoming choppers when they land. The third is that they're booby trapping the area right now and then taking off. We'll see."

Mazilli took off his helmet and looked at a photograph tucked inside.

"Your wife?" Duncan asked.

"Girlfriend," Mazilli said. "There were a couple of times today when I thought I'd never see her again."

Marzo thought of the "Dead Already" advice he'd received in training camp but didn't say anything.

"Ever think of loved ones in times like that, Captain?" Mazilli asked.

An image of Carrie's smiling face flashed before him momentarily, and he felt a crushing sense of loneliness. But he steeled himself and said casually, "Nah. I've got other things to think about."

Mazilli looked at Duncan and said, "How about you, Sarge. Do you have a family?"

"Divorced," Duncan said. "Two grown kids though. Great kids."

Mazilli said, "Ever think about dying in combat and leaving loved ones behind? It's natural to think like that, right?"

Duncan didn't reply at first. Then he reached into his back pocket and removed a photograph. He passed it to Mazilli without a word. It was an old black and white photo of a skinny little kid, maybe five or six years old, with disheveled hair and wearing a bow- tie. He was smiling and holding a rolled up piece of paper bound with a ribbon."

Mazilli studied it for a while and then said, "Who's this?"

"That's me," Duncan said. "That's my kindergarten graduation picture."

Mazilli looked at Captain Marzo, but Marzo shrugged.

"I don't get it," Mazilli said. "You carry around a photo of yourself?"

Duncan hesitated before replying and then said, "My mother was dying of cancer when that photo was taken. I didn't know it then, but I remember her standing behind the photographer when he took the picture. She had this scrawny little kid, and she knew she was dying. Every time I look at that photo I wonder what it must have been like for her, knowing she was going to leave her little boy behind. She died five months later, but never lost her spirit. That's what I think of when I go into battle. If she could handle the *certainty* that she'd be gone, my kids and I can handle the *possibility* that I will."

Mazilli nodded and handed the photo back. No one spoke for a few minutes. The wind picked up and the night grew colder. Then a slight smiled crossed Captain Marzo's face. He perked up, listened intently and said, "Sounds like no one's going to die tonight." Soon they all could hear helicopter rotors in the distance.

90- Thanksgiving

November 2001

Nothing was the same after the towers fell. September 11 was the last time Carrie saw Johnny, and she hadn't heard from him since. The media reported that the Taliban were being routed and that America would soon install a provisional government and sponsor democratic elections. In Washington, Brian was spending endless hours studying interrogation transcripts of captured al-Qaeda members. And in Bristol the deli crowd was mourning the loss of a childhood friend, Billy Moyer.

After playing football with Angelo, Nick, Big Frankie and Jimmy, Billy went to college at Georgetown and continued on for his law degree. He married his college sweetheart and established a successful practice in her hometown in North Jersey. They also owned a bed and breakfast on Long Beach Island that his wife, Trish, managed during the summer. In recent years the gang had gathered there for a late September reunion, but the 2001 get-together was never held because Billy lived his last day on September 11. He was in a meeting on the 97th floor of the North Tower when the first plane hit. Those who knew him prayed that he died instantly.

It seemed as if everyone on the East Coast knew a heartbreaking story of someone who perished when the towers fell; however, Billy's fate hit far too close to home, and the deli gang was devastated. The guys loved him as the brother who made good. They took pride in his accomplishments and appreciated his generosity. Now he was gone. His memorial service was a gut-wrenching experience as Trish bravely eulogized her slain husband as her emotionally shattered teen daughters and the deli gang looked on. In the following weeks, Angelo and Nick had trouble controlling their rage, and Jimmy had drifted into a persistent depression. Big Frankie and Donna coped by being strong for the others.

While the older generations could compare the New York tragedy to Pearl Harbor, World War II, or the turmoil of the Vietnam Era, younger people had no similar frame of reference. To say it was a defining moment in their lives would be an understatement. This was especially true of Mickey. His commitment to the fire service made what happened in New York all the more painful, and he planned to join the thousands of emergency personnel traveling to Ground Zero to assist in the search efforts. However, the city announced it was so overwhelmed with support that it couldn't accommodate any more volunteers. Mickey was disappointed until he read about St. Paul's Episcopal Church, located just across the street from where the towers once stood. The small, colonial era church had miraculously survived when the towers crumbled and had now been converted to a temporary shelter for Ground Zero workers. Apparently the church needed help in serving the rescue workers and rotated volunteers every couple of days. Mickey wanted to be a part of something and talked Bobby into going to New York.

For three days Mickey and Bobby ladled soup, made sandwiches, and slept on cots in the basement. They watched as the men dragged themselves in after each shift, filthy from their task and leaden-eyed from grief and exhaustion. They'd eat in silence, cat nap for an hour or two, and return to their grim work.

The Ground Zero site was illuminated by massive flood lights so that work could continue around the clock. On their final night, Mickey and Bobby visited the site when their shift ended at midnight, and they were struck by the utter silence of the area. They watched as workers sifted through the debris. Over two thousand victims were buried in the rubble, and it was regarded as sacred ground. They'd heard that each time a body was found, all work stopped as the corpse was placed on a stretcher, covered with an American flag, and removed from the site as the other workers stood silently at attention. Now, they had gotten close enough to see one of the makeshift ceremonies take place, and they cried openly.

Everyone in Bristol knew all about Billy Moyer and his relationship with the guys at the deli. When Mickey and Bobby returned from New York, they visited the deli to pay their respects. There wasn't a dry eye in the store as they shared what they had seen. After a while, Angelo closed the store early and passed out beers.

In Washington there was a strong view that additional al-Qaeda attacks were planned and a fear that more sleeper cells were in the United States. Brian was working longer hours than ever, including

415

weekends, and he was sullen and withdrawn at home. He realized that Jenny was feeling the strain of his behavior, but he felt helpless to change it. Finally, he assured her that the pace wouldn't last forever. Things would calm down. In the meantime he suggested she visit Bristol more often to see her parents and spend some time with Carrie. At first she resisted, saying she wanted to be there for him, but she relented eventually and began a routine of weekend trips home.

As the war in Afghanistan continued, media images of battlefield successes placated an angry public, but Carrie saw the images as constant reminders of the dangers her husband faced. She feared for his well being and struggled to maintain a positive outlook. She had landed a job as a part time writer with the *Bucks County Courier Times,* and she used it to keep busy. She had long-since graduated from fluff stories and had been given some investigative assignments that she felt had substance. There were other positives in her life as well. Her mother was doing fine and continued to receive encouraging reports from her doctors. Her father was landing consulting contracts and enjoying a lighter work load. Carrie was grateful for all of this, but she was still haunted by the war.

As Thanksgiving approached, Carrie dreaded another holiday without Johnny. Jenny was down in the dumps as well when she arrived for the long weekend. Brian had just told her that there was no way he could take the time off for the holiday. He wasn't permitted to explain why, but she knew it was related to information the agency was getting for the al-Qaeda interrogations. Every lead had to be followed; Brian would see to that.

She and Carrie took a walk to the riverfront for a glass of wine at the King George Inn. It was mid-afternoon and the place was empty. They sat at one of the high tavern tables, and Jenny had trouble keeping her composure as she explained her problems to Carrie.

"I don't want to seem selfish," Jenny said. "But I'm not sure how much longer I can take this. He's gone all the time, and when he's home, he's a different person."

Carrie was trying to console her when Jenny added, "Listen to me. I'm crying the blues because Brian works late and is irritable when he's home, but my problems are nothing compared to yours. My God, you haven't seen Johnny in ages. I'm so sorry."

"Don't be silly," Carrie said. "Both of our husbands are at war, Jenny. Mine just happens to wear a uniform."

"Still…" Jenny said.

Carrie interrupted. "We're all in this together, remember? That's what we said."

Jenny stared into her glass. "I know," she said softly. "But sometimes it's so hard."

"Real hard," Carrie said. She brushed some hair from her eyes and asked, "Do you realize that from the first day I met Johnny in high school until now, we've been apart more than we've been together?" She forced a laugh and added, "And when we're apart, we're really apart. I mean like half a world away."

Jenny shook her head and said, "I don't now how you do it."

Carrie forced a smile. "I guess I can do it because I have the greatest friends in the world in you and Brian."

"Ditto," Jenny said. She raised her glass, and Carrie raised hers before they took a sip.

"I just want him to come home safely."

"He will," Jenny assured her. "To hear Brian tell it, Johnny's the best damn soldier in the army."

Good soldiers can't stop bullets, Carrie thought.

Jenny was swirling the wine in her glass and said, "I'm so afraid that I'll never get Brian back emotionally. I mean, he's a different person."

"Don't say that. He'll be his old self again soon. You'll see," Carrie assured her, but in her heart she feared that neither of their men would ever be the same.

Carrie felt her spirits sinking. She glanced across the tavern to the piano in the corner and thought of her birthday dinner with Johnny so long ago. He had asked the piano player to play something from Les Miserables, and he had played *On My Own,* her favorite song from the play.

She closed her eyes now and sang just loud enough for Jenny to hear. *"On my own, pretending he's beside me. All alone…"*

Jenny recognized it and hummed along softly.

They stopped and Carrie sighed, "Some holiday this is going to be.

"Some Thanksgiving," Jenny mumbled. "It's just my parents and I. I wish Brian were coming."

Carrie visualized Thanksgiving at her house. It would be just she and her parents. They had much to be thankful for, but the day would be dull, which meant she'd dwell on Johnny's absence. Then an idea struck her, and she liked it right away. Her mood brightened and she called to Jarred, the bartender, and ordered another round. When Jenny looked surprised, Carrie said, "I have something to run by you."

It was cold but sunny on Thanksgiving Day, and the girls started their preparations early that morning. Carrie's house had a big kitchen and the girls were excited about their tasks. Neither of them had any idea how to prepare a Thanksgiving meal, but after spending most of Wednesday night reading cookbooks, shopping, and making preparations, they felt they were ready.

Jenny finished mashing the potatoes while Carrie basted the turkey one last time. "That looks fantastic," Jenny said.

Carrie slid the turkey back in the oven and said, "Remember how burnt the turkey was in the *Christmas Vacation* movie, the one with Chevy Chase?"

Jenny laughed. "I loved that movie!"

"Well, I had a dream last night that ours would look like that."

"No way!" Jenny said. "This is going to be a kick-butt meal."

Carrie was happy to see Jenny's spirits were up.

"How are things going in the other room?" Jenny asked.

"Great," Carrie replied. "The Boyles, the Kellys, and the Ryans are getting along well. It's like an Irish reunion. Dad's mixing drinks, and they seem to be having a good time. The moms are happy too because they don't have to cook." Jenny had invited Brian's parents and was surprised when they readily accepted. The same was true of her parents. She thought both couples would have preferred to have dinner in their homes, but it seemed as if everyone was looking forward to more companionship.

Jenny looked at the clock on the stove. "The real test will be at two o'clock."

Carrie grinned. "That's what Thanksgiving is all about. Fifteen people! It's gonna be great." Carrie thought back to her trip to the deli to invite the Marzos. Donna had said they appreciated the offer but had to decline because Nick and Jimmy ate at the deli every day, including Thanksgiving.

"I'm inviting them too," Carrie said, "and Big Frankie."

"That's so nice of you," Donna had said. "But you'd be wasting your time. Nick doesn't go to social events, and Jimmy does whatever Nick does. As for Big Frankie, he's got two kids to worry about."

"I'll include them!" Carrie gushed. "I'll invite the mailman if you want me to."

Donna smiled. She put her arm around Carrie and said softly, "What's this all about?"

Carrie looked at her and said in a low voice, "I have to do this."

Donna noticed Carrie's eyes begin to fill, and she understood. She stepped back, leaned against the counter and said, "Have you heard from him?"

Carrie shook her head.

"Neither have I," Donna said. "I tell myself every day that no news is good news."

It stayed quiet for a long time until Donna slammed her palm against the counter top and said enthusiastically, "Let's do it! Let's have that dinner, Carrie."

Carrie was startled, but her face brightened. "Do you think the men will come?"

"I'll make them come."

Carrie smiled. "Really? What about Nick?"

"Nick's afraid of me. If I push it, he'll come, especially for you. He's crazy about you."

Carrie's thoughts returned to the present when Jenny said, "Tell me again about Frankie's kids."

"Big Frankie married a girl who had two children. He adopted them and, a little while later, his wife took off and left him with the kids. They haven't heard from her since."

"So sad," Jenny said.

"Yeah," Carrie said. "Big Frankie was heartbroken and so were the kids. But it's kind of nice too, because he loves those kids and he's a great father."

Jenny shook her head. "I can't wait to meet them."

The doorbell rang at precisely two o'clock and the deli gang spilled in. The girls had feared the meeting would be awkward, but it went smoothly. Everyone seemed to enjoy meeting new people, and Mr. Boyle's drinks helped ease the mood.

Carrie gave Nick an extra special hug, and he said, "Boy, this is a warm reception." Then he looked at her in mock sternness and said, "But did you meet my demands?"

Carrie smiled, stepped back and counted on her fingers. "One. We have yams. Two, you get a whole turkey leg for yourself. Three, you can watch the football game when it comes on."

"And what about four?" Nick asked, straight faced.

Carrie looked lost. "Four?"

"Four," Nick replied. "I get to see you smile all day."

Carrie relaxed and said, "You got it, Uncle Nick!"

The group meshed easily. Jenny asked the kids to help them in the kitchen, and soon they could hear everyone howling from the living room as Nick told one of his stories. When dinner was ready, they all squeezed in around the table and cheered as the girls presented the food. They held hands as Mrs. Boyle said grace. When she was finished, Jimmy added a short prayer for "Our boys overseas, for Billy Moyer, and for the families of all the victims." That gave everyone pause for a moment, and Mr. Boyle broke the silence by inviting Angelo to carve the turkey. For the next two hours they laughed, shared stories, and enjoyed the meal and their new friendships.

After dinner Nick said, "So, Mr. Boyle, I hope you hate the Cowboys as much as I do," which was his way of saying it was time to watch the game. The men left for the living room while the women cleaned up and prepared the dessert.

When they were alone, Jenny said to Carrie, "This was a great idea. I'm so glad you thought of it."

"It was fun," Carrie agreed, "but a lot of work. Now I know why people go out to dinner so much."

Jenny said, "Hey, tomorrow is Black Friday. Wanna go shopping? President Bush said we should shop to stimulate the economy."

"Actually," Carrie said. "I had something different I wanted to run by you. My editor thinks my experience with the Nairobi Embassy bombing makes me a good candidate to do a story about the World

Trade Center Tragedy. He wants me to visit Ground Zero and do a first person account of what's happening there and how people are coping. I was reluctant to do it, but after hearing Nick's story about Mickey and Bobby's trip there, I'm thinking maybe I should. Why don't you and I take a train to New York tomorrow for the day?"

91- Calling from St. Paul's

They caught the train in Trenton for the ride to New York's Penn Station. Jenny seemed subdued all morning, and Carrie finally asked what was wrong.

"To be honest, I don't want to go," Jenny said. "I'm doing it as a favor."

Carrie was surprised and waited for an explanation.

"Look," Jenny said. "Yesterday was a great day. We had lots of fun."

"Right," Carrie said. "So why are you down today?"

"Because yesterday reminded me of how normal people live. They enjoy friends, family, love and laughter."

"Okay, but we were part of it. Wasn't that a good thing?"

"It was," Jenny replied. "But today we're plunging right back into that other world. What do you think this trip is going to be like? We should be going to Macy's and Rockefeller Center, not Ground Zero. This certainly isn't going to lift our spirits."

Carrie sat back and exhaled slowly. "I'm sorry," she said. "I guess you're right. It's just that I'm writing this article and..."

"It's not your fault," Jenny said. "I just feel as if I've had it. I've had it with tragedy. I've had it with the constant tension I feel around Brian. I'm...I'm..." She brought her hands to her mouth and shook her head slowly. When she composed herself, she added, "I've been trying to make it work with Brian; I really have."

"And it will work. What's happening to you guys is temporary. You know that."

"That's what I keep telling myself," Jenny said. "But these last few days...And now this trip."

"I'm so sorry," Carrie said. "I wish you would have told me."

"I was trying to be a good friend, but once we got on the train it just started to get to me."

Carrie searched for the right words. "I don't know what I was thinking. I know this won't be pleasant. It's just that with Johnny away, I feel like I have to do something meaningful. Aside from taking care of my mom, I haven't done anything worthwhile since Nairobi."

Now Jenny was conciliatory. "That's crazy. You're being way too hard on yourself. A year in Africa, a Master of Arts degree in journalism, you've been doing things."

"But I still don't have a real full time job. When my editor offered me the chance to do an article like this, I jumped at it. I need something to help me keep my sanity."

"So you asked your best friend to go with you, and here I am again acting like a self-absorbed boob. I wasn't always this way. I used to be the strong one, remember? I feel really stupid."

"Don't be silly," Carrie said. "Like you said, things just caught up with you a little. That's all."

Jenny let out a sigh. "They certainly have."

Jenny seemed fragile and Carrie was worried about her. "Listen," Carrie said,

"This whole thing was a dumb idea. Let's get off at Princeton and get a ticket for home."

"No way," Jenny said. "I'd never forgive myself."

"Really, Jenny, it's not that big of a thing."

Jenny forced a smile and said, "I'm better now, I really am. I think I just needed to vent again, and you're a good listener. Actually, I love New York and haven't been to Manhattan in years." She thought a minute and added, "How's this for a plan. We'll do your journalism thing. Then we'll stop at Macy's. It's just a couple of blocks past the train station. Going there is a must since it's Black Friday. After that we'll have a nice dinner in a little Italian restaurant, just like in the Billy Joel song, and then we'll come home. Sound okay?"

"Sounds great," Carrie said. "What about Rockefeller Center?"

"Nah. Every time I go there I think of the *Catcher in the Rye* and I get depressed. Window shopping and dinner are all I need."

"Are you sure?"

"Positive," Jenny said, forcing a smile.

They exited Penn Station at 7th Avenue and were immediately enthralled by their surroundings. Washington and Philly were nothing like The Big Apple. Manhattan was louder, wider, taller and far more crowded. Their eyes were immediately drawn upward to the countless billboards and soaring buildings. The Empire State Building loomed a block or so to their left, and for the first time Carrie realized that it was once again the tallest building in New York. On the ground, they were jostled by crowds of people speaking English, Chinese, Spanish and a myriad of Middle Eastern tongues. The languages blended with the incessant honking of taxi horns and formed a harmony unique to New York. Street vendors were everywhere, and the aroma of hot dogs, sauerkraut, and roasted peanuts competed with the exhausts from vehicles that jammed the avenue.

The sidewalks were lined with merchants whose tables offered five dollar watches, three dollar hats, and silk screened posters of Elvis and Marilyn Monroe. The girls were handed pamphlets asking them if they were saved and a flyer inviting them to an adult women's club. An elderly black man played *God Bless America* on the clarinet, while passers-by tossed coins in his opened instrument case.

Jenny looked up, spun herself around to take it all in, and exclaimed, "This is wild!"

Carrie agreed. The lower end of New York may have been the scene of staggering death and destruction, but midtown Manhattan continued to pulsate with life.

There was a line of taxis available, but Jenny suggested they walk for a while. They headed south down 7th Avenue toward Lower Manhattan for several blocks before boarding the subway, which they took to Chambers Street near the World Trade Center site.

When they climbed the steps to daylight, it was like they were entering a different world. The air seemed heavy and there was a pervasive smell of wet plaster. The streets and pavements still showed traces of gray-white cement dust from the crumbled buildings. But what struck the girls most was the eerie quiet, the almost total absence of noise.

They walked east on Chambers to Broadway and then turned south toward Vesey. They were a block away from Ground Zero when they first saw St. Paul's Chapel. Hundreds of people lined the sidewalk waiting their turn to enter the small church. The girls noted the demeanor of the crowd. People stood in silence or spoke in hushed tones. The scene reminded Jenny of the aura of quiet reverence she felt when she visited the Vietnam Wall in Washington.

An ornate wrought iron fence surrounded St. Paul's, and visitors had turned it into a makeshift memorial, leaving thousands of articles that covered every inch of space. In addition to hundreds of American flags, there were school hats and pennants from around the country. Tee-shirts with 9-11 messages, hand- painted posters and other works of art were fastened to the posts. There were rosary beads and a vast assortment of personal items, some spiritual, some patriotic.

Jenny read poignant letters written by children from schools near and far. Many were addressed to the fire department. Some included simple images of fire trucks, burning towers, or the Statue of Liberty. Most offered messages of hope or condolences. Some depicted fear. All were touching in their innocence.

Perhaps most moving were the posters of missing persons, complete with photographs that loved ones had affixed to the fence. Some pleaded for information and held out hope they would be found. Others accepted the fate of those who were gone and memorialized their lives.

Carrie occasionally took notes as she moved along the fence. She found a collage crafted in honor of Father Michael Judge, the New York Fire Department Chaplin. He was a Franciscan priest whose parish was less than two blocks from the World Trade Center. Father Judge had been one of the first volunteers on the scene. He was killed by falling debris from the towers, reportedly while administering last rites to a victim. The narrative stated that his body-bag had been labeled as the first officially identified victim of the attack. The collage depicted several photos of him performing his ministry and laughing with the men from nearby Station 10. There was a final photo of the beloved slain priest being carried from the scene by five grief-stricken firemen.

Carrie and Jenny walked to the side of the building and entered the graveyard. They saw a large uprooted Sycamore and listened as a tour guide explained that the tree had shielded the chapel from falling debris, allowing the building to stand undisturbed as the towers crumbled around it. The guide said it was nothing short of miraculous, and no one in the crowd was prepared to argue.

Next they entered the crowded chapel and saw that it had been completely transformed to a relief station, just as Nick had conveyed Mickey's story. The walls were lined with cots and food-serving stations, and banners hung everywhere. There was a huge one from Oklahoma City that read, *To New York City and all the Rescuers: Keep Your Spirits Up, Oklahoma Loves You!!* Elementary school children from Michigan fashioned an American flag in which the white stripes were formed from paper cutouts of children's hands, each with a short handwritten message of hope and support. Another hand-painted banner was stark red with a white star and the word *Courage* painted in bold blue letters.

Carrie found a priest's outer vestment mounted on display. An accompanying narrative explained that a visiting fireman had pinned the patch of his fire company to it, and the idea had caught on. The vestment was completely covered with fire, rescue and police patches from around the country.

People were milling around, and Carrie politely interviewed a husband and wife who had driven in from Ohio to see the place where their nephew had perished. They spoke of their pain and the healing nature of the improvised shrine.

A string quartet was playing in the front of the church, and Jenny stepped away to listen. She sat in a pew and scanned a brochure about St. Paul's Chapel. She learned that this was the same church where George Washington worshiped during the brief period when New York was our nation's capital. Jenny reflected that George Washington certainly was no stranger to adversity. She noticed that the pews of the colonial era church were scratched and marred, and the brochure explained that the damage was caused by firemen and rescue workers who slept on them in their gear between shifts. The congregation decided to leave the pews in that condition to preserve the memory of what took place there.

Jenny saw that Carrie was talking quietly with another couple now, and she took advantage of the time to reflect. She found the music comforting. Everything about St. Paul's was soothing. The chapel offered an incredible combination of sadness, reflection, love, and an unconquerable spirit. It spoke of the highly personal nature of the loss that had taken place, while at the same time reflecting that it was a loss that was shared by all, a loss that would be overcome.

Carrie touched Jenny on the shoulder to indicate her interviews were finished. They walked outside and neither of them spoke for a long time. They just stood, looking at the church, the fence, and the crowd that continued to form. Finally, Carrie said, "The last couple I spoke with lost a son when the towers fell. He was a fire fighter. They said they came here every day to volunteer while the search for survivors went on. Even after they gave up hope, they continued to come. They said they're at peace now, but they   still come frequently in the hope of consoling loved ones of the other three hundred and forty-two firefighters who died."

Jenny listened.

Carrie said, "No use in going to Ground Zero. They still have most of it blocked off. You can't get close enough to see much. Besides, I think the story is right here."

Jenny agreed. She folded her brochure and placed it in her pocket.

Carrie took out her cell phone and said, "My editor wants me to give him one word that will identify the theme of my article. He does stuff like that. I want to send it to him while it's fresh in my mind. Jenny watched as Carrie entered the letters of a one word text message. It read, RESILIENCE.

Carrie hit send and Jenny asked if she could borrow the phone. She dialed Brian's private number and Carrie began to step away to give her privacy, but Jenny grasped her arm and said, "Stay."

Brian answered and Jenny said, "Hi, it's Jenny."

Brian was surprised to hear her voice. He had called her the day before to wish her a happy Thanksgiving and they had spoken briefly. "Hi, Jenny," he said warily. "Is everything okay?"

"Yes," Jenny said. "I know you're busy, but I won't keep you long."

Brian sounded embarrassed and a little concerned. "Don't be silly. It's crazy here, but I have time for you. What's going on?"

Jenny cleared her throat. She was finding it hard to continue.

"Jenny?" Brian said. "Are you still there?"

"Yes, I'm here," Jenny said. She paused again and said, "Brian, I just want you to know how much I love you and admire you for what you're doing."

Brian started to respond, but Jenny went on. "I want you to know that no matter how much time it takes for you to do your job; I'll be here waiting for you. I'll always be here."

The phone went quiet for several seconds and then Brian said, "I love you, Jenny."

"I know," she replied hoarsely.

He added, "Come home, Jenny. Come home tomorrow. I'll take some time. I promise."

"I will," she said quickly. Then she flipped the phone shut so he wouldn't hear her cry.

Carrie looked at her friend and smiled. She waited for Jenny to compose herself and then said, "Are you ready for Macy's?"

Jenny wiped her eyes and said "No."

"Good," Carrie replied. "I'm not in the mood either. How about a quiet bottle of red and a bottle of white?"

"Yes!" Jenny said, "And some pasta."

They both smiled and walked arm in arm toward the subway.

92- Paddy's Pub

October 2002

It was Friday afternoon, and Carrie's editor finally approved her last draft for Sunday's paper. Usually she would join the news staff for Happy Hour at "The Tank" in Tullytown, but Carrie begged off this time. She was heading to Washington to spend the weekend with Jenny and Brian.

She was coping with Johnny's absence by keeping busy, but she also took encouragement from the news out of Afghanistan. The fighting had subsided after December, and Johnny was able to send an occasional letter. Although he was still characteristically vague about his exact location or activities, Carrie knew it was a good sign that he was able to communicate at all.

Jenny's life had improved as well. After her trip to ground zero a year earlier, she had returned to Washington for a heart to heart with Brian, and they talked for hours. Brian maintained that his obsession with work was necessary to protect innocent people like her. Jenny replied that his commitment was counter productive, at least as far as their relationship was concerned. "It doesn't much matter if you save me physically if you're killing me emotionally," she had said through tears. "Sometimes I feel dead inside," she added, "and I think you do too. So what's the use? You can't let the terrorists to this to us."

Brian had listened quietly as Jenny made her final point. "I know what your job entails, and I accept the long hours and the pressure. But when you're home, I need you to be the Brian I fell in love with. I need you to come back into my life."

At that point Brian conceded that Jenny was right and added that Dr. Blake feared that his intensity was diminishing his effectiveness. Brian promised Jenny he would change and would keep his job in perspective. To Jenny's relief, he finally did change. He still worked long hours and still experienced mood swings, but his lows weren't as low as they had been. Jenny now felt as though she had her husband back because of an understanding they had reached. Jenny wanted to see more of the jovial Brian she had fallen in love with. But she also made it clear that she didn't want him internalizing his problems. She wanted to be his partner in every sense of the word, and that included hearing what was bothering him. Life wasn't perfect, but it was much better, and she, like Carrie, was grateful for a fulfilling career that made the hard times easier.

On Saturday night Carrie and Jenny went to their favorite spot in Georgetown. Brian had worked that day but promised to meet them at the club. He seemed to be in good humor when he arrived and made a big fuss over Carrie. They ordered a round of drinks and he quizzed Carrie about her latest writing assignments. Carrie had just finished an article about the anniversary of the Yon Kippur War for which she had interviewed several prominent local Jewish leaders, as well as a spokesman from the Arab League in Philadelphia. Brian appeared to be listening; however, Jenny sensed that he was distracted. Soon he lost eye contact and was focused on his martini glass instead.

Finally, Jenny said, "Something's wrong, Brian. Tell me what it is."

Brian looked incredulous. "Are you serious? Do you really have to ask?"

"I guess I do," Jenny replied. "Has something happened?"

"Haven't you seen the news today?"

Jenny looked at Carrie and then back at Brian. "No. I met Carrie at Union Station. We took a walk, did some shopping, and came here. What's going on?"

Brian sighed, "Ever hear of Bali?"

"I've heard of it," Jenny said. "But I don't know much about it."

"Same here," Carrie said.

"Bali is a resort city in Indonesia. It's a popular vacation spot for westerners in Southeast Asia. Terrorists struck a nightclub there last night. They hit a place called Paddy's."

Jenny gasped, and Brian continued. "A suicide bomber detonated himself inside the place. As survivors rushed to get outside, another terrorist exploded a massive truck bomb out front. When the dust cleared, two hundred young people were dead and another two hundred were severely burned or wounded."

"Oh my God," Jenny said.

"Hospitals couldn't handle the volume. I read accounts that some of the burn victims had to be placed in nearby swimming polls to ease their suffering. It was a scene from hell."

Carrie had a flashback to the Nairobi Embassy and was reeling from the memory.

Brian hadn't intended to ruin the gathering, but the anger he'd been suppressing earlier was apparent now, and he continued with his voice rising. "Like I said, it was a popular spot for westerners. Eighty-eight of the dead were Australian, forty-four were European and seven were American."

Jenny shook her head at the numbers and said, "Who did this?"

"Who do you think?" Brian snapped. Then he caught himself and said, "I'm sorry, Babe. I didn't mean that. You can imagine the kind of day I've had."

Jenny put her hand on his and said, "That's okay, Brian. I understand."

He covered her hand with his and went on. "Islamic extremists did it. Eighty-five percent of the people of Indonesia are Muslim. It's the most populated Muslim majority in the world."

Carrie's reporter instincts kicked in and she asked, "So why attack there?"

"Indonesia is a secular state. Their leaders promise freedom of religion, but the extremists want an Islamic Republic, and they view the Bali resort as a gathering place for hedonistic westerners. They feel the visitors pollute the country with their sinful ways. I mean, after all, they dance and drink. So the terrorist bastards see no alternative but to slaughter them in the name of Allah."

Brian was seething now, and the girls didn't blame him. Carrie asked, "So how do we prevent these attacks?"

"You don't," Brian said, "at least not effectively. We uncover plots like this all the time, and we work with local governments to intervene before it's too late. But even if one in twenty is pulled off, the results are… The results are what I just told you."

"My God, Brian," Jenny said sadly. "Every time I think I know what you're going through…"

"It's okay," Brian said softly. "You've given me a better handle on things. It's kind of like being a doctor who loses a patient. You focus on the ones you save, or you'll go crazy. You just look ahead and keep doing the best you can."

"That's a good philosophy," Carrie said.

"Yeah, except we're not doing the best we can, at least not in America. There's a lot more we could do."

"Like what?" Carrie asked.

"I'm not sure you want to know," Brian said.

"Of course I do," Carrie replied.

"Me too," Jenny added.

Brian sat back and took a long sip of his martini. He exhaled deeply and began. "There are bad people in America, sleeper cells. We're pretty sure of that. They're here and others are trying to join them every day. We have to stop our tip-toeing around this problem. The sad fact is that the bad guys are all Muslims. I'd give the FBI far more power to operate in America. The CIA will track them oversees, but when we hand them off to the FBI, we need to give them more tools. I'd require every Muslim in America to be fingerprinted, men, women, kids, grandmothers, everyone."

Carrie's jaw dropped as Brian continued. "I'd also require each one to provide a DNA sample, just a quick Q-tip swab of the mouth. We need a national data base of who's out there."

Carrie said softly, "I understand your frustration, Brian, but the vast majority of Muslims in America are good people…"

"I know that!" he snapped again. "We need to catch the ones who aren't. I'm sorry, but I can't sort them out. Can you?"

Carrie pushed back. "But what you're proposing is grossly illegal-denying due process and equal protection."

"Sure it is, and the terrorists know that and laugh at our laws as they plot their next atrocity. We need to make the things I'm talking about legal. I don't give a damn how, but we need to do it."

Jenny began to protest, but Brian said, "Wait. I'm not finished." She sat back, and Brian paused for effect. "We should put suspicious Muslims on watch lists and monitor their calls. I'm not saying listen to their calls, at least not at first, but electronically monitor who they call and who calls them. If we find one bad guy, it could lead us to other suspects. Then we can get wire tape warrants and listen in. It's a big task because we're talking about thousands of people, but we have the technical ability to monitor them twenty-four-seven."

Brian was running on all cylinders now. "We should also issue torture warrants. We..." Brian!" Jenny exclaimed. "Listen to yourself. Torture warrants?" "Exactly," Brian said. "I'd do whatever it takes to stop these people."

Jenny said softly, "Come on, Brian. There's no such thing. We can't toss out the Constitution because we're scared."

"We don't toss it out, we change it. We have search warrants, so let's have torture warrants. I'm not saying we torture willy nilly. We go to a judge, make the case for probable cause, and get a very specific warrant if we feel a threat is imminent."

"I can't imagine that," Carrie said. Brian leaned forward and said, "Imagine this scenario. Let's say the cops have a guy in custody who they know has planted a dirty nuclear bomb in Manhattan. They know the clock is ticking and that thousands will die if it goes off. The terrorist in custody is laughing at them. He won't tell them anything. You're the judge, Carrie. Would you like to have a legal basis to issue a torture warrant, or do we let thousands die because it's against our principles?"

Carrie hesitated and then said, "That's a tough call."

"It used to be," Brian said. "But the world changed on September 11."

"These guys are willing to die. What good would torture do?"

"They're committed to die, but they're not committed to long periods of pain. There's a big difference."

The table got quiet for some time and then Brian added, "You guys think I'm nuts, right?"

"Of course not," Jenny said. "But you're sounding a bit extreme."

Brian smiled and said, "It's still me, guys. I haven't morphed into some kind of Dr. Strangelove. I'm taking about a paradigm shift. I may sound emotional... Well, I guess I am. I'm actually sick to my stomach thinking about American kids, thousands of miles away from home, being dipped into swimming pools to ease the pain of their burns until the hospital staff can get to them. Call me crazy, but stuff like that tends to put me in a bad mood. But I arrived at what I'm saying in a logical, rational way, and I'm not alone in my thinking."

Jenny said, "The worst time for a country to make decisions about people's rights is when they're frightened. Remember that exhibit I did at the museum about Japanese Internment in World War II?"

"Yeah, I do," Brian said.

"We rounded up thousands of innocent Japanese-Americans," Jenny said. "They were American citizens! We rounded them up without evidence of any wrongdoing, forced them to leave their homes and possessions, interrupted their careers, and put them in camps in Wyoming. My God! It was one of the darkest days in our history. We threw the Constitution out the window."

"That's true," Brian said. "By the way, the Supreme Court allowed it."

"That had to be one of the worst rulings in the history of the Court," she replied.

"Was it? I'm not so sure. The justices said that things are different during times of war."

Jenny started to say something, but Brian held his hand up to stop her. "Look," he said. "Tomorrow's Sunday and I have to go to work. We expect more details on Bali to be in by then, and I'll be busy. For now, I really want to enjoy the night with you. So let me leave you with something to think about, and then we'll drop the topic and have dinner. Fair enough?"

The girls nodded.

Brian cleared his throat and shifted in his seat. When he spoke, he had the demeanor of a lawyer making a closing argument. "A person could argue that the most serious threat to the United States took place during the Civil War. The southern states were in rebellion, and President Lincoln was committed to preserve the union. In the early days of the war, the area surrounding the capital was teeming with southern sympathizers, spies, and potential saboteurs. The President revoked the writ of habeas corpus, something he clearly didn't have the constitutional authority to do. But it enabled him to round up those who were considered a threat and detain them without due process. He also used military courts away from war zones to prosecute anti-war agitators. When critics challenged him, the President basically said that the Constitution was not a suicide pact. Lincoln was not prepared to sacrifice the long term well-being of the country to avoid short term and isolated violations of civil liberties. He did what he had to do."

Brian leaned back in his chair and took another pull of his martini. Then he said, "Think about that. The man most historians rate as our greatest president violated the Constitution on several occasions. I think he felt that in order to preserve our Constitution, we have to preserve our country."

Then he leaned forward and said softly. "Suicide pact. I like that term. I doubt the founding fathers designed the United States Constitution to be a suicide pact. I doubt they would have stood by with their hands tied behind their backs while their country was attacked. The primary function of government is to protect its citizens. Before we build a road or provide a senior citizen with social security, our main task is to protect the people from attack. I love the Constitution as much as you do, but we need to find a way to adapt it to the new realities we face."

Having said his piece, he smiled at the girls and said, "Let's have dinner."

93- Welcome Home

January 13, 2003

Johnny Marzo sat on the stage of the Bristol Riverside Theater with two other local veterans of the war in Afghanistan. Above the stage was a banner that read, "Bristol Welcomes Home Its Troops." There were several dignitaries and elected officials present. Mayor Joe Saxton had coordinated the event and was serving as master of ceremonies.

Johnny scanned the crowd as Mayor Saxton spoke. He'd only been home for two days and enjoyed seeing so many friendly faces. Carrie sat in the first row with Johnny's parents and the rest of the deli gang. Mickey was in the balcony with police, firemen, and rescue personnel from throughout town. Brian and Jenny were stuck in Washington but would be driving up the next day to join Johnny and Carrie for a quiet dinner. He hadn't seen them in sixteen months and couldn't wait for the reunion.

Bobby was there along with Tommy Dillon. Tommy was out of rehab, and Johnny had spoken to him briefly before the ceremony. He looked and sounded great. In fact, Johnny's biggest surprise since being home was to learn that Brian and Bobby had formed a partnership to open an auto repair shop. Brian provided the down payment and signed for the loan, and Bobby was set to run the place and share the profits. As part of the deal, Bobby would hire Tommy as an apprentice, which Bobby was more than glad to do. The guys were ecstatic about the arrangement, and Johnny was thrilled to see them so happy. The garage was on Farragut Avenue in Bristol, and Johnny promised to stop by later to see it.

Johnny had given up worrying about Brian's money management. Things always seemed to go right for him, just as it had with the town house in North Carolina. He leased it out when Carrie moved north, and his rent exceeded his mortgage payment. He was building equity and paying his bills. Johnny smiled at the thought of what the Kelly financial empire would do next.

The dignitaries had already said a few words, and Mayor Saxton was concluding his remarks. As a captain, Johnny was the highest ranking soldier on the stage, and the Mayor would introduce him for some closing comments.

Johnny deeply appreciated the outpouring of support, but he didn't want to be there. He didn't like the limelight, and Special Forces soldiers seldom acknowledged their work. But this was different. The Pentagon knew that the American people needed to feel a part of the war on terror, to know we were striking back. Johnny understood that ceremonies like this were cathartic. They offered the public a welcomed release of pent up emotions. But the biggest source of his discomfort was his feeling that things in Afghanistan remained unsettled.

The United States entered the war with three objectives: to eliminate the Taliban who had provided al-Qaeda with safe haven, to capture or kill Osama bin-Laden, and to sponsor democratic elections. To accomplish this, America relied heavily on ground forces provided by the Northern Alliance. However, the United States cultivated good will with its new allies by making several concessions along the way. The Afghan leaders readily welcomed American supplies, air power and money, and grudgingly accepted Special Forces tactical support. But, to ensure their future credibility and dispel any semblance of being a puppet of the Americans, they insisted on being in the forefront in the elimination of Taliban rule, and the United States welcomed the idea.

By early December of 2002 the southern city of Kandahar was the last major Taliban stronghold. After Johnny's team coordinated days of intense American bombing on Taliban positions, the tribal leaders launched their ground assault and Kandahar fell.

Johnny took satisfaction in the victory, but he still felt little reason to celebrate as long as the principal architects of the September 11 attacks remained at large. Osama bib-Laden and his inner circle had escaped the onslaught and were believed to be hiding in the rugged mountains of Tora Bora, and it was feared that the caves and obscure mountain passes would make his capture extremely difficult. Johnny felt someone in Washington or in CENTCOM had made a serious mistake by allowing the Afghans too much responsibility on the ground. He believed American forces should have been used to block the escape routes into the mountain ranges near the Pakistan border. But the United States had bowed to the wishes of its Afgan allies and left the task to them. In retrospect, Johnny wondered if the tribal chiefs were more interested in overthrowing the Taliban and gaining power than they were in capturing bin-Laden. The fact that the United States had purchased their support with hefty payments suggested the possibility that bin-Laden may have purchased his escape route in the same way.

After Kandahar, Johnny's team had moved north to join the operation at Tora Bora. The United States had bombed the area relentlessly, and Special Forces searched the elaborate cave structure, rooting out Taliban fighters. They gathered DNA samples of the dead in the hope one would match samples they had of bin-Laden's, but they didn't. Johnny spent the next several months training the new Afghan army and crushing lingering pockets of resistance.

Now he was home, and the people in the crowd looked happy. We'd just kicked ass pretty good in Afghanistan, but Johnny wondered if the audience's satisfaction was tempered by just the slightest bit of the same disappointment Johnny felt. He believed that the American people didn't care as much about Afghanistan's future as it did about killing bin-Laden. He was the symbol of what had happened in New York, Washington and Western Pennsylvania. The people wanted him, the government wanted him, and Johnny knew that wouldn't happen any time soon.

Mayor Saxton introduced him, and Johnny thanked the crowd. He spoke briefly about the bravery of the men he served with and reminded the gathering that the war on terror would not end until the terrorists were found and brought to justice, a long and daunting task.

After the ceremony, he mingled with well-wishers for a while, told his family he'd see them later, and left with Carrie. His family had held a party for him at the deli the night before, and he and Carrie had promised to set this evening aside for just the two of them.

They went outside and were alone for the first time since he'd gotten home. The weather wasn't bad for mid February. It was cold, but the sun was out and there was no wind. Johnny said he felt like walking, and Carrie draped her arm through his as they strolled down the hill to the river. The walkways were shoveled, but the grass still had a light covering of snow. The shoreline was frozen, and large chunks of ice floated upstream with the tide.

They walked to edge of the wharf, and Johnny looked out at Burlington Island. It had once been a vacation spot, but it was uninhabited now, and the land had become an environmentally protected area. Recently, people had spotted an eagle soaring over the island, and Johnny searched the sky in the hope of seeing it now. He didn't, and he wondered if eagles migrated for the winter. He and Carrie enjoyed the island view most in the fall when the lush green foliage transformed into a rich assortment of colors. But even now the snow covered branches of the bare trees painted a beautiful winter scene.

Johnny thought of the mountains of Afghanistan. They were both beautiful and foreboding. They were created by God but had become the shelter of the devil, the place where Osama bin-Laden might plan his next unspeakably evil deed. Johnny shrugged off the thought. The Taliban had been defeated and al-Qaeda had been seriously weakened. Beyond that, he'd have to accept the situation for now.

Carrie interrupted his thoughts. "Okay, lover boy. The evening is yours. I've scoped out some things we can do. There's a new restaurant in Langhorne, a converted farmhouse. It's supposed to be very romantic with a cozy fireplace and a nice menu. Or there's a new place in New Hope I read about. We can start planning the wedding and share our ideas with Brian and Jenny tomorrow. I've told Jenny a thousand times to just go ahead with her ceremony, but she insisted on waiting until we can do it together. She…"

Johnny interrupted her. "The first thing I want to do is kiss you." He did. It was the first real kiss they shared since he'd been home. When they parted he said, "How have you been?"

She diverted her eyes and said, "I've been okay."

He lifted her chin with his finger so their eyes met again and repeated softly, "How have you been?"

Her eyes began to fill, but she smiled bravely and said, "I've been fine." Then she broke down. He held her tightly as she sobbed into his shoulder. "I've missed you so much, and I was so worried about you."

"I'm sorry," he whispered over and over. "I hate leaving you."

"I know," she said as she stepped back and wiped her eyes.

He motioned to a bench nearby and said, "Let's sit for a minute."

Johnny's tone concerned her and she said, "Why? I don't want to sit."

"So we can talk," he said gently.

There was nothing Carrie wanted more for the past sixteen months than to talk with Johnny, to hear his voice and plan their future, but there was something ominous in his tone. She sensed bad news was coming and said, "No! I don't want to talk. Not like that." She looked frightened and her hands were trembling. "You're home now. We'll have dinner or go to the movies. Maybe stop for ice cream. We'll have fun. There's nothing else to talk about."

Johnny put his arm around her and guided her to the bench. She looked terrified, and Johnny was dying inside. He'd rather be pinned down in a Taliban ambush than have the conversation he was about to initiate. He exhaled slowly and began.

"You know what's been going on with Iraq."

Carrie followed the news as closely as anyone, but she refused to acknowledge Johnny's statement or the next crisis that loomed. He went on. "President Bush says that Saddam Hussein has weapons of mass destruction that he could conceivably use against us. There are also hints of a link between Hussein and al-Qaeda."

Carrie had an urge to cover her ears to shut him out, but she didn't.

Johnny continued. "The President put conditions on Saddam that he doesn't seem to be honoring. Bush says that if…"

Carrie stopped him. She knew what was coming next and didn't need to hear it. It didn't matter much why he was going back. She only had two questions. How long would he be gone and how dangerous it would be?

"I can't say how long because I don't know." Johnny said softly.

Carrie composed herself and said stoically, "You've been gone a long time, Johnny, and I've been a trooper about it."

"I know," Johnny said meekly.

"I got involved with my work. I wrote two articles a week. I spent time with my parents. I visited your family. I jogged. I volunteered at church. I did it all to keep my sanity until you returned."

"I know," Johnny repeated.

"Now you're telling me you're leaving again," The emotion was gone from her voice. "You've already fought in Afghanistan longer that most soldiers served in Vietnam. Why isn't that enough?"

Johnny rubbed her back and said, "We're at war, Carrie."

"We were at war then too, but a tour of duty was only one year."

"We had a draft then. There were plenty of people to go around. Things will be tight now if we go into Iraq."

"Then why don't we have a draft now?"

"That won't happen," he replied. "I don't think Congress would ever approve another draft."

"So what does that mean? We'll just keep using the same soldiers over and over?"

"I don't know," Johnny said. "Enlistments were up after 9-11, maybe they'll stay up. That will help."

"Maybe isn't good enough," she said, still without emotion. "And what will you be doing this time and how dangerous will it be? Tell me and don't sugarcoat it."

"You know I'm not supposed to say what I'll be doing, but I think you deserve to know."

"That's an understatement," Carrie said. "And you know I wouldn't tell anyone."

Johnny nodded. "If we go in, our job will be to secure the Iraqi oil fields in the north before Saddam can destroy them. I'll be working with the Kurds, which you know I was trained to do."

"Oil," Carrie said, shaking her head.

Johnny ignored that and said, "The inside word is that we'll bomb the daylights out of them for a while, I mean really blow them to pieces, and then the ground forces will take over. There won't be much left of them by the time we go in. It should be a short war."

"Should be?" Carrie said.

"The Iraqi people hate Saddam. Vice President Cheney says the people will welcome us as liberators. It won't last long."

Carrie laughed sarcastically. "Should be a snap, huh?"

"I'm not saying that," Johnny replied. "I'm just saying that the big shots think it will be a short one."

Carrie sighed and forced a smile. "Well," she said. "I said I'm in, so I'm in. Mr. Lombardi was away from his Angelina for three years straight in World War II. I guess I'll have to be as tough as she was. I guess if you have a man worth waiting for, you wait."

Now Johnny's eyes began to fill and he said, "I never dreamed I'd put you through this."

Her smile was genuine now as she wiped a tear from his cheek.

"So how many days leave was the army gracious enough to give you?"

Johnny didn't want to answer.

"How many?" she said playfully, trying to lighten his mood.

"Ten," Johnny said.

"Ten!" Carrie said. "What in the world will we do for ten days? I'll be bored with you after five."

Johnny grinned. He had the greatest woman in the world. "That includes travel time to and from Central Asia. Plus I've been home for two days."

"So that means?"

"So that means I have five days left in Bristol."

His words hit Carrie like a punch to the stomach, but she kept her spirit. "I guess I can put up with you for that long."

"I hope so," Johnny said.

"It would be nice if we could make a baby while you're home."

Johnny shot her a look and she burst out laughing. "Just kidding," she said.

Johnny stammered for a minute and said, "Do you want to? After all, we're married."

"I'd love to, but I still owe my mother that ceremony we've been talking about."

Johnny nodded. "A kid would be great."

"Here's the thing, Johnny Marzo. The next time you come home, and I don't care if it's for fifteen minutes or fifteen years, we're going to St. Theresa's, we're having that ceremony, and we're starting a family."

94- A Pre-Emptive Strike

March 2003

The public march toward war with Iraq solidified as early as October of 2002. That's when Congress authorized the Bush administration to take military action if the Iraqis failed to comply with United Nations Resolution 1441. Among other points, the resolution required Iraq to reveal the status of its suspected stockpiles of chemical and biological weapons and submit to UN inspection of alleged weapons facilities. Iraq repeatedly asserted that it had destroyed its stockpiles of such weapons and had no on-going production facility, although it could produce no evidence to that effect. Finally, under mounting pressure from the world community, Iraq allowed a UN inspection team, under the supervision of Hans Blix, to search the country for WMDs. The team began its work in late November of 2002 and by February of 2003, after over seven-hundred inspections, nothing of significance had been discovered.

Aside from some face-saving delays and assertions of sovereignty violations, Blix reported that Saddam was generally cooperating with the inspectors. Nevertheless, by late February of 2003 it was becoming increasingly clear that the United States would go to war. There was a military buildup in the Persian Gulf, National Guard and Army Reserve units were being activated, and the administration was putting pressure on the UN and its allies to take military action. In the face of this buildup, France took the position that it would veto any UN resolution that authorized military action as long as inspections continued and economic sanctions remained in place.

The Bush administration countered by declaring that it had all the authorization it needed to proceed with an invasion without additional UN action. In mid-March a meeting was held in the Azores attended by President Bush, Prime Minister Tony Blair of Great Britain, and Prime Minister Jose' Maria Aznar of Spain. The leaders declared that the time for diplomacy was over and that war was imminent if Iraq didn't immediately comply with all aspects of U.N. Resolution 1441.

Everyone at CIA headquarters worked late that night, and Brian had asked Dr. Blake to join him for drinks afterward. Instead of the usual watering hole, Brian suggested a quiet tavern not far from Langley. Everyone at headquarters had been on edge, but Brian had noticed that Dr. Blake was especially anxious and he wanted to know why.

They selected a booth in the back corner. The doctor ordered two scotches straight up, and Brian ordered a beer. They made small talk until the drinks arrived, and Blake tossed his first scotch down with one gulp. He was mid-way through sipping his second when Brian said, "May I speak freely?"

Blake shook his head. "Damn it, Kelly, I'm a busy man. I didn't think you asked to meet to discuss baseball. What's on your mind?"

Brian glanced at the widescreen television behind the bar. It was tuned to CNN, and the talking heads were all over the topic of Iraq. Brian looked back at Dr. Blake and said, "I wanted to ask what's on *your* mind."

Blake looked annoyed. "What's that supposed to mean?"

"It means I haven't seen you this much on edge in a long time."

"Really?"

"Yes, Sir. Really."

Blake finished his second scotch and looked for the waitress who was occupied. He pushed his glass toward the end of the table to signal he wanted a refill.

"Tell ya what, Wonder Boy, why don't you tell me what you think is on my mind?"

Brian sipped his beer and wiped his lips before speaking. "Okay, I will." He lowered his voice and began, "I think you're sick over the war that's about to start. I think you believe it's a big mistake. I think you've looked at the same intelligence reports I've looked at and haven't seen hard evidence that Saddam has WMDs. That's what I think is on your mind."

Blake ignored him and motioned impatiently to the waitress. They waited until she brought another scotch and then Blake said, "I have my doubts about what we're about to do, but you and I don't get to see everything. I guess someone else saw better information."

Brian could tell Blake didn't believe his own words. He was prepared to challenge him when Blake said, "What about you? What are you thinking?"

"Don't get me wrong," Brian said. "Saddam's an evil guy, one of the worst. I'd love to see him get kicked in the teeth, but not now, not under these conditions. We've got Saddam in check. The inspectors are in Iraq. The economic sanctions are in place. The whole world is breathing down his neck. There's no reason to go to war now, and, most importantly, there's also no evidence that he had anything to do with 9-11."

"What about the alleged meeting in the Czech Republic between Mohamed Atta, the leader of the 9-11 hijackers, and Iraqi agents?"

"With all due respect, Sir, you know that's a bunch of crap. The evidence we've seen on that is a joke."

Blake seemed detached as he responded. "Like I said, we don't get to see everything."

Brian put his elbows on the table and leaned toward his mentor. "I thought you respected me."

"I do. You're one of the best analysts I have."

"Then why not be honest with me? We're about to launch a pre-emptive war that changes our entire foreign policy. We're going it alone when the rest of the world, aside from Britain and Spain, is telling us to wait."

"It's not the job of the CIA to make policy," Blake pointed out. "We gather and analyze intelligence. The administration and the Departments of State and Defense, turn it into policy." Blake was mouthing the words, but his tone obviously lacked conviction.

Brian was growing agitated now, and he let Blake know it. "Does it bother you when what we hear the administration say in the news about *our* intelligence reports doesn't jive with much of what we've seen? Does it bother you when… "

Blake had had enough. He slammed his palm on the table and said, "It bothers the hell out of me! But what do you expect me to do about it?" He looked around the room and lowered his voice. "Maybe there's a bigger picture that we're not privy to, or maybe they're cherry picking intelligence to suite their goals. I don't know. What I do know is if they want a war, they're going to have it, and you and I can't stop it."

Brian sat back. He closed his eyes and exhaled deeply. After a time he said softly, "I read your report."

Blake nodded and said, "Do you mean the one on how the war will go?"

"Well, I read that too. Everyone knows that one is correct. Iraq's army is grossly weakened from what it was in 1991, and we're much stronger. We'll cut through Iraq like a knife cuts through butter. But I was talking about your assessment of what conditions will be like in Iraq after we defeat them."

"Oh, that one," Blake mumbled as he reached for his glass. The scotch was obviously taking effect.

"Yeah," Brian said, "that one. You said it would be impossible to control a country after the victory with the small force Secretary Rumsfeld is planning to use."

"I wrote that," Blake replied, "but I'm not a military analyst. I could be wrong."

"A lot of retired generals agree with you," Brian protested.

Blake shrugged and Brian continued. "You also said that Iraq's diverse religious and ethnic groups hate each other. You said that in the absence of a ruthless dictator like Saddam to keep the lid on, the country could erupt into sectarian violence."

"It's just a hunch," Blake said flatly. "We'll see."

Brian hated seeing Blake detached like this. He knew Blake didn't agree with what was going on and he wanted him to do something about it."

He softened his tone and said, "I got into this business because of you, Doctor Blake. You know I admire you."

"The sentiment is mutual," Blake said. "You serve your country well."

"Okay, we're two dedicated professionals. So how can we allow all this to happen?"

"*Allow?*" Blake said mockingly. "How can we *allow* this? My God, Brian. How can we stop it? The President wants it. Congress wants it. The American people want revenge. Hell, even the media seems to want it. I'm not seeing any great cry from the free press telling us to wait."

Brian knew all of that was true and he looked despondent. Blake sensed it and said, "Look. Maybe you're right about this being a mistake.

I think you are. But maybe there really is more information to go on than what we've seen. We're counter-terrorism. We were brought into this late to help identify targets if we invade. What does Rumsfeld call it, Shock and Awe?"

"Right," Brian said bitterly. "We should be spending our time finding al-Qaeda in Afghanistan instead of this nonsense in Iraq."

Blake waved him off. "I know. But the point is what if they're right? What if Rumsfeld and his assistant Wolfiwitz, Cheney, Bush, what if all of them are right? What if Saddam has WMDs? What if Saddam is working on a nuclear weapon? What if we can install a democracy in Iraq? What if a democratic Iraq leads to a democratic Iran? What if this war is a success?"

"That's a lot," Brian said. "But if all of that were true, then the war will go down as the right decision."

"That's right," Blake said. "And I think we're going start to find the answer in a day or two. Until we do, you keep your head down and do your job. Remember, we don't make policy at the CIA. We gather and analyze information. What the administration does with that information is out of our hands."

95- At a Time of Our Choosing

March 19, 2003

Brian sat at his desk glued to his computer screen. It was just after nine 2100 hours Washington time on March 19th, or 0500 hours on March 20 in Iraq. Two days earlier President Bush had announced that hostilities would commence at a time of our choosing. Now was that time. Central command had decided to open the war with a decapitation strike against Saddam Hussein. The goal was to end the conflict quickly by making Saddam the first victim of the war. To accomplish this, two F-117 Nighthawks were dispatched to his last known location, the Dora Farms area outside of Baghdad. Our latest ground intelligence stated that Saddam would be visiting his sons there at their compound. The F-117s would drop 2000 pound bunker-busters on the target. The F-117s payload would be supplemented by scores of

Tomahawk cruise missiles launched from submarines and surface ships hundreds of miles away.

The CIA had played a vital role in selecting the target by utilizing informants and agents knowledgeable of the dictator's movements. The assignment was tricky because Saddam moved frequently to avoid assassination attempts and often deviated from his planned itinerary. In addition, the aircraft and tomahawks would be traveling considerable distances and targets had to be programmed in advance. For these reasons, everyone knew the strike had a low probability of success, but all agreed that the possible reward was worth the effort.

Brian still had serious doubts about the wisdom of initiating the war, but if it was to be, then he hoped the decapitation strategy might lead to a settlement that would avoid the messy peacekeeping aftermath that he feared.

In the first gulf war, submarine based launchings accounted for only about four percent of cruise missiles used. In the war that was about to begin, plans called for subs to deliver almost a third of all missiles launched. Brian reviewed the list of surface that would be involved. Then he scanned the list of submarines scheduled to participate in the first strike. They were positioned in the Red Sea and the Arabian Gulf, far from their target. The list included the USS Boise, the USS Newport News, the USS Cheyenne, USS Montpelier…Something caught Brian's eye when he saw the Montpelier, and he stopped. It was a Los Angeles class nuclear attack sub equipped with Tomahawk missiles, nothing unusual there. Then he saw what had caught his eye. The commander's name was Bill Frake. The name swirled through Brian's memory bank until it hit home. Bill Frake was the naval officer who spoke to Brian's high school assembly back when he was a senior at Bristol High. Frake had been a lieutenant then.

More than ten years had passed since that day, but Brian remembered Frake's closing words to the students. *I don't know what the navy has in store for me, but I know my dream is to command my own submarine some day, and I've been fortunate enough to have pursued the training and experiences that could one day make that possible.*

Now Frake was the commander of a nine-hundred million dollar submarine and was about to launch a missile that could take out the man who was arguably the most ruthless dictator in the modern world.

447

Brian smiled. He had no doubt the missiles would hit their target. He prayed Saddam would be there when they did.

96- Shock and Awe at the Deli

Donna Marzo called Carrie on March 20th when the news broke that the full scale invasion had begun.

"I'm a nervous wreck," Carrie said. "How about you?"

"Same thing," Donna replied. "Listen, everyone is watching the news, and I'm the only woman here. Can you join us?"

Carrie's parents were away, and Jenny was stuck in Washington. Carrie didn't want to be alone, and she jumped at the chance to be with people close to Johnny. She raced over and found the gang focused on the TV.

"You're just in time," Nick said. "Things are about to heat up."

She hugged Donna and then took a seat with the rest of the guys.

Angelo was preparing sausage sandwiches and asked Carrie if she wanted onions and peppers. "Nothing, thanks. I'm not in the mood for eating."

"I'll take the works," Nick said. Then he said to Carrie, "Angelo and I have an arrangement. He cooks when he gets nervous, and I eat when I get nervous. It's a perfect match."

CNN was replaying segments of President Bush's speech from two nights before.

Iraq continues to possess and conceal some of the most lethal weapons ever devised... it has aided, trained, and harbored terrorists, including operatives of al Qaeda...

"Think he's right, Nick?" Jimmy asked.

"Don't know," Nick replied. "There seems to be a lot of disagreement. I guess we have to believe him."

Donna jumped in. "Are you kidding? People trusted Johnson in the sixties and look where it got us."

"This is different," Big Frankie said. "We've been attacked."

"Not by Iraq!" Donna shot back.

"Calm down!" Angelo yelled from behind the counter. "I want to hear the rest of this."

They turned their attention back to the speech.

...a broad coalition is now gathering to enforce the just demands of the world.

Saddam Hussein and his sons must leave Iraq within 48 hours. Their refusal to do so will result in military conflict commenced at a time of our choosing...

Speaking now to the Iraqi people, Bush said, *...As our coalition takes away their power, we will deliver the food and medicine you need. We will tear down the apparatus of terror and we will help you to build a new Iraq that is prosperous and free...*

Then he addressed a topic that hit home with Carrie.

And all Iraqi military and civilian personnel should listen carefully to this warning: In any conflict, your fate will depend on your actions. Do not destroy oil wells, a source of wealth that belongs to the Iraqi people...

Carrie caught the words "Oil wells." In a rare breech of secrecy, Johnny had told her he and his team would probably be helping the Kurds secure the rich oil fields in the north.

She tapped Nick on the shoulder. "Excuse me, Nick. If Johnny was doing something regarding oil, what would it be?"

"Everybody is doing something about oil," Nick said. "If you ask me, this whole war is about oil. It's about putting in a friendly government that will ship us all the oil we want at a decent price."

"Okay, I get that, but I'm wondering about Johnny."

"I apologize, princess. Here I am talking politics while you're worried about Johnny."

"She's not the only one," Donna said. "So what do you think Johnny is doing right now."

"Well," Nick said. "You have to remember, Special Forces rarely do the things you think of when you're thinking about conventional Army or Marines. If I knew what part of the country he's in I could..."

Carrie interrupted. "Let's just say he's going to be in the North, just for an example."

Nick looked at her and wondered if Johnny had told her something. He smiled and said, "Okay. Just for an example, let's say he's in the North."

The room got quiet. On the TV screen, the sky over Iraq looked like a fireworks display.

"See that? That's just the beginning of what is expected to be the most concentrated barrage of firepower unleashed in half a century."

"Yeah," Jimmy said. "Blow up their asses."

Big Frankie gave him a light tap to the head and said, "The girl is concerned about her fiancé. Take it easy."

"Sorry, Carrie," Jimmy said. "I didn't mean to be... whatever I was being."

Nick shook his head and went on. "We're not just dropping bombs willy nilly. Those are either fixed targets identified months earlier or they're active targets identified more recently. I guarantee you that our Special Forces infiltrated Iraq days ago getting ready for this. Johnny may be painting targets with lasers or calling in coordinates right now."

Carrie stiffened. She didn't like that option.

"The other possibility is that his team has been assigned to capture and protect something of strategic importance. It could be a weapons stockpile, power grid, oil pipeline or refinery. As Saddam's army retreated from Kuwait in 1991, they set every oil well they could find on fire. Johnny's mission could be to infiltrate and secure a site before the enemy even knows he's at war and then hold it. That's why I'm pretty sure they've been there for days in advance of what you're seeing now, hunkering down and waiting to strike."

Carrie didn't like that option either. "Are there any other possibilities?"

Nick rubbed his chin in thought. "Well, when the ground fighting stops, and believe me, it won't take long after three days or so of this bombing, the Special Forces may get involved in training friendly Iraqis to become soldiers. That's one of their specialties."

Carrie looked at Nick, and he could see she was looking for reassurance. He was about to give it to her when Angelo broke in. "Can I say something here?" He took off his apron and came around from behind the counter. He put his arm around Carrie's shoulder and said softly. "I'm sure you know my history with the draft."

Carrie said she did.

"Sometimes I can't shake the feeling that Johnny got involved in all this to compensate for what I did by going to Canada."

"You shouldn't think that way," Carrie said. "He's never even hinted at that. I think he just believes in what he's doing."

"And I hope he knows how much I respect him for it."

"I know he does, Mr. Marzo. He's told me how much it means to him."

Angelo nodded. "I won't lie and say I'm in favor of this war, because I'm not sure that I am. And I don't trust that…"

Donna touched his arm and said, "Not now, Angelo."

"You're right," Angelo said. "That's another topic. I just want you to know that I think my son is one of the best trained soldiers there is. And I know he'll return safely. I know you're worried. Hell, we're all worried, but I just wanted to say that we're here together and our Johnny…your Johnny will be okay."

"Damn right he will," Jimmy said.

"Guaranteed," Nick added. "And we'll all be here waiting for him."

Carrie turned to face Mr. Marzo. He was a hard man, not given to emotional displays, and they had never shared an intimate moment. She draped her arms around his neck and whispered "thank you." She could see that his eyes were filling and knew hers were too. She kissed him on the cheek and everyone cheered.

Nick lightened the mood by saying, "I've got a warm feeling in my tummy right now and an empty feeling too. Can a guy get some food around here?"

"Absolutely," Angelo said. "Jimmy, get a couple of six packs from the back room. We've got a war to watch."

Donna took Carrie by the hand and said, "How about if you and I leave these guys alone for a while and go into the house for a nice cup of hot tea."

"That would be great," Carrie said.

Donna led her to the family kitchen and put the kettle on. "We spend so much time in the deli that people sometimes think we don't have a residence."

"I guess it's convenient having the house and store attached, but I have to admit that the deli is one of my favorite spots in the world."

Donna smiled and said, "Mine too." She got their cups from the cabinet and said, "You know those guys love you like a daughter. There aren't too many women that frequent the store."

Carrie smiled and said, "I love them too." She was beginning to feel a part of the family. She loved Johnny's parents and appreciated the way they treated her. She suddenly had an urge to tell Mrs. Marzo that she and Johnny were married. She missed him so much and felt that confiding in his mother would somehow bring him closer.

Donna poured their tea and sat next to Carrie at the table and said, "Johnny is so lucky to have you."

Carrie smiled and Donna said, "I want you to promise me something."

"Sure," Carrie said.

Donna took Carrie's hand and admired her engagement ring, and Carrie felt guilty that she kept her wedding band in a drawer. "Angelo and I got married when we were nineteen," Donna said. "We were so much in love. Even though we were so young, I've never regretted it. Not for a minute. He's a good man with strong convictions."

"I can tell," Carrie said.

Donna released her hand and said, "I do have one slight regret though."

Carrie was surprised and asked what it was.

"We were married in a half-assed ceremony by a magistrate in Montreal with no friends or family around. It was one of the happiest and saddest days of my life."

Carrie didn't know what to say.

"So I want you to promise me that when Johnny comes home, and I know he will come home, promise that the two of you will have the biggest damn wedding Bristol has ever seen. I want to see dresses, bridesmaids, flowers, balloons, doves, centerpieces, people dancing, booze, food, limos, three priests on the altar, the whole bit. It will be the wedding I never had and the wedding you and Johnny deserve. Do you promise?"

Carrie took her hand and said, "Absolutely, Mrs. Marzo. I promise."

97- Oil!

Turkey was a member of NATO, and consequently one of America's allies. The United States had hoped to launch a two-pronged invasion of Iraq, with one prong entering from Kuwait in the south and the other from Turkey in the north. However, the Turkish government was under intense pressure from its Muslim population to avoid the appearance of being America's lap dog. So in the end, Turkey refused to allow an all-out assault from its soil. But that didn't prevent the Turkish military from allowing small groups of American Special Forces to operate from their country under cover.

In the days preceding the bombing of Iraq, while American and British forces massed along the Kuwaiti border, Captain Marzo's A-Team, along with several other Special Forces units, quietly assembled on the Turkish border. Then, several hours before the bombing of Saddam's suspected location, they slipped into Iraq under cover of darkness.

Their mission was to secure a key junction along the oil pipeline that ran northward from Mosul in Northern Iraq to Turkey. The oil fields around Kirkuk and Mosul held some of the richest reserves in the world. Both areas had refineries, and the Iraq-Turkey pipeline ran north toward the massive Ceyhan line in Turkey. In the first gulf war, Saddam's forces, retreating out of Kuwait, had set oil wells ablaze and destroyed pipelines as a way to disrupt the oil supply and punish the world. The dense black smoke from the burning rigs caused an environmental emergency and obscured Iraqi forces from the allied air assault.

Marzo's team was charged with protecting the flow of oil this time by securing a main pipeline junction and its shut off valves. Other teams would do the same at other junctures. It would be impossible to prevent Saddam's forces from damaging the pipeline somewhere along the hundreds of miles it covered, but if the junctions and shut off valves were protected, then repairs would be quick and disruptions kept to a minimum.

Marzo's team traveled in three armored Humvees. Under difficult conditions they covered ground quickly, assisted by their GPS and night vision equipment. They avoided the main roads that posed the danger of checkpoints and booby traps. Northern Iraq had been a no-fly zone since the first gulf war, and America owned the skies. Infra red sensors on air force drones kept the team informed of possible enemy detachments in the area. Each man was equipped with a chemical warfare suit with a charcoal liner designed to filter out the kinds of lethal substances Saddam was known to have used in the past. Every soldier in the Iraqi theater was terrified of the possibility of chemical or biological attack, but they had trained for it and felt prepared.

Marzo hadn't slept for longer than two hours in the last twenty-four. Once the action started that would become the norm. They were operating on adrenalin now, adrenalin and fear. They drove in silence, each struggling to keep his focus, but each inevitably drifting to thoughts of home. Images of Carrie, the deli, Brian, and Jenny flashed in Marzo's subconscious, but he pushed them aside. There was no time for them now; besides, he reminded himself, he was fifty miles deep into enemy territory with only thirteen other men, and a war was about to begin. He steeled himself against thoughts of home by relying on his practice of believing he was already dead.

Sergeant Steve Bauer, an engineering specialist on the team, drove Marzo's lead vehicle. With him were Mazilli and Perez. Duncan was in the second vehicle with Farina and Dobbins. Everyone else on the team was in vehicle three. Marzo checked his equipment, the GPS had them on course and the drone's infrared sensors detected no enemy in the area, at least not yet. It was 0300 hours. They were moving in almost total darkness in an area free from civilians. Hopefully, that was the case, Marzo thought; because the team might be forced to treat anyone they encountered as hostiles and take them out quickly. Marzo hoped that wouldn't happen.

The air was warm and dry, and Captain Marzo knew that by mid April temperatures would soar to well above one hundred degrees. They drove south over the barren landscape, traveling parallel to the pipeline but remaining at least five miles to its east. They'd gone another ten miles now, and Marzo checked his watch to assure himself they were still on schedule. They were.

Nothing had gone wrong so far, and if something did, Marzo knew they weren't totally alone. There was a squadron of Blackhawk helicopters locked and loaded at the Turkish border and ready to lift off for a rescue and extraction mission if needed. Still, the deeper the team penetrated into Iraq, the longer the time it would take for help to arrive. In a firefight, thirty minutes could be an eternity. If the team encountered trouble, they'd have to handle it quickly and decisively.

They turned when they were five miles away from the target and headed toward the pipeline. At three miles they exited their vehicles and began the final approach on foot. No doubt the junction and pumping station were booby trapped to be detonated if necessary, so the element of surprise was crucial. The team had to eliminate the enemy before anyone could destroy the facility.

Assisted by their night vision gear, they moved quickly, guided now by hand held GPS that identified the pipeline and terrain before them. When they were within a mile, they circled to the south and stopped five hundred yards from the target. The plan called for a southern assault because it was the direction guards would consider the least likely approach and was therefore the least likely to be booby trapped. Then they waited.

The command post relaying the information from the drone to Marzo reported eight guards at the site. Sergeant Ricky Bond, the team's communications specialist, now had the image of the site on his computer screen. Four of the infrared dots showed slight movement, while the other four remained stationary. It was the best situation Marzo could hope for: four of the enemy were on guard duty and four were apparently asleep. The team spread out, advanced to within two hundred yards, and inched forward. All were in radio contact, and all knew the plan. The four most accomplished snipers on the team would each select one of the patrolling sentries. Another four would arm their grenade launchers with stun grenades aimed at the guardhouse where the remaining hostiles were sleeping. Marzo and the rest of the team would then storm the target to take out survivors of the initial attack before they could damage the pumping station.

At 0525 hours, just minutes before missiles would commence falling on Baghdad at Saddam's last known location, Captain John Marzo kissed the medal Mr. Lombardi had given him and then gave the word to fire. The war against Iraq had begun.

98- Phone Cards for Our Troops

November 2003

The Deli had become Nick's newsroom. He sat at the card table and watched war reports on CNN for hours each day, interrupting his viewing only when an irritated Angelo ordered him to do a chore.

"If ya wanna eat, ya gotta work," Angelo would say, and Nick would grudgingly perform the task quickly and return to his seat.

Jimmy was by his side as always, watching as Nick took extensive notes and delivered the latest news to anyone who entered the store. Jimmy developed the habit of repeating everything Nick reported just in case the listener missed it the first time.

One issue they were keenly interested in was the search for weapons of mass destruction. Day after day they waited patiently for news of their discovery, but nothing came. Angelo had long-since decided that the threats of WMD's had been a ruse used by the administration to justify a war they wanted to fight for other reasons. Every so often, to ease his boredom and lash out at the President, he would shout to Nick from behind the meat counter, "Did they find anything yet?" and Nick would shout back sarcastically, "Nothing yet." To which Jimmy would shake his head and add innocently, "They just can't find them."

On slow news days Nick would refer to his past journal entries, and he and Jimmy would deliver a chronology of major events to date. If no one else was around, Nick would just read his notes out loud as Angelo filled food orders, rolling his eyes as Nick droned on.

March 20, hostilities began…Saddam eludes early missile strike… April 3, Americans capture Baghdad Airport…April 9, Baghdad falls and Saddam's statue is pulled down…April 13, American led Kurdish forces take the northern cities of Kirkuk and Mosul…

Nick especially liked that reference because they had learned from Brian that Johnny had been operating with the Kurds in the North.

Nick also alerted the gang to major events about to unfold and encouraged them to watch on television. He had summoned everyone to the deli for President Bush's May 1st announcement that major combat operations were over. Angelo, Donna, Big Frankie, Nick and Jimmy were all there. Donna even invited Carrie.

They watched as President Bush, flying as a copilot in a Lockheed S-3 Viking, landed on the aircraft carrier USS Abraham Lincoln and emerged from the plane wearing a flight suit, with his pilot's helmet tucked smartly under his arm.

As the deck hands cheered wildly for the President, Donna said, "Who the heck does he think he is?"

"He must have seen that *Top Gun* pilot movie with Tom Cruise," Angelo said, dripping with sarcasm.

"Trust me," Donna said, "He ain't no Tom Cruise."

"I don't know," Jimmy said, "I think he looks handsome."

Nick shot Jimmy a look and Jimmy said, "You know what I mean."

"I never know what you mean," Nick replied. "But that's okay because you don't either."

"Anyway," Jimmy said. "Bush is a jerk."

"Why don't you guys give the President a break?" Big Frankie said. "He just won a war."

"The soldiers won the war," Angelo retorted, "not that dimwit."

Carrie had tuned them out as the exchange grew into another pro Bush- anti-Bush argument. All she cared about was how events in Iraq impacted on Johnny's future. She watched as the President later appeared before microphones on the flight deck and announced to the assembled crew:

"*We have difficult work to do in Iraq. We are bringing order to parts of that country that remain dangerous...*" But then he said the words she'd been waiting to hear, "*In the Battle of Iraq, the United States and our allies have prevailed.*"

Behind him was a large red, white and blue banner that read, *Mission Accomplished*, and seeing it gave Carrie a tremendous sense of relief. One hundred and seventy-six Americans died since the conflict had begun, and Johnny wasn't one of them. Hearing the President's words gave her hope that Johnny's time in Iraq would be coming to a close. She was wrong.

That was May of 2003, and as the months wore on Johnny's letters and calls became more frequent and his duties less secret. Possibly as a result of his success in training the Kurds, Johnny's team had been assigned to train what was to be an elite corps of Iraqi Special Forces.

Once trained, they would participate in rooting out growing pockets of resistance as Americans attempted to turn over control of the country to the Iraqis.

Carrie felt that training missions sounded safe, but she was still troubled by the steady number of American deaths. There were thirty in June, forty-eight in July and another thirty-five in August. Violence was on the rise again, and it was apparent that not all Iraqis viewed the Americans as liberating heroes.

Carrie kept herself busy with her writing, and had been awarded her own weekly column. It was devoted to the war from the perspective of those on the home front who had loved ones in Iraq or Afghanistan. She did an article on the medical, psychological, educational, and job placement services veterans would need upon their return and used Nick as resource. An article she wrote on the difficulties faced by army wives and girlfriends left behind led to the formation of a woman's support group which she continued to facilitate. She also saw Brian and Jenny every other weekend. They would come to Bristol once a month to visit their parents, and she would go to Washington once a month to stay with them.

In mid November Carrie was spending a quiet evening at home when she received her weekly call from Johnny. People were still sending phone cards to servicemen, and Johnny made use of them whenever he could. He assured her he was fine and then listened as she brought him up to date on her work, their parents, and the guys at the deli. Then she said, "You'll never guess where I got my car inspected today."

"Let's see," Johnny replied. "Would it be Bobby's new service station?"

"Bingo!" she said. "It was so much fun. The place is called Honest Bob's Service Center. The sub message on the sign reads, 'We drain your oil, not your wallet.' Cute huh? It was crowded that day too, so I guess business is good."

"Brian's a marketing genius," Johnny said. Then he asked, "Is Bobby happy?"

"Are you kidding? He's ecstatic. Brian bought all state-of-the-art tools and equipment."

"How about Tommy? Is he doing okay?"

"That's the best part," she gushed. "Tommy is great. He looks good, he's working hard, and he's learning the trade. He asked me to send his regards. Bobby did too. And I saw Mickey at the drug store about a week ago. He's doing well too and asked me to say hello."

"And what about you?" Johnny asked. "How are things going?"

She got quiet for a time and then said, "I told you. I'm working hard and enjoying my job."

"I know that," Johnny said. "Mom, Nick, Mickey, everyone who writes to me sends me your articles. They're terrific."

"Thank you," she said softly.

"But I'm not asking about how work is; I'm asking how *you* are."

Her voice lowered and she said truthfully, "It's been ten months, Johnny. I miss you so much, and I worry all the time. Sometimes it's pretty hard."

It tore Johnny up each time he thought about what he'd put her through. He took a breath and said, "I've got some news."

The words stung Carrie, and she was immediately apprehensive. She didn't want any more news. She was close to her breaking point already and wasn't sure how much more she could handle. The only thing she wanted to hear was that he was coming home. Her mind raced as she considered what on earth the army could be asking him to do next. Finally, in a voice that was barely audible, she said, "What kind of news?"

Johnny could sense her tension and said evenly, "I'm being transferred."

Bang! There it was again. It was like an explosion had gone off inside her head. Where would they be sending him this time? Back to Afghanistan? Turkey? Maybe on a secret mission to a place he couldn't even tell her about. She summoned her strength and said, "Where?"

In a crystal clear voice he said, "Carrie, I'm being transferred to Belgium."

Carrie thought she misunderstood him. "Belgium! Did you say Belgium?"

"That's exactly what I said," Johnny replied lightheartedly. "I'm going to Belgium."

Carrie brightened. It wasn't home, but at least he'd be out of harm's way. "My God, Johnny, that's terrific. What in the world will you be doing in Belgium?"

"Believe it or not, the war in Afghanistan is showing signs of heating up again. Some NATO countries are sending limited numbers of peacekeeping forces to help us. My job will be to work on joint training exercises with our NATO allies. We'll work on how to coordinate US and NATO forces. My whole team is going."

"When do you go?"

"It won't be for two months yet. That will give me and the team a full twelve months in Iraq."

"Don't worry Johnny, I know how long it's been!" Carrie said emphatically. "In fact, you've been on this tour for ten months, two weeks, and four days as of now."

"Yeah," Johnny said with a hint of regret in his voice. "I suppose you do know."

She wished his transfer would be sooner, but she wasn't complaining. She sounded giddy when she said, "This is too good to be true, Johnny. Will I be able to see you?"

"Absolutely. There may be some scattered field exercises, but we'll be on a base ninety percent of the time. It's mostly showing each other how we operate."

Carrie wiped her eyes and said, "You have no idea how happy this makes me."

"Me too," he replied. Then he said, "I have more news."

"More news! Don't spoil this, Johnny Marzo," she said half kidding and half seriously. "Please don't spoil this."

"I'll try not to," Johnny said lightly.

"So what is it?"

Johnny had dreamt of this moment for a long time, and now he struggled to choke back his own emotions. When he gathered himself he said, "I'm coming home, Carrie."

Carrie's heart leaped. "You're getting a leave?"

"No," Johnny said. "I'm leaving the army and coming home."

Carrie was too stunned to speak, so Johnny did. "I've thought about doing it for a long time. This has all been so unfair to you, and I can't put you through it anymore. I've done my job. I've served in Kosovo,

Turkey, Afghanistan and Iraq. I've done my duty to the country I love. Now it's time to take care of the woman I love."

Carrie was still too numb to speak, and Johnny continued. "I have no idea what I'll do for a living yet. But I know a lot of Special Forces guys who go into law enforcement when they get out. Some work for security companies too. You know, high tech corporate security stuff. I have some skills; I'll find something."

He could tell she was crying now, and she said, "I don't care if you shine shoes for a living. Just come home."

"I will," he replied, "and we're finally gonna have that beautiful life we've dreamed of together."

Carrie felt a sudden wave of panic. She said, "Are you sure you can do this? Nothing can go wrong. No bureaucratic mess-ups? Don't get my hopes up unless you're sure."

"There won't be a problem," Johnny assured her. "As an officer, I can give up my commission and leave active service as long as I don't have outstanding commitments. The army is like a cell phone carrier. It gives you extra benefits if you sign up for a longer contract. My current commitment ends when these two months are up. So it will be a good time to leave. I would never do this while I'm in a war zone. I could never allow myself to walk away like that. But once they decided to transfer me to Europe, it gave me the opportunity, and I'm gonna take it.

"When I get to Brussels, I'm going to give the army my sixty-day notice. So, I'll spend two more months here, and two months in Belgium. I'll be home by spring. Count on it."

With that she broke down completely and Johnny said above her sobs, "Listen, Carrie. I want you to visualize something, okay?" When she didn't answer he said, "Are you all right?"

She managed a weak "yes," and he went on. "When I get home, we're gonna do all the things we used to do. We'll take long walks together. We're gonna eat pizza at Cesare's. We're gonna drink Espresso martinis at the bar at the King George. Are you hearing this?"

The best she could do was to nod into the phone, but Johnny could hear her breathing. "Remember that bed and breakfast we stayed at on Long Beach Island, the one with the balcony?" She managed another "yes" and he said, "We're going back there, Carrie. We're gonna get take-out and a bottle of wine and spend all night on that balcony, just like we did before. And we're gonna eat ice cream at that place where the waiters sing. We're gonna have a home, and we're gonna spend long nights together reading books and drinking tea. And when we go to sleep, we'll be right next to each other, and we'll be able to reach out and touch each other whenever we want. We'll visit Mr. Lombardi in the summer and stock up on tomatoes. We'll stop by the deli for some laughs. We'll go to church on Sundays, just like normal people. We'll do everything together, and after a while, we'll forget we were ever apart."

He waited for her to gain some composure, and then he said, "I need you to see all of that, Carrie. Tell me you can see it."

She finally replied in a choked voice, "I love you, Johnny Marzo, and I can see it. I can see all of it."

"Good," he said, "Because I've been seeing it for a long time."

She was more composed now and said, "Me too. I just wish we didn't have to wait five months, but we'll make it."

"One more thing," Johnny said jokingly.

Carrie was laughing through her tears now and shouted into the phone, "Stop it! What else could there be?"

"I know five months is still a long time to wait, but I thought it would help pass the time if you talked to Brian, Jenny, our parents and Father Morris. Start planning our wedding ceremony. I'm thinking a May wedding would be nice."

99- Pre-Nuptial ...

Carrie was terrified that something dreadful would happen to Johnny before his tour ended in Iraq. The wait seemed endless, and she passed the time just as Johnny had suggested, by making wedding plans and keeping up with her work.

She gave her parents the news and never saw them happier. Carrie's mother told her there was a time during her illness when she feared she'd never see her daughter's wedding. Now, healthy and vibrant, she scanned bride magazines and led Carrie on the mother-daughter ritual of searching for a wedding dress. They visited malls in Quakerbridge,

King of Prussia and Cherry Hill and still hadn't put a dent in the possibilities. Mr. Boyle stayed clear of the process and happily gave the ladies a generous budget which Mrs. Boyle privately told Carrie she intended to ignore.

"Your father is a wonderful husband and a practical man. He's earned a handsome living and always valued the importance of saving," she confided. "Now, it's about time I teach him the importance of spending."

Of course, Johnny had shared the whole plan with Brian first, and when Brian told Jenny the news she could hardly contain herself. She called Carrie right away, and the two were like school girls who'd just been asked to the prom. She made plans to come home to meet with Father Morris and join Carrie in the hunt for a reception hall. Brian had suggested someplace swanky like one of the stately mansions along the river in Andalusia or Bensalem, or someplace in Philly like the Crystal Tea Room or the Art Museum. But the girls vetoed all of them. This wedding was a homecoming of sorts, and they wanted the celebration in Bristol where it would be convenient for the guests. Eventually, they chose the large banquet hall at Mickey's firehouse, Goodwill Hose Company #3. Brian balked at first, but relented when the girls said they'd allow him to rent linen, china, and silver for the tables, have white gloved servers, and adorn the room with plants and flowers from every florist in Bristol.

Selecting a May wedding date became problematic because there wasn't a day in May when the church and hall were available at the same time. Reluctantly, they moved the date to Saturday, June 19, and it didn't take long to realize that their mothers would welcome the extra time to plan.

They met with Father Morris, and he was wonderful. He was actually excited about the idea of a double wedding. This would be his first, and he thought it would be fun. The girls agonized over whether or not to tell him the unusual nature of their ceremony and their civil marriages. In the end, they decided to tell him the truth. Father smiled and said it was not a problem. "Technically," he said, "you're not married in the eyes of the church. The church respects the legal nature of your relationship, but I have no problem keeping your civil ceremony our secret. Besides, I think your mothers deserve this, so don't give it another thought."

As the days and weeks passed, conditions in Iraq worsened. Since President Bush's mid-summer assertion that the U.S. had sufficient forces to suppress the insurgents and his "Bring 'em on" taunt in front of the media, eighty-three more Americans died in the summer and another one-hundred and fifty-seven were lost in the fall. The rate continued throughout December and January. The insurgents were making effective use of improvised explosives and rocket propelled grenades to attack American convoys. The Pentagon and the American public learned a painful lesson about the vulnerability of the unarmored Humvees. In addition to the rising death toll, American men and women were being maimed in the unprotected vehicles.

In December Secretary of Defense Donald Rumsfeld visited American Troops at their staging area in Kuwait, hoping to boost morale. Instead, the troops peppered the secretary with embarrassing questions about the lack of protective armor on their vehicles. A national Guardsman from Tennessee spoke of troops resorting to what he called hillbilly armor. He said soldiers were relegated to searching through junkyards for sheets of scrap iron that they could bolt to their vehicles for added protection. Rumsfeld was taken off guard by the exchange and promised that the supply of more heavily armored vehicles would increase.

Foot soldiers had armor problems as well. Most of the troops had been issued Vietnam era flack jackets that were of little protection against the modern penetrating ammunition used by the enemy. As word of this reached home, the networks broadcasted cases of American parents purchasing and sending their sons and daughters state-of-the-art Kevlar vests with ceramic inserts.

The general public was shocked and outraged, and so was Carrie. She interviewed parents and spouses of soldiers in the war zone and wrote an angry article that drew widespread attention. The premise was that a disproportionately small percentage of Americans was shouldering the bulk of the war effort. At the very least, we should give them the proper equipment. The result of her article and others like it across the country had elected officials falling over each to rectify the problem.

The days passed until Johnny's exit from Iraq was just two weeks away. His orders arrived instructing him to report to Brussels by March 2. He would spend a week with his NATO counterparts, after which he was entitled to a week-long leave. Following his leave, he would submit his sixty-day notice and spend his final two months assisting NATO's preparations for their peace-keeping mission. He expected to be out of the army and home by May 20.

Brian put a call through to Johnny in mid-February when he heard about Johnny's pending leave. He began with his customary ribbing. "Hey, Captain, did you get your AARP card yet? I hear they offer lots of benefits."

"Drop it, wise guy. It's a sore subject," Johnny replied.

"Mixed feelings?"

"Very," Johnny said. "I know it's the right thing to do, especially for Carrie, but I just don't feel good about leaving the team. I'll feel different once I get to Brussels."

"You've paid your dues, Johnny boy, big time."

"I know," Johnny said. He was eager to change the subject and said, "So what about you? What are you up to?"

Brian's tone became more subdued. "I've got some thinking to do. Your decision to leave the army has Jenny suggesting I reconsider my future. There was a time when I thought this would be my life's work, but I've been at it for eight years now, and I have to admit I'm fried. The Agency is going crazy. We've got a war in Iraq, a brewing problem in Afghanistan, and we're tracking terrorists around the world."

Johnny let Brian vent.

"I don't know…I guess I'm a little disillusioned," Brian admitted. "No WMDs, the Taliban's regrouping, Iraq is deteriorating."

Johnny knew Brian was discouraged, but his friend sounded even more frustrated than he anticipated. Brian went on. "Do you know that we have fewer troops per capita to control Iraq than New York City has policemen to control its population?"

"I'm in Iraq, remember, Brian? I get it."

"Right. Sorry about that. Anyway, we massed a half million troops for the first Iraq war, and we weren't even planning on occupying the country later. Why did Rumsfeld think we could handle this one with so small a force? And how did he convince everybody else in the administration he was right?" His voice was rising now. "I mean, who plans this stuff. I'm in the damned CIA. I'm supposed to be part of the solution but…"

"Hey, take it easy," Johnny said. "Planning the war wasn't your job, remember? Your assignment was to avert terror plots, and you've rolled up quite a record doing that. How many did you head off, fifteen, twenty?"

"Twenty-two, if you're really counting. But it's those one or two that you don't head off that get you." Brian got quiet and then added, "Like I said, I used to think I'd make a career of this. I used to love it…Now, I just don't know."

"What would you do if you left the agency?" Johnny asked.

"I'm a millionaire, remember? Brian joked. "I don't have to do anything but eat grapes if I want to." He laughed at himself and added, "Maybe I'll open a string of auto repair shops. Did I tell you that Bobby's place is booming? Honest Bob's Auto Repair. He's got appointments now, and they're backed up. Bobby says Tommy loves it and is doing great."

"Carrie told me," Johnny said. "That's real good news."

Brian was animated again. "I can franchise the Honest Bob's idea. I'll open an Honest Joe's, Honest Ralph's. Hell, I'll open the first female owned shop. I'll call it Honest Jane's or whatever. You know how single women feel mechanics cheat them on their auto repairs. I'll make a fortune."

Johnny was relieved that Brian didn't sink too deeply into the funk he was in just a minute earlier. "Be careful," he said. "I don't want to see you on food stamps in your old age. How's the stock market?"

"I'm out."

"Out of money or out of the market?"

"The market, wacko. I've got plenty of money."

Johnny was more than surprised. Playing the market was Brian's hobby. "You pulled out?"

"Completely. I read some experts who convinced me we're overextended. I think we're in for a downturn. It may not be for a few years or so, but some savvy people say it's coming. So I thought, why be greedy? I've made a lot of money. So I pulled it and put it in some no-risk instruments. I'm feeling good about it. I'm much more relaxed."

"Sounds like you know what you're doing," Johnny said.

"Let's just say things have gone very well, and no one ever went broke taking a profit."

When it got quiet again, Brian cleared his throat and said, "Speaking of spending money, I have an idea."

"We weren't speaking of spending money," Johnny joked. "We were speaking of saving it."

"Well, now we're speaking of spending it, Captain Marzo."

Johnny sighed and said, "Here we go again."

"Just hear me out, okay?"

"Sure, Brian. I'm listening."

"Well, first of all, we've all been working very hard, and ..."

Johnny interrupted. "Can we please skip the rationale and just tell me what you want to do?"

"No," Brian said. "The rationale is always important."

"Fine," Johnny replied. "But give me the short version."

"I'll do my best. Point number one, we've all been working hard. Two, Carrie hasn't seen you in fourteen months. Three, none of us has ever seen Spain before. Four..."

Johnny jumped in again. Spain!"

"Yeah, none of us have been there and the girls are excited to see it."

Johnny was still processing that as Brian went on. "I've been thinking about what to get you guys for a wedding gift and decided on a trip to Spain for the four of us."

Johnny started to protest, but Brian cut him off. "With all due respect, Captain Marzo, just shut up. You can pay for all the drinks when we get there. Fair enough?"

Johnny laughed and said, "I have a job you know. I can pay for me and Carrie."

"You're getting married, my friend, for real this time. You're gonna have some start-up costs. Save your money for that."

Johnny knew it was useless to fight with his friend over money, but to save face he said they'd talk about payment later. Then he asked, "So when would we take this trip?"

"We go in three weeks," Brian said flatly.

"Three weeks!" Johnny thundered. "Are you serious? I assumed you meant we'd go this summer or fall, sometime after the wedding."

"Too long to wait," Brian said. "Carrie misses you now, we all need a vacation, and you'll be on leave. This is perfect"

"I don't know," Johnny said warily.

"You know how I like to think out of the box, right?"

"Yeah, I know," Johnny deadpanned.

"I'm calling this a pre-nuptial honeymoon. Good huh?"

"Terrific," Johnny said sarcastically. "It's guaranteed to start a trend."

"That's what I think," Brian said proudly. "Maybe I should open a travel agency. We'll..."

"Knock it off," Johnny snapped. "I guess I'd be wasting my time if I offered some ideas about the trip, right?"

"You're absolutely right. The trip is totally planned. The only thing you get to do is come and have a good time."

Johnny smiled to himself. He knew Brian was happiest when he was in control, especially when he was planning vacations.

"Okay, so fill me in."

"The girls are flying to Madrid on March 7th. I've got some work to finish up here and they want to experience the countryside before they visit some museums in Madrid. Jenny wants to check out their displays for ideas she can use here in Washington. Anyway, I'll be taking a red eye that will get me into Madrid very early on March 11th. You're flying in from Brussels the same morning. We'll hook up at the airport, meet the girls, and spend one night in Madrid. Then we take a short flight to Barcelona where we'll stay for five days. I'm told it's a beautiful seaside city with lots of restaurants and clubs. It won't be warm enough for the beach or swimming, but it has a spectacular view of the Mediterranean. We'll have a blast."

100- Madrid

March 11, 2004

Carrie and Jenny quickly fell in love with Spain. They began their visit in the ancient city of Toledo known for its mosaic of Christian, Muslim and Jewish faiths. Carrie had become fascinated by the extensive influence of Muslim culture after the Moorish conquest, and Jenny was enthralled by the panoramic view from the elevated city. Toledo's medieval character was most evidenced by the fortified palace, Alcazar, that loomed above the narrow cobblestone streets and the magnificent, seven-hundred year old Gothic Cathedral that had taken three centuries to build.

They spent a full day touring the walled city and watched the sun set while dining on roasted lamb at an outdoor restaurant overlooking the Tagus River. They found the city to be even more spectacular at night, and they lingered at their table long enough to finish a bottle of full-bodied Cebreros.

The next day they headed north toward Madrid, stopping overnight at a small town thirty kilometers south of the city, where they sampled Castilian bread and cheese made from sheep's milk and, of course, more wine. They took a small room in the village and Jenny wrote post cards while Carrie drafted an outline for an article.

When they were finished, Jenny made tea and poured each of them a cup. Carrie said, "I can't believe I'm going to see Johnny tomorrow."

Jenny smiled and said, "I can't wait to see the two of you together again. But this vacation is only a teaser. Soon you'll see him every day."

"And," Carrie gushed, "We will publicly be Mr. and Mrs. Johnny Marzo."

"Your mom is already engrossed with the wedding arrangements and loving it. She's going to be so happy."

"Yours too," Carrie said. "It's going to be great."

They sipped their tea, each lost in thoughts of the wedding ceremony, the reception, and the life that would follow. Jenny broke the silence. "I can't believe I never said this before, but I just want you to know I consider you the sister I never had."

Carrie smiled. "I've felt the same way for a long, long time."

Jenny added. "I admire you for holding up so well after all you've been through."

"Thank you," Carrie said. "It would have been impossible without you. By the way, your life hasn't exactly been a box of chocolates. You've had a rough time and you've been pretty strong yourself."

"It hasn't always been easy," Jenny conceded, "but even in the worst of times I still had Brian with me, and we had our good moments. But you…" she shook her head at the thought, "with Johnny gone so much, and worrying about his safety, and your mom's illness. I just don't know how you did it."

"Well, it's over now," Carrie said. "Tomorrow is a new beginning."

"And tomorrow comes early. We're catching the 6:45 train to Madrid. We'll have to be up by five-thirty."

"Five o'clock for me," Carrie said. "I want to look extra good for Johnny."

"I think you'd look good in Johnny's eyes no matter what."

Johnny's flight from Brussels to Madrid's Barajas Airport arrived at 6:55 the next morning, and Johnny found Brian waiting for him at the gate. They embraced for a long time without speaking. When they parted Brian wiped his eyes and said, "It's good to see you, man."

"Same here," Johnny replied.

"You look great," Brian said. "Looks like Iraq agrees with you."

"Yeah," Johnny laughed. "It's kind of like a health spa. You get to sweat out the impurities." Then he said, "You look a little tired, my friend. How was that red eye flight?"

"Don't ask," Brian said. "I left Washington at five-thirty yesterday afternoon and landed here about an hour ago. With the time difference, my body's telling me it's time for bed."

"Did you sleep on the plane?"

"Nah, I worked. I wanted to get some stuff out of the way before we partied in Madrid."

"And that's what we're gonna do," Johnny said. "From what I can tell, you and the girls have a full day planned."

"I have my itinerary right here." He unfolded the paper that he had e-mailed Johnny and the girls. The plan was to meet them after they arrived at the Atocha train station at 7:45. The nineteenth century station also housed a twenty-one thousand square foot tropical garden under a glass canopy. It was considered to be one of the must-see sites in Madrid. They would have breakfast there before leaving for the world famous Prado Museum less than a half mile away. The Prado was the main attraction that had enticed Jenny to visit Madrid, with works by Bosch, Velazguez, El Greco, and Caravaggio.

Johnny nodded. "I don't know, Brian. I mean, I know Jenny is interested in the whole museum thing because of her work, but I can't see myself looking at a bunch of paintings."

"I know," Brian agreed. "We're going for Jenny's sake. But there's one painting I want you to see. It's Goya's masterpiece, *Execution of the Rebels,* also known as *Executions of the Third of May 1808,* which depicts the death of Spaniards who resisted Napoleon's invasion of their country. It's a harsh topic, but it's brilliantly done and says something about patriots. I think you'll find it moving."

Johnny shrugged, "If you say so."

"I do," Brian said.

"Okay. Let's get my bags and grab a cab."

Brian smiled. "No need for a cab." He motioned to a man who had been standing off to the side, and the man stepped forward. "This is Carlos Alfaro, our driver for today. Carlos, this is my friend, Captain John Marzo."

Carlos smiled and the men shook hands. He had a strong handshake and looked more the military type than a Madrid limo driver.

"I took the liberty of arranging transportation for the day," Brian said. "Madrid's a wonderful city, but, like any city, it has its crime element that preys on unsuspecting foreigners. Carlos can help in that regard. Keep us off the back streets."

Johnny shook his head. "I just spent a year in a war zone and you hired us a body guard?"

"You're here to relax, my friend. Now let's get the bags."

The train traveled north toward the city as Jenny studied her map of Madrid. "It looks like we have a nice day planned," she said. "After we visit the museum we're going to a park for a stroll and a light lunch. It's called Parque del Retiro."

"Well, the Spanish certainly know how to relax," Carrie said.

"Maybe Brian will learn something from them," Jenny added. She turned to her map again. "Brian said dinner is a surprise, but I'm sure it's somewhere along Paseo Del Prado or Paseo De Recoletos. They're both known for their shops and restaurants."

"One thing is sure," Carrie said. "Brian will pick a winner."

The train stopped at a small station and more commuters boarded. "This is the last stop before we get off at Atocha Station," Jenny said.

The passengers squeezed in, and Abdul-Hadi Halabi was among them. He took a seat several rows in front of the girls. He was young, no older than twenty. He was dressed in jeans and a light jacket and carried a back pack. If anyone was paying attention, they would have noticed he seemed nervous as he checked his watch frequently, but no one did.

The train was uncomfortably crowded now with the addition of the new passengers, and Carrie was grateful that she and Jenny were getting off at the next stop. She checked her watch. It was 7:25, and they were due at Atocha at 7:35.

Halabi was silently praying now. Praying and sweating. He felt privileged to be a part of what would be a glorious day. He had studied under the Tunisian, and the Tunisian was a genius. If everyone did his part today, the result would be spectacular. The Spanish had supported the Americans in the war in Iraq. They were part of the western plot to humiliate Muslims, and they would pay a price. The Spanish people would curse their government and its policies when this day was over, and he and the Tunisian and the others would meet that evening to celebrate and praise Allah. He was sure of it.

The train approached Atocha and Halabi knew he would have to move quickly or be caught up in the crowd. If he became trapped, he would perish. He was at peace with that prospect if it was Allah's will, but that was not the Tunisian's plan.

As the train pulled to a stop, Carrie was placing the postcards she'd been writing into her pocketbook and Jenny was gathering her things to leave. "No use fighting the crowd," Carrie said. "Let's let the people in the aisle get off before we stand."

Jenny agreed.

The train arrived at 7:36, one minute behind schedule. Not bad, Carrie thought. When it stopped, Abdul-Hadi Halabi sprang from his seat and rudely pushed past passengers standing in the aisle. No one noticed that he'd left his backpack behind.

Seconds later a cell phone rang and the backpack exploded. The explosion ripped through the train shattering windows and throwing bodies in every direction. Commuters on the platform were hit with shards of glass from the windows. People on the train were lying on top of one another, and smoke filled the compartment. The main force of the explosion had been out and up, blowing a hole five feet in diameter through the side and roof of the compartment. The blast and the horrifying screams from the victims created a panic in the station as commuters trampled each other while fleeing the platform.

Inside the train, those who could groped their way to safety through the smoke and mangled bodies, some using the very hole created by the blast to exit the train. Others, too injured to move, cried out for help.

It was 7:45 by the time Johnny had retrieved his bags and was walking through the terminal with Brian and Carlos. A minute later all hell broke loose. People were shouting and heading for the exits while others stood in shock in front of TV sets along the concourse. The three men rushed to the nearest monitor and watched in silence as the commentator spoke of the explosion. He was speaking in Spanish, but both Brian and Johnny understood enough to realize what was going on.

They looked at Carlos who motioned for them to follow as he broke into a run. They raced for the exit and Carlos' waiting vehicle. They jumped in, and Carlos took a portable red light from the seat and attached it to the roof as he sped out of the parking lot with lights flashing and sirens blaring.

Brian explained quickly that Carlos was an off duty detective with the Madrid police and also on the CIA payroll. Dr. Blake had suggested Brian use him and he did. Brian didn't have time for a longer explanation, but Johnny got the general picture.

Brian, Johnny and Carrie had international phone service for years and Jenny had just obtained it for the trip. Brian flipped open his phone and dialed Jenny's number while Johnny dialed Carrie. Neither girl answered. They tried again as Carlos used his siren to spread traffic as he raced along the Madrid-Barcelona Highway toward the city. The cell towers were overloaded now and there was no service. Carlos turned on the radio. The broadcaster was speaking so rapidly that Carlos decided to translate. There were reports of multiple explosions. As many as ten bombs at four different stations: El Pozo, Tellez, Santa Eugenia, and Atocha. The words hit like a bucket of ice water to the face.

Casualties were high. Emergency vehicles from all over the city were converging on the stations and rushing victims to nearby hospitals. The broadcaster mentioned at least seven hospitals. Police had cordoned off the stations, and civilians were ordered to stay away. Nevertheless, Carlos could get them there. The question was should they go to the station or the hospital? Brian was pounding his fist on the dashboard while Johnny was trying to think. "What if they're hurt?" Brian screamed. "What if those bastards got them?"

Johnny's combat training took over, and he grabbed Brian's arm to make him stop. "Knock it off," Johnny said stoically, "and think."

Brian quieted down but wondered how he could think when images of Jenny being injured or worse flashed before him. Johnny remained calm but prepared himself for the worst.

Johnny said. "If they're unharmed, they'll be scared as hell, but they'll be okay, and they'll contact us when service is restored. If they're injured, they'll need us at the hospital. I say we go to the hospital. But which one?"

Carlos said, "The two closest to Atocha Station are Hospital Gregorio Maranon and Hospital del Nino Jesus."

"Pick one," Johnny said.

"We'll get to Gregorio Maranon first," Carlos replied.

"Okay. Move it!" Johnny said.

They exited the highway and headed southwest on Calle De Alcala, then turned south on Calle Del Doctor Esquerdo. Madrid is the third largest city in Europe, and traffic is always bad, but it was almost impossible now. Still, Carlos moved them quickly, using his siren and the opposite lane when necessary. They arrived at the hospital and found chaos, with ambulances parked haphazardly and rescue workers pushing gurneys toward the emergency room doors. The radio was now reporting casualties in the hundreds and a rising death toll. A doctor came running from the hospital and told policemen to stop allowing non-critically injured people into the facility. That was easier said than done. Scores of common citizens had joined in to assist the injured and they needed direction.

Combat medics were forced to make similar treatment decisions in the field all the time, and Johnny's Special Forces training took over. He pushed his way to the doorway and began giving orders while Carlos flashed his badge and assisted. Head and chest injuries received immediate attention, as did traumatic amputations and severe bleeding. Broken bones and soft tissue wounds were forced to wait, despite their wild protestations. It was difficult to turn anyone away, but Johnny knew that the indiscriminate use of vital medical resources would only add to the death toll. As each gurney approached, he prayed that it didn't hold Carrie or Jenny.

Brian looked helpless, and Carlos directed a uniformed policeman to escort him inside so he could look for the girls. They roamed the trauma ward, and Brian thought he might vomit. The carnage and horrifying screams were unbearable. He searched for a half hour and then stopped. Jenny and Carrie could be anywhere in the hospital or one of the other six hospitals serving the victims or...worse.

Brian tried the cell phone again, but there was still no service. He was dazed now, dazed by the incredible suffering and his fear for Jenny and Carrie's fate. He leaned against a wall and sobbed. This couldn't be happening, he thought. Why were they here? Why did they have to be at this place at this time? Why couldn't they all be back in Bristol, eating pizza at Cesare's and enjoying a beer? Why did they have to be wrapped up with Washington, and Iraq and the CIA, and this?

He forced himself to be analytical. There was no sense looking for Jenny and Carrie under these conditions. It was useless and unfair. In the hospital he saw children separated from their parents, and elderly victims disoriented and alone. It wasn't fair to use this time for his personal needs. He would have to wait. Wait for cell phone service to be restored. Wait for the authorities to develop casualty lists by hospital. Wait for news of where healthy but displaced survivors could gather to be reunited with loved ones. He'd wait until things calmed down and then he'd check all the lists.

The horrible thought crossed his mind. What if one girl survived and the other didn't? He pushed that prospect aside He'd heard inside the hospital that the exhibition center at Juan Carlos Park had been set up as a temporary morgue. He decided he'd wait as long as he could, and if he didn't hear from the girls, he'd check there too.

The injured continued to stream in, and Brian saw Johnny and Carlos still at work. Johnny seemed to be drawing his strength from the activity while Brian relived the horrible possibilities each time another gurney was wheeled toward him. He took a deep breath and walked out to join them.

101- Six Months Later

Saturday, September 18, 2004

Six months after the Madrid bombings, Johnny found Mr. Lombardi near the back of St. Theresa's Church, standing in front of the stained glass window the boys had bought when Mrs. Lombardi died. The brass plaque beneath the window read *In Loving Memory of Angelina Lombardi,* and Mr. Lombardi visited there often. Johnny stood next to him and saw that the old man was praying the Rosary and had tears in his eyes. Johnny rubbed his back gently. Lombardi kept his gaze on the glass portrayal of the Blessed Mother and said, *"It's too hard when dey leave you first."*

"I know," Johnny said softly.

"Da more you love dem, da more it hurts," the old man added.

Johnny nodded. His eyes were filling now, and he tried to comfort the old man. "You were together for a long time," he said.

"I know." Lombardi replied. *Some are not so lucky."*

Johnny's mind flashed to the scene at the hospital in Madrid, a scene he'd relived every day since the attack. One hundred and ninety-one people died in the explosions, and another two-thousand and fifty-one were injured. He'd seen combat in Afghanistan and Iraq, but March 11,

2004, loomed as the worst day in his life. He forced it from his mind and thought instead of all the visits he had made to the old man's house over the years, the lessons he'd learned, and the strength he'd drawn from him, especially in these past few months.

Lombardi turned to face him and regarded him as the grandson he'd never had. Johnny was wearing a tee-shirt and Lombardi squeezed his arm, forced a smile and said, "Strong sum-a-na-bitch."

Johnny laughed, shushed him, and whispered, "We're in church!"

Lombardi shrugged, pointed up to the ceiling, and said, "Da man upstairs knows how I am."

Johnny smiled.

Lombardi examined Johnny in his white tee shirt, tuxedo pants, and shiny black shoes. He checked his watch and said, *"Hey, Mr. President, Captain Marzo, whatever I call you now. Get dressed. Da guests will be coming."*

"I know," Johnny said. "My shirt and jacket are in the sacristy. It's hot today and I'm a little nervous. I didn't want to get sweaty and wrinkled before the ceremony so I took my shirt off. Anyway, I wanted to see you to say thank you."

"For what?"

"For everything. For…"

Lombardi cut him off with a bear hug that choked his breathing. Then he said, *"I'm glad you try to steal da tomatoes, and I'm glad I didn't kill your friend. I'm glad you save my life. Now go dress."*

Johnny entered the sacristy and found Brian pacing. "There you are," Brian said. "Where've you been? The Mass is in thirty minutes."

"Relax," Johnny said. "There's plenty of time. Besides, I can't have my best man looking like a nervous wreck."

"Don't worry about me," Brian said. "Just get dressed."

While Johnny put on his shirt and fastened his bow-tie, Brian occupied himself by reviewing his checklist: money for Father Morris, the rings, the petitions for Mickey to read…

Johnny watched Brian and thought back to the horrible days in Madrid. The cell phones had remained out of service the entire day of the bombings, and neither of the girls had been brought to Maranon Hospital. That evening, after things quieted down, Carlos drove both men to the temporary morgue at Juan Carlos Park. He flashed his credentials and brought them inside hoping to examine a list of the dead. At that point one-hundred and sixty-three bodies had been brought to the morgue, with more arriving each hour. But only eighty-four had been identified, and the majority of them were men who had wallets and identification in their pants. Women, who tended to carry their identification in their purses, were more difficult to identify. Brian's hands shook as he reviewed the list of names. Jenny and Carrie weren't on it. Carlos examined the list next, and for the first time it hit home with Brian and Johnny that Carlos might have had a friend or loved one who was victimized by the bombings. Fortunately, he didn't.

Now they were faced with the grisly task of examining the bodies of the unidentified female victims. Carlos volunteered to do it instead and collected photos from each of them. He came back in a half hour with news that he'd found four female bodies whose faces weren't recognizable, but who fit the size and weight descriptions they had given him. Terrified, they followed him as he led them to the bodies. One by one they dismissed the possibilities, and Brian collapsed in sobs as the last body was cleared. Their girls weren't dead, at least not yet.

Next, Carlos drove them to the central police station where a list of displaced persons was being compiled. The names of those hospitalized who could be identified were phoned in to headquarters along with their current location. Johnny's heart leaped when he saw Carrie's name. She was a patient at El Nino Jesus Hospital and was in serious but stable condition. Jenny's name was not on the list.

El Nino Jesus was a small hospital less than a half mile from the larger Maranon facility where they had worked earlier. Carlos drove as Johnny tried to assure Brian that Jenny would still be okay, but Brian was detached and unresponsive.

It was almost midnight when they reached the hospital and Carlos got them past the front desk and secured a room number. A nurse accompanied them to the room, and Carlos interpreted as she explained along the way that Carrie had a fractured hip, a severely lacerated cheek, a mild concussion, and multiple bruises. Early tests revealed no internal injuries. She'd been lucid, but in a lot of pain. Of course, the nurse added, she was deeply traumatized.

They reached her room, and Carlos and the nurse stayed at the doorway as Johnny approached the bed with Brian two steps behind.

Johnny's eyes filled when he saw her. One side of her face was heavily bandaged. She had an oxygen line in her nostrils and IV tubes hung from her arm. Her eyes were closed, and he stroked her forehead gently. She gasped at his touch, and Johnny pulled his hand away. Then her eyes focused on Johnny and she let out a whimper of relief.

He stroked her uninjured cheek as he whispered that she was going to be fine, and he would not leave her side. She squeezed his hand lightly, and he said, "Brian is with me."

Brian stepped forward, ashen faced, and Carrie forced a faint smile. "Where is Jenny," she said almost inaudibly. When Brian said he didn't know, Carrie squeezed her eyes shut and mumbled, "The train… explosion."

Johnny's heart ached for his friend. Brian had always prided himself on his resourcefulness, but he seemed powerless now and paralyzed by his anguish. Carlos told Brian he would drive him to each of the five remaining hospitals if necessary. "I believe she's alive my friend, and we'll find her if it takes all night."

Carlos said something to the nurse in Spanish, listened for her reply, and told Brian, "The nurse says that they have patients here from all four stations, but many are from Atocha. We might as well start our search here. She'll give us a list of rooms with unidentified female patients."

Johnny had nodded his encouragement and watched as the three of them filed out of the room.

Father Morris entered the sacristy all smiles. "Well, gentlemen, are we ready?"

"More than ready," Johnny beamed.

Father turned to Brian and asked, "Do you have Johnny's rings?"

"Yup," Brian replied, patting his breast pocket. "They're right here."

"And how about you, Johnny? Do you have Brian's rings?"

"Got 'em," Johnny said.

The priest beamed. "My first double wedding! By the looks of the parking lot, this is going to be a big one. Take a peek at the church."

The sacristy opened to the altar, and Johnny and Brian leaned out the door to take a look. The church was full, but people were still crowding in.

"This should be one of Bucks County's biggest weddings," Father Morris said. "Certainly one of the biggest Bristol has ever seen. You guys have gotten pretty famous."

"I guess we have," Brian said. "Thanks to Carrie."

Following the Madrid attacks, the two couples had spent eight weeks in Spain while the girls recuperated with Johnny and Brian by their side. The army acknowledged Johnny's circumstances by granting him a month's paid leave followed by the processing of his discharge papers. Brian took a three month leave of absence from the Agency, with the understanding that he would work with Carlos in Madrid investigating the bombers, their explosives, and their tactics. On April 3, less than a month after the attack, Spanish police traced the alleged mastermind of the plot, Serhane ben Abdelmajid Fakhet to an apartment in the southwest part of the city where he was huddled with others who executed the bombings. Faced with their imminent capture, the terrorists chose to detonate a bomb killing themselves. Although he could never be sure, Brian hoped the man who injured the girls was among them.

As it turned out, Brian found Jenny shortly after Johnny had found Carrie. She was also a patient at El Nino Jesus, just as the nurse had suggested. She had been brought to the hospital unconscious, with a broken right arm and leg and a collapsed lung. Brian was there when she regained consciousness and refused to leave her side until her condition was upgraded from critical to satisfactory.

They stayed in Madrid while Carrie's hip and Jenny's limbs healed and remained while the girls completed physical therapy. But after two weeks Carrie felt good enough to ask for a laptop, and she began wiring stories back to her editors at the *Bucks County Courier Times*. Carlos arranged interviews with survivors and family members of the victims, and Carrie recorded their first hand accounts. It made for captivating reading back home.

Nick, being the hopeless romantic that he was, leaked a side story to the local press about the hometown boys who had grown to be a Special Forces captain and a CIA analyst respectively, and the planned double wedding which had to be delayed. By the time the four returned from Europe, everyone in Bucks County knew their story. Now it seemed that just about everyone in the county had turned out for their wedding.

Father Morris said, "Well, we have the rings, a priest, a big crowd, and two grooms. All we need now are a couple of brides and we're set to go."

Brian continued pacing while Johnny closed his eyes and thought about the rehearsal dinner from the night before. They had it at Cesare's in Bristol, and their four families, the guys from the deli, and the Pac Men were there. It was an intimate gathering before the big bash planned for the following evening at the firehouse. Donnie Pit, the proprietor of Cesare's, reserved the back dining room and offered to put out a big spread. "I'll do some vodka rigatoni, meatballs, some veal scaloppini, sautéed vegetables, whatever you want, just name it."

"Pizza," Brian said.

"Sure," Donnie said, "We'll do some pan pizzas. I'll cut them in small squares for an appetizer."

"Not as an appetizer," Johnny said. "We just want pizza."

Donnie looked puzzled. "Just pizza?"

"Just pizza," Brian said. "Pizza and beer. Maybe a little wine for the girls. That's it."

Donnie looked uncomfortable. He was honored to be hosting the dinner and wanted it to be just right. "Hey, this is a big night for you. Friends, family. How about…"

"Just pizza," Brian said.

Donnie tried one last time. "Look," he said. "You guys have been in Europe for two months. If you're a little short on cash, it's not a problem. Let me take care of it."

"I appreciate it, Donnie," Johnny said. "But money is never an issue with my friend here. It's just that we've been dreaming about this for a long time. I thought about it in Turkey, Afghanistan, Iraq, Spain… This is what we want."

Donnie smiled and said, "Then you got it. We'll have every kind of pizza you can imagine."

It turned out to be the most fun they'd had in a long time. The deli guys sang a few of their old doo wop songs. Big Frankie sang some Frank Sinatra, and Nick and Jimmy argued about who would sit closest to the aisle for the ceremony. The four sets of parents sat together, and it was hard to tell which was happier.

After a while the party had settled down. The parents were talking quietly at their table and the deli guys had broken out a deck of cards. Carrie, Jenny, Johnny and Brian found themselves alone at a corner table taking it all in. The laceration on Carrie's cheek was healing nicely but the scar would never fully disappear. There had been no time for plastic surgery on the day of the explosions, but Johnny didn't care. It would always be a reminder that he'd almost lost her. In that regard, it simply made her more beautiful. Jenny still had the slightest bit of a limp from her broken leg, but the doctors assured Brian that it would continue to improve with time.

Jenny offered a toast to the four of them and their new lives together.

After they drank, Carrie announced that she and Johnny had some news.

"Let's hear it," Jenny said.

Johnny interrupted by saying, "You better give them some background first."

"Good idea," Carrie said. "Okay. Well, when we first got home I was thrilled that Johnny was out of the army. Not because I didn't want him to serve in some way, but because I just couldn't take him being half way around the world any more. He seemed at peace with his decision, but I knew it would just be a matter of time before he grew restless. Then, when Brian announced, with Jenny's approval, that he wasn't leaving the CIA until in his words, he caught, 'every terrorist bastard that walks the earth' I knew Johnny would have to do something. So I downloaded an application to the FBI, gave it to Johnny, and told him to fill it out. His eyes lit up when he saw it, and, after I convinced him that I sincerely wanted him to join, he completed the application and sent it in."

"Wow!" Jenny said.

"Keeping secrets from your friends, huh," Brian said.

"Sorry, Pal," Johnny replied. "I wanted to keep it quiet in case I was rejected."

"Anyway," Carrie said, Johnny received his reply yesterday," She decided to be a tease and freeze her conversation on the spot.

"Well?" Brian said. "What was the verdict?"

"The verdict," Carrie said proudly, is that Johnny Marzo, my man, has been accepted into the FBI. He leaves for Quantico for training next month."

Brian and Jenny were on their feet offering Johnny congratulations.

Carrie waited for everyone to sit down again, and then she added, "When he completes the course, he'll live in an interesting place called the United States of America. He'll have a fairly normal job. He'll have a house that he comes home to almost every night after work. He'll have a wife waiting for him, and a handful of kids greeting him at the door. And if he's good enough, and we know he will be, he'll qualify for the counter-terrorism unit."

Johnny smiled, winked at Brian, and added, "And I won't quit until I've caught every terrorist bastard who tries to operate in the USA."

Father Morris brought him back to the present by announcing that the girls had arrived at the rear of the church, and it was time to take their places at the altar rail.

They entered the church and stood facing the crowd. Johnny saw his parents in the front row and smiled. His mother winked and Angelo gave him a thumbs up. Brian's parents were sitting next to them. The mothers of the girls sat beaming across the aisle. Both looked great, but Johnny thought Mrs. Boyle looked especially healthy and vibrant.

Seated behind Johnny's parents were the deli guys: Nick, Jimmy, and Big Frankie, all of whom had been his unofficial uncles since the day his parents brought him home from Canada, and he loved them like family. Johnny saw the Pac Men and nudged Brian to look in their direction. Mickey was there with his girlfriend. Actually they were engaged now and planning a spring wedding. They spotted Tommy Dillon. He looked like a million bucks, scrubbed and polished, with his new girlfriend sitting next to him. At the party the night before, Tommy had told Brian and the rest of the guys that they'd saved his life. Brian said it was the best wedding gift he could hope for. Bobby, the new entrepreneur, came stag but was dressed to the nines as he basked in his newfound prosperity.

They continued to pan the audience as they waited for the girls to appear. They saw faces they hadn't seen in years. Mr. Baxter, Mr. Swilli and Ms. Quattrocchi were there from the high school. They saw other teachers too, and friends they had gone to school with.

Johnny's eyes were drawn to the back of the church where he saw Mr. Lombardi, standing alone by his wife's window. At that moment Johnny Marzo felt a level of contentment he hadn't felt since he left high school. He was home again with no plans to stray very far.

Finally, the music began and the girls appeared side by side at the vestibule of the church, each escorted by her father. As they made their way down the aisle, Johnny and Brian each focused on the girl they were about to marry- again.

Johnny locked eyes with Carrie, and images of their past flashed before him. He thought of their vacations in Israel and Rome, and he snickered at the sight of Emilio splashing in the fountain in Berlin. He saw Mr. Lombardi at his kitchen table telling him to go to Europe to get the girl. He remembered his first awkward meeting with Carrie in front of the high school. He remembered Brian's description of Carrie at the 5th Ward Pool. Brian had called her Helen of Troy, and Johnny had no idea what that meant at the time.

The girls reached the last pew and kissed their fathers. As they took their final steps forward, Johnny whispered to Brian, "Don't plan any trips for us for a long time."

"Not a chance," Brian said.

Then they offered their girls their arms and the ceremony began.

The End.

About the Author

Bill Pezza has taught history and government for four decades, specializing in interdisciplinary studies and incorporating oral, grass roots history into his work. He currently teaches at Bucks County Community College. He and his wife Karen reside in Bristol, Pennsylvania. They have three adult children, Leighann, Bill, and Greg.

Readers may contact the author at bpezza@comcast.net or visit his website at www.billpezza.com.

CPSIA information can be obtained at www.ICGtesting.com
Printed in the USA
LVOW08s0932150813

347927LV00001B/53/P

9 781438 967141